WE * UNLEASH THE MERCILESS * STORM

ALSO BY TEHLOR KAY MEJIA:

We Set the Dark on Fire

TEHLOR KAY MEJIA

WE UNLEASH THE MERCILESS STORM

KATHERINE TEGEN BOOKS
An Imprint of HarperCollins Publishers

Katherine Tegen Books is an imprint of HarperCollins Publishers.

We Unleash the Merciless Storm
Copyright © 2020 by Tehlor Kay Mejia
All rights reserved. Printed in the United States of America.
www.epicreads.com

ISBN 978-0-06-269134-7

Typography by Molly Fehr
20 21 22 23 24   PC/LSCH   10 9 8 7 6 5 4 3 2 1

First Edition

To the lovers and the fighters,
and every hero who dares to be both.

⊹⇝✳⇜⊹

"*It* is said that only two living souls saw the Salt God leave the earth for the last time.

At the edge of the island, where sand met sea, what had once been a glorious and peaceful land lay in ruins. The neatly painted homes with their abundant gardens had been destroyed, the white sand pockmarked with craters that children played in and old women clucked their tongues at.

It had all come to nothing, they said, this last stand by their once-benevolent god. In the end, the Sun God had taken what he wanted and cast the Salt God and his chosen people into shameful shadow—all for the love of a fickle woman.

But still, when the Sun God banished his brother, the outer island believed. That he would set right the wrongs his rage-filled heart had visited on their land. That he would leave them with peace and dignity, to watch over them from the skies. That they would have a chance to say goodbye to his mortal form as he climbed the ladder to the heavens.

They were wrong.

A vulture, picking apart the carcass of a fish as night gave way to morning, watched as the divine man who had been the outer island's protector walked barefoot from his village. Fury was etched in the lines of his face.

As he marched down the beach, it is said his brother's banishment burned on his skin like a brand, embers falling to make glittering glass beads of the sand where they landed. A crow, attracted by the shine, followed behind, gathering the beads up to weave into her nest, her eyes curious as the god's strides became longer.

Sea spray trailed from him like smoke as the flesh and bone that held his mortal body together loosened and unhinged, revealing the pure light of the god-being within.

Jealous of the crow's bounty, the vulture approached, oblivious to the transformation happening before him. But just as he beat his massive wings at the slender crow, it is said that the Salt God's eyes—terrible and awesome as they took their divine form—turned on them like a lighthouse's lantern, freezing the two scavengers in place.

In those eyes, the birds saw all that had passed in the world, and all that would come to be. With that knowledge, they rose up, a man and a girl, naked and unashamed in the god's divine presence.

Eyes drawn by the transformation, the god bent down, taking the beads from the girl's hands, the last of his mortal form still curling away from him like paper set aflame. In his own glowing hands, he made of them a silver ring, set with a stone of turquoise.

Handing the ring to the man, it is said that the god looked him once more in the eye, and in it he saw the boy's soul. His true nature.

'El Buitre y La Cuerva,' he called to him in the gods' tongue. The spirits within them came forth, meeting the god's spirit of pure light as at last his human form was abandoned forever. 'You will care for them,' said the air where the god had only just stood. 'They are yours now.'

In the water where he disappeared, a glow remained, fading slowly as the sun rose. Attracted by the light, other animals came to drink from it, and as they did, they, too, stood up, men and women, boys and girls.

El Buitre held the ring aloft. 'We will protect the people,' he said, the first words in his human tongue.

The glow disappeared from the shore, the god's last farewell.

'We will protect the people,' the rest replied.

'We will be their voice,' La Cuerva said, her long black hair blowing in the breeze.

'We will be their voice,' the rest repeated.

And so it was . . ."

—The Legend of La Voz, A People's Oral History

From this moment, I pledge my life to the service of La Voz. I will hold no other person or organization in higher esteem. I will accept no responsibilities or roles that conflict with the mission of rebellion.

—*La Voz Membership Pledge*

╌╫⪫✳⪪╫╌

CARMEN SANTOS HAD IMAGINED HER homecoming a thousand times.

During sleepless nights, unnerved by the quiet of the government complex, she'd lain with her eyes closed, picturing it in detail so vivid her heart squeezed with longing for the salted earth. The ghostly beauty of the barren trees. The colors and sounds and smells of home.

In some of her fantasies, she returned victorious, someone's blood (usually Mateo's) on her hands. In some, she stole away in the dead of night and slipped in like a shadow, sliding back into her old role as easily as she slid into silk dresses and heavy silver rings.

But she'd never imagined it this way. In the dark hour before the sun painted the horizon pink and gold. Exhausted, dehydrated, delirious from fear and travel and hunger. Fleeing the scene of a botched fire in the capital's biggest marketplace after a rescue attempt gone wrong.

She'd never imagined herself hunted, broken by the choices she'd made, clinging to Alex's tattered shirt with the last of her strength as the dirt bike sputtered over the invisible boundary line.

When it stopped, Carmen slid off the bike face-first onto the hard ground, her muscles finally giving up the fight, tiny rocks pressing into her skin like knives. The earth beneath her cheek smelled like metal. Or was that sweat? Blood? Her thoughts swam; her chest felt tight.

"Get up," said a voice. Alex's. Images swam in front of Carmen, her ears ringing from the explosion, from the drone of the engine over countless miles.

She couldn't get up.

"Santos, *get up.*"

Why? Carmen wondered as more bodies crowded around Alex's. There was shock in their expressions. Suspicion in their tight lips and the whispered words Carmen couldn't make out.

"There were three of them behind us a mile back." Alex

was on her feet again, turned away from Carmen, though her voice carried. "I thought we lost them, but . . ."

"What's the matter with her?"

The words penetrated the haze around Carmen like nothing had since she'd fallen. Maybe since before then, when she'd left Dani on the side of the road. This voice was sharp but weighty. A voice that had lived beneath Carmen's ribs for as long as she could remember. A voice that told her she was really back.

Every muscle screamed as she pushed herself up off the ground. The rocks falling away from her cheek now bit into her palms, drawing blood. But Carmen was no stranger to blood.

She could feel him moving toward her, even through the darkness, even through the sting of sweat and dirt that made her squint to make him out. She turned toward him like a flower to the sun.

"Cuervita," he said, closer now. "Is it really you?"

In the harsh light of the torch he carried, the Vulture looked older. The fine lines beneath his eyes reached for the corners of his mouth. There was a little more white in his eyebrows, and in the bushy tangle of the hair he refused to trim.

As he stepped closer, Carmen realized he was as tall as she remembered from childhood—though she had grown taller, too. He still had that hunter's grace that age could not rob him of; it was present in the way he held his shoulders, the way his clothes hung, the way the light played off scars and knotted muscle.

Even here, with her vision swimming and everything inside her splintering to pieces, Carmen remembered: this was a man worth believing in. A man worth following. A man worth the consequences of everything she had done and more.

"El Buitre," she said, not bothering to hide her sudden tears. "I'm back."

His gaze softened as he took her in, and Carmen imagined how she must look to him. Defeated, the remains of her silk Segunda costume hanging from her in filthy ribbons, barely able to face him.

Behind him, two men helped Alex lift Jasmín's lifeless body from the motorcycle's trailer, and Carmen braced herself against a wave of emotion as it all came flooding back. Jasmín, unconscious and vulnerable; Alex, masked, armed, ruthless as ever.

And Carmen, caught between two worlds, tackling Dani to the ground as the explosion rent the air around them, turning everything they'd known to shrapnel on the roadside.

Dani, the truth dawning like a new day on her face.

Dani, Alex's gun pointed at her temple.

Dani, looking at Carmen like she'd never seen her before. Never laughed with her. Never kissed her dizzy.

The pain in her chest was searing, worse than any amateur explosive attached to the engine of a sedan. Worse than anything else she'd ever felt, and Carmen was no stranger to pain, either.

"I'm back," she said again, more to herself than El Buitre.

But something of her memories—and the things they had begun to unravel in her chest—must have shown, because El Buitre's eyes narrowed, his gaze calculating now where it had been welcoming a split second ago.

Reaching forward, he took Carmen's chin between his finger and thumb, looking at her as if he could read her thoughts. Her motivations. Despite everything, Carmen forced her mind to quiet, her heart to calm. For a moment, she had felt like his daughter. But she was a soldier first and foremost. It was what he had raised her to be. And soldiers were obedient. Soldiers didn't let their commitment slip. Not even for a second.

"Back?" he asked, his voice quiet, inaudible to the growing crowd pretending not to listen. "I suppose that remains to be seen."

Carmen's heart dropped into her stomach, the haze of pain and exhaustion clearing as cold terror took its place. El Buitre's gaze, still searching, said she'd been away too long, living among the enemy. It said he'd heard tales of her exploits.

It said he didn't trust her more than any other outsider, and he didn't intend to start until she proved herself to him. To all of them.

A gunshot split the night, and Carmen (who had once been so steady under pressure) dropped to her knees at the sound, the memory of the explosion too recent, her heart beating a jackrabbit's rhythm in her chest.

Return shots, and El Buitre shouting as the border patrol agents who'd followed them from the wall entered the camp, guns blazing, torchlight flickering on their shining helmets and boots as the camp prepared to fight back against the intruders.

From the ground, Carmen tried to quiet her heartbeat. How many times had she been woken in the night to gunfire and shouting? She was a soldier, not some weak-kneed girl in need of rescuing. If she was going to prove she was really home, she'd have to start here. Now.

Your home is under attack, she told herself, rising on shaking legs.

But as she called out for a weapon, steeling herself, she knew: this was no longer her home. Her home was a million miles away, beating in the body of a girl she might never see again.

And if anyone found out her loyalty was divided, she'd be killed. Or worse.

The officers were outnumbered, unprepared for what they would encounter in the eerie light of La Voz's nomadic hideout. Taking it in for the first time, Carmen saw they'd chosen this location well. A grove of long-dead trees, their trunks bleached white with the salt in the ground, hid the rebels as the border officers stumbled between them, firing wildly at plant and person alike, hitting neither.

With a weighty, bladed staff in her hand, Carmen felt her

pulse begin to slow. She had never been the most aggressive fighter, but she'd trained with weapons since childhood, and every member of La Voz was expected to fight. Despite her Segunda training, and her years of using more subtle weapons to achieve her goals, she still remembered the feeling of a heartbeat at the end of her blade.

Following the sound of shuffling footsteps, Carmen caught the light of a nearby torch off one of the officers' polished buttons and moved silently in his direction, the bladed end of the staff in front of her.

He never saw her coming.

She was behind him, her staff between his shoulder blades, ready to strike when the wind shifted, and something squeezed tight in her chest. The smell of the burning torch. The fire. Dani across the flames confessing everything, telling her she wanted more than just almost-kisses and lies.

What would she think of this Carmen? The one ruthless enough to leave her behind. The one ready to kill a man just because she had been trained to. Could Dani ever love someone like that? And did it matter? Could Carmen change? Or was it already too late . . .

Her moment of hesitation cost her. Sensing her presence, the officer turned, and Carmen froze. It was kill or be killed now. The girl she had been, the one Dani had wanted, wasn't strong enough to survive here.

And still, Carmen hesitated—even when his eyes met

hers, even when he drew his gun level with her chest. Her heartbeat was too loud in her ears, the grove going blurry in her peripheral vision.

Had she come all this way just to die because she didn't know who she was?

When the officer crumpled to the ground before her, Carmen felt a moment's relief. Maybe this wasn't her moment after all. But when her rescuer stepped forward, gray mane glinting in the torchlight, she knew the bullet would have been safer.

El Buitre hauled the dazed officer to his feet, never breaking eye contact with Carmen. He had looked at her tenderly first, like a daughter. And then with confusion, like a stranger. But the story his expression now told was one Carmen had learned by heart.

One that was much more dangerous than any bumbling officer with a shiny new pistol.

He had seen her waver. Seen her doubt. And that made her a traitor.

Carmen had only been eight the first time she saw a La Voz agent accused of treason, but she'd never forget his hearing around the table, or his punishment.

Exile. Total excommunication from La Voz and all their resources.

The accused man had wept when El Buitre handed down the verdict, the sound wild and terrible, and Carmen had understood. It seemed like a mercy, letting him live, but excommunication was just another kind of death sentence. The only thing more dangerous than being a La Voz agent on this island was being a *former* La Voz agent.

And that man had been *captured* by border patrol. Cracked under interrogation. Passed along information that was functionally useless by the time they got ahold of it.

If El Buitre thought Carmen had actively conspired with a highly placed operative within the government complex? Given her classified information that would go straight to Mateo and his father? Jeopardized active plans?

She'd be lucky if excommunication was the worst they had in store for her.

But there was more than just distrust in the Vulture's eyes tonight. As Carmen held his gaze, she saw something new, too. Something like mania. Something with an edge of uncertainty to it. A hint of fear.

The marketplace fire had been sloppy work, lazy. Carmen had thought so even before it led to the end of her residence at the Garcias'. But was there more to it than just poor planning? What had been going on in La Voz since she'd left?

She wasn't the same girl she'd been, but maybe this place had changed, too.

"Drop that, and come with me," he said to Carmen, and she obeyed. In order to discover what he was hiding, she'd have to survive the night.

El Buitre pushed the officer roughly toward the crowd beginning to form, Carmen following behind him. The other officer had been killed by someone with a steadier hand than Carmen's, his body laid out at the center of the circle, seeping blood into the thirsty ground. Beside him, two men were building a fire, already glowing faintly against the predawn darkness.

"Tie this one up," the Vulture said, pushing the second officer into the center of the circle, where he looked at his partner and went ghostly pale.

Alex made quick work of the ropes. Jasmín was nowhere to be seen. The ghost of their long ride to the outer island was with Carmen as she stayed close to El Buitre, not restrained, but aware she was far from trustworthy in his eyes.

She awaited her sentence. Had he seen enough to excommunicate her? To lock her up? To kill her? Growing up in the nomadic resistance camp, she'd seen worse punishments for lesser crimes. To survive here, you had to hold loyalty sacred.

Had Carmen betrayed them?

Her heart, still aching for Dani, still wondering where she was and whether she was safe, made a pretty compelling case. But how much of that had El Buitre seen?

He turned to her, the crowd still growing as the commotion woke the camp.

"Carmencita," he said. "Come here."

The flames were flickering, the officer was struggling against his bonds, and the eyes of La Voz were on her as she faced him, her warring loyalties snapping behind her like a flag in the wind. How could she hide her feelings from them when she didn't understand them herself?

"When you were six years old, La Voz took you in," the Vulture said, his voice deep and solemn, carrying across the fire and into the crowd. "On that night, you made a vow to us. To the resistance. To the people. Do you remember?"

"Yes," Carmen said, the word stinging her throat on the way out. Of course she remembered. It had been the proudest moment of her life. The moment she'd found her family.

"We have asked much of you these past eleven years," he said, looking her in the eye now. "You've lied, committed betrayals and crimes too numerous to count, risked your life, and taken the lives of others."

Carmen nodded, but she knew he was far from finished.

"Most recently, you've gone into enemy territory. Become someone else. You've changed the very fabric of who you are for this organization, and we value your skills. Your devotion."

"Thank you," Carmen said, waiting for the tide to turn.

"But you've been away from home a long time," El Buitre said. "Living among strangers, wearing their clothes, learning their values and their ways, joining their *families* . . ." He let this last word ring out, and Carmen could see its impact on the shifting figures beyond the fire.

"I've never had any family but La Voz," she said decisively, though Dani was still a living, breathing contradiction in her blood. "Everything I've done has been for the good of the cause."

Murmurs spread through the crowd, and Carmen didn't try to decipher them. There was only one opinion that mattered here tonight.

El Buitre appraised her as the man at their feet struggled in his bonds. She wasn't the only one conflicted. Carmen fought the urge to plead, to explain her behavior with the officer, to swear by everything she believed in that she had never wavered.

But it wouldn't help. It would only make her look like she had something to hide.

"They dressed you in these gowns," El Buitre said after his long silence. "Made a plaything out of you. They dulled the blade we've been honing since the moment we found you. You're home now. Are you ready to sharpen it again?"

Carmen nodded once, solemn and sure, but inside the war waged on.

"You know what you have to do," El Buitre said, and she did.

Hands betraying nothing of the unsteadiness in her knees, none of the stuttering in her heartbeat, Carmen reached out for the dagger he offered her. The ornate one he wore on his belt. She'd never been allowed to touch it before, though it had often preoccupied her attention as a child. Set into the hilt was a shining stone, said to be the very one from the ring the Salt God had presented to the Vulture on the day of his transformation.

A hush fell over the grove. As a Segunda, Carmen had been taught to always be aware of her aesthetic, and right now she knew she was frightening. Feral. Wild. Her silk dress in tatters, her hair matted and tangled, her duty eclipsing her desire in the shadows across her face.

It was time to make a choice. The one she hadn't made with the officer's back bared to her. The one that might mean leaving Dani behind forever.

Carmen stepped up to the kneeling officer, using the strange electricity she knew crackled around her to her benefit. An animal fear that transformed him. Something that made them both seem less human.

"I know no master, no lover, no family but the cause," Carmen said, her voice ringing clear as she reached forward without hesitation and opened the officer's throat.

He slumped to the ground, his blood spreading slowly at their feet.

The now silent crowd could see nothing but Carmen as she wiped the dagger on her ruined dress, smearing blood across her stomach, her hips, until the blade was clean once more.

There is nothing more important than the impression you leave behind in a room, came the voice of her maestras as she took the dagger between her teeth and pulled the Segunda's dress over her head.

Naked, filthy, worn and exhausted and scarred, Carmen closed her eyes for a moment, feeling the heat of the flames on her skin, feeling the metal of the blade in her mouth.

Goodbye, she said, to every piece of her that had loved being Carmen Garcia, bride of silk and silver, chosen daughter of the Moon Goddess. To the part of her heart that had once hoped to win the love of a girl like Dani.

To every kiss, every caress, every shared smile.

She was a soldier. A survivor. There was no room to be anything else. Not if she wanted to live.

With the attention of La Voz on her alone, Carmen threw her Segunda's dress, the last piece of her old life, into the flames, and together they all watched it burn until there was nothing left but ashes.

When it was gone, she took the knife from between her teeth and turned back to El Buitre, presenting it to him hilt first.

If he was uncomfortable with her display, with her exposure, he didn't show it. He took the knife back and nodded once. A short, sharp thing that said she'd earned another night of life.

Tomorrow, his silence seemed to say, was still uncertain.

Women approached with blankets, clothes, bundling Carmen up and leading her on shaking legs to the nearest tent, laying her down. She drifted in and out of consciousness as they bathed her and treated her wounds, dressed her in the all-black uniform of the resistance.

But when they'd gone, when Carmen was alone, the dawn painting faint purple streaks down the walls of the med tent, something broke open inside her, tears sliding down her cheeks until her hair and the pillow beneath it were soaked.

She had tried to leave it all behind at the fire, and she would claim she had until her dying breath. But here, alone, she was forced to reckon with the weight of it. With the whisper of Dani still here in the air she breathed.

Carmen was home, but loving Dani had altered her past the point of no return.

She got to her feet, wincing at the ache in her bones and the sting of the cuts on her skin. Alone, barefoot and furtive, she snuck back to the firepit, now just a bowl of embers on the ground, and with a stick dug through what remained until she had found what she was looking for.

Blackened, unrecognizable, but still precious. A braided piece of silk from the strap of her dress. The last dress Dani had ever seen her in. Ever touched her in. Carmen knew it was foolish, that it could mean death if she kept it and anyone guessed what it meant, but she tucked it into the pocket over her heart nonetheless.

Dani was part of her now, and try as she might, there was no fire hot enough to burn the memory of her—or the desire to get back to her—away.

I pledge my life to my brothers, my sisters. On our linked arms will the resistance rise.

—*La Voz Membership Pledge*

⊹⫍⟩✳⟨⫎⊹

"I'M NOT GOING IN THERE," whispered a child's voice outside Carmen's tent. "She's scary."

"I heard she glared at Emilio yesterday and his arm broke. Like, just spontaneously broke. Just from her looking at him."

Carmen groaned, rolling over in her bed. She would have laughed if she wasn't so annoyed.

"That's ridiculous. *I* heard she grabbed his arm. Broke it with a flick of her wrist."

"Kind of makes you wonder," one of them said, and Carmen knew her voice. One of the older girls. Almost ready for a sword and a seat in the Vulture's meeting hall.

"Wonder what?" the first one asked. A little boy, barely nine, but still older than Carmen had been when she'd been brought to La Voz for the first time.

"How anyone in the capital ever believed La Cuerva was a Segunda."

Carmen sighed, getting to her feet, stalking across the tent and flipping open its door before they could scatter. "Emilio tripped on his own clumsy feet," she said, trying not to smile at the expressions of terror on their faces. "And it's a sprain, not a break. If you're gonna be out here talking chisme, at least get it right."

"Lo siento, señorita," said the girl. "You asked to be awakened at . . ."

"I know what I asked. And one more thing:"

The children looked at her like a tree that had just been struck by lightning.

"Don't call me La Cuerva."

When Carmen closed the tent flap in their faces, they scampered away immediately, fear quickening their steps. Like she was an adult herself. Someone to be respected, even feared. It was the kind of moment she had dreamed of before she left home. But she'd been a child herself, then.

Children didn't understand what it took to earn those looks. How much they would wish for the innocence of their fear when they were the ones wearing battle-weary expressions and thousand-yard unseeing stares.

At least they feared her, Carmen thought. That meant her

display at the fire had done its job. But it had been two days, and she knew she couldn't coast on it for much longer. Not with this secret still buried in her chest.

At the long, low table beside her bed, Carmen lifted the lid of a woven basket. Inside, beneath torn scraps of linen for cleaning and binding wounds, was the braided piece of violet silk. Such a tiny thing, but still enough to damn her if anyone recognized its significance.

Every time she looked at it, she told herself she'd throw it away.

And every time, she put it back in the basket and closed the lid. It was the only thing that even began to soothe the feeling of an open wound. It never faded. She carried it with her everywhere.

This was her proof that it had all been real. Dani. Carmen and Dani. The fledgling thing between them that had never had time to take flight.

Where was Dani now? Carmen wondered, splashing salt water from a bowl on her face, rubbing mint paste across her teeth. Was she safe? Did the only girl she'd ever loved hate her for what she'd done? Carmen left these thoughts in the basket with the last fragment of her old life. She couldn't take them where she was going.

Out in the already sweltering morning, Carmen headed for the mess tent, looming ahead in silhouette. A few people were up, loading metal bowls with corn porridge and settling down, talking among themselves. The chattering stopped as

Carmen passed. More nods. More glances that said she'd be the topic of all conversations that rekindled after she'd passed through.

It had been like this since her return.

Ignoring the stares, Carmen ladled a bowl of corn porridge for herself, settling alone in a darkened corner of the tent. But she was never truly alone. Placed in a tent near the Vulture's own, Carmen was, ostensibly, in a place of honor within the camp.

She knew better than to trust appearances.

El Buitre wasn't rewarding her; he was observing her. Even when he wanted her to believe he wasn't.

There, Carmen thought grimly. Beside the clay jugs of water and cerveza was a sly-featured boy. Eleven, she judged, green-eyed, his hair pulled back. He watched her intently, not speculatively. Like he was taking notes.

Carmen knew she was a curiosity even among cutthroats and rebels, but there was something different about the gaze of a Vulture spy. She ought to know; she'd been his most promising one herself not so long ago.

The boy's steady eyes stayed on her as she ate. He was good, Carmen thought, trying to shrug off the feeling of being observed now that she knew where it was coming from. But it wouldn't fade. And what the boy was looking for couldn't be found on the surface.

Looking across the flames at El Buitre that night, Carmen had felt at home. She had felt like herself again. But she hadn't felt cold and ruthless, or like she was capable of anything. Because despite the content of the whispers swirling around her at every turn, she hadn't just manipulated a promising new recruit for the sake of the cause.

She hadn't cast Dani aside when she'd run out of uses for her.

Carmen Santos had developed feelings for the last person she should have, utterly without premeditation, and spent weeks trying to make it look like it was all part of the plan.

Carmen Santos had betrayed everything she'd ever believed about putting the cause first, one night in the firelit living room of her husband's mansion, and every night after.

Carmen Santos had barely forced herself to walk away from the wreckage of a ruined car, even though staying would have meant losing her life and delivering a crushing blow to the only family she had ever known.

Carmen Santos, the little crow of La Voz, the most promising operative in three generations, was in love. But she was good enough to make sure the little boy with sharp eyes couldn't read it in her expression, at the very least.

As she finished her porridge, she lifted the bowl in salute to the boy, who'd let his gaze linger just a second too long. He flushed to the roots of his hair and left the tent.

Carmen's smugness didn't even last to the door.

"Cuervita," said an icy voice just on the other side of the tent flap. Carmen stiffened at the name. The little crow from La Voz's legends. She had loved it as a child, something tying her to the family, to the mythology of the resistance's origins. But things had changed. It sat different now, like someone else's name.

"My *name* is Carmen," she said, emerging from the tent, a young man falling in step beside her. She tried to keep as much distance between them as possible. "Just Carmen."

"If you say so."

Ari Vasquez was barely nineteen, but he carried himself like someone with the keys to the kingdom. He was tall, his black hair swept off his forehead in long strands that occasionally broke loose and fell into his face. His features were sharp and angular, and his eyes—which Carmen had overheard at least five women in the compound discussing at length—were the palest green.

The other women seemed to think these green eyes made Ari handsome. Carmen thought they looked a little fishlike. But, she was forced to admit, this wouldn't be the first time the charms of a supposedly handsome man were lost on her.

They'd been introduced her first morning back, and Carmen had understood at once that he was at the heart of the changes to La Voz. The authority in his stance, in his stride, was the very thing she'd found missing from El Buitre when they'd locked gazes across the flames.

By all appearances, the Vulture ran La Voz, as the legends said he had for centuries. Of course, he wasn't truly immortal—only the mask was, handed down to a new La Voz operative when a Vulture reached the end of his ability to lead. But it was good for the people to believe he knew their history, had seen everything.

El Buitre led every meeting, observed every training skirmish, and presided over every grievance session. But Ari was never far from his side, making pointed asides for no one's ears but El Buitre's, taking the right-hand chair at meetings and sitting up in the commander's tent by candlelight long after the camp had gone to sleep.

The Vulture Carmen knew would never have allowed someone so much influence, especially someone so new. So young. So what did Ari have to offer? Carmen wondered. Or what secrets did he know?

"As much as I appreciate the escort," Carmen said as they walked, "I'm assuming you're not just here for the pleasure of my company. What can I do for you?"

"So suspicious," he said, moving closer to her. "I only wanted to see how you were settling in. Camaraderie is the heart of the resistance, after all."

"I've been La Voz since you were still a snake under a rock somewhere," Carmen said, keeping her tone as pleasant as she could. "I'm well aware of what's at its heart."

Ari's false friendliness faltered, his pale eyes narrowing. "You may be fooling everyone else, but I see right through you, *Carmen Santos.*" He said her name like it was whispered around campfires. "We both know you won't be getting any closer to your old position as long as your *prized recruit* doesn't prove she's not a traitor. Or did you have a better pet name for her? 'Recruit' isn't very romantic, is it . . . ?"

The mention of Dani hit her like a punch to the stomach. Carmen fought to keep her face clear, counting to ten in her head.

Ari took advantage of the silence. "Things have changed around here, little crow," he said. "This place isn't just a story your abuela tells at bedtime anymore, it's a rebellion. An army. You better get used to it."

He walked away, but this time he left Carmen with a distraction. The proprietary way he'd mentioned the changes to La Voz was right in line with her theories that he was somehow manipulating the Vulture. But how? And why would El Buitre ever allow it?

Regardless, as Carmen walked toward the center of camp, she was forced to confront the truth in his words.

Dani hadn't responded to multiple attempts to make contact. She'd missed a scheduled meeting with Sota. No one, not even Carmen, knew where she was or what she was doing.

Despite the grave stakes for both of them, Carmen's initial reaction was fear that Dani no longer had the same feelings for her. That her silence toward La Voz was a symptom of a more personal silence toward Carmen herself.

But there were other options, too. Much more dangerous ones. Dani was a double agent in very precarious circumstances. If anyone on either side considered her a traitor, it would mean the end of her life.

The thought made Carmen's stomach twist and knot. It

was all she could do not to race out of the compound right now to see for herself that Dani was alive. That she was safe.

Of course, an action that rash would have consequences of its own.

And Carmen was responsible for more than just herself.

As she neared the medical tent, she did her best to push her fears aside. La Voz had made no judgments on Dani's loyalty. Daily attempts were being made to establish contact. There may come a time to panic, but if Carmen put her emotions aside, if she thought like an operative and not a girl in love, she knew that time wasn't now.

Not yet.

Inside, the tent for long-term medical care was bright, flaps open to let in the light.

Jasmín lay in a cot near the center, alone until someone else was gravely injured. This tent was rarely so quiet. It made Carmen uneasy.

She'd been here every day, casting withering glares at the kids assigned to help out in the med tent—orphans picked up during raids, or the children of long-time La Voz members. Most notable among them was Emilio, who had taken it upon himself to trip and sprain his wrist, igniting the chisme machine.

Since she'd returned, Carmen sat beside Jasmín as much as she could bear, counting the hours.

"Good morning," said Alicia, the healer looking after Jasmín.

"No change?" Carmen asked.

"Sleeping poison is tricky," said Alicia. "Her vitals are the same, but there's no way of telling when she'll wake."

She had said the same thing the day before, but Carmen knew the longer Jasmín went without waking up, the slimmer the chances grew that she would be the same when she did.

Just as she had since she'd been brought here, Jasmín lay motionless on her cot, chest rising and falling with her shallow breath. Her forehead was beaded slightly with sweat, and her face was peaceful, serene.

But it was day three, and she hadn't woken up.

She didn't need a doctor to tell her that wasn't a good sign.

Carmen wanted to scream, tear at her hair, kill everyone who was responsible for doing this to her. Most of all, she wanted to cry. But Carmen Santos, ruthless soldier, could not be seen crying.

Especially not over the first girl she had ever kissed.

So instead, she took the seat next to Jasmín's bed, tried to look concerned but composed, and continued her vigil. She wouldn't give up hope until there was none left to cling to.

There was still time.

As if she had heard Carmen's thoughts, Alicia bustled out of the tent, leaving Carmen alone with Jasmín, tying on a white armband with a red cross around her black canvas uniform before departing.

At La Voz headquarters, everyone wore the same uniform.

25

Only their armbands differentiated them. White with a red cross signified a healer, gray with an orange falcon was a scout or messenger, and red with a black vulture's skull was a soldier. The rest wore no armbands at all; they worked in the mess tent or did camp setup and maintenance; they made weapons or clothes or minded the children.

Carmen had left too early to get her assignment, and of course there was no insignia for a spy. She'd worn silk dresses and gold bangle bracelets the way the others wore their ranks and symbols. Once she'd thought she was bound for a warrior's band, or that maybe they'd invent a whole new category for her when she became the best spy in the organization's history.

Now, five years later, she sat at a girl's sickbed and wondered if she'd make it through the next week without being branded a traitor.

Life was full of surprises.

"Sleeping poison is tricky," Carmen muttered with disdain. That was the best she could do? Maybe La Voz needed a better healer.

Like a reflex, Carmen patted the pouch around the leg of her blacks, feeling for the vials that were always there.

They were no strangers to poison in La Voz; they carried it with them wherever they went. The first one, a pale, innocuous green, induced a temporary state of madness, which would cause confusion and grogginess at first, but would gradually progress to full hallucinations and hysteria, and finally death, if not neutralized quickly.

The second was a colorless, odorless sleeping poison. It guaranteed two hours of unconsciousness if taken orally, but it varied based on height and weight. Obviously whatever Jasmín had been given was much stronger.

The third poison was blood red, so you couldn't mistake it for the others. It was only one dose, but it wasn't intended for use on an enemy. This poison was for a quick and painless death, and was kept as a last resort. As she watched Jasmín lying unconscious on the bed, Carmen felt the vindication of knowing that the people who had attempted to kill this girl had died in ways that were far from painless.

For all the time she'd spent at Jasmín's bedside, Carmen hadn't spent much of it looking at her. It was too difficult to see her like this, wan and wasted, kept alive with droppers of sugar water and rags soaked in milk and honey. Her swallow reflex was good—a development that had seemed exciting on the first day—but solid foods were dangerous, and her cheeks were hollowing out by the hour.

If she didn't wake soon, there would barely be anything left of her when she did.

In the beginning, there had been long scratches across her face and down her arms. They looked intentional, like the work of a madman with a blade and a desperate gleam in his eye. The scratches and bruises were healed or healing now, but Carmen had memorized them all.

When she got her hands on Mateo, she would start by re-creating them. But that's not where it would end.

Jasmín's breathing grew shallower, and she panted like a terrified animal for a few seconds before it evened out again. Carmen gripped the edges of her chair until her knuckles turned white, waiting for it to pass. It always did. For a moment, she missed her long Segunda's painted nails. At least they felt like something when you dug them into your palms.

But she'd cut those, too, the morning after she threw the dress into the fire. To hide the ash that had gotten trapped beneath them when she dug for a last memento of Dani.

The red stain had taken days to fade, but it was gone now. The last vestige of her Segunda beauty regimen. Why did that make her sad?

Dani would barely recognize her now. Bare-faced, dressed in black canvas. Would she even want her without her lip stain? Her tinted brows? The berry paste she'd used to redden her cheeks?

Her hair was coarse; it frizzed from the sea air and the salt water she washed it in. They couldn't waste the filtered stuff on something as useless as haircare. The women here wore it short for the most part, just for ease of upkeep. Carmen had as well, before she'd been sent to the capital. But now she couldn't bring herself to cut what had grown there.

A Segunda's hair had been part of her armor, and Carmen

Santos was never unarmed.

Jasmín stirred, a groan escaping her lips. This, just yesterday, had brought Carmen so much hope. But it hadn't led to more. She adjusted Jasmín's pillow and sat back down, her muscles already itching with restlessness.

For anyone else, a cursory check-in would have sufficed. Not this lingering bedside visitation. But Carmen liked the quiet, the lack of prying eyes. Plus, they said you never forgot your first. Anything done to Jasmín felt personal to Carmen. Like the debt was hers to settle.

God willing, it would be settled soon.

But had it *all* been Mateo's doing? Carmen wondered, reaching for Jasmín's hand. Whose idea had it been to have her arrested? To send her into the belly of the beast with no clear plan for extracting her once the information had been gathered?

Ari's boastfulness came back to her then, and she dropped Jasmín's hand as quick as she'd taken it, standing up, pacing the tent as her thoughts raced. The arson at the marketplace had been Carmen's proof that La Voz was changing, but hadn't Jasmín's assignment borne the same brand of recklessness? Lack of forethought?

El Buitre had been the methodical type, an information gatherer, a calm, steady hand holding a deadly blade. His plans had taken time, yes, but they'd been airtight. They'd gotten people rescued, not killed. They'd struck blows; they hadn't opened La Voz up to take them.

Carmen was still pacing when the tent flap opened again.

"Nurse Santos," said a voice she would have known anywhere. "Not sure it fits."

Carmen turned to face Alex, hoping the manic energy of her thoughts didn't show on her face. "Just plotting vengeance, you know," Carmen said casually.

"Better to do it with a weapon in your hand." Alex's keen gray eyes gauged the distance between Carmen and the bedside, sizing up the expression on her face.

"Depends who's responsible," she replied.

"Does it?" Alex asked, raising a brow.

"Why send Jasmín in to be arrested?" Carmen countered, unable to keep her suspicions from bubbling over.

"It was a reconnaissance mission. We needed intel on the interrogation facilities." Alex's tone held a warning. One that Carmen ignored.

"But why do it rashly, with no extraction plan? Especially when we already had so many other balls in the air? It doesn't play like an El Buitre strategy, does it?"

"Careful, Cuervita," Alex said. "You've been gone a long time."

"Exactly my point," Carmen said. "I'm asking you when ill-conceived, rushed plans became part of La Voz's legend. You were here. I wasn't. So what happened?"

Alex looked at Carmen in that cool way they'd both learned in childhood. It was an appraising stare. A leader's hallmark.

"El Buitre wants us in the ring. Now. Maybe you should focus on your own shortcomings instead of digging for things that aren't there. There's no mystery to unravel here, Carmen. If you want to be one of us again, you have to earn it like everyone else does."

They had once been as close as two people could be, but while Carmen was away learning silk and silver and subterfuge, Alex had been here. At El Buitre's side. In the dust and salt, becoming a warrior.

As much as Carmen wanted to pretend things hadn't changed between them, she couldn't. Alex didn't look at Carmen with the same reverence and fear the others did. She knew her, in the way only girls raised like sisters and soldiers could know each other. She had been there in the final moments. Carmen's confession. Dani's look of utter betrayal. The way she'd pleaded for Dani's life and stayed until it was almost too late for all of them.

"You're right," she said, breaking the long silence, getting to her feet. Alex could have this one if it kept the peace, but Carmen didn't believe there was nothing to dig for. Not for a second. "The healers said I should take it easy for a few days, but I feel fine."

"When has Carmen Santos ever let a *medic* tell her what to do?" Alex asked, with a half smirk. "Remember that time you tore your arm open trying to climb that tree when we were on the west coast?"

Carmen smiled. She still had the scar, right where her

upper arm met her shoulder. "Hurt like hell."

"How long did they try to keep you out of the ring that time?" Alex pressed.

"Three weeks."

"How long did you stay out for?"

"Four days. I made Sota steal a mask for me, like my height wouldn't give it away."

They both laughed. "Don't tell me you're less brave now than you were at eight."

Carmen held Alex's eyes, sensing a question beneath the statement. "Wiser, maybe," she said. "But no less brave."

Alex let her response hang in the air for a moment, something swirling unsaid between them, kicking up a storm in Carmen's nerves that she hid with steady hands.

"Care to prove it?" Alex said finally, gesturing out the tent door, smiling again.

"Who do you think I am?" Carmen asked.

Alex didn't answer.

Jasmín stirred again.

Carmen didn't look back.

✥✥✳✥✥

THE FIGHTING RING WAS ALWAYS at the westernmost edge of the camp, and Carmen and Alex reached it quickly, uneasiness trailing them.

They didn't speak, but it was the silence of people with too much unsettled between them. Carmen knew it wouldn't last.

Ahead of them, El Buitre stood before a crowd of early morning trainers, his own long rifle at his back, the ceremonial dagger returned to his hip. Carmen averted her eyes, not wanting to think about what she'd done with it. The dark red of the officer's blood as it fed the earth.

What would Dani think of her if she knew Carmen was a killer?

Would she ever get the chance to find out?

In the sky, the sun had risen in earnest, and the heat was already building, cut slightly by the breeze off the sea. Carmen let her dark thoughts float away, rooting herself in the moment, ready to prove she had nothing on her mind but making herself back into the soldier La Voz had trained.

"The locals claim this place is cursed," El Buitre was saying as they approached. He gestured around at the grove, which had probably once been glorious.

All that remained now were the trees, ghostly, jagged at the tops from the lightning strikes of hundreds of years ago. The roots clung stubbornly to the salted earth, though they'd stopped drawing anything but dust from it long ago.

"They forbid their children from playing here," he went on, "scared of the whistling through the branches or the dancing shadows." He looked at Carmen as she took her place beside him. "Legends aren't often true, but that doesn't mean we can't use them when they benefit us."

Carmen nodded, seeing the wisdom in it. The grove was haunted, so they became the ghosts. No nosy children, no gossipy village wives to report to the border officers. It was an ideal hideout.

But as the early risers of the resistance chose their weapons and prepared to train, Carmen knew he was talking about more than the legend of the haunted grove. Carmen herself was mostly legend, tales of her exploits exaggerated since before she'd been waist-high on a true La Voz operative.

El Buitre knew it, and allowed the rumors to flourish. So far, they had benefited him. But the look on his face said he wouldn't hesitate to change his opinion—or Carmen's status—if she stopped being useful.

Her stunt by the fire three nights ago had bought her time, but he was still suspicious of her. She thought back to the piece of her Segunda dress in the basket on her bedside table and selected a weapon, aware of his eyes on her back.

"The goal of true resistance is not violence," he said, his booming voice reaching out to the scattered group as they stretched, adjusted weapons, and began lightly sparring. "It's not about blood, or death. The goal of true resistance is peace. Abundance. Violence is only a means to an end."

It was what Carmen had always told herself. The first time she wounded a man, the first time she killed one. That the violence was leading them to peace. That there could be no victory without sacrifice.

As the swords began to ring out and knives slashed through the crisp morning air, she felt something stirring. An excitement, an eagerness. This was what she'd been made to do.

No matter what Dani (or anyone else) thought of it, Carmen also couldn't deny it felt good to have that electricity in her veins. A purpose for her muscles and her pounding blood.

"The Garcia mother has been murdered!" El Buitre's voice

rang out. "Three of our operatives fled the scene, and were followed into our camp by border officers! One of the most powerful families in the country now knows there's been a traitor in their midst!"

Carmen closed her eyes against the picture he painted. Against the memories it brought up, and the fears. Dani was in that house, with all those people who now knew Carmen to be a traitor. Was she safe?

"How long do you think they will wait before they come for us?" El Buitre asked, and his words were like flint sparking into dry grass. Anyone on the sidelines stretching rushed into the ring. "WILL WE BE READY?"

The ringing of steel was the only answer he needed.

Never one to rush, Carmen took her time. She couldn't let the Vulture's scrutiny make her reckless. He wanted the Cuerva he'd trained; he would get her on her own terms.

Carmen sized up the area. Even at this early hour there were people milling around outside, watching, getting ready to head in. Carmen took note of where the fighters inside clustered.

Before she'd been there a whole minute, she had a strategy in place. It was like breathing, putting the pieces together, seeing the holes in defenses and the places she'd need to craft a plan that ensured her victory. The familiarity fed the buzzing in her blood until she felt it at last. The thrill. The draw to the fight. It had been a long time.

"Having second thoughts?" Alex asked, but her smile was

teasing. This was a place they could meet—a place where nothing was left unsettled but the victor.

"Calculation isn't the same as hesitation," Carmen said, scoffing. "Some of us have strategy."

"Some of us have strength."

It had been a common battle between them once—which was better, brains or brawn. Carmen had never had Alex's raw physical power, but she'd had a mind for the bigger picture that kept her three steps ahead. Their overall record when Carmen left had been a draw.

Alex, true to form, had already headed for the weapon rack. Carmen lingered a few minutes more.

"Adapting to a fighting space can be challenging," El Buitre said, moving between the soldiers, correcting grips and stances. "But we must be well-versed in combat on every type of terrain. You never know when trouble will find you."

Everyone fought more fiercely with his eyes on them. It was one of his great assets as a leader—he brought out the best in all of them. Carmen felt the pull to impress him, and the awareness of his attention, which never strayed from her for long.

This was her chance to prove that she hadn't gone soft. That she wasn't right now betraying him by wondering what a short-haired, brown-eyed girl would think of her ruthlessness.

"Our enemies practice in gated training facilities," El Buitre was saying now, his tone disdainful. "The same raked, pristine enclosure day after day. They stay in one place. They stay comfortable. But comfortable doesn't win battles."

After spending the first six years of her life on the move with the resistance, Carmen could account for the lack of comfort, at least. Though she'd never have admitted it, it had felt almost decadent to stay in her room after the first three months at school.

But a year into her Segunda training, the restlessness had kicked in. Carmen had felt stagnant, exposed. She'd never quite gotten used to the feeling of living in one place.

The moving schedule she'd been raised on was practical for a number of reasons:

First, it kept them novel. A story for villagers to tell rather than a nuisance that would have them contacting the authorities. Next, it kept them resourceful. Packing light, ready to move, without the comfort and laziness that came from getting used to one location. And last, it kept them insulated. Relying on each other rather than forming attachments to people who would only become liabilities.

The irony of this last one was not lost on Carmen.

She stretched as she continued to watch, limbering up muscles that still held the echoes of explosions and the tightness of too much mandated rest.

"As most of you already know, there are no rules in the ring!" El Buitre shouted as a skirmish got more intense just inside the boundary line. "There are no rules in war! We must be prepared for any tactic, any eventuality. Fight with all the creativity you can muster—your opponents in the field certainly won't be passing up any advantages."

Though she'd heard them a million times, El Buitre's instructions made Carmen feel calm, centered. A familiar soundtrack.

Weapons stood in racks just outside the ring beside two buckets of armbands—half dyed red, the other half white. You wore them to cover up your existing insignia. The only thing that mattered in a fight was the victor. Status was irrelevant.

Once Carmen had taken in the terrain and gotten a sense of the flow of combat, she walked up to one of the bins and took a red band, closing her eyes as she wrapped it twice around her upper arm, letting everything fade away. Dani. Her silence, her motivations. Alex and her silent judgment, her resistance to answering any of Carmen's questions about the new direction La Voz had taken.

El Buitre, watching from across the clearing. Waiting for a mistake. Waiting for a reason.

None of those problems could go over that line with her. Her mind had to be empty, focused, ready to strike and react. There was no room for distraction in a fight.

The crowd inside shifted, thinning and swelling as people were defeated, as more arrived. Carmen watched for the other red armbands, her team. You didn't always know their faces, or their names, because that's the way it often was in a real fight. Bodies coming and going, alliances shifting, people joining and dying and defecting with every passing day.

In front of the weapons rack, Carmen hesitated. Before she'd left home, she had always fought with a short sword. But it didn't feel right. She wasn't that girl now, any more than she was a Segunda, or the wife of Mateo Garcia. They had been roles, and Carmen Santos was on to the next.

From back in her tent, the tiny piece of her Segunda's dress seemed to taunt her, undermining her commitment. She closed her eyes again, willing the thought of Dani away. But she never went far.

Finally, almost at random, she chose a staff with a bladed end, nearly as tall as she was. It would do for now. With a weapon in hand her blood was buzzing, synapses firing in a way totally devoid of worry for the first time since she'd returned home.

El Buitre's eyes were drawn to her again, something like pride in his features as he took her in, back in her La Voz uniform, armed and dangerous just like he'd raised her to be.

She needed to show him he was right. That she belonged. Otherwise she wouldn't live long enough to find out what had happened to him. To La Voz.

Beside her, Alex selected a two-handed sword, the metal warped and dinged in places like so many of their weapons. The camp had only one skilled blacksmith. They were notoriously hard to recruit, and even harder to train, so weapon repair and refinishing was a slow business. Mostly members took what they could from skirmishes with desperadoes and policia, treating them as disposable when they broke or wore out.

Carmen was grateful that the staff she'd chosen was straight at least. After so long away from home and training, she would need all the help she could get.

In front of her, a man staggered out, bare-chested and spitting blood. He seemed to be missing a tooth. Carmen nodded at him, but she did not smile. He returned the nod, but dropped his eyes quickly. Intimidation, or disrespect? Carmen wondered. But she couldn't tell.

Centering herself briefly, Carmen let it pass. This man was nothing compared to what they'd be facing. The capital, in an uproar over Mama Garcia's death. The grieving chief military strategist marshaling his troops. Mateo, cruel and closed-minded, looking for any excuse to obliterate the threat beyond the wall.

Carmen's face was what they all dreamed of at night. Her name was on their lips as they trained, as they planned. She was the reason they were coming. To kill her and everyone she'd ever loved.

Well, almost everyone.

It didn't take long before she was ready, the thrill of the coming fight pounding in her pulse. Out of the corner of her eye, Carmen saw El Buitre smile slightly, like he could feel the bloodlust coming off her in waves.

Inside the ring, the fight was underway, the teams pitted against each other, single skirmishes and groups clashing, coming apart, re-forming and clashing again. No one glanced

Carmen's way as she stepped over the line into the ring, but that was fine.

She had always taken pleasure in being underestimated.

A mace swung for her the moment her left foot crossed the line, and she brought the staff up to meet it, hearing the wooden handle groan a little under the heavier weapon's weight, adjusting as best she could to compensate. The girl swinging it had a feral scowl Carmen was immediately drawn to. She looked a little older, but the top of her head barely reached Carmen's shoulder.

Another underdog, she thought, grinning now. But the girl's scowl did not give way.

Carmen twisted before the mace could do more damage, her body remembering how to dance this way. The twist broke the contact, but before Carmen could strike a blow of her own, the girl was shoulder checked by a man Carmen didn't know sporting a red armband.

"Welcome," he grunted before engaging with the scowling girl, leaving Carmen free to move deeper into the fray.

The next flash of white that came her way was a boy who looked to be only a year or two older than her. He was tall, with hair that flopped into his eyes and a grin that said he was a little frivolous. He hesitated when he saw her, the flash of fear obvious. Carmen's first instinct was to punish him for it, but her Segunda training slowed her blade.

She knew now that the easiest way to get what you wanted was to give a man what he wanted. It was knowledge she hadn't had the last time she'd stepped into this ring.

Throwing her full force at a man bigger and more experienced than she was would never work. But that didn't mean she had to lose.

She smiled, just a small one, luring him in. *I'm not as scary as you've heard,* the smile said, and she made her first strike intentionally feeble.

Don't ever show strength exceeding that of a man's, her maestras had said. *It will put him on the defensive and make the road ahead rockier.*

The boy was strong, his muscles defined, but when he blocked he held back. She could feel it. Her next strike was a little harder, but this time she subtly tossed her hair, watching him follow the long line of her neck, the mane that was still effective even ravaged by salt and lack of proper moisturizing.

He took his eyes off her weapon. Her smile turned feral. By the time he noticed, it was too late. Carmen hoped El Buitre was watching now; this was the kind of show he enjoyed.

With the center of the staff she sent him sprawling, spluttering in the dust cloud that rose up around him. By the time he came to his senses, the blade of Carmen's staff was at his throat, her legs on either side of him, pinning him down.

"Think with your *brain,* not your little friend down there," she said, increasing the pressure until she just nicked the skin. First blood. The end of any fight in the ring. "Do you know what's coming for you?" she asked. "For all of us? Because I can guarantee you it's harder to beat than me."

He swallowed instead of answering, the words trapped somewhere below the blade.

"Next time you make a mistake like that," Carmen said, "you'll be more than just humiliated. You'll be dead."

She watched her words sink in for a moment too long.

"Move on!" came El Buitre's barking voice from outside the line. "Each fight is a link in a chain. Never lose sight of the battle!"

Carmen swore under her breath, "accidentally" kicking the boy in the ribs as she stepped over him. It had been a rookie mistake, stopping to congratulate herself—and the Vulture's gaze, heavy on her back, knew it better than she did.

She tried to tap back into her anger, the sense of urgency that an army of soldiers on the trail of her scent had stirred to life just a moment ago. But there was danger here, too, and it could get to her much quicker than any army.

Divided, Carmen gripped her weapon tighter and charged back in, looking for someone to punish.

There was a narrow miss with a slim-hipped woman who danced just out of Carmen's reach until she managed to slice her bare forearm. Then a bear of a man easily twice her size who came at her with a two-handed hammer. She barely managed to nick his neck at long range with her spear while he was winding up for another strike, and he glowered at her for half a minute before stalking over the line.

From there, they blended together, people coming and going, Carmen's head swimming with the strain and the lingering injury she'd sustained during the blast. *Where is Alex?* she wondered, sweat running down her face as she sidestepped a three-on-two engagement, searching for the familiar short hair and angular features.

She could beat anyone in this ring twice, but it wouldn't be worth a thing until she squared off with the girl she'd learned to fight beside. The girl who knew her every move. They never left the ring until they'd faced off, and today was not a day for breaking traditions.

And then, without warning, there was a sword point at her chin. "Where's your strategy now?" Alex asked, her voice low. But Carmen dropped to the ground, sending the sword bouncing harmlessly off her collarbone as she spun to strike out at Alex's ankle with her spear.

Alex blocked the attack easily, but her sword was slow to pull back, and Carmen used the extra seconds to get on her feet. They squared off, sizing each other up like they'd done a million times before. But Alex had a new edge to her today.

Distrust.

No matter how often they'd gone blade to blade, worn different colored armbands, they'd always left this ring on the same side. Today, Alex's look said she wasn't sure they would.

Carmen put a hand on her hip, tired of being questioned, forgetting the piece of silk in her tent and the army descending on them, and remembering only that this girl—her sister, who had promised to always believe in her—was now looking at her like she was a stranger.

Alex adjusted her stance, not backing down.

"Enough."

The voice barely made it through the blood pounding in Carmen's ears, but her body obeyed instantly, shoulders relaxing, weapon dropping.

El Buitre surveyed the two of them, his expression inscrutable.

"Clean yourself up," he said to Carmen. "I want to see you in my quarters."

He walked away before she could reply, the letdown of adrenaline mixing with her fear until she felt less like herself than she had before the fight.

So much for proving myself, she thought, careful not to let the fear show on her face.

In front of her, the other girl's pupils were still dilated, her weapon struggling to settle at her side.

For a brief second, Carmen imagined hitting her anyway.

"Don't be late," Alex said.

Carmen tossed her hair irritably and tossed a passing boy her staff. He barely caught it. Tomorrow she'd hear that Carmen Santos buried a spear in a boy's chest with the force of her annoyance alone.

"Put that away," she said to him, and to Alex: "This isn't over."

Carmen stormed out of the ring, heading for El Buitre's tent without pausing to clean up. She was sweaty and grimy from nearly an hour of hand-to-hand combat. He wanted a soldier? He would get one.

But she had a nagging feeling today hadn't been enough.

That maybe nothing would ever be enough.

She took the long way toward the center of the grove, moving through the trees, giving herself time to calm down before she reached El Buitre's tent. She passed children at play, men sewing rips in clothing, and women sharpening knives.

Carmen had been shocked, arriving at the capital, when she found duties divided by gender. Men who didn't cook or clean, women who had never held a weapon. In La Voz, in the outer island in general, there weren't enough hands to be fussy about whose did what.

She passed stalls before reaching the mess tent with hand-made goods and meager dried food offerings. No one used money here, but the barter system was popular, and there was a lively trade—from old women who wove blankets and tapestries to children running around with sweets they made from stolen sugar.

Carmen had loved it when she was young, ditching lessons to come down and play jacks in the dirt with the potter's younger daughters, or steal sweets from the pockets of the cook's sons and run from them when they chased her.

El Buitre had always come for her before long, though, reminding her that her place was at his side. In her lessons.

Learning the business of running the resistance, of fighting, of negotiating, of spying.

She should have been worrying that it could all be wiped out at a moment's notice. That the military was likely on their way. Scouts had been sent to the capital the moment Carmen and Alex returned, but they hadn't returned, and without more information, the resistance was little better than sitting ducks.

But despite the overwhelming odds and the sea of unknowns, Carmen wasn't focused on worry. Not even about the obliteration of her home.

She was too busy wishing Dani were here, hand in Carmen's, taking in the sights, giggling over Carmen's memories.

Carmen missed Dani so much it caught her off guard sometimes, made her lose her breath. The longer she went without seeing her, touching her, kissing her, the less sure she was that any of it had been real in the first place.

You're a fraud, and a traitor, and a thief, said a cruel voice in her head. *The only you she could ever love was the lie. . . .*

She didn't want to believe it, but where was Dani now? If she believed in the cause, believed in Carmen, if she had truly loved more than just the facade, why hadn't she made contact?

The center of the compound loomed in front of Carmen long before she was ready, marked as always by the blood-red stamp of a vulture's skull on black above the doorway. It was the only thing that indicated his place was different from the rest. It was no larger, no more extravagant.

There are no kings in La Voz, he always said. *Only soldiers.*

Of course, statements like those only made people revere him more. Carmen had never wondered as a child, but now she did: Whether he knew the effect of his supposed humility. Whether he used it to his advantage.

"Come in," he said through the open flap of his tent when she approached.

Carmen ducked slightly into the tent, her hips brushing the fabric of the narrow doorway as she stepped inside. It was dark, candles burning low despite the brilliant sunlight outside. At a makeshift table of crates and scrap wood in the corner, El Buitre bent low over what looked like a map, making a mark and rolling it up as she entered.

She wanted to believe the gesture was a coincidence, but she knew him too well.

This was more proof that he didn't trust her.

The implications of his actions were troubling enough without the way they made her feel. Like she was still a little girl. That her own personal sun had turned away from her, leaving her in the cold.

When he faced her, Carmen felt the same way she always had in his presence. Humbled. A little afraid. Grateful for him and everything he had done to give her a life worth living.

This was the man who had raised her. The closest thing she would ever have to a father.

She wanted him to trust her because his trust went hand

in hand with her survival, but she wanted him to love her, too. Nothing could ever be easy.

"You wanted to see me?" she asked.

"How are you settling in?" He rose to his feet, moving to another small table with two chairs near the doorway of the tent. He sat in one, and gestured her into the other.

"No need to settle in," Carmen answered as breezily as she could. "I've been looking forward to my homecoming for a long time, Jefe." Despite her best efforts, there was an edge to her tone.

"The circumstances were less than ideal," he said, pouring himself a drink.

Carmen declined the one he offered her. She needed her wits about her here.

"Yes," she said. "I was out of communication, but someday you'll have to tell me about the marketplace fire. La Voz has changed tactics since I left." She was pushing it, and they both knew it, but Carmen wasn't going to sit here and pretend to be the only one at fault.

"We're in the business of calculated risks, Cuervita; perhaps you remember."

"I've taken a few of my own," Carmen said, nodding. This wasn't the time to dig for information. The mystery of La Voz's new, sloppy maneuvers would remain a mystery awhile longer.

"That's why I asked you here," he said, his eyes sharp as they focused on hers. "One of your calculated risks is giving us a good deal of trouble."

Dani, Carmen thought, her pulse jumping even as she kept her gaze steady on his.

"Sota's report came in just an hour ago. Your friend has missed two check-ins. Hasn't sent word. She's in the wind, m'ija, and I need to know what she knows before things get any worse."

"First of all," Carmen said, "she was an assignment, not a friend." The truth in her chest fought with the lie on her lips, but Carmen kept it silent. It was the only way.

"I'll confess I'm relieved to hear it," El Buitre said, his eyebrows raised.

"You doubted me?"

El Buitre considered her. "A fool trusts blindly. The wisest man is full of doubts." It wasn't the first time he'd said it, but it was the first time he'd said it about Carmen. "When you left home you were a girl, molded by the world you had been exposed to, raised at my knee. It was easy to trust you then. You were a tool in my hand."

"And now?" Carmen asked coolly. She wasn't thrilled with the metaphor.

"Now you're a woman. Grown in the eyes of the world. You have been away, absorbing another world, making choices I was not there to supervise or advise you in. Am I wrong to wonder if those choices have truly brought you back to me?"

"Not wrong," Carmen admitted. "But I hope I can ease your mind now. I belong to the cause, Jefe, as I always have. Not a tool, maybe, but a comrade. Nothing about my absence has changed what I believe."

It was the truth, she thought as she waited for him to respond. Even though there was more to that truth than she had told him.

"There was more in Sota's report," he said, rewarding her show of loyalty with more information. "The Garcia house is empty. The family has fled, and none of our informants know where they've gone."

"You think they're sequestering her?"

He nodded. "But why?"

When Carmen was a girl, he'd often thrown scenarios at her this way. Hypotheticals. A whetstone to the blade that was her developing talent for strategy.

But this was no hypothetical.

"There are two options, as far as I can see," Carmen answered levelly. "One, she's turned, promised them information in exchange for safety, and they're keeping her isolated to prevent us from finding out."

El Buitre nodded, impressed by her ability to face the worst-case scenario head-on.

Just as she'd known he would be.

"And the other?"

"They've discovered her betrayal," Carmen said, trying to hide her fear, the way it felt like a cold current lurking beneath the warm waves. "And they've imprisoned her. Or they're torturing her for information. Or . . ." She couldn't hesitate. She had to be clinical. Detached. Even though she was screaming inside. "They've killed her already."

"And if they're torturing her?" El Buitre asked, his face as impassive as Carmen hoped she'd kept her own. "What songs will this little bird sing them?"

"She could do damage as an informant, but not nearly as much as Jasmín could have," Carmen said, as if she were considering it for the first time. "As far as I know, Sota kept her mostly in the dark."

"And what about you?" El Buitre asked, watching her face like a hawk. "Did you keep her in the dark as well?"

"She discovered my true identity two minutes before we were separated," Carmen said, as if it were a question of little consequence and not the heart of the tension between them. "I believe Alex's report on that was thorough."

"She seems to believe it," El Buitre allowed.

Carmen bristled. "I was sent into enemy territory *alone* at twelve, to accomplish a task no La Voz agent in a hundred years has been equal to," she said, her words controlled but simmering with something that seemed to heat the small tent around them. "I used the tools at my disposal to accomplish that task. I secured allies, I gained access to locations and information. I followed every order given to me."

He waited, his expression placid as she said her piece.

"I'm happy to answer any question you have, Jefe, but if I'm being accused of something, I at least deserve to know what it is."

For how close to the line she'd just stepped, El Buitre

didn't seem upset. There was a gleam in his eye Carmen couldn't quite define. It made her uneasy.

"If I'd intended to make an accusation, you'd know," he said. "I brought you here to inform you that the council will convene at midnight to decide on a course of action regarding the Vargas girl and the trouble she has caused this organization. I would like you present at that meeting. I hope you will take the time between now and then to recall any detail about your . . . acquaintance with the girl that may prove useful in our decision-making process."

Carmen knew this tone well enough. She was being dismissed.

"I appreciate the courtesy," Carmen said, "but it's unnecessary. I'm ready."

"I hope that's true."

There was a time when she would have stayed, gotten the last word, but Carmen took the dip of his chin as permission to leave and walked out, careful to keep her footsteps soundless, not to show her irritation.

Or her fear.

Because as frustrating as his assumptions were, Carmen knew they weren't unfounded. He wanted proof that Dani had been nothing to her, proof he hadn't found in her denials today. More than that, he wanted proof that Dani hadn't been enough to sway Carmen from her obligation to the cause. That she hadn't taken its place as the most important thing in Carmen's heart.

As Carmen walked back toward her tent, dreading the coming night, she wondered: Why hadn't she admitted it? Said the feelings had been real, but they hadn't changed the way she felt. That the cause was still the only truth in her heart.

There was only one answer to that, and it was one Carmen wasn't nearly ready to face.

I pledge my honesty to my brothers and sisters in the cause; no lie or mistruth will I utter in their presence.

—*La Voz Membership Pledge*

+‡>✳<‡+

BACK IN HER TENT, instead of preparing, Carmen slept, waking from strange dreams to find night had fallen.

She was disoriented, head ringing from her exertion during training and her dreams. Winding snakes curling in on themselves, whirlpools that exposed the inky black nothingness at the depths of the sea.

There had been no answers in sleep.

But there were none in waking, either.

Rising from her bed, Carmen pushed her sleep-tangled hair from her face and walked out into the night. The air was still, and in this section of camp—so far from the buzzing epicenter that was busy any time of the day or night—it was quiet. Peaceful, even.

At least, it would have been if Carmen's thoughts weren't more tangled than her curls.

Midnight was approaching. It was time to answer for her final night as a Segunda at last.

Though her eyes strayed toward the basket that held the charred piece of braided silk, she didn't dare open it tonight. She was already too close to losing everything.

"I'm sorry," she whispered across the room. To the talisman. To the girl it represented. An apology for every lie she'd have to tell tonight.

Outside, she closed her eyes against the gentle breeze playing through the haunted grove, the hollow trees singing in it, creating a cocoon of darkness and gentle lullaby that Carmen almost believed would hide her forever. But the moon had finished its ascent in the sky, and she was out of time.

"You ready?" Alex's voice was soft, but Carmen had to will herself not to jump.

"Are you?" she asked mildly.

Alex held her hands up, palms facing Carmen. A peacemaking gesture.

"I get it, I get it . . . it's just been a while since you've been part of the ranks, hermana. And everyone has a lot to say tonight. . . ." Alex's tone said she was only stating the obvious, but Carmen had known her too long and too well not to know there was something thorny lurking beneath her too-calm exterior.

"I *know* it's been a while, Alex." Carmen had known this moment was coming, but justifying herself to both Alex and El Buitre in one day was a tough pill to swallow. "It's not like I was on vacation."

Alex just raised her eyebrows, her palms still open.

"If you disagree," Carmen said, crossing her arms, "feel free to share. Or would you rather wait for El Buitre to summon me and let you off the hook?"

Alex's eyes narrowed. "You want to hear it? Fine. No one *ordered* you to play at puppy love with the baby spy. You're hiding behind the idea that it was beneficial to the cause, but you've got a long way to go to convince anyone of that."

Carmen waited, knowing there was more, keeping her face impassive as fluttering wings of panic brushed her insides.

"You were out of control when we left her," Alex said. "You took your sweet time saying goodbye. You almost destroyed everything we spent five years building with you in that school. . . ."

Carmen had had enough. "*We* spent?" she asked, incredulous. "*We* built? Were you there, Alex? Surrounded by people who would kill you or worse if they knew who you were? Being groomed like a farm animal to be sold to the highest bidder?"

"You're missing the point," Alex said with a dismissive

wave of her hand that made Carmen see red. "You let your feelings for that girl cloud your judgment. You were more concerned with apologizing and making sure she forgave you than you were with debriefing her and getting the hell out of there. It was reckless, and it wasn't like you."

Carmen took a deep breath through her nose, the sound hissing in the empty space, calming her pulse before she spoke. Alex was all earth. Timeless and stony. Fighting her with fire had never gotten Carmen anywhere.

"I was making sure she didn't feel betrayed," Carmen explained, the truth almost too noisy beneath her lies. "I was supposed to have weeks to gracefully extricate us from that situation, and I barely had two minutes. I did the best I could with the resources I had, which is exactly what we were *all* trained to do."

Another deep breath. Alex didn't interrupt.

"With the information Dani has, in the position she's in, her hating me was more dangerous than spending a few extra seconds on that roadside. I was *acting*, Alex. Protecting what *I* built."

I'm sorry, Carmen thought again. To the last piece of her old life. To the girl she had lived it with. A girl who deserved better than violence and deception and betrayal.

"So, you're telling me it was all an act? The relationship? Just a way to pull her closer when you felt her slipping away?"

Carmen couldn't afford to hesitate, even though the answer tore her apart. "*Yes*," she said emphatically. "And I'm trying really hard not to be offended that you even had to ask me that question."

It was the answer Alex expected, Carmen thought as she met her gaze unflinchingly. The one she had to give if she wanted to survive.

"If they decide tonight that she's a liability," Alex began finally, watching Carmen closely, "or even if it's too dangerous to extricate her, there won't be anything you can do to save her. You'll have to be on board with her termination."

Carmen took her time answering. Not even Alex would expect her to be casual about human life. She tried to think of how she would feel if Dani were someone else, someone who didn't feel necessary to her survival. Someone who wasn't somehow part of her soul.

When she was finally ready to answer, she faced Alex without apology. "The cause comes first," she said, slowly and clearly. "If she's a risk to us, I won't get in the way."

After the words were out, Carmen felt empty. Hollow. She hadn't realized she was harboring hope of seeing Dani again, of explaining, apologizing, picking up where they'd left off.

But how could she ever do that now?

Carmen had expected to have to lie, but she hadn't been prepared for how it would make her feel. For the truth it would expose—one she couldn't bend or manipulate or ignore.

Dani deserved better than Carmen. Better than all of this.

Alex's and Carmen's eyes stayed locked for what felt like an eternity. Carmen wore the ruthless rebel like a mask as she fell apart inside, needing Alex to believe, needing to stay alive even if she wasn't sure what for.

At last, *at last*, Alex stepped forward, cuffing Carmen on the shoulder. "I'm sorry, hermana," she said. "But you know I had to make sure."

Carmen nodded, trying not to show the relief turning her knees liquid. "I would have done the same if it were you," she said, like a girl who knew who she was. Knew where she belonged. But as Alex turned to lead the way to the meeting, Carmen felt the emptiness threatening to take over.

Could she really do nothing if they voted to let Dani die?

Before setting out, she patted her poison pouch, strapped beneath her pant leg.

She never went into a room full of enemies without it.

✦

IN THE LONG MEETING TENT behind El Buitre's quarters, Ari was alone in the seat at the leader's right hand. Carmen glared at him, but he was unfazed. His expression said he knew something she didn't.

Alex took the seat across from him, to the left of El Buitre's chair. Carmen sat beside her, as her usual chair was occupied. She tried to keep thoughts of Dani at bay, to focus on getting through the night, but her conversation with Alex had dragged up too many demons. They wouldn't rest.

Instead, she focused on her elaborate fantasy of giving Ari a bloody nose. It was the best distraction she'd found so far.

They waited as a few more people came in. Two older men in soldier armbands Carmen didn't recognize, and a bandless woman, a streak of gray in her hair, who looked only vaguely familiar.

Within minutes, the table had filled, but the top seat was still empty.

Ari got to his feet.

"Our leader has been indisposed, but he's instructed me to begin this meeting in his place. Please, take your seats."

"Are you kidding me?" Carmen asked, barely under her breath. Alex shot her a warning glance.

"We have a lot to discuss, and not a lot of time," Ari said, raising his voice to cut through more whispers than just Carmen's. "So." He clapped his hands, then turned to Carmen. "We'll start with you and Daniela Garcia. Tell us what happened your last week in the house."

The tent went very still and quiet. Ari watched Carmen, a predatory gleam in his eye.

"We received no correspondence from you," he pressed, clearly more for the benefit of the crowd than for Carmen. "You missed regular check-ins. Why?"

Little as she liked this turn of events, Carmen had no choice but to play along. "I had grown closer with Daniela," she began, as if she were addressing a leader and not a jumped-up weasel with a power complex. "She was conflicted, but very close to making a full commitment to La Voz. One that wasn't contingent on Sota's blackmail. One I felt we could benefit from when my usefulness in the Garcia house had run its course."

"Go on," said Ari, like baiting an animal into a trap.

Carmen took a deep breath, let it out slow. "She knew nothing of my involvement, per my orders, and I was afraid sneaking off to make a report might raise suspicion that would distract her from the process of committing on her own. I made a judgment call."

Truthfully, the last week of her residence in the Garcia house had been one of the most terrifying of her life. She had spun constant webs of deception, knowing she needed to give Dani up—and any hope of a future with her—but for the first time in her life she'd been unable to do what was expected of her.

"No one is accusing you of anything," Alex said, her tone light. "*Right*, Ari?"

"Of course not," Ari said, matching her tone but not meeting her eyes.

"As I've said, I'm happy to give you all the information you'd like about my mission and its execution," Carmen said. "This isn't my first time at the table. I know how it's done."

"How was it that you ended up in the marketplace that day?" Ari asked, nearly talking over her. "Especially with much more convenient ways to get in contact at your disposal."

Carmen willed her heart to slow, paranoid suddenly that it was audible in the enclosed space of the tent. Ari was getting desperate, and he was right to be. Carmen had much more goodwill built up with the people at this table than he did, and with Alex on her side . . .

"With all due respect, Ari, all these questions have the same answer. I couldn't reach out to our better placed contacts without blowing my cover and spooking my asset at a pivotal moment."

"You say you were close to Daniela," Ari said, rapid-fire. He was making his way to his point. "But close enough to be missed at any hour of the day or night? That's *very* close. . . ."

Despite herself, Carmen felt her cheeks warm. Not the warmth of shame—she'd never been plagued by that particular affliction—but the feeling of this slimy boy rifling through her memories was almost more than she could take.

As close to the truth as possible, she reminded herself. It wasn't Ari she needed to convince. It was the rest of the people at the table.

"We had a romantic relationship," she said, like she was discussing a classified document and not a frantic kiss in a rainstorm.

"And *that's* how you recruited her?" His tone was laced with harsh judgment. He looked around at the table, inviting them to condemn Carmen alongside him.

"Sota did the recruiting," Carmen said, careful not to react emotionally. "The relationship was one of convenience. The closer we got, the more she confided in me. His access to her was limited, and we needed to know as much about her state of mind as possible."

Alex nodded her approval. Slowly the people around her followed suit.

Ari's plan had backfired, and Carmen felt her confidence growing. She hadn't forgotten how to play this game. Maybe she would make it out of this after all.

But who will you be once you're out? a small voice asked.

Carmen ignored it.

"When it became clear Daniela's feelings were more than platonic," she continued, "I took the opening. It allowed me to keep track of her loyalty, find out if she was truly devoted or just responding to the blackmail."

"Not very convenient when the *relationship* prohibits you from making contact or receiving orders," Ari snapped. "Not to mention the risk if you were caught."

This time, she didn't have to think. The lie was ready.

"The marketplace fire was an unexpected complication," she said, shooting a glance at Ari. "It was a very public demonstration at a time when there were a lot of pieces in motion. Before that, the risk made sense. After, it became an unmanageable situation for all of us."

In the tent, the mood shifted. Glances that had been directed at Carmen now moved to Ari, who looked murderous.

"If you'd checked in, or even managed to not be *miles* from where you were supposed to be, the demonstration in the marketplace—which was an unqualified success, by the way—wouldn't have affected your mission. Don't try to lay your mistakes at our feet."

He was overcompensating, reaching; he was losing the room. Carmen could have laughed if she wasn't so busy being cool and collected. Making a show of strength and professionalism as he floundered.

"What mistakes were those, Ari?" Carmen asked. "Just so I understand why you're suddenly so . . . upset."

His face was flushed, and he gaped for a moment before he answered.

"*You* had a relationship with an asset! You jeopardized an active mission! You probably fed secrets to a stupid girl who probably gave them right to the Median government!"

"If you'd like to provide proof for any of these emotional accusations, I'm happy to discuss them," Carmen said, one eyebrow raised at his outburst. "But otherwise I'll continue to tell you what I've been telling you: I made the best decisions I could with the information and skills I had, just as I was trained to do."

"Oh, that's not the whole story and you know it, you *all* know it!"

Ari got to his feet. Carmen remained seated, her gaze cool in a way that only seemed to infuriate him further.

"That's enough."

El Buitre crossed the tent, taking his seat at the table, looking pointedly at Ari, who took his seat.

"I apologize for the delay. I trust Señor Vasquez has managed to keep things on track?"

Ari, Alex, and El Buitre all turned to look at Carmen, who smirked across the table.

"It's been positively civil." Let Ari wonder why she'd stood up for him, Carmen thought. Let him be unnerved.

"Good," said El Buitre. "We'll go over the minutes at a later time. We have pressing business to attend to now."

Everyone sat up straighter as he spoke, the uncertainty of Ari's meeting melting away. Even Carmen couldn't deny the effect of his authority. Not even when he might be here to condemn Dani once and for all.

"As you all know by now," El Buitre began, "Daniela Garcia failed to arrive for her meeting with Sota. We received word this morning that when he traveled to the Garcia house, it was empty. The family has relocated. We aren't sure at this point where they have gone, or why."

He presented the facts without commentary, but around her, people shifted uneasily. They were drawing conclusions that spelled out Dani's fate in creased eye corners and lips pressed tight together.

Carmen had explained her own intentions well enough, but how could she protect Dani? How could she keep her safe from this?

"I'd like to add some context here," Carmen said, unable to keep quiet, ignoring a pointed look from Alex that said she was about to undo all the good she'd done. "Daniela sustained extensive injuries in the explosion. I wouldn't be surprised if they've made it impossible for her to travel yet."

"And if that were the only factor at play, I would agree with you," El Buitre said, shaking his head regretfully. "But the emptying of the house gives us . . . significant pause."

Ari smirked at the term *us*, and Carmen avoided his eyes. How much influence did he really have here? Enough to orchestrate a poorly planned demonstration, sure, but could he get Dani killed?

The Vulture she knew was pragmatic but fair. He wasn't cruel. But he wasn't the only one on that side of the table anymore.

"There could have been any number of reasons for a move." Carmen tried to sound logical, like the closest agent to the situation due to her mission and training, and not like a lovestruck seventeen-year-old trying to protect her girl-friend from being executed for treason.

El Buitre inclined his head, allowing her to continue.

"The Garcias are under suspicion for the disappearing sympathizers. Even during the marketplace fire, they were holed up in one of their coastal properties. It's not much of a stretch to think that they'd move Daniela there as well, to keep the family together in the wake of their most recent struggles."

"It's a stretch," Ari said, finding his voice again. "Far more likely that our lovesick new recruit wanted to punish the girl who left her, and became an ally to anyone who could help her get revenge."

"That's speculation." Carmen's voice was closer to a growl than the level tone she'd been aiming for. "You have no way of knowing—"

"Oh, and you do?" Ari interrupted. "You just painted a pretty picture of Daniela and her family fleeing the capital because of an internal threat. Was that more than speculation?"

"I was *there*." Carmen leaned toward him across the table. "I knew her. I knew all of them. My speculation is based on experience, not my own agenda."

"Really?" Ari rose to his feet, performing for them all even as he stared right at Carmen with those cruel pale eyes. "Because we haven't talked much about that *agenda*, have we?"

"I'm right here," Carmen said, her voice deadly.

"Enough," El Buitre said, placing his palms down on the table. His voice was quiet, his gesture soft, but there was no questioning the authority in it.

Ari sat down, but Carmen could see him fuming. She leaned back into her own chair, crossing her arms. She never should have let him get to her. Her calm, cool exterior had been what swayed the room before. No one wanted a volatile spy.

"For the moment," El Buitre went on, "we will have to consider her out of our reach. But a decision must be made, whether or not we can count on her input to help us make it."

"Just to be clear," Carmen said. "What decision is that?"

Ari scoffed. The Vulture Carmen had known would have dismissed him from the table, but this man in front of her did nothing. Something rebellious stirred in Carmen's heart. Something that didn't recognize what had happened to its home in her absence.

"Regrettably, we must assume that one of two outcomes is currently playing out," El Buitre said, echoing Carmen's hypothetical from earlier that day. "Either Daniela Garcia has been discovered, or she has turned."

"She hasn't turned," Carmen said firmly, hating the way Ari's eyes crawled over her when she said it. "I'm not sure what's going on there, but I know she's committed. And if we can assume it's the other option, we owe her our protection."

Carmen held her head high as the accusatory silence pressed around her like fog.

"I think what Santos is trying to say . . . ," Alex began, weighing in for the first time. She got to her feet beside Carmen, a counterbalance to Ari's performance. ". . . is that there are a lot of moving parts here, and that rushing a decision would be unwise."

Alex looked at Carmen, though she spoke to the two men, and Carmen knew this was her way of being loyal. Of honoring what the two of them had shared. She was well-respected at this table. Her support made an immediate and visible difference.

El Buitre looked to Carmen to corroborate Alex's statement.

"I've known Dani since she was twelve years old," Carmen said, palms up on the table, defenseless, accepting. "I lived with her at the Garcias'. She confided in me." She took a deep breath, needing them to believe this, if nothing else. "By the time we left her on that roadside, she was a hundred percent committed. If I had had any doubts, we would have taken care of the problem right then."

"I had a gun to her head, Jefe," Alex said. "Whatever you believe about Santos and her connection to the girl, I still believe we made the right call."

El Buitre considered this, the weight of his pause filling the room. No one dared break it.

Carmen fought the urge to shift her weight, to touch her hair. Her heartbeat spelled Dani's name again and again as her old home and her new reservations did battle in her chest. Ari's gaze bored into her from across the table, trying to see what was beneath the surface.

As if she'd ever give him the satisfaction.

"I have no doubt Carmen was persuasive," the Vulture said at last. "But I remain concerned about the nature of her emotional relationship with Daniela as it relates to her ability to be objective in this situation."

The words landed heavily on the table, and in the pit of Carmen's stomach.

How many more times would she have to tell this lie?

How long until it wore thin?

"I've never had a problem with objectivity, Jefe," Carmen said. "You of all people should know that."

"Well," said Ari, the fire from their argument before still lingering behind his eyes. "That was before you were sent to a school that trains people to be unstable and emotional and spent your sensitive resistance mission developing an inappropriate relationship with an asset. Forgive us if we don't—"

"Forgive *us*?" Carmen asked, cutting him off, getting to her feet before she even knew she was. "Where did you even come from? And where do you get off speaking to me like that?" She turned to El Buitre. "Are you going to let him talk to me like that? I was on a mission given to me by this organization. I used the tools at my disposal to accomplish the goals I was assigned to achieve. I fail to see what I've done to deserve this distrust, or *that* disrespect."

Carmen knew she was out of line, and El Buitre's eyes flashed at her insolence. Ari was on his feet now, too, and they glared daggers at each other while waiting for the hammer to fall.

"Sit. Down. *Both of you.*"

They obeyed.

"Ari, in case you haven't noticed, your seat is somewhat west of the head of the table," El Buitre began, his tone not nearly as chastising as Carmen would have liked. "As such, I will ask you to leave the task of speaking for the collective to its leader."

"Apologies, Jefe," Ari said, though his expression was insolent. "It won't happen again."

"Cuervita," El Buitre said, turning to her. "This is an organization that listens to every viewpoint at the table, no matter how much we may disagree. Though his delivery left much to be desired, I won't undermine Ari's right to an opinion."

"So you feel my relationship with Daniela was inappropriate," she said, refusing to apologize, knowing it didn't go unnoticed. "Even aware of the fact that it was a calculated risk undertaken in service of the mission *you* gave me."

"I didn't use the word *inappropriate*," he said. "That was Ari's choice. But I do wonder whether it was the wisest course of action, yes. And I wonder more whether it's colored your judgment on the matter at hand."

Carmen pretended to be choosing her words carefully, but in truth she was just searching for an explanation that would make sense. One that didn't involve completely unplanned, dangerous feelings for a girl that could be the ruin of both her and the resistance.

"I was cut off from everyone," she said, unsure where she was going, trusting she'd get there. It was what she had been trained to do as a spy. Lie on her feet. She had just never expected to be doing it at this table. "For years. I had to make my allies where I could, trust the people who earned it."

The table was quiet now, and Carmen felt something start to crystallize. Something that was wholly truthful, but not

74

the whole truth. No one interrupted her. Not even Ari.

"Dani was one of those people. I know none of you have gotten the chance to know her, but I did. I trust her as much as I trust any of the people here. And in my well-informed, objective opinion—which I assure you, I am still capable of having . . ." This part was directed straight at Ari. ". . . she wasn't at risk of turning. If she's gone, if Mateo has discovered even a hint of her allegiance to us, she's in danger, and we owe her protection in exchange for the loyalty she has already shown us."

Ari looked like he was ready to interject again about the objectiveness of Carmen's opinion, but with El Buitre's reminder of his position still fresh in everyone's memory, he thankfully held his tongue.

"I understand being close to the situation is part of what makes you valuable to us," El Buitre said. "But we make decisions together, to avoid any one person's judgment being compromised at the expense of the whole."

"I understand that," Carmen said, trying to keep her composure. "But none of you worked with her. None of you knew her. Why wouldn't you defer to my judgment on this?" She was testing the limits here, and she knew it, but leaving Dani's fate in Ari's hands was as good as pulling the trigger herself.

Her loyalties played chicken with each other, daring, pulling back just before she said something she couldn't take back. But as the people assembled spoke in low tones to each other, as Ari made his case with a look as clearly as if he'd made it in words, Carmen felt one side starting to take over the other.

If they wanted to kill Dani . . . if someone gave the order . . .

"I propose," said Alex finally, breaking through the whispers, "that we pause on any major decisions regarding the asset until we can gather more information. Santos is right. She's well placed and valuable, and it would be unwise to make a rash decision without all the facts."

Carmen felt a fierce swell of gratitude for Alex, but across the table, Ari snorted.

"Something to say?" Alex asked, voice as cool as her silver-gray eyes.

"Is no one else concerned that this untested new girl is running around the government compound just full of resistance secrets? If she has turned, doesn't it make sense to neutralize that threat as soon as possible?"

Carmen was on her feet again, and not even a harsh look from El Buitre could force her back down. She was dizzy with anger, her cool facade cracking and crumbling. For the first time since she'd returned, she didn't care what the consequences were. "You're really going to stand there and criticize *her* for being new? When it's been *how long* since you crawled out from under your rock?"

"Cuerva," El Buitre warned.

"I'm sorry, Jefe, but Alex just proposed something completely reasonable, and this guy is over here shooting down every idea but slitting Dani's throat without even considering it. Since when is that the way La Voz operates? I know I've been away from the table awhile, but I thought taking care of our people was something pretty integral to the cause."

Ari tried to interrupt, and Carmen dared him to with her glare, the jut of her hips. She was ready to make stew meat out of this skinny boy.

"The fact remains," said El Buitre, louder than usual, hushing everything but Carmen's increasingly murderous thoughts, "that no matter what we'd *like* to do regarding Daniela, we don't currently have the option of contacting her. Our first order of business, regardless of what follows, needs to be locating her."

"And then what?" Carmen asked El Buitre, getting to her feet. Ari stood, too.

"We do what needs to be done to protect La Voz," said Ari.

"*And then what, Jefe?*" Carmen asked again, ignoring Ari, looking directly at the head of the table.

"That will depend on the information we have when we find her," he said at last.

"I want your word there will be a vote before anyone hurts her," Carmen said, not caring what anyone thought, needing the assurance that she'd at least be notified before things went any further.

But what good was El Buitre's assurance when Ari was here, speaking for him, undermining everything Carmen had once loved about the cause she'd pledged her life to?

El Buitre's searching look lasted a beat before he said: "You have it. But Cuervita . . ."

"I understand," Carmen said curtly, walking away from the table without being dismissed, unable to erase the look in Ari's eyes as she passed.

The one that said he didn't give a damn about El Buitre's assurances.

6

My skills, interests, and resources I pledge to the cause of resistance.

—*La Voz Membership Pledge*

᛭⟩✳⟨᛭

CARMEN HOPED THAT THE NIGHT air would settle her, but outside the meeting tent, her reckless thoughts only had more room to spiral.

El Buitre's word had once been as good as law, able to make Carmen feel sure no matter how chaotic their circumstances. But things had changed, and tonight's meeting had only made that clearer. The marketplace fire, Jasmín's poorly planned mission and rescue . . . Not to mention the way he'd let Ari completely vilify Dani inside . . .

How long before he dropped the pretense of community? Of fairness? Of valuing their members like a family? How long before this poison spread to the rest of the organization and more lives than Dani's were in danger?

Could Carmen really wait for them to hand down a decision with this kind of distrust brewing inside her? She had been a law unto herself for so long that she no longer knew how to take orders without questioning them.

But if that made her a bad soldier, did she really want to be a good one?

That's when she noticed the dirt bike, leaning against a tree just behind the meeting tent. It wasn't the same one they'd ridden across the country, but it was similar enough. Someone in the meeting tent must have ridden in from the field and left it before the meeting.

I'm not doing anything, she told herself. Just sauntering over and placing a hand casually on the engine casing. Still warm. That meant it ran. The keys weren't in it, but Carmen had known how to hot-wire a bike since she was eight. This one already had the wiring all exposed where the casing was cracked. She could have done it in her sleep.

Inside her, the battle was reaching fever pitch, and it was anyone's guess which side would be victorious.

If Carmen could no longer trust the integrity of her organization, she had only her own judgment to rely on. The only person she trusted to find Dani and gauge her circumstances was herself.

Yellow wire to the red. Carmen wouldn't have to cut them, just pull them out a little farther from the plastic.

You'd be throwing away your whole life, said a panicked voice in her head. One that remembered being a scared six-year-old with no family, no protection. Her parents had promised to return, but hours had passed. Days. The only people who had come were desperadoes. Until El Buitre.

If you do this, she told herself, almost like a dare, *you can never come home again.*

She was loosening the wires before she decided to. La Voz had always been more than just a place to rest her head, more even than the people who made it all mean something. It had been a calling. A passion. A purpose.

Could it really be home if she didn't believe anymore?

And could she really believe in a cause that no longer valued the lives and loyalty of the people who served it? That saw members as disposable? Let them die during careless missions undertaken just to prove a point?

The answer was clear. It was pounding in her pulse, racing in her chest.

Carmen judged the distance between the tent flap and the bike. These things were loud as hell; she would only have seconds after it started to get far enough away not to be followed. But the makeshift lean-to where they stored and repaired the bikes and trucks was at least a mile west of here, and no one could chase her without a vehicle.

There would be time, if she was smart.

There would be time, if she didn't look back.

Sota was the only trusted operative in the capital. Carmen

knew he would be the one charged with finding Dani. Could she get back to the capital before he fulfilled his mission? Could she use what she knew to save the life of the girl she loved?

Jasmín had almost died when she was sent into Mateo's torture cell prematurely; now Dani was in danger of being abandoned to the most dangerous family in Medio—or worse. Carmen was a soldier, loyal to the cause above all. And the leaders had strayed too far from it. If they wouldn't right these wrongs, she would have to correct their course herself, consequences be damned.

Carmen slung her leg over the bike and removed the casing, the red wire visible, the yellow one tangled underneath. That's when she heard the tent flap open. She recognized Alex's shadow before she turned, but when she did, it was to meet the still, wary eyes of her former best friend.

"Where are you going?" she asked, voice as even as her gaze, and Carmen knew in that moment what Alex's choice would be. It was in the square of her shoulders. In the set of her lips. The angle of her chin. In the battle between the cause and its leadership, she'd chosen wrong.

"To do what's right," Carmen answered.

"You're making a huge mistake." There was regret beneath her words, but no uncertainty.

"One of us is," Carmen replied, taking the red wire in her hand, barely breaking eye contact to locate the yellow. She pulled them from their plastic sockets with an audible crack, live metal exposed, ready to start the engine as soon as it made contact. "I'm not running away," Carmen said. "I'm just doing what I have to do. For all of us. I'll be back."

The wires were a millimeter apart, Carmen's eyes still trained on Alex, when the other girl reached for her gun. Carmen's blood ran cold, but she kept her gaze steady, not giving away a thing.

"You're going to shoot your oldest friend?" Carmen asked when the barrel was pointed squarely at her chest, turning to face Alex, opening herself up into an even wider target.

"You know the rules," Alex said, barely betraying the effort keeping calm was costing her. "No loyalties before the cause."

Carmen held her hands at her sides, palms facing upward, offering peace. "The cause isn't a person, Alex. It's the movement. It's what we've believed in all our lives. Just because they've forgotten that doesn't mean *you* have to."

The gun was still pointing at Carmen when she turned, trusting Alex's loyalty even if she couldn't trust her temper. Baring her back to the chambered bullet, Carmen connected the wires, the bike's engine roaring to life between her thighs.

"Santos!" Alex yelled as shadows began to rise inside the tent, frantic movement silhouetted against the canvas as they all moved toward the door too late. "Don't walk away from your family for some girl."

Over the growl, Carmen gave Alex and the barrel of the gun a sad smile. "I'm not walking away from my family," she said, loud enough to make sure Alex heard. It was the very closest thing to the truth. "I'm protecting it, for all of us."

Tents and makeshift shelters crowded the road out toward the camp's boundaries. There was nowhere to go but straight past the meeting tent's door. Past El Buitre's tent. Through the center of camp, past Jasmín's still-sleeping form.

In front of the tent door, Alex was still holding the gun steady, the sinking moon glinting off the barrel. Over the snarling engine, Carmen didn't hear Alex cock it, but she saw her finger move, saw the light in her eyes go out.

Carmen had said all she could say. She opened up the throttle, shooting through the light spilling out of the tent and past Alex, her hair whipping in the dust the bike kicked up. Chickens beside the kitchen tent scattered, clucking sleepily at the interruption.

The first shot barely missed the tire, burying itself in the dirt as Carmen swerved, her heart beating too fast.

She was only trying to pop the tire, she told herself, but the words sounded hollow even in her head. Alex had chosen a side, and the next shot went over Carmen's shoulder, the sound nearly deafening her as the tent flap opened at last and the house emptied. El Buitre was shouting now, reaching for his own weapon.

But Carmen, tears stinging her eyes against the night, was already passing him, passing the medical tent.

The camp, which had seemed so large and sprawling when Carmen first arrived, was gone before she could decide whether the sob lodged in her throat would dare to break free. The grove was quiet and still in the light of the high moon.

It would sink soon, and then it would be just Carmen and the darkness, all the way to the sea.

It was almost sunrise by the time she made it to the place where the wall and the waves intersected.

It was a secret place, and a dangerous one. If there was one thing she could count on, it was that El Buitre would stay as close to it as he could. The rocky cliffs dropped a hundred feet to the water here, and the Sun God's chosen had relied on them to do some of the work when the terrain became inhospitable for building walls.

Here, the wall relinquished its burden to the sea, leaving an expanse of impossible, rocky coast about a half a mile wide before it picked up again. It was the least guarded place on the wall, because to attempt a crossing here meant nearly certain death.

But Carmen had never been afraid of death.

Not her own, anyway.

She abandoned the bike beside a low scrubby bush at the edge of the world. She wouldn't be able to take it where she was going.

An outlaw in the capital, a fugitive from the most powerful force on the outer island, Carmen couldn't risk crossing the wall at any of their normal checkpoints. Not alone. Not

unprotected. Not with both sides of the island likely screaming for her head.

Sitting in the dirt, her heels planted in front of her, Carmen stared up at it. The wall. Each block so massive people
had made up stories about a god helping humans build it. It
was the only way they could fathom it. But Carmen had seen
what people could do when they were desperate, when they
were afraid.

She didn't believe gods had built the wall.

She believed men had made other men do it.

Some people called it beautiful, forty feet tall, the blocks
carved with likenesses of major and minor deities. From here
Carmen could see the goddess of secrets and the god of the
harvest. Next to them, the four capricious children of the god
of fermentation and fertility, who were said to be present at
every feast or festival ever held.

Carmen had never seen the behemoth as anything but
what it was. A mandate, leveled by men with everything
against men with nothing. A symbol of prejudice and hatred
and fear.

The gods were only stories told by people in power to
make oppression seem glorious, fated. Carving their likenesses into the very thing keeping the people broken and
suffering? Cut off from the resources that could save them?

It was nothing more than a cruel joke.

Along the sand-colored stone, above and below the faces
of the gods, were hundreds of years' worth of scribbles and

scrawls, names drawn or painted or carved into the side. Hearts around some, joining them together. Among those were slogans, symbols, made by rebels long forgotten by time. Servants of another Vulture.

Carmen had never seen the point, though she'd often gone along when people snuck out of camp to add their own contributions. She didn't see why anyone would want to make themselves a part of this monstrous, terrible thing.

Turning away, Carmen made for the silhouette of a massive tree just north, listening to the waves all the way. She had always felt most like herself near the beating heart of the ocean. And to do what she was about to do—to justify what she had already done—Carmen needed to be sure.

The tree was a behemoth of a thing, clinging to the edge of the cliff like it had been here longer than the stones. Around its trunk were hundreds of ropes—some just a knot at the base, their lengths worn away by the wind; some still strong, new, like they'd only just been tied.

It was a lonely place. A desperate place. But tonight, Carmen wasn't alone.

Beneath the tree, against the backdrop of the night sky and the tossing sea, was a slim silhouette, hair tossing like a banner in the breeze off the water.

A girl, Carmen realized as she drew closer. Her shoulders were narrow, her face still round and soft. Carmen's heart squeezed in her chest.

"Here for the view?" she asked softly, not wanting to startle the girl. Unfortunately, this place wasn't only used by people desperate to cross into the capital. But when the girl turned, Carmen saw fire in her deep brown eyes. Determination.

"No," she said, and nothing more.

Carmen sat beside her, finding comfort in a silence that demanded nothing. They had each been driven here by their own demons. They couldn't take them from each other, but they could share the burden in this small way.

"My sister brought me here when we were younger," Carmen said, not sure if the girl was listening, or if she needed her to. "With our . . . little brother." Sota and Alex weren't exactly her siblings, but resistance identities were secret, and this got the point across well enough. Alex had been fourteen, Carmen and Sota ten.

"Did you go through?"

Carmen shook her head. "We just came to look. I remember the waves, my sister holding my arm so I didn't fall. I was terrified."

"I'm not," the girl said, but her voice refused to hold steady.

"Me either, anymore."

There was more to the story that Carmen couldn't share. The way the three of them had climbed this tree, its gnarled roots clawing the cliffside, and sat in the cradle of its branches as Alex told the sad story of her parents' crossing.

"There's a tunnel under there," the girl said, the trembling gone from her voice. "They say if you can make it through there, you can get to the other side."

Carmen nodded. "You have to get there first."

Alex's parents had tied their ropes to this tree, descended down the cliff easily. But a woman who'd been traveling with them and survived told Alex things had taken a turn when they hit the water.

"A lot of people drown," said the girl, her brave, jutting chin breaking Carmen's heart. "But I won't."

"I believe you." Carmen remembered the way she'd been intoxicated by the danger as a child. The lack of equipment, grappling hooks, nets. The stark loneliness of being alone with a rope and your desperation, knowing you might not make it to the other side.

Alex, Sota, and Carmen had cut into their palms that day, pushing them together one by one, letting their blood mingle. They had been born with families, Alex had said, in the somber tone of a wedding or a baptism. Those families had been lost. That day, they had chosen each other. Sworn to each other. They would be each other's family now. No matter what. The Crow, the Wolf, and the Fox.

But today, the sea spray mingling with the single tear that escaped, Carmen knew it had been a fantasy. A child's silly, dangerous game. Alex had fired a gun at her today, and there was no guarantee Sota wouldn't do the same when she reached him.

"We'll go together," Carmen said, and when the girl turned, her eyes had widened, fear finally visible in them though she did her best to mask it with stubborn pride.

"I don't need your help. I'll make it on my own."

Carmen smiled. "Good, you can keep me company while you do."

After a long moment, the girl nodded. Just once.

The girl reminded Carmen of herself, before she'd seen the things she'd seen. Before she'd loved, and lost. Before she'd been forced to make choices that made her almost unrecognizable to herself.

"What's your name?" Carmen asked, and the girl looked at her suspiciously. "We're going off the edge of the world together," she said with a wry smile. "I think that's reason enough for first names anyway."

The girl didn't look away, but she didn't speak, either.

"I'm Carmen."

After a few tense seconds, the girl's expression softened a little. "Cielo."

Carmen nodded. "It's nice to meet you," she said, not expecting a response. She didn't ask any further questions. She didn't need to know where Cielo had come from, or what had brought her here.

In this place, they were the same. Desperation had made equals of them, but it was hope that would send them over the edge.

Carmen had just walked away from the only family she had ever known in a rain of bullets. She was on her way back to a city that had branded her a murderer and a traitor to its government. And all to find a girl who might slam whatever door she opened in her face. If she was even alive to open it.

But in the midst of it all, Carmen had hope. Hope that it wasn't too late for Dani. Hope that there was still a way to keep the cause she loved from turning into something she couldn't believe in.

Whoever Cielo had been, she was hoping for something, too. Something that made whatever horrors were behind her a springboard for what came next.

Not that she would have admitted it, but in the moment, Carmen was glad she wouldn't have to go alone.

Carmen closed her eyes one more time, feeling her own imprint in the wind. In the salt spray. She was alive, and as long as she was alive, everything was still possible. She had never believed in gods or legends. She was supposed to be one of them, after all, and she was more mixed-up girl than cuerva's spirit.

But she believed in freedom.

She believed in people, taking care of each other, doing what was right.

That was what would carry her through this moment. Not prayer. Not stories about special, chosen people. Not gods that came and went as they pleased. But her *own* divinity. Her own ability to create the world she wanted to see.

"Ready?" Carmen asked.

"Ready."

Carmen checked the ties on her La Voz blacks, quickly braiding her hair down her back, taking off her shoes. Cielo watched her, clumsily braiding her own hair as well.

"You won't be able to swim in them," Carmen said, gesturing at the boots still laced onto the girl's feet.

She cast a reproachful look at Carmen, and Carmen wondered what they'd cost her, these shoes. Why she was so hesitant to give them up. They had sturdy soles, but they fit poorly, and suddenly Carmen remembered taking the shoes off a soldier she'd killed. The way she'd had to force her hands not to shake.

"There will be other boots," she said gently to the girl, and finally Cielo removed them, placing them beside Carmen's own at the foot of the tree.

From the belt at her waist, knowing the knot she tied was responsible for her life, Carmen added her own rope to the tree, letting it fall down the cliff, the bright red of it standing out against the rest.

Cielo tied hers as well, copying Carmen's careful twists and passes until they were both satisfied.

"Here's to hope," Carmen said, before checking her knots one last time.

"To hope," the girl muttered, her lips stiff with fear.

Fingers clenched around the rope, Carmen turned her back to the sea, and took her first step down the long, vertical road to the bottom.

7

No fear, no grief, no struggle will keep me from serving my cause.
— *La Voz Membership Pledge*

+‌⊱✳︎⊰+

THE CLIMB WAS DIFFICULT, TREACHEROUS, and wherever a rope ended, frayed and flapping in the breeze, Carmen tried not to think of whoever had fallen to the rocks and their death.

Ghosts didn't make the most pleasant companions.

But slowly, painstakingly, with confidence in her feet and her reason for climbing, Carmen made her way down toward the water, the girl beside her, matching her steps, her knuckles white on the rope.

Too soon, the time came to let go, the waves tossing violently beneath them. The tunnel was said to be just a few yards below the surface, but they'd have to dive for it, and to do that they had to brave the treacherous water.

Carmen closed her eyes, centering herself, trying not to think of Alex's parents, or all the other desperately hopeful people who had met their ends here.

When she opened her eyes, Cielo was reaching out for her hand.

Carmen took it gratefully. Something warm. There was no way she'd be heard over the rioting waves, so she squeezed the hand in hers again.

Once.

Twice.

They dropped into the water on three, hearts full, Carmen imagining the deep blue waters of the beach she had been born on, the sand almost silver in the sun. The way she'd dive down to the bottom for shells. Her mother had watched her, Carmen thought. She remembered her presence, but her face had long been lost to time.

This water was nothing like the water of her early childhood. It was deep, dark, shockingly cold against her skin. "No!" Carmen shouted when the current wrenched Cielo's hand from hers, but the sound was swallowed by the waves, salt pressing into her open mouth, choking her, dragging her under.

Carmen panicked, not knowing which way was up, wondering if she'd made the last mistake of her life. She thrashed around, flipping over and over, looking through the shock of the salt in her eyes for the light that would tell her which way was up, casting around all the while for Cielo's slender silhouette, her cloud of curls.

There was nothing. Only the darkness. Only the weight of the water pressing in on all sides.

She let out a stream of air at last, giving in to the stinging protest inside her chest, the bubbles shooting straight down her chin, tracing her body toward her outstretched toes. Carmen chased them, flipping herself upright, kicking for her life.

A voice inside her screamed not to go too far from the place the other girl's hand had been taken from hers, but she couldn't save her if she drowned. She had to breathe first.

I'll be back for you, she promised.

When Carmen's head broke the surface, there was relief like nothing she'd ever felt, and she dragged in a glorious, punishing breath like it might be her last. The relief was momentary at best. Below the water, she hadn't felt the current, but now she saw that in the few seconds she'd been under, it had taken her far from the cliffs. Much too far.

All around her was the black of the water. There was no sign of Cielo, but the waves obscured everything, dousing Carmen again and again.

The cold seeping into her bones, her legs going numb from it, Carmen realized with a sinking heart that she had to get to the cliffs, or she would die. She could do no more than hope Cielo was a strong swimmer. That she wouldn't give up.

Salt from Carmen's tears mingled with the salt in the sea

as she battled and kicked and fought, growing closer to the cliffs by inches, not feet.

More than once, she let herself go under. Just briefly. Just for a moment of rest.

The cliff face was growing closer, but not fast enough. Were her legs still moving? They must be, if she was. But her lungs were burning. With the world shrunk down to that burning and the surging sea all around her, Carmen prayed to the water itself, wild and free, more powerful than any god.

And then the rock face was there, or was it just a trick of the waves? Of the prickling almost-numbness in her finger-tips? Delirious with exhaustion, pain, and humility, Carmen reached for it again and again, never quite making contact, the water dragging her back mercilessly as if to say *It's here, but you'll have to fight for it.*

If she could cling to it just a moment and catch her breath, she could dive for the tunnel.

Cielo will be there, she told herself. *She'll make it, just like she knew she would.*

But Carmen had to make it, too. So she swam, and thrashed, and pushed onward through the freezing cold.

Just when she thought there was no more fight left in her, that one more kick or reach or breath would kill her, the sea changed its mind. Rearing up like a jungle cat ready to strike, it dragged Carmen's nearly lifeless body up into the air and hurled her toward the rocks.

The impact was so jarring she barely felt the pain, just the rattling of her every bone. As the water receded, her fingers and toes clung to the cliff face, leaving her twenty feet above the water with nothing but slippery salt-stained rock to keep her from falling to her death.

She thought of Alex's parents now. She couldn't help it. Closing her eyes for a moment, she beseeched their spirits, the salt-prints of their hands in the rocks. Carmen had been cavalier, and too sure. She didn't deserve their help, but she needed it now unless she wanted to join them, haunting the spray around these cliffs for the rest of her days.

The sea was back, tearing her from the rock, dragging her back to the water.

That was when she saw it.

It was a hole carved in the rock, only exposed when the water pulled away from it, readying another assault against the uncaring rocks and Carmen's broken body. But she wasn't going to let that happen.

Taking the biggest breath she could, Carmen dove below the waves, pushing down, down, away from the air and the light, eyes open even as the salt stung. Above her, the surge of the wave she'd been floating atop slammed into the wall with a force that surely would have killed her. But under the water it was a gentle push, and Carmen used it to propel herself forward, feeling for the break in the stone, clinging for dear life, knowing she wouldn't make it back if she didn't find the tunnel now.

When her hand caught on the lip of the opening she nearly gasped, but instead she pushed her way in, held breath on fire in her chest, sure she would lose control at any moment and suck in the water like air.

It was dark inside, and she closed her eyes, feeling her way forward, frantic, trying not to panic as red spots bloomed in the blackness and her chest heaved and struggled against her stubborn refusal to breathe.

She stood on the bottom, pulling herself along as best she could, face tilted upward, praying for air until the moment she was sure she'd lose consciousness. The floor was slanted upward. Any minute she would break the surface. Any minute.

When Carmen did, for a moment her mind couldn't grasp the significance, holding on to her breath, her scrambled wits struggling to catch up with reality. But then she breathed. She breathed like it was the first thing she'd ever done, or the last thing she would. She clutched at her chest and her throat, stumbling up the now steeper slope until at last the water was shallow enough to collapse.

It was like being born again. There, in the tunnel, she pulled herself forward, face in the tiny space above the dark water until the space grew larger, until the tunnel floor sloped up and she lay down on the cold, wet stone floor.

The moment she could lift her head she cast around, searching for movement, for a slim silhouette in the darkness.

When she saw nothing, she listened for the sound of breathing, of coughing, of anything.

Despite her salt-ravaged voice, despite the futility of it, she screamed Cielo's name again and again.

But as much as she hoped, as much as she screamed, she knew she was alone. There was no life in this place. The only shapes around her were white, still. When she realized they were bones, her skin crawled, her stomach heaving, but every last muscle in Carmen's body was spent, and among the dead she sobbed into her arms like a baby.

"Come on," she choked between sobs, staring at the entrance to the tunnel, waiting for the girl to surface. "Come on, Cielo!"

Time passed. An hour? Two? Five?

No one came.

Carmen sobbed harder, screaming into the echoing cave, remembering Cielo's reluctance to remove her boots, her stubborn jaw clenched against her fear. The way she'd reached for Carmen's hand at the moment she needed it most.

The grief overwhelming her turned to rage. Rage at this wall and the people who had built it. Rage at every person who sat at a table in a suit and talked about Carmen and Cielo and everyone like them like they didn't matter.

They had built a wall to keep Cielo out, made her so desperate she risked a life she'd barely lived just to escape it. It wasn't her hope that had killed her. It was these men.

Mateo's face swam before her in the darkness, his smug smile, his cruel eyes.

He would pay for this life, too. If Carmen had to swim through a hundred more hells to get to him.

She got to her feet then, knees aching, chest still tender from protecting her breath. She pressed one hand against the wall of the cave. A silent promise that she hadn't forgotten what she'd seen. That she wouldn't. That she'd carry this desperation and the heaviness of Cielo's sacrifice with her for the rest of her life.

And then she turned toward the light.

8

Though the fight may wound me, test me, knock me down, I will rise again in service of La Voz.

—La Voz Membership Pledge

⊶⊹⊱

WHEN SHE EMERGED FROM THE hole in the ground, knees and palms scraped and bruised from climbing, Carmen was alone in the center of a grove not unlike the one she'd fled.

Only here, the trees were alive.

It had been years since she'd been to this part of the island. She walked toward the tree line to get her bearings, taking stock of herself in the light. She was filthy, bruised and scratched, barefoot. Her hair was probably horrifying. On the bright side, she would be hard to recognize as Carmen Garcia, wanted killer of the chief military strategist's wife.

Her clothes were torn, damp from the water and the cave air that hadn't let them fully dry. But inside her pant leg her poison vials were still intact—protected by the cushion of her thighs and wax seals made to withstand the water and the salt.

She could be thankful for that, at least.

Carmen's head spun. She thought back to her last meal: corn porridge in the mess tent. Almost twenty-four hours ago now, though it felt like a lifetime.

Her grief over Cielo and her anger at the wall's defenders sat heavy in her stomach. She didn't feel hungry, she wasn't sure she ever would again, but she had to take care of herself. Fainting in a nameless grove this close to the crossing point would be like painting a bull's-eye on her back. She'd be in prison by nightfall.

That, at least, was reason enough to find sustenance.

Up ahead, the trees thinned out, and Carmen found she wasn't alone. Two little girls hid (mostly) behind a wide trunk, pointing at her as they giggled.

They looked to be all of maybe seven years old, almost identical, with two black braids apiece hanging down over their shoulders. Sun-blessed skin, sparkling wide brown eyes.

"Una nadadora," they whispered back and forth, and then louder. "Nadadora?"

Swimmer, Carmen remembered. She nodded.

"Come with us," one of the girls whispered, beckoning her closer.

"Where?" Carmen asked, instantly on her guard. She had

been a six-year-old in the custody of desperadoes once; she knew youth wasn't necessarily a marker of innocence.

"Food," one of them whispered. "Water," said the other.

When they turned to scamper away, Carmen followed. She had no other choice. Without help, she would never make it to the capital. And she had come too far to fail now.

Intuition, El Buitre had always said, was the most important sense a resistance fighter could possess. Knowing who to trust was often the difference between life and death outside the compound, and Carmen had always prided herself on trusting herself.

Today, it said these girls were too playful, too innocent, to have been set on a sinister task by the kinds of people who used children to do their bidding.

She hoped she was right.

The girls stopped every few yards, smiling shyly back at Carmen, who walked slowly due to the stiffness in her arms and legs. They seemed to expect this, and with little gestures and encouraging words they led her to the east, the trees thinning before opening up into a tiny village.

There couldn't have been more than seven or eight huts total, walls crumbling, roofs badly thatched. It was a good thing it never rained this far out, Carmen thought as the girls gestured to her once more before approaching the largest tent and ducking inside.

Great, Carmen thought, walking closer, but slower than before. *Adults.*

Adults would want a story, to know where she'd come from and why she had crossed the wall in such a dangerous place. Adults might recognize her resistance uniform—send her back to El Buitre or turn her in to the policia.

At this point, Carmen didn't know which would be worse.

But she was here, exhausted, starving, her lips cracking and parched from lack of water and an excess of salt. Little as she liked the idea of giving up control, the idea of dying on the road was worse.

When a man and woman stepped out of the tent, Carmen didn't run.

"Nadadora," said the woman to the man, and he nodded.

"You swam?"

"I swam," Carmen agreed.

"Most people don't survive that journey."

His words were a knife between Carmen's ribs, the memory of the empty tunnel still too fresh to share. "Just stubborn, I guess," she said around the pain.

There was a long silence. A held breath.

And then the man laughed, a big, booming thing that set the children shrieking and chasing each other around the fire. Carmen felt her shoulders relax a fraction of an inch, the grief loosening its hold on her heart. When was the last time she'd heard someone laugh?

Her traitorous memory was only too eager to remind her: Dani, in the government compound's marketplace, spinning to the beat of the drummer, her laugh flying loose and care-free into the crowd.

That was when I knew, she thought sadly. And then: *Please, don't let it be too late.*

"She's got spirit," the man said, his form as large as his voice. "No wonder the tunnel spat her back out again. Too salty for its taste, aren't you? Alright, alright, sit down, you look half dead. Juana, get her some soup."

A flurry of activity sprang up around her, and Carmen (unsure how her legs had even carried her this far) sank down with shaking knees beside the fire.

"I'm Bemabe, and you're welcome here, Nadadorita."

She was fed a seafood stew that stuck to her ribs while not being too rich for her tender stomach and then allowed to bathe, her wounds tended to with an outer-island salve. The smell of it made her dizzy with nostalgia.

They even found clothes for her—though none of the slim-hipped girls or women here had anything to fit. Carmen double-belted men's linen pants instead, unbothered, strapping the poison pouch to her thigh again beneath them.

When he saw her in his hand-me-downs, Bemabe the booming man laughed again. "You're a spitfire," he told her, more than once.

As the sun reached its highest point in the sky, Carmen was shown to a cot in one of the smaller huts, promised privacy, and left alone to rest. Every ounce of her training told her not to let her guard down in the company of strangers, but sleep was inevitable, and though she fought it, this time she fell.

When she woke, the sky was dark, and the voices outside sounded merry—if a little drunk.

Carmen emerged from the tent feeling restored, braiding her tangled hair as she approached the fire. Bemabe sat on a low stump, Juana on his knee. Other men had gathered, other women, and a jug was passed around, filling little cups. One of them was offered to Carmen. She accepted it, and a place by the fire.

But she was already wondering how soon she could move on. Forces on both sides of the island were hunting her, and Dani was running out of time. Not to mention every day she delayed was another day Mateo walked free.

And Carmen wouldn't stand for that. Not after everything he'd done.

"She's a thinker, this one," said Bemabe, when Carmen had been silent too long. He laughed again. A few of the other men laughed with him.

"I hear thinking helps with this whole survival thing," Carmen replied dryly, sipping at the cup. Fermented pineapple juice. Sweet and tangy.

"Depends where you're trying to survive," the man said, the woman getting up off his lap and disappearing toward another hut, glowing with candlelight. "Here we're more the 'enjoy life while you're living it' type."

"Sounds nice," Carmen said, and it did. For a moment she imagined herself here, wearing loose skirts and letting her hair hang long, chasing children, making stew. It was a lovely dream.

The conversations at the fire quieted. The man moved closer, leaning over on his elbows.

"It's better to travel by night," he said, raising an eyebrow at her.

"Kicking me out already?" Carmen asked with a wry smile.

"It's not my choice," he said. "It's yours. But it looks like you've already made it."

"Why did you help me?" Carmen asked, genuinely curious, sipping again at the sweet drink.

"It's what we do," he said, spreading his arms out, shrugging.

"You just wait here for people to survive the tunnel?"

"I swam through that tunnel myself, you know," he said, eyes far away. "Almost ten years ago now. I choked on that seawater, crashed against the rocks, woke among the bones."

"Why?"

"Adventure," he said. "Glory, money. I was from a mud hut on one of those nameless beaches. I wanted to fight in the rings on the middle island, to gamble and win, to make a big life for myself."

Carmen had heard of the fighting rings. El Buitre spoke derisively of them. Glamour and gambling for puffed-up fools. She kept this to herself as she looked around at the huts. The community. The way they seemed to flourish. "Did you find what you were looking for?"

"What do you think?"

She didn't know how to answer, so she didn't.

"The swim, it changes you," Bemabe said, his eyes far away now. "When I came out of the ground, there was no one. I almost died from the thirst. Suddenly, the adventures seemed less important."

"So you stayed?"

"It took me a while to gather what I needed. But in the tunnel I promised the god of the bones I would return if he let me pass through unharmed, and I did."

Carmen thought about this, sipping at her drink, watching the firelight flicker and dance. Bemabe had sat in this spot for years, devoting his life to quenching the thirst and filling the bellies of the few people to survive the tunnel.

After five years of spying in the capital, and another six living at the heart of La Voz, Carmen thought she had never seen such true resistance before.

"You saved my life," she said, standing, setting down her empty cup. "I won't forget it."

"You might," he said, winking. "It's all the same to me and the god of bones."

Carmen smiled. "I suppose it is."

"I don't know where you came from, girl," he said. "And I don't need to know. The black clothes? We burned them.

Whatever you're running from, it's over there now." He gestured toward the wall, looming just a mile or so away. "You can start again."

Her smile turned sad. "I wish that were true."

When she walked away from the fire, he didn't call after her. Didn't try to stop her. His resistance was here, and Carmen's felt a thousand miles away, but she thought the feeling of his fight would stay with her a long time.

The journey toward the capital wasn't always as easy as that first night.

On the motorcycle, even with unconscious Jasmín and the trailer to pull, they had done it in two days. Now Carmen had no friends in the world. She avoided known resistance allies as surely as she avoided the places loyal to the Median government. Mostly she slept outside, anywhere she could conceal herself during the day.

At night, in Bemabe's borrowed linen pants, usually with a rumbling emptiness in her belly, she pointed her inner compass toward Dani, toward Mateo and justice. With them driving her, she covered as much ground as she could.

There was the occasional kindness, of course. A doe-eyed, willowy boy who'd found her sleeping in his family's pig enclosure and offered her a loaf of stale bread, watching her go with a wistful expression.

An old beggar in one of the rural markets who had given her his clay cup of coins.

Carmen fell asleep dreaming of Dani. She wished she had the piece of her Segunda's dress to run between her fingers. Something to anchor her to the memory of the girl she loved. But she'd left it behind with everything else.

As she traveled barefoot up the island, Carmen's illusions about who she was, about what it meant to resist, were burned away, replaced by these kindnesses. These faces. She wouldn't forget. She had no god to swear it to, but she swore just the same.

In the same breath she cursed the men who had made resistance necessary, made it dangerous. She cursed Mateo with every waking breath, the twin desires to save Dani and destroy him drawing her up the island slowly but inexorably.

It was four days before she reached the outskirts of the capital, a few hours before dawn. She paused near a small creek to take stock, and in the pool there, lit by the moon, she looked at herself for the first time since she'd left La Voz.

Her face was sun-darkened, every strand of her hair matted and tangled. Her linen clothes were in tatters, and her feet were cracked and sore from the road. Bruises and scrapes scattered her arms and legs, tender to the touch, souvenirs of her collision with the rocks.

She had left this city a powerful man's Segunda, a murderer and a thief and a spy.

She entered it again a nameless girl. A girl no one recognized. A girl destined to be underestimated.

As she waited for daybreak, she washed her face and

hands, combed through her hair with her fingers. A beggar girl hadn't looked out of place on the road, but in the city she'd be a magnet for the policia. They didn't treat the poor kindly in the capital.

Who are you? Carmen asked her reflection, winding her somewhat more orderly hair into a twist at the nape of her neck, patting her face dry on the cleanest part of Bemabe's tunic.

She'd always had someone to tell her before.

Cuervita the La Voz agent had been El Buitre's right hand, the princess of the nomadic La Voz city. Carmen the Segunda student had been cruel and aloof, punishingly beautiful. Carmen Garcia had been emotional, feisty, but with the nurturing heart that made her a perfect partner.

When she'd returned to camp, there had been no choice but to sink into her old, ruthless reputation. To prove she belonged or suffer dire consequences. As a beggar on the road, she'd walked in shadows, wide-eyed, grateful for any kindness that helped her to survive.

But now she was back in the capital, back where it had all started. Survival wasn't enough. Carmen was ready to create, to destroy. And she had the tools to become a girl who could.

She needed to be the invisible beggar to get through the streets without being recognized.

She needed to be the girl who had left the outer island at twelve, to convince Sota she was worth helping. She needed to be the beautiful Segunda Dani had fallen in love with, to remind her why their love was worth fighting for.

She needed to be the ruthless revolutionary who loved no one and nothing more than her cause, to make Mateo and the men like him pay.

As the sky began to lighten, Carmen made her way through the capital's south gate on foot, keeping her face in shadow whenever she could. She didn't pass many people. Mourning flags flew for the Garcia Segunda above every large building on the horizon.

Ahead, just a few hundred yards from the hull of the burned marketplace, a knot of officers stood in conversation, and they weren't the only ones visible by far. The capital had been attacked. They were taking no chances with security.

Without allies, without backup, Carmen was exposed to them all, but she walked on anyway. Chin high. On one thing, her Segunda maestras and El Buitre had agreed: success was so often about making people believe in who you were.

And to make them believe, you had to believe yourself.

With all the training she'd received, Carmen watched the capital come to life around her, watching for a chink in the city's armor, somewhere she could slip in and blend in. *There*, she thought at last, joining the ranks of servants heading toward the smaller households. No one batted an eye. To them, her small steps and slumped posture marked her for what she was—even more than the tattered clothes she wore.

No one important would ever make themselves so small.

"Perdóneme, señora," Carmen said as they reached the

gate to the city's center. "I forgot my apron and hat, and I'm afraid Señorita will be upset. Do you have an extra?" She bit her lip, painting fear across her expressive features.

This woman didn't have an extra, but she whispered to the woman in front of her, and the message spread through the ranks until a starched white hat and apron made themselves available among the brown hands reaching back for her.

Resistance, Carmen thought, and abruptly she was fighting off tears. They could be punished for helping her, and Carmen knew if the policia ever found out who she was, they would be.

She vowed, for their sake as much as her own, that she wouldn't be caught. She added their faces to the old man's, the beggar's, the doe-eyed boy's. To Bemabe and Juana and the god of bones. To Cielo. She wouldn't forget them.

With her head down, apron and hat securely tied, Carmen could have passed for any number of servant girls. She would move effortlessly through the city, so long as she stayed vigilant and kept her face in shadow. Nodding her thanks to the women around her, Carmen split off from them, joining the crowds on their way to the city's center.

She had made it this far. It was time to find Sota, before it was too late.

9

My bonds to my La Voz comrades in arms are eternal, and cannot be torn apart.

—*La Voz Membership Pledge*

╾╂❥✳❃╂╾

CARMEN MANAGED TO PROCURE A basket with some sleight of hand in the chaos of stands and stalls and tents that had sprung up to replace the marketplace. Now she was just any maid running morning errands for her household.

When she reached the plaza where the demonstration had taken place, Carmen couldn't help but give herself a moment to stop and stare.

It had been dark when she and Alex sped by it on the bike to make their escape. But in the daylight, there was no mistaking the effect of the twisted, charred beams, the gaping spaces where the well-ordered and massively populated shopping center had been less than two weeks ago.

From the moment Cielo had been taken by the water, Carmen had let two things drive her—the twin desires to reach Dani and destroy Mateo. But with the consequences of La Voz's ill-conceived plan before her, Carmen realized there was enough room in her heart to detest Ari, too.

People had died here. Innocent people. And if she'd ever had any doubt that Ari was responsible, his reckless behavior in the tent before she'd left was enough to make her sure.

He was a cancer spreading through La Voz, Carmen thought. But why? She took in the scene in front of her, remembering the chaos, the screams. What did he have to gain?

And whatever his reasons, why had El Buitre let him?

Along the charred outer wall, vigils had been set up. Rings of orange flowers, drawings, paintings, letters, candles. Knowing she should keep moving, that staying in one place too long put her at greater risk of being discovered, Carmen walked over and knelt before the closest altar.

She had only one of the beggar's coins left, and she placed it in front of the smallest cluster of flowers. It was all she had to offer. A single tear fell, and then a second, but then Carmen was standing, brushing off her knees.

The sooner she got moving, the sooner she could get back and burn Ari to the ground.

Despite her anger, Carmen knew she couldn't do this alone. Her first order of business was to find Sota, and hope La Voz hadn't already turned him against her.

She knew he traveled between the safe houses, but that was all she knew. She'd have to work through them one by one and hope she found him in time.

The first location was too close to the fire site. Carmen didn't bother with it. It had been abandoned when the officers came to account for the wounded and dead.

There were three more that she knew of, but by late afternoon she was hungry, hot, and had struck out at two of them. They were empty—and not just temporarily. They looked like they'd been vacant for weeks.

Outside the final location (just as empty as the others), Carmen sat on the steps for just a moment, weary and demoralized, nearing the end of her rope.

Sleeping outside in the country, on the road, had been one thing, but Carmen didn't know how she'd survive a night outside in the city without protection. Even if the policia and La Voz weren't all after her head, there were also gangs of criminals that roamed the capital's streets at night. A woman alone wasn't safe on the streets after dark, especially one without a weapon.

Just as she was starting to truly panic, Carmen felt the well-worn prickle at the back of her neck that meant she was being watched. She'd never had more enemies than she did at this moment, and instead of reacting, she stayed perfectly still, breathing normally, trying not to betray that she knew she was under observation.

A good spy doesn't need advance warning; her brilliance is in her reaction to the unexpected.

"Reciting El Buitre quotes in your head isn't gonna save you from me," said a voice that would have been familiar if not for its dangerous edge. It had been foolish to stop here, to give in to her weariness. "I'm going to need you to stay very still."

There was no mistaking it now. That voice, which had been preternaturally serious even at eight years old. Carmen could almost see the somber eyes, contrasting with the fox-like smirk. She had not managed to get to Sota before La Voz's version of the story did, and now it was anyone's guess how this was going to go.

"I'm not going anywhere." Carmen was careful not to move anything more than the muscles it took to speak. "I came here to see you, Sota. I'm not trying to run."

He didn't reply, and Carmen didn't dare turn her head to look at him. The tense silence stretched on, and Carmen's nerves stretched with it. Had Sota been following her from safe house to safe house, waiting for her to reach this one?

It was the most remote, Carmen thought. On the outskirts of the capital, bordering the jungle that separated the city from the walled government complex inside. The best choice for a secret meeting with a high-profile source.

But also the best choice for an off-the-radar execution.

Carmen watched the coin flipping over and over in her mind's eye as it descended toward the ground.

Her patience ran out before it hit.

"Well," she said, standing swiftly, every muscle tensed, waiting for the shot or the tackle. Waiting for death or forgiveness. "If you're not gonna kill me, can we go inside? I'm starving."

"I told you to stay where you were!" Sota said, but when she finally turned to face him, she could see the indecision on his face. The place where his orders were warring with what he knew was right.

"And when have I ever listened to you?" She smiled, a crooked, smirking thing that only this boy could bring out. Sota had walked into La Voz's supposedly secret hideout at eight years old, past all their best guards, past traps meant to snare officers and wayward villagers and wild animals alike. With his serious eyes and grief weighing down his narrow child's shoulders, he'd asked to speak to the man from the stories.

No one had known what to do with him, or how he'd found them, so they let him in.

Neither the leader nor the boy had ever divulged the details of that meeting, and Carmen—who had also been eight at the time—remembered seething with jealousy at the responsibilities Sota had been given at such an early age. But he had been family from that day on, and when Carmen looked at him now, unarmed, torn, she knew he still was.

"Get up," he said, his voice only wavering a little. "Inside. Now."

"You don't have to do this," Carmen said, but she complied,

letting him take her wrist and lead her through the door without a fight.

"Sit," he said, and she did, spreading her hands at her sides in a gesture of surrender.

"What now?"

"What *now?*" Sota ran his hands through his hair until the curls looked like kelp in a strong current. "I'm supposed to turn you in, Santos! Send you back to await trial for being a traitor to the cause!"

Instead of restraining her, Sota flopped into the chair opposite her. Carmen relaxed, but only a little. They had been trained together. Carmen was a little stronger, but Sota was faster. If he decided he wanted it, the fight wouldn't be an easy one. And Carmen would hardly win popularity points with La Voz by harming him.

She watched him as he deliberated, not sure she'd ever seen him indecisive. He didn't look so good, either, his face pale and drawn. Underfed, unrested; Carmen wondered where he'd been. What he'd been doing since he'd found the Garcia house empty.

"I'm not a traitor," she said simply, meeting his eyes, her own open and unguarded. *The closest thing to the truth*, she thought, willing him to see that she was still that girl he'd raced across the seaside cliffs, the one he'd competed with to see who could eat the hottest dried pepper. Because part of her still was that girl. Hopefully, it was enough.

Finally, Sota looked away for the first time, putting his

head in his hands, giving Carmen the edge if she chose to flee. He was showing her he had seen that girl. That he honored the family they'd chosen.

She stayed right where she was.

"I'm not a traitor," she repeated.

"You have a really counterintuitive way of showing that," he said, his voice half angry and half incredulous. "You *fled* the compound against orders on a resistance bike to rescue your lover, who may or may not have turned on the cause."

Carmen would explain, in due time, that she hadn't betrayed the cause—only the people leading it into the ground. But for now, he needed to be on her side despite the dire circumstances. There could be no hesitation.

"Don't forget the armed La Voz operative pursuing me," Carmen said dryly.

Sota's head came up, his hair flopping into one eye, making him look impossibly young.

"*Armed?*" Sota asked. "Did he shoot at you?"

"She," Carmen said, trying to sound nonchalant. "Alex."

Sota's eyes were too wide, but Carmen shrugged.

"She missed."

"She wouldn't have missed if she hadn't meant to."

"Not much of a comfort, honestly," Carmen said.

The silence stretched, but it grew easier with every minute that passed without Sota tying her up and sending her back. She had trusted her instincts, and it seemed she had chosen right.

"So, now what?" she asked him again, and he got up, lighting lamps, pulling the dust cover off the low chairs in the small living room, making sure the curtains were closed and the doors were locked tight.

But which side were they hiding from? Tonight, it was anyone's guess.

Sota stood in the circle of light beneath a tall lamp, his angular features thrown into harsh relief. He was the boy she had grown up bickering with, yes, but he was also the Fox, a La Voz agent who would do what was best for the cause, no matter what it cost.

"What the hell happened to you on the road?" he asked, gesturing at her bruises, her tangled hair. "And how did you even get across the wall? They obviously weren't letting you use the water trucks. . . ."

Carmen hesitated, and for a moment she was back there, drowning, smashed against the rocks, dragging her battered body through the remains of those less fortunate than her. "The tunnel of bones," she said, and she didn't have to fake her haunted tone. *Cielo.*

"Carmen . . . ," Sota said, and now she could see him at ten, leaning over to bandage her cheek when she'd fallen face-first out of a tree. "How did you survive?"

"I'm stubborn," she said, but Sota didn't laugh like Bemabe had. Maybe he could see Cielo in the crease between her brows. Either way, he didn't ask any more questions about her crossing. Carmen, exhaustion blurring her vision, was grateful.

"I'm supposed to get you back to El Buitre, one way or another." Sota paced back and forth, frustration in every jerky step. "They told me you were out of control, that you'd lost your perspective and couldn't be trusted on your own. The fact that I haven't tied you up yet would probably be considered a betrayal."

"So why haven't you?"

"Because I don't think I believe them." Sota exhaled around the words, like it was a relief to admit them. "You're a lot of things, Santos. Headstrong, reckless, vain, *irritating* . . ."

"Can we get to the point here?" Carmen snapped.

"You're not a traitor. The cause is your life, just like it's mine. I don't think you would have left unless you had a damn good reason."

"Do you want to hear what it is?"

Sota cracked a smile. "I have a feeling I don't have a choice."

"I mean, you could gag me . . ." Her smirk matched his own, and for a minute the years between twelve and now folded in on themselves. They were just two kids, same height, same intensity. Two lost children who could have died or worse, who instead had been given a chance to be part of something. Bickering and scrapping, but protecting each other when they got in trouble, each refusing to give the other up.

"Was it really all for her?" Sota asked.

"No," Carmen said, thinking of the flames that had driven her here, Ari's flickering the brightest now. "It's still the cause for me, before everything. But you should have seen it, hermano. . . ." She shook her head sadly. "This new right hand of El Jefe's, he planned the marketplace fire, he got those people killed, botched Jasmín's extraction, and no one is stopping him."

Sota listened, his face giving away nothing. Carmen, tired and filterless, continued.

"I would never abandon the resistance," she said. "But as long as the leadership is acting this way, they're my enemy. My loyalty is to the cause, not to any man."

"But why?" Sota asked, half to himself. "What does he have to gain?"

"That's what I keep asking myself," Carmen said. "That's what we need to find out if we're going to stop him. But first, we have to save Dani. We owe her that much."

Sota's eyes focused again at the mention of Dani, like they were finally getting to the heart of things.

"They were going to kill her," Carmen said, not waiting for him to ask. She tried to keep the emotion out of her voice, not sure if her heart was breaking for the girl or the cause she loved. "He kept suggesting it, and no one was stopping him. I did everything I could to convince them she wouldn't turn, that we owe her our protection if she's in danger. But they wouldn't listen. Even though I was the only one who knew her."

"I knew her," Sota said quietly, and Carmen knew she had him.

"Yes," Carmen said. "You and me. We're the ones who

should decide. To them—to *Ari*—she's just a liability. But that's not what La Voz is. We don't use people and throw them away. And if we start, we're no better than Mateo and all the rest of them."

Sota had gone inward; that thousand-mile stare that had made him so unnerving as a child looked better on him now. He looked like a man.

"I didn't run away from La Voz, or justice there," Carmen said. "I ran to you. You're the only one I can trust. Please, help me save us, Sota."

Carmen could feel every heartbeat between them, Sota caught between his timeless stare and her gaze. Around them, candles jumped and flickered as darkness settled beyond the windows. When he stood, Carmen followed suit, and they met in the middle of the room.

Sota raised a palm, and something in Carmen unraveled as she raised her own. She wasn't alone. Or, if she was, at least they were alone together.

When she brought her palm to his, they stayed that way for a moment, pressing fiercely against each other, holding each other up. When he dropped his hand, Carmen felt she'd gotten a piece of herself back from the god of bones.

They were here now, among the living, and they had to live. Maybe that's what Bemabe had meant all along.

Though I will train, raise arms, and fight for my cause, the true weapons I bring to my fight will be determination and loyalty.

—*La Voz Membership Pledge*

⊹⊱✶⊰⊹

"SO," SOTA ASKED, TAKING HIS seat again. "What do we know?"

Carmen's head swam with exhaustion, but he was right. With this many people against them and so much at stake, they had very little time to waste.

"When you reported in about the house being empty, El Buitre assumed Dani had either been found out or turned."

"A reasonable assumption."

Carmen nodded. "It was what I expected. But at the meeting, Ari seemed to have already decided betrayal was the only option. He basically told them to execute her on the spot and shouted me down every time I suggested something saner."

"I wish I knew him better," Sota said, chewing his lip, lost in thought. "I've been in the capital so long I haven't had much of a chance to read him. If we just knew what his endgame was, maybe we could figure out how to smooth this over."

"Forget smoothing things over," Carmen said. "He was the one to suggest I wasn't being objective because of my relationship with Dani. The things he said . . ."

Sota didn't ask if they were true, and Carmen thought she might be grateful to him for the rest of her life for that. "Peace is off the table, then," he agreed. "But what else is there?"

"Even if she's innocent," Carmen said, "I don't know if they'll approve the resources to extract her. Ari will fight tooth and nail against it, and El Buitre is either unwilling or unable to disagree . . ."

"So, she's dead either way," Sota said, his voice hollow.

"Unless we can find a way to get to her," Carmen said, coming around to the plan she'd been half formulating during her long, treacherous journey from the wall. "If we can just talk to her. Find out what's really going on . . ."

"What if . . . ," Sota began, hesitating. "What if she *has* turned? What then?"

She met his eyes. To anyone else she would have said *I'll kill her myself.* But she had been as honest with Sota as she could be, and she didn't want to break his trust now by acting certain when she wasn't.

Carmen loved the resistance. She loved the fight. But

126

could she kill the girl she loved? Even for the cause she swore to love more?

"I don't think she has," she said instead. "And regardless of what anyone thinks on that subject, she's sacrificed for us. She's fought for us. We owe it to her to know the truth beyond a shadow of a doubt before we let anyone hurt her."

Sota sat thoughtfully for a moment before saying: "When she came to see me that day, after the demonstration, when I was shot, she was all in. It didn't seem like an act."

"Exactly," Carmen said, vindication and relief flooding through her. "That's why I came to you. You're the only one who knew her like I did."

"Well, not *exactly* like you did." He smirked at her, and Carmen threw the closest thing she could grab at him. It was a candleholder. A heavy one. He caught it effortlessly.

"Pendejo," Carmen muttered, getting to her feet and crossing to the low sofa, unable to remain upright any longer. Now that immediate death seemed to be off the table, her body was no longer negotiating with her sense of urgency. She lay down carefully, feeling the ache in every individual muscle. She closed her eyes.

Between spies, there was no security, no sure knowledge that you'd be safe from harm or retaliation. But there could be trust, if you chose it, and tonight Carmen would.

It was Sota's turn to ask, "What now?" and though Carmen's eyes were closed, her mind was already racing.

"Write to them," Carmen said. "Tell them it would be a

127

risk to get me out of the city right now, and that I have information that you believe will help you locate Dani. Be vague about the rest but tell them I've agreed to cooperate and you'll be keeping a close eye on me in the meantime."

"I'm going to have to give them a timeline, or they'll come here and put us both in chains." The weight of Sota's words hung heavy in the room.

"As long as you can manage," she said, hating how small her voice was. She had been running on pure adrenaline since the bike's engine had sparked; there had been little time to consider the consequences if she failed.

You're fighting for what's right, she told herself sternly. *The consequences don't matter.*

"I'll do what I can," he said. "But then what?"

Carmen sat up, no longer tired, thinking of how much there still was to accomplish.

She wanted to show La Voz that it was worth prioritizing the people who had been loyal to them. That her path of radical empathy was better in the long run than a mercenary approach where you used people and threw them away.

She wanted to save Dani. She wanted to save the resistance. She wanted Mateo to suffer for what he had done.

It was a lot to ask of a few days, and she'd be foolish to bank on any more time than that.

"Where do you think Dani is?" she asked Sota as he sat down beside her on the sofa.

"My guess is that they've moved her to one of their more remote properties," Sota said. "It keeps them all out of the public eye while they deal with the scandal, and they can contain her if she tries to reach out."

"Good point," Carmen agreed. "If they haven't discovered her. But if they have . . . if they're trying to get information from her . . ."

"It's possible they've taken her somewhere more dangerous," Sota finished for her. "And if that's the case, it's going to be a lot harder to get her out."

The beginnings of a plan were starting to form in Carmen's overtired mind, but she knew she would need sleep, and food, and a moment of quiet to pull the strings together. "Send the letter tonight," she said. "We need to make sure they're not out hunting for me. In the morning, we'll start looking for her."

"Where?" Sota asked.

"Let me rest," Carmen said, losing the fight against her memories of Dani, needing to escape into sleep before she gave anything more away. "I'll tell you in the morning."

Her hands in my hair, Carmen thought. *Her lips on mine.*

She couldn't think of those hands going still forever. That smile dying on those perfect lips. Not if she wanted to stay focused on the mission. On saving her.

"You're going to get us both killed," Sota muttered, stalking into the kitchen.

"You better hope not," Carmen replied, and then she let sleep's sea pull her and Dani's memory under.

In the morning, Carmen woke to furious cursing from the other room. She was on her feet before she was fully conscious, sliding into fighting stance.

"Oh yeah, great, maybe we can *punch* the world's worst news." Sota rolled his eyes as he came into the living room. He was gripping the newspaper in his hands so tightly his knuckles were turning white. How had he gotten it? Carmen wondered. Had he really left her alone?

"Right, because pulverizing the newspaper holding the world's worst news is a way better idea," Carmen bit back irritably. "Give me that."

Sota threw the paper at her. "I swear to every god, Santos, if I get killed for this, I'm going to haunt you for the rest of your natural life."

"Cállate," Carmen said, sinking to the couch as her heart sank to somewhere around her knees. The photo and headline were worth every creative curse word Sota had employed.

On the front cover, a black-and-white photo of Dani and Mateo took up half the page. Their dark heads were bowed as they stood at a podium, Dani leaning into Mateo, his arm around her shoulders.

"*Garcia Family Breaks Silence*," Sota recited. "It looks bad. It looks worse than bad."

"I *know* it looks bad." Carmen focused on Sota, trying not

to let her eyes flicker again and again to the photo. Hoping the tensing in her muscles and the burning rage in her eyes appeared political, because right now she was blind to everything but him touching her.

El Buitre's and Ari's doubts from the table came creeping in like a toxic, chemical fog. What if she had been wrong? What if Dani really hated her enough to turn against the resistance? How well had any of them really known each other?

She shook the thoughts free, focusing on the words of the headline, trying to forget the image.

"She's doing exactly what we told her to do," Carmen said, her voice hollow in a way she hoped didn't sound like heartbreak. "She was supposed to get closer to him after my betrayal, become indispensable."

"Read it," Sota said simply, and Carmen did, her stomach sinking further with every word. Every glance at his hand on her back.

Sota was right. From a political standpoint, the article was much worse than the photo.

Mateo Garcia, grieving after the tragic attack on his innocent mother by a resistance group (known on the outer island as *La Voz*), would be throwing a benefit. Along with his loyal wife, Daniela, they would raise funds and awareness for a program that would use *newly gathered information from a source close to the resistance group* to form a task force within the Median government that would deal *unprecedented blows* to resistance efforts in Medio.

The standard language was used, the kind that made everyone born on the other side of the wall look violent. Barely human. All while the poor, innocent Medians clutched at their pearls in distress.

At the bottom was a smaller photo of Carmen, taken during her first week as a Garcia Segunda, with a brief tally of the accusations against her. They were laying the murder solely at her feet, but the blame for her radicalization was laid at La Voz's. It was ingenious, really, the way they managed to condemn the individual *and* the group without using a single fact or witness.

Except an anonymous source. Which may or may not have been real.

Which might or might not be Dani.

Just beneath the picture was a line that made Carmen's stomach turn. The Garcias were offering an exorbitant cash reward for any information on Carmen's whereabouts. She should have expected it, but it still made her deeply uneasy to see it there, in print, like a death sentence.

El Buitre would have this paper soon, if he didn't already. With Ari whispering in his ear, he would draw a conclusion that unfortunately looked all too logical.

One Carmen wouldn't be there to talk him out of.

Of course, the one detail they hadn't included was the location. Everything was on lockdown after the attack, Carmen assumed, but damn, it would have come in handy.

"What are they trying to do . . . ?" Carmen wondered

aloud. The question had two possible answers, and the correct one depended entirely on how well a brokenhearted Dani had been able to lie upon her return to Mateo.

If they had discovered her, they were likely using her as bait. They wanted to use Dani to lure more members of La Voz to them. If they believed she'd betrayed them, they would send someone to take care of the leak, and the Garcias could use her as leverage.

If they hadn't discovered her, this was retribution for Mama Garcia's death. They'd put this out hoping La Voz would consider *Carmen* the leak, and kill her. Or come looking for more information.

Either way, this was lazy, cruel Mateo using La Voz to do his dirty work, and Carmen felt her hollow chest filling with all the anger she'd rediscovered in the tunnel of bones and more.

"There's another option," Sota said, like he'd rather not.

"That's not an option," Carmen said flatly. But of course, it was.

"If she was angry enough at you, it could have overridden her commitment," he said, almost gently, none of that brotherly teasing or chastising in his tone.

"She wasn't like that," Carmen said, her voice gaining conviction. "She never would have let romantic feelings decide something like this for her. She's much too ambitious for that. If she's angry at me, it will only make her work harder."

She wanted to believe it. She wanted to believe it so much.

Sota didn't speak, and his silence was worse than skepticism.

"This was never about me," Carmen said. To him. To the silence. To herself. "She joined for the same reasons any of us did. She wouldn't give up on them just because of a relationship gone bad."

"And she told you that?" he asked.

"I knew her," Carmen snapped.

"First love is a powerful drug." He didn't say it like an accusation, but it didn't matter.

Carmen tore the photo in two and stalked out back to where the safe house's small patio butted up against the jungle.

What was happening to her? Even with Sota as her only witness, she shouldn't have been so blatant about her feelings. This had to stay about the integrity of La Voz if she expected anyone to side with her.

And it was. *It was.* But was it really her fault that it was hard to remember when she'd just seen the girl she had risked everything for being publicly cozy with the person she hated most in the world?

She took a deep breath of fresh air, listening to the white noise of the city waking up. Her thoughts spiraled, growing darker. She worried about El Buitre, and what he'd think when he got Sota's letter. She worried that Dani was being forced into photo ops through blackmail. She worried that she wasn't.

Through it all, she fixated on that hand. That horrible hand that had been so close to cracking Carmen across the mouth when she didn't give him what he wanted. The one that had tried to inch up her thigh every time they were alone in a room together.

The one she'd escaped, and left Dani to endure.

Carmen's breath came harder and faster until she wanted to take apart her skin and climb out, emerge as some heartless, winged thing that could drift away from caring on the island breeze.

Until then she wanted to rewind her life, be the single-minded, ruthless spy she had been trained to be. The one who didn't let anyone get close. The one who never cared about where men placed their hands, or where girls placed their loyalties. As long as the cause was being advanced.

But there was no going back. She and Dani had tied their fates together in a hundred ways since Carmen was capable of being the girl she'd once been. Carmen had to save her if she had any hope of saving herself or her cause. It was all one mission now.

And Mateo daring to touch Dani was just one more thing she vowed to make him pay for.

When Carmen opened the door again, Sota was waiting in the same place. "Ready?" he asked, and she nodded.

For the next hour, they planned.

They wrote coded notes to their highest-placed operatives

135

in the government complex. They gave them staggered meeting times for the next day, making sure they understood the invitation wasn't optional.

Carmen and Sota spoke to each other little, and when they did it was in terse, fragmented sentences. All the while, they waited for El Buitre to kick in the door. For the next inevitable disaster.

But when it didn't come, the quiet was almost worse. It felt disingenuous, for things to be still when the whole world was threatening to implode around them.

It was nightfall when a messenger tapped at the back door. By the time Carmen reached it, the deliverer was gone, and a square note sat on the ground at her feet with a vulture's curved talon stamped into the back. Pinned to it was the front cover of the newspaper.

It was coded, and she handed it wordlessly to Sota, waiting for the verdict. In the meantime she averted her eyes from that damn photo, back from the dead to haunt her.

"I have four days to send you back," he said, and Carmen just nodded. It was a blow, but what had she expected? She would have to work another miracle. Keep Dani alive. Keep her protection, and her cause, and her family. Keep the girl she loved.

Take down Mateo.

Prove Ari was a venomous snake.

Four days was the blink of an eye with all that staring her down, but hadn't she done more with less?

"Santos . . ."

"Don't worry," she said. "I won't let them punish you for my actions, no matter what happens."

"That's not what I was going to say," Sota said, and took a step toward her, reaching out to touch her cheek. "You're doing the right thing. This is La Voz. It's a family, not just a cause. You're looking out for your people. That doesn't make you a traitor. It makes you worthy of the title of rebel."

Carmen threw her arms around him as he stood stiff and awkward, eventually reaching out to pat her back. She didn't cry—she couldn't let herself start—but the feeling of the walls closing in lessened a little with him there. He seemed to know it, because he didn't step out of the embrace until she was ready.

"Thanks," she said, and he smiled that fox's smile.

"Someone has to take care of you while you're taking care of everyone else."

The informants started trickling in the next day. Carmen wanted to be part of the interrogations, but Sota outright refused.

They were mostly staff members of high-profile families, but there were a few politicos as well, and a few more wives. The one thing they all had in common was the blackmail that had brought them here.

Blackmail was a fickle source of influence. There was always the chance they'd be offered a better deal. Not one of these people was truly loyal to the cause; they were just afraid. And fear was not as powerful a motivator as duty, or loyalty, or love.

Sota was afraid the temptation to turn Carmen in to Mateo would be too great for most of them—not just because of the reward money, but because they believed her to be responsible for the death of someone they knew much better than they knew the shadow-faced boy at the edge of the jungle.

As much as Carmen despised the outcome, she couldn't argue with the logic, and so she sat in the cramped closet for most of the day as Sota asked the same questions again and again:

"Where have Mateo Garcia and his wife been moved?"

"What is the location of the benefit referred to in the newspaper?"

"Has there been any talk of resistance activity by the Garcia Primera?"

"Has she been seen in public since the death of the Garcia Segunda?"

On and on, until she wanted to bang her head against the wall in frustration. No one had seen Dani. No one knew anything. Sota always gave them a chance to volunteer the information, but he soon moved on to reminders of their weak points, how easy it would be to let it slip that this meeting had occurred to their employers, their spouses, their friends.

When that didn't work, he moved on to deeper threats. To

expose the blackmail they'd used to bind them to La Voz in the first place.

He raised his voice, if he had to get to that point, banging his fist on the table (sometimes going a little overboard with the theatrics, in Carmen's opinion) but none of his techniques yielded a whispered word about Dani's location, or any of the other information they needed so desperately to find before both their futures were destroyed along with hers.

When the sun had set on the first day, Carmen emerged from hiding for the sixth time feeling more deflated than ever.

"Do you think they're covering something up? Or do they really not know?"

Sota shook his head. "It's not a cover-up," he said. "They're too unified. There's no way he got to all of them. They must just really be hiding her well. . . ."

"Or imprisoning her," Carmen said, rubbing the kinks out of her neck with one hand as she took a seat at the kitchen table.

"We have eight more people to see tomorrow," Sota said, sitting down across from her. "One of them is bound to know something."

"What if they don't?" Carmen asked.

Sota shook his head. "We have to hope they do. For both our sakes."

But all Carmen could think was that one of her four days

was already gone, and she was no closer to Dani. No closer to discovering what kind of danger she was in, or to helping her, or to changing anything at all.

Carmen woke at the crack of dawn, soaked in sweat, reaching out for a ghost that was no longer beside her. Dani had been so real, her hair close-cropped on the sides but flopping into her eyes, her bottom lip between her teeth, her eyes sparkling with the kind of mischief Carmen had been delighted to learn she was capable of.

In the orange light from the streetlamp outside, Carmen twisted her hair up in a bun on top of her head, fanning her face and neck as she woke up fully, the knots of anxiety settling back into place as they remembered what was at stake today.

She had to pretend not to care that Dani was surprising and beautiful and unlike anyone she'd ever met. At this moment, Carmen's only objectives were to save an innocent girl, and prove to El Buitre that the resistance was about people, not personal glory.

That's all.

That's all, she told her heart, which stubbornly refused to slow.

There was no guarantee that Dani would even want her when she knew what she was. All the things she'd done. Yes, she remembered the way it had felt to be together—the dream proved those experiences were burned into her skin.

But she also remembered the way it had felt to slit the border officer's throat. The satisfaction. Could Dani ever love someone who was capable of that?

Either way, she deserved to live. That's what Carmen had to focus on now. The rest would come later.

In the kitchen, she hoped splashing water on her face would dispel the last of the lingering dream. But when she turned toward the window, the shadows outside told her she wasn't alone.

Sota was unmistakable, even in silhouette, but there was a girl with him, short, plump, familiar somehow. They were engaged in a whispered conversation outside, but Carmen couldn't hear a thing. Sota was too smart to leave doors open, especially if—as Carmen suspected—he didn't want her privy to this conversation.

But Carmen was smart, too, and Sota didn't expect her to be awake. With the way sound would bounce off the fence, maybe the kitchen window would be close enough to pick something up. She slid it open noiselessly, climbing onto the sink, pressing her ear against the tiny crack she didn't dare widen for fear of being discovered.

". . . a sensitive situation," Sota was saying. "I'll need to reveal this information at the right time, do you understand?"

"I came to tell Mistress Carmen," came another voice—a girl's voice, as familiar as her shape against the window. It was Mia, she realized. The serving girl from the Garcia house.

Immediately, Carmen was swept away into memory. Dani across from her at the otherwise empty dining table, their ankles brushing against each other beneath it, eyes catching, teeth worrying at lips, Mia checking in too often while they dreamed of being closer. . . .

"I'd like to speak with her," the girl was saying now, her voice determined.

"Listen to me," Sota said, and Carmen heard the shuffling of footsteps as they moved away from the door. Unfortunately for Sota, they only moved closer to the window. "Carmen and I are a team. I will tell her whatever you tell me. I'll just need to do it at a time that won't endanger any of us."

"You promise she will find out exactly what I tell you? And soon?"

"You have my word," Sota said, and a chill started at the base of Carmen's neck, traveling down. Why hadn't Sota woken her? Had he been lying all along?

"Señor and Señora Daniela have moved to a house very nearby. They do not leave, and when they do, Señor uses a secret entrance and exit. Señora Daniela has not been seen. I think she stays inside the house."

"Where is the house, exactly?"

"Sombra Lane." Carmen's stomach sank. It was the most highly guarded section of the complex. "A large white stone house. Señora is under constant supervision. No one is allowed in or out without Señor's approval."

"Is she in danger?" Sota asked, and Carmen, holding

142

her breath, thought she heard concern in his voice. It was something. He was lying to her, but maybe not about everything.

"I do not know," whispered the girl. "I must get back. They will miss me."

"Thank you," Sota said. "We will do everything we can."

"Señora Daniela and Mistress Carmen are kind people," said the girl. "I don't know what to believe, but I don't think they would do these monstrous things."

"Your instincts are good," Sota said, and Carmen could almost see the gaze he was turning on her now. The one that made people feel worthy and strong, seen. The one that made him such an expert recruiter. "Don't let them take that away from you."

"Thank you, señor," she said, her blush almost audible.

Carmen closed the window, hopping down like a cat, landing silently on the balls of her feet and creeping back toward the couch, where she stretched out in her own imprint and waited for Sota to make a sound loud enough to "wake" her.

Maybe her suspicions were unfounded. Maybe he would tell her the truth right away, and the cloak and dagger had just been for effect.

When the door slid on its track, Carmen sat up, stretching, running her fingers through her hair.

"Good morning," he said, his face betraying nothing but mild amusement at the state of her curls.

"And to you," she said, getting to her feet and padding

toward the kitchen, making more noise than usual to put him at ease. "Taking a walk?"

"Hardly," Sota said. "I don't have a death wish. Just making sure the perimeter is secure before people start showing up."

"And is it?" Carmen asked, trying to keep her tone light.

"As good as it's going to get," Sota said, heating water for café on the tiny stove. "The first one arrives in twenty minutes. Ready to disappear?"

Normally, Carmen would have whined, or at least made a joke, but today she was quiet. "Whatever it takes," she said, and if Sota noticed something was off, he didn't show it.

But the tension was back in the house, the trust they had earned together that first night gone as it built and thickened in the air around them.

He was lying to her, and there was little time left to figure out why. With only two days left, another full day of interviews seemed like such a waste. Carmen had been willing to endure it when there were no other options.

But now, whether he liked it or not, Carmen had enough information to decide to act. Whether that included Sota or not would be up to him.

For the cause, I will lie and I will cheat, but to my comrades in arms, I will value honesty and forthrightness above all.

—*La Voz Membership Pledge*

CARMEN SPENT THE FIRST FEW hours of her day feeling every atom of air between her body in the closet and Dani's in the Shadow District, setting them on fire one by one with her longing.

Around midday, they had what Sota called a breakthrough. One of the janitorial workers from Mateo's father's building had divulged the time and place of the benefit, and finally, luck was on their side.

"It's tomorrow," Sota said excitedly. "We'll have time to prove everything before you have to go back to El Buitre."

"Still no news on Dani's location, though?" Carmen asked innocently. "It would have been nice to get to her before the event, speak to her without all those prying eyes."

"At this point, I say we take what we can get," Sota said, his gaze steady on hers.

He hadn't quite lied, Carmen thought. That ability to play with the nuance of the truth was part of their training. He had always been better at it than she was.

In her hiding place, she had nothing to do but let her thoughts spiral to their most terrifying places. If Sota would lie to her about Mia's information—about something this vital to their mission—what else was he lying about?

She'd been consumed with the task at hand, with her ticking clock, but in the quiet hours of Sota's interviews, Carmen returned to the marketplace fire. To Jasmín's role, and the danger she'd been placed in unnecessarily. Carmen might have been certain Ari was the architect of this new era, but he couldn't have done it alone, could he?

Sota was Jasmín's contact person while she was living with the Flores family.

Sota had been there, in a mask, the day of the fire.

Sota was the one in charge of finding Dani after Carmen's rushed extraction.

The thoughts sank into her stomach like stones, weighing her down during the long hours of hiding. Alex had pulled a gun on her, chosen the leadership over what Carmen knew was right. Was it really such a stretch to believe Sota had betrayed her, too? That he was humoring her while helping Ari bring about the destruction of the cause she loved?

In this small, dark closet, cut off from the vital information being mined from La Voz's key sources, it didn't seem like a stretch at all.

Sota performed the rest of the interviews as a formality, but by sundown he claimed there hadn't been any more significant developments. Carmen stayed quiet as he briefed her, and this time she could tell he noticed. She watched his every gesture, looking for proof.

"We only have one night before the party," Sota said. "I say we make preparing for that our main priority."

"Of course," Carmen said, but she didn't meet his eyes no matter how long his gaze rested on her face. He shifted uncomfortably, and Carmen couldn't help but wonder if it was a reaction to her stony demeanor or a guilty conscience.

Overcoming the awkward silence, Sota launched straight into planning and details for the benefit, with Carmen playing along to avoid suspicion. But as darkness settled around the house, a more vital plan started beating its new rhythm through her veins.

She had been good so far, sticking to the plan, hiding when he told her to, sitting through hours of boring meetings instead of charging in and taking action. She had done it because she felt she owed it to Sota, because he had been on her side when no one else was.

But if she couldn't trust him, what was to stop her from doing things her own way?

As Sota discussed catering schedules and uniforms and key entry points, Carmen nodded along, formulating a much riskier plan of her own.

There was no way Sota was going to allow her to attend the benefit, and he was right not to. Carmen Garcia had lived with these guests, dined with them, socialized and laughed and clinked glasses with them. Disguising herself wouldn't be as easy as staying in the shadows, even though she had only been Mateo's Segunda for a few weeks.

But she hadn't come here to sit on the sidelines and wait for a judgment to be handed down. She had come to find out for herself. Both the things she had admitted to Sota, and the things she hadn't. She had been robbed, by Ari and his fire, of the chance to tell Dani how she felt. To find out how she felt in return. And now she knew where the answers were.

It would be beyond stupid to go to Dani alone. Carmen knew that. But the possibility of getting to Dani *now*, instead of waiting in this stuffy room for someone else to decide? Someone she wasn't sure she trusted?

It was too intoxicating to pass up.

They had the beginnings of a passable plan for the benefit when Carmen feigned tiredness, sending Sota to bed in the house's lone bedroom. He hesitated with his hand on the doorknob, and Carmen knew he was reviewing her strange demeanor tonight, wondering what she knew. In the end, he left the door wide open. He didn't say a word.

But an open door wasn't going to stop Carmen.

Silently, she dug into the wardrobe lining one wall, stocked with clothing in various sizes for the operatives who rested here during missions. She chose black everything, pinning her hair close to her neck so it wouldn't wave like a flag behind her. She would be the night. She would be the sombra. The cuerva. She would get to Dani. She would find out the truth, once and for all.

And afterward, she would pick up the pieces.

Carmen lay down on the sofa again, covering up with a thin blanket, feigning sleep as restless, reckless energy coursed through her body, demanding action. It was an eternity before she heard Sota snoring—even louder than usual. Only then did she cross the small room and ease the door open, every nerve on edge until she was in the courtyard, alone, comforted by the new moon whispering assurances to thieves and spies everywhere. There would be no illumination tonight.

She paused, watching a lone figure in the distance wend its way stumblingly home. While she waited for the coast to clear, she turned her face up, the night breeze playing across it. In that moment, she let herself imagine it, if only briefly.

Dani, alone in a room.

Dani, sitting on the floor, tears running down her face.

Carmen would walk up behind her noiselessly, and when Dani opened her eyes at last, she wouldn't be afraid. There would be a moment where everything was understood, where the only thing left to do was cross the space between them and let their lips meet.

Again and again and . . .

The man was gone. Carmen opened the gate with barely a rasp. Her longing, even in the face of every obstacle between them, was strong enough to carry her to Sombra Lane. To carry her anywhere. When she looked down, she was surprised to see her feet still touching the ground.

"Going somewhere?"

She hadn't heard the door open, but her heart sank. Sota was nearly invisible in the doorway, slender as a sword leaning against the frame. It was anyone's guess how long he had been there.

From limitless and full of potential, the night suddenly became a cage. A stone, tied to her ankle, dragging her to the bottom.

"Just getting some air," she said, knowing it was feeble.

"Testing the gate for squeaky hinges, too, I guess."

She didn't meet his eyes. The ache in her chest was almost too much to bear. She had believed she would see Dani tonight. She had *needed* to see her. But there was no way Sota would understand that. No way she could even attempt to explain it to him.

The pounding in her pulse from remembering Dani's kiss screamed that she should fight him, do whatever it took to get her to Dani.

But the distance between them was unspooling now, the obstacles—which had looked so manageable while she daydreamed about stolen kisses and the things that came after—too much to overcome. Carmen had been foolish. Reckless. She had been everything she'd sworn she wasn't at El Buitre's table.

She sighed, dropping her chin to her chest, defenseless before Sota.

Yes, she believed in the resistance. In its potential. In the danger of men like Ari to their cause, and the damage Mateo and his father could do. But she had been lying to herself if she thought that was the only reason she'd left the outer island.

"I don't even know who I am anymore," Carmen said, her throat hot and tight with the tears she wouldn't let herself shed.

"Come inside," he said, and she could hear it in his voice. He wasn't sure she'd come. He didn't trust her, either, not entirely. Could she really blame him, all things considered?

Carmen didn't have to worry about what he would do if she ran. The restlessness was gone. All that remained was a deep exhaustion.

Back inside, Sota boiled water and placed a cinnamon stick in it while Carmen curled up in a ball on the couch, mourning, though she wasn't sure for what.

When he returned, steaming clay cups in hand, he looked reflective, not angry.

"I lied to you," she said, taking the cup he offered, making room for him to sit beside her. "I lied to all of them."

"I lied to you, too," he said. "But you already know that by now."

Carmen shrugged.

"Do you want to tell me the truth?" he asked, his eyes wide and liquid in the glow of the candles that lit the room. Outside, the wind tossed the moonless night, and Carmen could see it in his face. He wasn't demanding. He would still help her, even if she refused. He was asking for her, not him.

Suddenly, she felt ashamed for doubting him.

"I love her," she whispered, hoping her confidence now would make up for her earlier suspicion. "I loved her the whole time. But I thought she'd never . . . I didn't think . . ." Carmen sighed.

"But then she did."

"Then she did. And it was everything. I thought I had enough, before, that I didn't need more, but then she looked at me and it was like turning the lights on in a dark room." Carmen knew how it sounded. She couldn't even look him in the eye when she said it. "And now everything seems smaller, and dimmer, and I can't turn the lights back off."

Sota didn't call her a traitor. He didn't say anything. He just waited.

Finally, Carmen looked at him. "They wouldn't have understood."

"No," he said. "They wouldn't have."

"But you do?"

Sota hesitated. "No," he said. "But I know you. And I don't believe you're a traitor. Being confused doesn't make you wrong."

The words made a nest in her chest, and she held them tight. "But?" she asked when she was ready.

"But . . . it is dangerous. Especially now, with Ari trying to destroy everything we've built, with the military ready to start a war over Mama Garcia. You and I are the stone in the dam keeping this whole thing from falling apart. We can't afford to make mistakes."

"I know," Carmen said, and she did.

"Tonight would have been a mistake."

"I know."

"If you'd been caught . . . Alex has allied herself with El Buitre, and if what you've told me is true, Ari is pulling the strings somehow. Do you really want to leave them to their own devices? We both would have gone down for this. There would have been nothing standing in their way." Sota was up now, pacing, his hair on end where he ran his fingers through it in agitation. "And with sloppy plans being made, loyalties compromised, how long do you think it would take Mateo to destroy us?"

Carmen didn't say a word. How could she have let herself forget what was at stake?

"It's not just you, Cuervita. It's all of us."

"Okay," she said. "I get it."

"Have you been in contact?" Sota asked gently, after a moment had passed.

"No. I swear. I haven't spoken to her since we left her on the highway."

"And she really didn't know about you?"

"I told the truth about everything except the feelings." Carmen appreciated this fuzzy midnight space he'd made for her honesty.

"So you don't even know if . . ."

"If she hates my guts? If she'll ever let me near her again? If there's any future at all after everything that's happened between us?"

Sota smiled, spreading his hands in an apologetic gesture.

"No," Carmen said. "I have no idea."

"Is it worth it?" he asked. "Risking everything? Running away? Sneaking out of here? With all that uncertainty . . ."

Carmen smiled. "Have you ever fallen for someone?" she asked, meeting his gaze. "Like, really fallen for them?"

Sota's normally pale face pinked slightly along the sharp angles of his cheekbones.

"Once."

"So you already know the answer to that question."

They sat in silence for a while, each wrapped up in their own thoughts, their own doomed love stories. Carmen watched the candle nearest the window flicker and dance, thinking, of course, of Dani. Of tomorrow. Of every day after.

What if Carmen's betrayal was too much for Dani to

overcome? If the ruthless rebel Carmen wasn't who she wanted? If she had really moved on. . . .

But what if she hadn't?

"We have to stay focused," Carmen said, Sota's eyes still far away. She wondered who he was thinking of as she imagined Dani. "We have to figure out what Ari has to gain from creating chaos. We have to find out what Mateo is up to. We have to . . ."

"What?"

"We have to fix it all. Just the two of us." She remembered the protest in the government complex, the day gunfire had interrupted her and Dani's first kiss. The anger in the eyes of the people.

And then the fire. The way the charred bodies had looked as they carried them into the hospital's morgue. She would never forget it.

"Yes," he said. "You and Dani are just two people. One story."

"And what's that compared to all the stories in the world?" Carmen asked, her voice small and sad.

"I won't tell anyone about tonight," Sota said. "I promised to help you, and I will. But I want you to think, *really* think, about what you do next. Because I know, love is big, and it feels like everything. But it isn't. Life is everything. That's what we're fighting for here."

He got up, kissing her on the forehead in a rare gesture of affection.

"Thank you," Carmen said. "For believing in me. For not sending me back."

"You know, I used to be so jealous of you." Sota leaned against the wall that led into the hallway, running a hand through his long-on-top curls as he laughed at himself.

"Well, I mean, who isn't?" Carmen asked, flipping her hair.

"No, I mean it, when I first came to the hideout . . . you were exactly where you belonged. Everyone loved you; you were everyone's family."

"Oh, come on, you were the one to be jealous of!" Carmen remembered him then, the serious eyes, the way adults had deferred to him even as a child. "I was so sick of being everyone's little girl. They were sending you on missions at eight!"

"They sent you at nine."

"Still. A year is a long time to hate someone that much."

They laughed then, a soft one, lost in the memory. There had been good things about growing up the way they did, of course, and so many orphaned children had met worse fates that it seemed monstrous to complain.

"It was hard sometimes," Sota said then, and Carmen bowed her head.

"I don't think it's ever easy to make your own family," she answered. "You're not supposed to have to."

Sota nodded. "But we did alright, didn't we?" His eyes, for once, weren't serious or masked with painted-on mischief. They were open, almost vulnerable. Carmen had never seen him this way.

"We did great." Carmen stood, stepping forward. This time, when she reached for him, he reached back, and they hugged like the children they had been when they found each other.

"Alright, enough of that," he said, stepping away, sniffing. "We have a big day tomorrow. Get some rest."

Carmen didn't answer, just nodded good night and sank back down into the sofa, knowing sleep wouldn't come within a hundred yards of her tonight.

Alone with her thoughts, Carmen sipped at the cup that had finally cooled enough to drink. It was comforting, warm and spicy. The feeling of it curled up in her chest like a purring kitten, the perfect companion to the long night of stormy thinking awaiting her.

Behind Sota, the door closed with a click that told her he was as good as his word. If she left again tonight, risked it all, he wouldn't stop her.

But she didn't.

I will trust my comrades. I will trust myself.

—*La Voz Membership Pledge*

⊹⊱✳⊰⊹

THE NEXT MORNING, EXHAUSTED FROM sleeplessness and fear, Carmen slept too long.

Her dreams, of course, were only of Dani. Her hands and
lips, her whispers in the dark room Carmen had imagined
for them, her kisses turning to warnings, her warnings to
screams.

They replayed again and again until Carmen woke, the
sun high in the sky, past remembering details but carrying a
deeply ominous feeling in the pit of her stomach.

Sota was in the kitchen, already dressed in his caterer's
outfit, ready to catch the bus into the complex in less than an
hour. Carmen was always astonished by how easily he could

turn himself into someone else. This Sota wasn't cunning or wise or serious; he was bedraggled and downtrodden, on his way to yet another day of grueling work for little pay and less appreciation.

Between his disguise and their lucky break with the catering schedule, the first part of the plan was the least of Carmen's worries.

"Ready?" Carmen asked, and Sota grinned, transforming back into himself if only for a moment. He lived for the high-pressure days. Carmen had lived for them, too, once, but today there was too much at stake, and too little for her to do. "Let's go over it again," she said, the words easing the knots in her stomach just a little.

"Santos, I know what I'm doing."

"I *know* you do, but I don't get to be there, so you *will* humor me. Those are the rules."

Sota rolled his eyes, but obliged. "I take the bus into the complex and lie low during setup. Once the guests arrive, I'll identify our informants, and keep them in my sights in case I'm made and need to signal for a distraction."

"Good," Carmen said, jiggling her foot up and down. "Then what?"

Sota didn't fidget. He didn't hesitate. This helped, if only a little. "Once the guests of honor arrive, I'll move among them, paying special attention to any behind-the-scenes talk of Mateo's new initiative or the identity of his informant. I'll also watch Dani closely. If I determine it's safe

159

for her and for me, I will approach her."

Carmen felt almost calm again. It would work. Dani would be in charge of the event, so speaking with a caterer wouldn't look all that out of the ordinary as long as Sota timed it right. With any luck, Dani's name—and Carmen's—would be clear with La Voz by the time the sun went down.

"It's a good plan," Sota said, coaxing her out of her thoughts. "You should know, you came up with most of it yourself."

"If you want something done right . . . ," Carmen muttered.

"And where will you be, Cuervita?" Sota asked.

"I'll be here, making no noise, pretending I don't exist."

"That's right." He patted her on the head in a way that would have made her strangle him at twelve, but today she was too busy worrying. Worrying about Sota, about Dani, about herself. Worrying about the plan.

What if it all went wrong? What if Dani was found out? What if Sota came back with the news that she really had turned on them? What if another of the three million things that could go wrong went wrong?

A knock on the door froze them both. Sota was halfway into his caterer's apron; Carmen was on her third circuit of pacing the kitchen. He unfroze faster than she did, moving smoothly to the door like this wasn't at all out of the ordinary.

"Stay out of sight," Sota said quietly, and Carmen retreated to the bedroom, noiselessly taking the false mirror off its hinges to reveal the weapons hidden beneath. Every good safe house had a weapon stash. Carmen had just hoped they wouldn't need them.

Unfortunately, the stock was depleted, and the only thing left was a pouch of throwing knives. Carmen almost rolled her eyes. They were the least accurate, flashiest weapon she could think of. So impractical. But Carmen Santos was always armed, one way or another, so she took them anyway.

The voices from out front were muffled, and when she heard footsteps, she took one of the knives in hand, thinking she'd use it like a dagger if she had to. But as Sota led the man right to the door of the room, she slid the knives in a drawer instinctively before facing the resigned expression on his face.

"What's going on?" Carmen asked.

Sota pointed a thumb behind him at the man, who was massive, tattooed, and scowling. He looked slightly sheepish. "He's here to sit with you while I'm gone."

Carmen's anger flashed, heating her face. "What?"

"I'm sorry, Carmen, I want to trust you, but . . ."

"Sota, you can't honestly think I'm going to try anything."

He just looked at her. She had to admit he had a point.

"He's going to stay with you during the benefit, just to make sure all that worrying doesn't get the best of you. And if things go . . . less well than we'd hoped, he's here to protect you, too. Don't fight me on this, please?"

"This is completely ridiculous," Carmen said through gritted teeth. "I do not need a babysitter."

Sota shrugged. "So prove it. I have a bus to catch. And you weren't going anywhere, right? This way you'll have some . . . company."

Carmen gritted her teeth. "Fine."

Sota took a step closer, and Carmen felt it all come back. The worry, the helplessness. It should have been her out there risking her life. Her taking on the burden. This had been her terrible plan, her reckless insistence on fleeing their help and resources and doing it all herself.

"Be good, okay?" he asked her.

"I'm always good," Carmen grumbled.

Sota rolled his eyes affectionately and turned, saluting the scowling tattooed man on his way into the front room.

Carmen followed. There was something in her throat, something she wanted to say but couldn't find the words for. It built to a fever pitch as he took the doorknob in his hand, the feeling that she should say it before he went. The perfect thing. Something worthy of what he was risking today, and worthy of the gift he had given her by believing her when no one else had.

In the end, she stayed quiet. There would be time for that when it was all over. For better or worse.

Sota opened the door, and Carmen watched his posture slump, his face change in a way that was somewhere on the border of physical and magical until he was just any other bedraggled outer-island caterer.

He smiled back at her once more, and she raised her hand. There would be time.

After two hours, Carmen started to understand why Sota had recruited a bodyguard.

Her thoughts were a tangle of panicked warnings and tortured longing. Every muscle in her body was tensed against the feeling that she shouldn't be here, her instincts and her intellect engaged in a primal screaming match that drowned out everything else.

The bodyguard sat, solid and unmoving, in a chair by the door as Carmen slowly unraveled on the inside. She thought he looked familiar.

In the third hour, Carmen's intellect lost the battle. Dani was there. Sota was there. He was going to approach her, and *he* would be the one to decide what happened next. What if he decided wrong? What if Dani tried something stupid? What if, after everything she'd thrown away for this mission, Carmen never saw her again anyway?

What if she never got to know, *really* know, how Dani felt?

And Mateo would be there, seeking support for his newest, most insidious plan. Wasn't Carmen best suited to read between the lines of whatever speech he'd planned to impress the donors? Hadn't she endured his advances and half-drunken rants and life at his side for long enough to earn the chance to thwart his plan?

What if Sota was too careful, too objective? What if he missed something and they lost their chance to stop him because of it?

The feeling that had sent Carmen off on a dirt bike and into the tunnel of bones was welling up in her again, pricklier and more persistent because of her proximity to her goal. This wasn't a weeklong journey promising almost certain death.

This was barely a walk across town.

And again, from the most illogical place inside her, the place El Buitre and all his spy training couldn't repress completely, Carmen asked herself: Could she live with herself, would she *want* to live with herself, if things went poorly today and she'd done nothing to prevent it?

Dani's life was at stake.

The legacy of La Voz was at stake.

They had all been foolish—herself included—if they thought Carmen would be content to sit here and do nothing.

Covertly, she sized up the bodyguard. There was no way she was getting past him with physicality alone. Luckily, size and strength weren't the only things in her arsenal.

Use personal connections to trigger sympathy and under-standing in others, her Segunda maestras would have said, so Carmen stilled her fidgeting limbs and settled into the sofa across from him.

"I guess this is basically the worst assignment you can get, right?" Carmen dipped her chin just slightly, looking up through her lashes in a way that would attract attention without being overtly suggestive.

The man grunted.

Carmen subtly stretched her legs in front of her, just a casual shifting of position on a seat of awkward height. "Wait until you've been here for days," she said, rolling her eyes, lengthening her neck ever so slightly. "I'm so bored I've started talking to the plants. You wouldn't believe what they've seen."

This time, the grunt came with half a smile.

People misunderstood being a Segunda, Carmen thought. They always thought it was about sex. About seduction. But it wasn't. Not always, anyway. It was more about attention. About the ability to use physicality—your own or that of your atmosphere—to command and direct attention. To divert it. To make it bend around you or light you up or move in a certain direction around a room.

What they didn't tell you in Segunda school was that this skill had much farther-reaching applications than placating your husband when he'd been slighted by another politico. When you controlled people's attention, you could influence their reactions. If you influenced their reactions, you could affect their decisions. And that was power.

Carmen didn't know what she was going to do yet. All she knew was that this man had power over her at this moment, and no matter what she decided, she would need to change that dynamic as quickly as possible.

"Do I know you from before?" she asked.

"We've met." The smile didn't return. This wasn't good.

"When was that?" Carmen asked, lowering her voice just a little.

"When I dragged you to El Buitre by your ear for putting itching powder in my pillow."

Carmen deflated, as did any hope of swaying her bodyguard this way. Her ear still stung when she remembered it. She had distracted Gloriana the potion maker while Sota stole the powder. Juan Carlos here had just been the first person who'd left his bunk unattended after they escaped.

"You know . . . I'm not sure . . ."

"You remember."

For once, Carmen was the first to look away.

"I'm just gonna hang in here for a while," she said dejectedly, heading for the back bedroom.

"Don't try anything funny. You don't fool me twice, you hear?"

"Yeah, yeah . . . I hear you."

In the bedroom, Carmen paced as frantically and noiselessly as she could until she remembered: the throwing knives—she'd jammed them haphazardly into the top drawer when Sota came for her.

They were in her hands again before she'd really given it any thought, the building-disaster feeling writhing in her stomach, growing more urgent. It would be stupid to leave this house, with or without the guard. To expose herself to a crowd of people who would recognize her without question.

But wasn't she a resistance spy? A trained Segunda? If she could use the techniques of beautifying herself she'd learned at school in reverse, maybe she could stay close enough to get Dani alone, or to find out what Mateo was planning. . . .

You'd be back before Sota even knew you were there, said a too-persuasive voice in her head.

The babysitter would tell him when they got back, of course, but by then it would already be done. If she was successful, who could fault her?

In her head, the persuasive voice roared its approval. It was validation enough. Now she just had to figure out how to get out of here.

Carmen stood at the mirror with the knowledge she had gained at school and turned herself older. More tired. Downtrodden. She mussed her brows and drew her hair forward so it fell into her eyes, but it wasn't enough. The knife came back out, as did a stub of a charcoal pencil, and Carmen darkened beneath her eyes, smudging the black dust along the tired lines that had just begun to show after a week of sleepless nights.

Once her face was passable, she looked at the knife, such a tiny thing, and without another thought she wrapped her thick, dark mane around one hand and sliced it off at the nape of her neck. It was uneven, and it took a few minutes to track down the long strands the knife hadn't caught the first time through, but soon enough, she was done. There was a strange, uneven fringe across her forehead, the ends choppy, already curling

167

away from each other as they settled near her shoulder blades.

She had kept the hair for Dani. To be the girl she remembered. But the Carmen Dani remembered had broken her heart and left it bleeding and concussed on a roadside in the middle of the night.

If that was the alternative, maybe unrecognizable wasn't so bad.

The Carmen in the mirror was no glossy-haired, made-up Segunda with a vanity the size of a car's back seat. She was no powerful woman with the ear of one of the most promising young politicos in the country. She wasn't even a spy, with resistance contacts and survival skills born of a lifetime of running.

This girl was exhausted. This girl was utterly underestimatable.

And that was exactly what she needed to be.

All made up—or down—Carmen returned to the bedroom, spreading the apron and cap she'd been given out of kindness on her first day back in the city out on the bed. They would complete the disguise, but that was only half the problem.

She sat on the bed with the knife resting on her palm, feeling the weight of it. Like it was a piece to a puzzle she hadn't quite solved. She couldn't kill the guard, of course, or even seriously hurt him. Not if she wanted to end this caper looking like the disastrous-but-forgivable girl who would do something reckless to resist.

But there had to be something she could do to take him out of commission for a little while. . . .

That's when it hit her. The knife. The poison in the pouch on her thigh. She knew Juan Carlos would never accept a drink from her—that was La Voz 101—but it would barely take a prick of the knife into his skin to deliver the sleeping potion. With even a tiny amount of that in his bloodstream, she'd have plenty of time to get out.

Carmen Santos was ruthless, it had been said again and again, on both sides of the island, in the government and the resistance and everywhere in between.

Now, when she felt so far from the person who'd left for a dangerous mission at twelve, who'd been feared and respected when she returned at seventeen, it was almost comforting to remember that was true.

Or that it could be.

She felt every bit that ruthless girl now, dipping the tip of the razor-sharp blade into the vial, seeing the liquid shine like a diamond drop against the dull luster of the metal. She palmed it, careful not to puncture her own skin, and slid back into the room on silent feet.

The decision was carrying her now, fizzing in her veins, screaming that it was right even while the details remained murky and hard to pin down. How would she get into the compound? How would she find Dani before Sota and somehow avoid the Garcias and everyone she'd ever met as one of them? How would she stay invisible while Mateo gave his speech?

Most importantly, how would she escape without getting herself—or anyone else—killed?

But she was in the room, smiling a sad smile, and Juan Carlos wasn't on guard even though he really, really should have been.

"Hey," she said, moving closer, eyes downcast, repelling attention this time instead of drawing it. It was the same basic concept, if you did it right. "I just wanted to say I'm sorry about what happened back then. We were kids, it was silly, but I really want to prove to El Buitre that I'm still part of this family, and part of that is making amends, you know?"

Gruff, Juan Carlos waved her off as she shuffled a little closer. "It's not the end of the world," he said.

"Sure, but still. I'm sorry. Friends?" She held out the hand without the knife for him to shake, and when he reached for it, she grabbed his arm with the other. His sleeves were short, and she felt the small pressure before the give, felt the tiny bead of blood against her hand.

"What the—"

Carmen smiled again. "Sorry, friend."

But he was slumping to the ground, his eyes rolling back, and Carmen was grabbing the apron and the hat, tying them on in a near frenzy, and her heartbeat was screaming that it was time. Past time.

Go, go, go, whispered every beat of her pulse.

So she went.

13

When chaos strikes, I will use it. When silence settles, I will fold myself into it.

—La Voz Membership Pledge

-+>*<+-

CARMEN JOINED THE LINE AT the gate to the complex, knowing she would have to run the moment someone even raised an eyebrow in her direction. But she didn't have time for a plan, and the bus was long gone. She couldn't afford not to try.

The officers were out in full force, but they were spread thin, half of them on guard detail at the party, the other half frazzled, moving from one place to the next. Carmen took advantage, watching for openings, waiting for uniform backs to turn her way, for brief scuffles to command the attention of the officers nearby.

She moved through the blind spots when they formed, deflecting light and attention away from herself just as she'd once been taught to draw it.

In this way, slowly, she made her way through the city, until the iron bars of the government complex gate were in sight. An elaborate checkpoint had been set up, of course, and guests were being screened rigorously. But as she watched, Carmen realized the staff members had a separate line, and it was moving much faster.

Anyone in a service uniform was shouted at, intimidated, patted down aggressively. But the men in charge didn't look at their faces. They treated them like dogs.

That kind of unbridled egoism had cost them so much, Carmen thought. So much information, so many lives, and yet they clung to their superiority like there was no other way to live.

In this way, the most wanted woman in the country—barely disguised by tired eyes and an unkempt, self-shorn mane—made her way unrecognized through the crowds just arriving for Mateo's benefit.

They shoved her once, twice, glanced at the house insignia on her apron, and let her pass through with little more than a "Clean yourself up, don't you know the president will be here tonight?"

Carmen kept her head down, winced when they shoved her, shrank in on herself when they spoke, but inside she could barely believe she'd made it this far.

If she was being honest with herself, it was this egoism that was the real reason La Voz had been able to maintain a foothold in this world—to keep getting information and placing people in the right locations. Far more than any skill of their own. They had been exploiting this weakness for decades, and would continue to as long as it was there to be exploited.

Maybe one day, inner-islanders would wise up and learn to look their servants in the eye.

Carmen would keep praying that day didn't come for a long, long time.

"You're late!" snapped a sour-faced woman in the tent that had been set up for catering. It was a bold choice, Carmen thought, to hold the event in the open so soon after the market demonstrations, the fire in the capital.

But Mateo was nothing if not bold. The purpose of this benefit was to send a message. Make the statement that they would not be cowed. And if he did it right, that's exactly what it would do.

"Lo siento," Carmen said to the woman, looking at the floor instead of her face, letting her hair fall in her eyes, her shoulders slump. The woman threw her a different apron, one with starched creases, black with the Garcia family crest on it. Carmen tried not to laugh aloud at the irony.

Branded again. When she'd worn Segunda silk and flaunted her powerful husband, she'd been nothing but a well-monitored bird in a cage. But here, short-haired in a server's uniform, she was more dangerous to them than she'd ever been.

It was a good thing, she told herself when someone bumped into her from behind, sending her stumbling forward into a table. She needed to be dangerous today.

"Watch where you're going," the man snarled, already past her. When she turned around to apologize, his back was to her, moving toward the raised platform where he'd no doubt be speaking. His back was so familiar in its well-cut linen suit, his hair curling at the nape of his neck.

Carmen's blood heated almost past endurance. She hadn't expected to see him so soon. The table beside her was covered in cutlery, meat saws and knives and a hundred other things that would end him before he drew his next breath.

For a moment, she pictured it. His blood on the ground, pooling beneath him, the shock on his face when he recognized her.

But a quick death at the height of his power was more than he deserved, Carmen told herself. She would make him pay first. She would take away everything he had ever cared about. And then, if he was *lucky*, she would end it.

So he passed without noticing, and Carmen cooled the fire in her veins.

For now.

As the next hour passed, Carmen stayed on the fringes, keeping her back to everyone remotely familiar, making sure her hair was in her eyes and her face was downcast. For an absolutely awful plan, it was going almost scarily well so far.

When the guests began to arrive, it would be harder to stay out of sight but easier to do what she'd come to do. Listen to Mateo's speech. Watch Dani. Wait for the ideal moment to take her aside.

Try to get out of here alive.

It felt like a workable plan until, without warning, she saw her.

There were three tables and several roaming staff members, but the air grew heavy and sparkling between them, time slowing as Dani turned, the skirt of her long black dress flaring, her long arms the only skin visible below the neck in her modest Primera's cut.

Carmen had thought she knew her own mind. She had thought she had a handle on how she felt for Dani, and what it would mean if she had betrayed La Voz—or worse, if she hadn't, but she didn't want Carmen after all that had happened. But she knew, now, in this slow-motion moment, that she had known nothing.

Nothing at all.

The sight of her was like fire to gasoline. Like madness poison. Like falling.

Even her most elaborate imaginings—the room, the glade—hadn't done a second of justice to this girl. The strong lines of her cheekbones, the slim, boyish way her hips carried her dress. The hair, longer now on the top, just a little.

It was all Carmen could do not to sob, to run to her, to run away.

But she was invisible here, and all she could do was stand, frozen, as Dani smiled at Mateo, taking a seat next to him, pressing close enough to read a single piece of paper between them.

There was intimacy there, like Carmen had never seen before, and her blood couldn't decide whether to freeze or boil.

Either Dani's acting skills had responded well to the dire circumstances . . .

Or they were all in very big trouble.

Back in the kitchen tent, Carmen waited for the sun to set, for the guests to become sufficiently tipsy, for the speech to begin.

She was lucky there were so many staff members in place tonight. She hadn't yet been noticed by Sota, but she kept track of him as much as she could. Mostly, her struggle was maintaining awareness of Dani's position without daring to look at her directly.

After the effort it had taken to look away, she knew it was for the best, but the other girl's beating heart seemed to pull on her like the tide, and she found her gaze was never far off. Lovingly tracing the shapes of trees she had passed, glasses she had discarded, an overturned chair she'd righted before moving away.

The plaza filled with people dressed in evening gowns, the sliver of moon bright above them. She knew she wouldn't get close to Dani until after the speech, but even when she was out of sight, Carmen felt the pull of her.

She would be ready, when the time came.

Resisting the pull for now, Carmen observed the rest of the party, careful not to let her eyes linger on anyone for too long, but she kept returning to Mateo's father. There was something strange about him tonight.

He looked grim and pale, speaking little, his mouth a hard line even when he attempted to twist it into a smile. It was understandable, of course. He was grieving the loss of his Segunda. The mother of his son. But the more Carmen watched him, the more it seemed like something else was troubling him.

It took a while before she realized: Señor Garcia's anger was to be expected. But it didn't seem to be directed upward, at a cruel god that had taken his wife too soon. Or directed inward, either, at some thought of his own.

No, when his eyes moved from the person speaking to him, no matter who it was, his glare focused in on Dani and Mateo. On their casual closeness. On the trust Mateo had obviously placed in his remaining wife. The Garcia patriarch looked like he wanted nothing more than to pry them apart with a crowbar.

Carmen could relate to that sentiment more than she'd ever admit, but the implications of it coming from Señor

Garcia set Carmen's mind racing.

Distrust coming from the head of the Garcia family was tame compared to what Carmen had been expecting. Dani was alive, and seemingly unharmed. On top of that, Mateo appeared to genuinely believe in her. Even with his father's influence, that would take time to undo.

Time was the only commodity that mattered on a mission like this, and Dani had bought them more of it. Carmen's heart swelled with pride.

If *she's still loyal to La Voz*, said the nagging voice she had grown to dread.

Carmen ignored it.

"Stop lurking and get out there!" With a bony hand, the sour-faced woman pushed Carmen out of the tent just as Mateo smiled at Dani and they took the stage. "These drinks aren't going to fill themselves!"

Lost in thought, Carmen hadn't been prepared for the push. Hadn't planned her next hiding place. And worse still, she was immediately caught in the shuffle, propelled by moving bodies who pushed past her like an object until she was close to the stage. Too close.

"Ladies and gentlemen," said Mateo in a heavy voice. A voice that said he had seen tragedy, and he didn't intend to sit idly by. "Friends. Welcome. And thank you."

Everyone faced the stage, and polite applause scattered through the crowd. Carmen was only a few rows from the front. Close enough to see Señora Garcia hissing into her husband's ear. Close enough to see the way Dani's arm was touching Mateo's casually as she stood beside him.

Close enough to see Medio's president waver on his feet as he took another goblet of wine and downed it in one gulp before grabbing another.

This last thing focused Carmen for a moment—it calmed the rage heating up once more in her chest. She could understand what was wrong with Mateo's father, but what did the president have to drink about tonight? One more thing Carmen would keep an eye on while she was here.

You can never know enough pressure points in enemy territory. El Buitre again.

"As most of you know, our family recently lost a member," Mateo said when the noise had died down. "The tragedy has wounded us deeply, and though my instinct is to stay at home and mourn my mother's death in traditional fashion, this tragedy is more than just personal. It's political. And it affects us all."

The applause had ended, and all chatter around them died down immediately. Carmen could hardly believe she was standing here in the middle of this crowd. Her heart raced, and she scanned the area for any available hiding place, but there was nothing. Just a wall of people on every side and an absolute tangle of tables and chairs anywhere they were not.

Even the other servers had paused out of respect for the dead. Until they started moving again, Carmen was trapped.

"My mother, Señorita Pilar Garcia, was murdered. And

not just by anyone. By a rebel in our midst. A member of the savage organization La Voz, who I was foolish enough to let into my home unknowingly."

He cast his eyes down in a faux-remorseful way that made Carmen want to wrap her fingers around his throat. But it seemed she was the only one feeling that particular sentiment. The crowd was rapt, transfixed.

"I will never stop blaming myself for my mother's death. She was a beautiful woman, inside and out, a model Segunda in a world where so many of our oldest traditions are threatened by outsiders who can't understand them."

This time, the murmuring around them was approving rather than pitying, and Carmen listened closely, still looking down at her hands, hoping she could trust the self-absorption of her former peers to keep her invisible to them just a little longer.

"Which is why, with the help of my father and the unwavering support of my wife, Daniela—" He gestured to Dani here, and she looked up at him with a mixture of pride and pity that made Carmen's stomach twist. "I'm pleased to announce to you all that I'll be heading a new division of the Median government. One that will seek to undo all the harm that has been done to my family, and to countless others."

Dani was still looking at Mateo, and when she smiled at the crowd it was the smile of a woman perfectly aligned with her husband and his cause. Carmen had grown up watching what loyalty looked like, and Dani had it mastered tonight.

Her anger only built as Mateo touched Dani's shoulder, sharing a private word with her, too soft for the crowd to hear. When she smiled, it was with her whole body. Could she possibly be this good an actor?

And if she was, what did that mean for Carmen? For the million looks they'd shared just like this one. . . .

But more than that, what did it mean for Dani's life? If Mateo believed Dani, if *everyone* believed her, what evidence could Carmen possibly present to El Buitre to exonerate her?

Suddenly, Carmen was more alert than ever, feeling foolish for believing El Buitre had left this task to Carmen and Sota alone. What if there were other La Voz members in the crowd tonight? What if one of them believed the adoring gaze Dani now fixed her husband with?

Her head swam with fear and helplessness as Mateo looked back at the crowd, but still no one had moved.

"The Rebel Eradication Division will be making unprecedented strides in the investigation, capture, and punishment of La Voz agents and their sympathizers. We will seek to accomplish what no one before us has so far been able to—"

As he spoke, the president took another goblet of wine from the table in front of him, this time swaying on the spot as he drank it in two gulps that were almost audible. Mateo glanced at him. So did everyone else.

But no one looked harder than Carmen, who had just

watched her pressure point become a bull's-eye.

"We will do more than just defend ourselves from attacks like the one that happened in this very marketplace only a few weeks ago," Mateo went on, like nothing had happened. "We will do more than stop these people from infiltrating our staffs and our homes and our families." He paused here, for effect, and Carmen knew no one around her was even breathing.

For a moment, she forgot herself. She looked up at the stage. And not to the left at the president, her hair hanging in her eyes. But right at the happy couple, her newly severed fringe falling dangerously out of her face. Luckily, Mateo was busy basking in his moment of anticipation.

Dani, on the other hand, was looking right at her.

At first, Carmen thought she had looked through her like all the others. She waited for the gaze to lose focus or pass. She waited in vain.

Dani was frozen, her eyes open a fraction of an inch too wide, her wan politico's-wife smile too fixed to be natural.

All the reasons she had risked her life and her cause and everything else to come here disappeared, leaving just this one. Carmen knew she had to look away, but even though it was selfish, and dangerous, she didn't.

Dani did. She looked back at Mateo, who was breaking his dramatic pause at last.

"We are going to do what no one has done since the Sun God himself relinquished his human form to fight his accursed brother. We are going to find these rebels where they live, and we are going to make sure they can never hurt us again."

Something shifted in the crowd at these words, and Carmen finally looked away from the girl in front of her. Instead, like something was breaking inside her, she looked at Mateo. She looked right at him as he promised, in front of all these people, to kill her and everyone she loved.

"We are going to fight back." He thrust an open palm into the air, a bastardization of the La Voz palm salute. Around Carmen the crowd, whipped into a paranoid frenzy by his words, mimicked the gesture, though it had had no significance to them at all before this moment.

That was the power of fear when manipulated by the right hands. It made rallying cries of lies. It made murderers. It made wars.

Mateo, it seemed, had chosen the right time to light the fuse.

"With your help, we will enforce more rigorous screening procedures!"

Cheers split the air.

"We will offer incentives in border communities for giving up illegal residents!"

Even louder now.

"We will build centers where the criminals we catch in our midst will be forced to repay their debt to society!"

Across the square, a table was flipped end over end. Several glasses crashed into the stone of the ground under their feet.

"But most of all, we will be training a special military team to go beyond the wall. To use the intelligence we've gathered here and mount an offensive that will *wipe out* the organization that has plagued our community for generations!"

Suddenly, like a moving picture was playing in front of her, Carmen could see it. Men more terrifying than the military police she had spent her life in fear of, torturing the contacts they had gathered, using that information to destroy safe houses, to kill allies to the cause. To discover the whereabouts of La Voz's hideout. To end what the resistance had spent generations building.

Flames leapt in her mind's eye; screams echoed. Their organization was built for subterfuge, for spying and sneaking and intel gathering. But on a battlefield with the might of Medio's military and all their resources? They would be helpless.

The sounds of the crowd were growing louder, wilder, Mateo's hand was still in the air and the police standing around the perimeter of the square did nothing to stop the crowd from building on the frenzy.

This was no longer a high-society benefit. The masks were off. The monsters had been let loose.

For the first time since Carmen had hot-wired that dirt bike outside the meeting tent, Dani was the last thing on her mind. She had to get home. To hope that the knowledge of what was really coming would force El Buitre to retake the reins of his organization. To solidify the resistance into something that could withstand the storm.

Mateo had just declared all-out war on La Voz. The only thing left was to survive it.

Sota's words from the night she'd tried to sneak out of the safe house came back to her now, and even though Dani's pull on the tides of her heart hadn't lessened, even a little, there was something more now.

Carmen and Sota had placed themselves between the cause they loved and destruction, and destruction was coming as sure as the waves crashed against the tunnel of bones. It was time to take her place at the mouth of chaos. To beat it back with all the tools she had.

It was time to grow up.

In the frenzy building around them, Carmen looked up at Dani where she still stood beside Mateo on the makeshift stage. She had crossed an entire country to find her. She had disobeyed and betrayed the only people who had ever mattered to her.

And now she was going to leave without a word. Without a single moment where they were allowed to do more than stare as the world broke down around them.

Carmen's chest felt like something had shattered inside it, and every last shard was slicing into something vital. She could barely breathe. She could barely move. Everything was fuzzy outside the place where their gazes were locked.

Around them, the polite voices rose to shouting, and near the edge of the crowd Carmen saw a slim, boyish silhouette disappear into the trees.

Sota, she thought. He had heard what he needed to hear. It was time to go.

Carmen would be right behind him.

She lifted her hand to Dani once, briefly, the only goodbye she would be allowed tonight.

The only goodbye she would ever be allowed.

She knew, in this moment, that she loved Dani. Truly loved her. That maybe she would never love anyone else again. But if she didn't leave this place right now, if she didn't get home to play her part in what was to come, Carmen would never forgive herself.

Some people had lives. Others had causes. Her die had been cast long before this moment.

La Voz would find out what side Dani was on. Hopefully they would be merciful. But if there was any part of Dani still holding back, or any part of Carmen that didn't believe she was all in, she was the wrong person for this job. Maybe they had been right about that all along.

Dani didn't return the wave, or even acknowledge that she had seen Carmen in the crowd. But Carmen liked to think there was something sparkling in the corner of one eye as she turned away. She would keep the image with her.

It was the only thing she would get to keep.

Carmen fought her way through the crowd, holding back

tears, already pulling off her apron and her hat. She wouldn't be branded by that monster for one more moment.

When she reached the kitchen tent, she turned once more to look at the scene, remembering another riot in another square. The night Carmen had snuck down to the Medio School for Girls gate to let the protesters in.

That was the night it had all begun. Carmen and Dani and their doomed collision course.

But it was over now. Time to let go. To go home, to be a soldier in this war. To give the best counsel and fight the best fight she could. To trust the man who had raised her to do the job he was born to do.

It was what La Voz needed from her now, and she owed them that much. She owed them everything she had.

Out of Dani's sight line, Carmen's bitter sadness turned to anger as she played Mateo's words over and over in her head. It was what he had always wanted. The chance to attack La Voz openly, without fear of casualties or crossfire. An event so horrible it would force the people to accept his extreme views.

And it had been handed to him on a silver platter.

Carmen tossed the balled-up apron in the corner and bent down, checking her knife pouch and the vials beside it. She was alone in the tent, the rest of the staff fleeing or cowering in the face of the riot outside. For good measure she dipped a few of the knife tips in her final vial of poison. The one that would kill instantly. Just in case.

"Hey you! Girl!" The sour-faced woman was back. She didn't seem to notice Carmen was missing an apron, or see the weapons she had just hastily hidden under her long skirt. "Take out the dishwater, then come back!"

Though the woman had been rude and pushy all night, Carmen felt a pang of pity for her. Washing their dishes while they waged war on her and everyone like her. It was too fitting a metaphor.

The tub was right in front of her, gray with use, soap bubbles floating listlessly on the surface.

"Out in the trees! Go now!"

Carmen nodded, keeping her eyes down. Ridiculous as it was, the errand was the perfect cover. She would be the serving girl for one more moment, carrying dirty dishwater to the trees. Once she reached them, she would disappear.

"Sí," Carmen said. "I'll be right back."

Feeling the comforting bite of the poison pouch at her thigh, Carmen took the dish tub. Under the watchful eye of the sour-faced woman, she pushed through the tent flaps for the last time.

Slump-shouldered, hair in her face, Carmen hid her righteous rebel's heart as she moved apologetically through the crowd. The grove of trees was just ahead, and her heart nearly stopped when she realized where she was.

This wasn't just a grove of trees.

It was *the* grove. The one Dani had led her to after their day-out-of-time in the marketplace. The one where they had asked each other again and again, where they had inched closer, where their lips had almost, *almost*...

But then there were footsteps behind her, the trailing of a skirt on the leaves, and tears sprang to Carmen's eyes because she knew. She didn't even have to turn.

"Wait."

I will allow no other loyalty to sway me from my place.
—La Voz Membership Pledge

THE VOICE WAS AS SHARP as one of Carmen's blades, and it went through her completely.

Behind them, there were rallying cries, glass breaking, but here, there was quiet. Here, they might as well have been completely alone.

Carmen turned to face Dani, and it was so much more than just eyes meeting across a crowd. It was more than a goodbye. It was stars colliding. It was a storm where there had never been rain, lightning splitting the sky where they stood.

It was a quiet sigh. A whisper. It was coming home.

There was something fated in the air, something that felt

protected, even though somewhere far off, Carmen knew that was impossible. That she couldn't be safe here.

Carmen wasn't a Segunda or a spy when she stepped forward, cutting the space between them in half. She wasn't responsible for a world or a war or any lives but the two stretching toward each other here and now.

"I . . . ," she began, but Dani stepped forward, too, and the words died in her throat.

There were so many questions, so many things to know and understand. She wanted to warn her about La Voz, tell her to watch her back, no matter what her loyalties were.

But as they moved toward each other like magnets, Carmen saw the truth plain as day.

She was glad she had come. She had been the perfect person to judge Mateo's speech, to take an action plan back to La Voz. But she had been the exact wrong person to sit in judgment of Dani.

Carmen knew, in this moment, that it didn't matter what Dani had done. Who she had betrayed. What she had kept or sold. Who she was. She would have forgiven her anything. Loved her despite anything.

And if this was the last time they were ever going to see each other, what did it matter what the answers were?

"Is this a dream?" Dani asked, and suddenly Carmen was back in that doorway, and Dani was about to ask her to build a fire, and everything was different, but everything was the same.

"You dream about me?" Carmen asked, playing the part, walking in heart first.

"When I'm lucky." Then there was no more space between them, and Carmen knew she shouldn't be here, that the clock was ticking and she had to go, but for this one precious moment, she didn't care.

"You never should have come." Dani was close enough to reach out and touch now. "You could have been killed. You could have been worse than killed."

"I almost never do what I should," Carmen said, and Dani's laugh was half a sob.

"You have to go," Dani replied, but she was still moving closer. The smell of her was sharp and citrusy, clean, so familiar it brought tears to Carmen's eyes.

She tried to say she knew, but Dani was reaching for her, pulling her in, their lips meeting so softly Carmen wondered if she had imagined it. But there they were again, stronger now, and Dani's hands were in her hair, and Carmen was pulling her closer by her hips, and they had to stop because the world was burning around them, but they couldn't stop. They had never learned how to do it right.

It was Dani, as always, who pulled away. "Go," she said. "I can't watch you die."

And Carmen had told herself she didn't need to know, that La Voz would sort it out, that she was the wrong person to judge, but there was one question she couldn't leave without knowing the answer to, and it left her lips unbidden now:

"Did you choose him?" she asked.

Dani's eyes widened, just a little, and despite her proclamation, she stepped forward again.

"Never," she said, her lips against Carmen's. "Never."

Then they were kissing again, and Carmen could taste the truth on Dani's tongue. There was no stopping now; there were only hands and lips and hair and hips and the feeling of drowning and coming up for air all at once.

But then a stick cracked beneath a boot, and they sprang apart too late.

The president of Medio was standing in the entrance to their grove, his fly comically open, swaying on the spot, the look on his face saying he had no doubts about what he'd seen.

Carmen froze, her hand still brushing Dani's until the other girl stepped forward, voice already smooth.

"Hello, Señor Presidente," Dani said, walking toward him. "I was just checking for my house staff, and I found this one hiding in the trees." She chuckled, as if to create an intimate space between them, one that didn't allow for the cowardice of the lower class.

It was a valiant attempt, and a few seconds earlier it might have worked, but the president's eyes were open too wide. He backed away from Dani like she was a wild animal stalking him through the jungle.

Carmen kept her head down, willing herself to be the girl Dani had described. A poor, terrified girl, hiding from the benefit-turned-riot outside.

"You . . . ," he spluttered. "And . . . you. I knew it, I *always* knew . . ."

He was drunk, shocked, and he stumbled over a tangle of roots. Her camouflage gone, Carmen took the opportunity to stare him down. She couldn't help but assess his weaknesses, size him up as a target.

He would be an easy one tonight. His deficiency made her despise him. What right did he have to rule? This slob, this drunken, cowardly fool. He wasn't even a worthy adversary.

"Please calm down, señor," Dani said, moving closer still. "It seems you've had a bit to drink tonight. Would you like me to help you back to the party?"

"Unnatural," he snarled. "And *she's* a traitor. Don't think I didn't see. I told him again and again that *you* couldn't be trusted." His anger was clearing the wine haze from his eyes. In Carmen's expert estimation, the target was shrinking.

"Señor, please," Dani said, but Carmen knew it was useless.

"We spent weeks telling him, his father and I," the president said, like he hadn't even heard her. "That if one is spoiled you throw out the bunch. But he *believed* you, Daniela. He believed you were pure, and righteous. He fought for you. And just look what he was fighting for."

From weak and sputtering, he had turned dangerous. Carmen felt the prickle of fear trace featherlight down her spine.

"Wait until I tell them," he said, an almost manic gleam in

his eye now. "Not only are you a traitorous bitch, but you're a whore, too."

Something in Carmen broke at the word. Like being a whore wasn't condoned by the government this man claimed to run. Like girls weren't sold to the highest bidder to warm the beds of men who would never deserve them.

Like being a whore was so much worse than being a bigoted, prejudiced murderer who had just allowed war to be declared on half his own country. The poor half. The starving half. The half most in need of mercy.

Yes, Mateo was rotten to the core, and Carmen would make him pay. But had she cast her net too narrowly?

Mateo had been taught by other men. And this one was the most powerful of them all.

The images from before were back. Bemabe's camp at the gate to the tunnel of bones destroyed. La Voz on the run as their compound was torched. It was all because of him. This despicable, unworthy man who leered at her and Dani even as he was condemning them.

He thought their lives worthless because of who they were, who they loved, and where they had been born. And he was wrong.

Carmen was reaching for a knife before she knew it, like it was something happening to her rather than something she was choosing. The air seemed to slow down around her, everyone locked in their positions, no one noticing the lethal petals unfolding in their midst. Carmen's hand was at her thigh now, reaching into the folds of the pouch, careful to take the handle and not the tip. . . .

You have time, she told herself as the president tried to gain his drunken footing in the rocks and roots of the grove and Dani went from approaching to backing away. Everything was happening underwater. There was a line of light between her fingers, holding the knife, and the exposed, wrinkled skin at the president's neck.

On the other side of him, crashing through the trees, a silhouette approached. Time sped up at the sound, too fast now. Carmen's heart was beating out of her chest. Was it Mateo? His father? She only had time for one shot; how would they get out? But when the shape came into focus, it was the last person she had expected to see, and the most welcome.

Sota, a scratch along one cheek, his caterer's apron in tatters, got close enough to see what was happening and froze like he'd just found himself in someone else's dream.

She tried to see it as he must. Dani and Carmen, hair rumpled, shirts and dresses turned sideways. The president, turning, drunk and furious. And the knife in Carmen's hand, poised, ready to fire.

"No," Sota said, but the president had spooked, and in his enraged, drunken state he lunged for Dani.

Carmen didn't give herself permission to let go of the knife. She didn't ask for anyone else's. Its path across the glade was paved by the coming war, by every outer-islander who had ever died, or been tortured, or lived a life never knowing that hunger wasn't forever because of this man's cruelty. His prejudice.

It was paved by his pig's eyes open too wide, his lecherous leer as he called Dani a whore.

It was paved by every moment of hatred Carmen had felt in the tunnel, mourning the loss of Cielo, cursing every man who had upheld the wall and what it stood for.

The knife traveled along it, every stone that had built it so clear in her mind's eye.

It did not miss.

In a lopsided triangle, as the world went on turning outside, Carmen, Dani, and Sota watched the president of Medio reach for his throat, his eyes uncomprehending, and pull out the blade.

It wouldn't have killed him on its own; the cut had been shallow enough. But it wouldn't be the bleeding that killed him. He turned to Carmen, a bull that had seen red, but he didn't make it a single step before he fell to his knees, the poison already spreading through his veins.

"You . . . ," he croaked, and the look on his face was pure hatred.

"What did you do?" Sota whispered as President Ignacio Lorenzo Matos Valdez slumped onto the ground, his lips turning purple, the desert sand of his skin already graying. "What did you do?"

By the time his weight settled on the damp, mossy ground of the glade, the hatred had left his face along with the light. He was gone.

Carmen's hands were steady until she remembered Dani.

Dani, who knew her as a flighty Segunda, a girl with privilege and a hidden heart of gold. A girl who kissed sweetly and fed her strawberries and held her hand through busy marketplace streets.

But she had seen the real Carmen now. A girl who had killed. A girl who sometimes relished in it. A girl who had been trained by a legendary rebel and held a blade for the first time at seven.

"We have to run," Dani said, her voice as steady as Carmen's hands, her expression inscrutable.

There was no time to find out what this had cost.

"We have to run," Carmen echoed, her voice sounding far away to her own ears.

The knife was on the stone where he'd thrown it, tip still glinting dangerously beneath the blood. Dani reached for it, but Sota snatched her hand out of the air. He wasn't gentle.

"Are you insane?" he hissed. "Leave it."

"Into the trees." Carmen's words were quick, efficient, her emotions held at bay for the moment in the name of surviving the night. "We can't be seen on the streets. We'll stay in the jungle, travel by night until we're outside the city, and then . . ."

Sota's look stopped her. He was right. There was no point in planning further than that. Not now.

But they hadn't even begun before another player joined their terrible scene. The sour-faced woman, in search of her dish girl, her criticism dying in her throat as she processed what was happening in front of her. What this collection of bodies and their arrangement meant.

A scream split the air. She stared at the president's body, looking between him, the bloody knife, and their faces before screaming again. "He's dead!" she screamed. "The president is dead!"

They ran. Together, hands sometimes brushing, the three of them never separating as they moved too slowly down the road, to a place where they could take to the woods without being waylaid by dense jungle.

"Here!" Sota shouted, and they plunged inside without thinking twice, their footsteps too loud as they crashed through leaves and branches, pushing any obstacle aside. Moving, because if they stopped they would die.

The crashing of military boots pursued them, too close.

The shouts of men, too loud over the forest's soundscape, urged them on.

Carmen's heart beat too fast as one voice rose above the footsteps, above the voices of other men.

"I want them alive if possible, but do not let them escape!"

Mateo. Mateo was leading the soldiers. Mateo already knew Dani had betrayed him, and that Carmen was here. This game had just turned even more deadly.

"Carmen . . . ," Dani said, and it was the first time since they'd met on a bus at age twelve that Carmen had ever heard fear in her voice.

"It'll be okay," she told her, reaching out as they ran to touch the back of Dani's hand with her own. Dani didn't take her hand, and as dire as their situation was, Carmen felt it in her chest.

Would it be okay? she wondered as they ran. She had just murdered the president at a benefit full of the Median upper class. Where her cruel, vengeful ex-husband was only looking for a reason to kill them both.

She had given him a reason, tonight.

Behind them, the footsteps were getting louder, and Carmen could feel her strength starting to ebb, the length of the day and the shock worming their way in, turning everything heavy.

Dani tore the sides of her dress up the thighs so her legs could move freely, kicking off the flat shoes that had been practical at a party but slipped and slid on the leaves. Carmen thought privately that it wouldn't do much. Glancing sideways at Sota, she confirmed her worst suspicions in his grave face. The way he glanced back every few seconds even though it was slowing him down.

The soldiers gained ground with every moment that passed, at home in this terrain like three kids from the salt never could be.

"We should split up," Sota said, the strain of running evident in his voice.

"Are you crazy?" Dani asked. "They'll just pick us off one by one."

There was no argument against that. Not that any of them had the energy to make one anyway. Carmen had wanted to move quietly, to use the jungle to disguise them until they'd left the city and could contact resistance allies for help.

Mateo's quick reaction had robbed them of their best chance.

The soldiers adapted to the jungle as Carmen, Dani, and Sota lost steam. The realization settled gradually. They weren't going to be able to outrun them. And after the way they'd just humiliated Mateo, there was nothing but a death sentence at the end of whatever came if they were caught.

When they were caught.

Carmen wondered, as her heart hammered and sank, as she got used to the too-slow rhythm of her feet and the constant burning ache in her chest that meant she couldn't run forever. Would it be worth it? Her death in exchange for the president's?

Everything in her screamed that it would. But she hadn't only doomed herself tonight.

Carmen looked at Dani, laboring on bare feet through snaring vines and twisted roots, her face flushed, her hair alive as her body was jolted and jarred by the terrain. She was so beautiful. It was tragic, Carmen thought, how much of her life she had spent not loving this girl.

On the other side, Sota was determined, his olive skin barely flushed despite the exertion. The hunted fox. Her brother. The first friend she ever remembered having.

"We have you in our sights! If you surrender now we won't hurt you!"

This old lie, she thought, every muscle screaming at her to slow. To stop. But she clambered over a fallen log, checking to the left and right, making sure she was still one of three. None of them answered the soldier's shouts. None of them stopped.

"If you don't stop we will be forced to open fire!" This was Mateo's voice, performing even here, with no one to see him but three dead people and the men he paid to obey him. It was sad, Carmen thought. Better to die with dignity than live like him.

They did not stop.

The first gunshot hit to the left of Dani, and she gasped, veering into Carmen, who caught her and stumbled. Sota stopped as they tried to untangle, to get moving again.

"Go!" Carmen screamed, and the next gunshot hit right where he'd been standing.

They got up, pushing on, and Carmen and Dani didn't let go of each other's hands even when the connection slowed them. If they were going to die before they had ever found out what they truly meant to each other, Carmen was glad they would be together.

More gunfire, this time closer. Carmen's heart raced with the knowledge that any one shot could be the last. Sota was ahead now, looking back at them, shouting something Carmen couldn't hear over the pounding of her heart and the ringing in her ears. She thought of the knife pouch, and how useless the few remaining ones would be against armored soldiers and guns.

They were out of options, out of luck, out of time. Dani tripped again, going down just as a bullet whizzed over her head.

Carmen helped her up, but she could hear them breathing behind her now. Sota was ahead, and she thought it was good that at least he'd make it out. He'd tell everyone what had happened to them. That in the end they'd died for the cause, not in opposition to it.

Maybe it would be easier, she thought, with the president gone. Maybe it would be the thing that turned the tide. Could she live with that? Her final sacrifice?

Together, clinging, tears streaming down Carmen's face, they turned to each other, keeping up the pretense of running without much hope.

"Dani . . . ," Carmen said, but Dani only shook her head, pulling her behind a tree as more bullets barely missed their marks.

"Don't," she said, pushing on, knowing to stop was to die, knowing they would die anyway, unwilling to accept it.

But when the first cry of pain rang out, it wasn't either of theirs.

It was Sota's.

15

I will lay down my life, if required, in service of La Voz.
—*La Voz Membership Pledge*

⊱✳⊰

"SOTA!"

The scream came from Dani, but Carmen thought she could feel it in her lungs, too. In her throat. They couldn't stop, but when she looked to where she'd last seen him, there was nothing.

"We have to go back!" Dani said, pulling at Carmen's arm, slowing them both.

But Mateo was so close they could hear him screaming at his men: "He's down! Make sure he's dead. We can question the others." And Carmen knew, though the knowledge tore at every fiber of her, that this would be their only chance to escape.

She thought she had learned her lesson during Mateo's speech, the one Sota had tried to explain to her just a few nights ago. About the cause and the individual. About fighting for the good of all even when the system was flawed.

Apparently the lesson wasn't done with her yet.

Tears stung her eyes as she fought with Dani, who was still pulling her back, but Sota, though his cries could still be heard, didn't call for help. He knew what they had to do. What *he* had to do. Now, while all of Mateo's confused soldiers were running to the spot where he had fallen.

But still, Carmen hesitated, racking her brain for any way to save him without dooming them all. Without letting the knowledge they had just gained about Mateo's plans die with them.

They were supposed to do this together, she thought desperately. Stand shoulder to shoulder between La Voz and destruction. The resistance had never needed Sota more than it did now. There had to be a way to save him.

Her thoughts ground to a halt when the second shot sounded. The third. After that, there were no more cries.

"We can't go back," she said, her voice hard even though her heart was splintering under the weight of her guilt. Her grief.

"What do you mean?" Dani asked, digging in her heels.

"I mean he's gone, Dani. If we go back we're gone, too. We have to get back to La Voz, tell them what happened. We have no choice."

"There's always a choice!" Dani said, but Carmen was through arguing.

"He's gone, Dani. He's gone."

And they were out of time. If they wanted to take advantage of the opening Sota had left them, if losing him was going to mean *anything*, they would have to take their chance now. It was what he would want them to do.

It was what he would have done.

She pulled Dani as hard as she could, veering off the course they'd been on and into a dense tangle of trees, zigzagging through as Dani sobbed openly behind her. But she had stopped trying to turn around.

As they ran, Carmen prayed that he died quickly. That he wouldn't suffer for her choices. The guilt would come, she knew; she could feel it threatening like the low growl of a deadly predator. But guilt was no use if you were dead.

For now, there was no time. They had to keep running.

"Where are they?" came Mateo's voice, farther away than Carmen anticipated. She pushed harder, kicking off her own shoes to move more quietly, pulling Dani back and forth, sticking to the long shadows cast by the trees in the moonlight.

"Water," Dani whispered.

"I know," Carmen said. "I'm sorry. We'll stop soon and . . ."

"No," Dani said, pulling at Carmen's hand. "*Water.*"

She allowed Dani to pull her to a stop, throwing herself

behind a towering tree as her legs burned and her breath caught. But under it all, Dani was right. Water was running nearby. If they could reach it, maybe . . .

"They went that way!" Mateo yelled, closer now, but still not too close. If they moved quietly, if they were careful, they could reach the water. In the dark it would carry them much farther than their tired legs could.

"Come on," Carmen whispered, trading stealth for speed as they followed the sound of the current through the trees, listening to the sounds of Mateo and his men searching behind them.

The rushing grew louder, the sounds of pursuit falling away as they moved toward it, a hopeful bubble inflating in Carmen's chest. She had prepared herself to die, but the idea that she could save Dani kept her moving despite the crushing weight of Sota's loss, the specter of it stalking them more surely than the soldiers.

"Up here," Dani said, picking up speed as the trees thinned. There was no noise coming from behind them now, and it made them faster, taking advantage of the momentary absence of pursuers. Faster and faster, the trees still thinning, Carmen took Dani's hand once more, this time with the hope that they could do something more than say goodbye. That maybe it could all mean something.

The crescent moon was visible through the trees ahead, and Carmen pictured a river, deep enough to dive in and be carried far away. But when they finally reached the tree line, it was only to skid to a desperate scrabbling stop in the shallow earth.

In front of them, like a tear right through the center of the hope Carmen had managed to build, was a cliff. Fifty feet down, at least. The river to their left flowed right off it into a massive waterfall that splashed against the rocks below.

There was nowhere to go.

"No," Carmen muttered, squeezing Dani's hand, looking wildly around for anything that could save them. But there was no tree with a hundred years of climbers' ropes here. No easy way down. No way down at all.

Death in front of them. Death behind them.

"They're coming," Dani said, and Carmen saw her swallow once, hard, before her eyes turned to steel. She was right. Behind them, the footsteps were back, fewer this time. Carmen took Dani's other hand, looking into her eyes.

"Dani, I . . ."

"Shh," Dani said, looking back, her eyes desperate and wide, reflecting the sliver of the moon twice. "Not like this, okay? Later. When we're safe."

"A pretty story," came a voice from behind them. "But then, those always were your forte, weren't they, Daniela?"

Flanked by two soldiers, Mateo stepped into the clearing, his voice soft, his steps slow. Carmen knew better than to think he had calmed down. From even her short time as his

Segunda, she knew this was when he was his most dangerous.

"Out of exit strategies, are we?" He waved the soldiers away as Dani and Carmen backed away instinctively, knowing there was nothing there but empty air, the river on their right now offering nothing but an alternate way over its edge. "Out of lies?"

He waited, looking from Dani to Carmen as they reached the cliffside. There was nothing Carmen could say. She'd already shown her true colors, but Dani might still have a chance. Would she take it? Carmen wondered as Mateo sized them up with his cold, calculating gaze. Would she denounce Carmen to save herself?

The seconds passed, and Dani didn't speak. Even though the circumstances were as dire as they got, Carmen felt a fierce joy at the fact that Dani would rather die by her side, die for the cause, than continue to lie to Mateo about who they were.

"You," Mateo said, walking closer to Carmen. "You I knew to be careful with. The way you throw all that around . . ." He gestured to Carmen's physique. "It was obvious you weren't to be trusted. Any woman who's that eager for attention is obviously hiding something vile."

Carmen's rage, which she usually attempted to keep from taking over, flowed through her veins like poison. She had never wanted someone dead so much. Not even the man she'd just killed herself.

"You were enjoyable, though," he said thoughtfully. "An ornament. It's just a shame I never got to discover what was between those . . ."

"Enough," Dani said, her face flushed.

"Ah, yes," Mateo said, turning to Dani, his eyes sparkling even more maliciously. "Daniela." He paced back and forth in front of them like a jungle cat, poised to strike, with the absolute confidence that he had the upper hand.

Carmen had no hope of living now, but she wished with every ounce of determination in her that he would die, too. If not today, then soon. And painfully.

"I can only admit this now since neither of you will live to repeat it," Mateo said, with a chuckle that made Carmen's fists clench at her sides. "But I'll confess you had me fooled. That prim exterior, the passion lurking underneath it. The lies were so clever, so calculated. But there was too much of a man in you, wasn't there? That's why you went and found yourself a cheap whore and threw away everything you could have had."

"Carmen isn't a whore," Dani said, her voice trembling with rage. "And throwing you away was nothing. You are nothing. You're a bitter, small man with no one but the smarter, crueler men before you to thank for your so-called success. You'll die alone, Mateo. Alone and miserable. I can only hope it'll be soon. Now, if you're going to kill us, stop showboating and get it the hell over with." She paused. "Or can't you even murder a couple of defenseless girls without asking someone to show you how?"

The silence that followed was deadly. The cruel humor was gone from Mateo's eyes, and in its place was cold, sharp fury. Carmen laughed. What did it matter? This was the end of it all. Their whole twisted love story.

Mateo's revelatory villain speech seemed to have come to an end—either that or he didn't want to give Dani any more ammunition to use against him in her final moments. Carmen had never been so proud to be right.

But her pride was short-lived, replaced again by boiling rage when Mateo stepped forward and backhanded Dani across the face, sending her stumbling sideways, away from Carmen, clutching her mouth as blood seeped between her fingers.

"Mouthy bitch," he said. "You two deserve each other. But not as much as I deserve to make sure you both die today."

Carmen glared at him for a brief moment before leaning down to Dani, helping her to her feet. "I'm so sorry," she whispered, touching her split lip tenderly, blood staining her fingers. "This is all my fault."

"Shh," Dani said again, eyeing Mateo.

"Yes," he said. "You'll die. But not before I make you spill every worthless secret those mangy resistance dogs ever entrusted to you. Not before you both feel the pain you deserve."

He was still facing them, but his eyes were unfocused with anger, like he was trying to collect himself. Dani's were wide, and in that moment, her lip swollen and gaze darting from Mateo to the river and back, Carmen understood.

The river. The drop. There was every chance that it would kill them. But weren't they going to die anyway? Wouldn't it be better to end it on their own terms?

And what if . . .

But she didn't let herself finish the thought. Cielo had taught her this lesson: sometimes the hope was more dangerous than the fall.

"Tie them up," shouted Mateo, his voice still strained with anger, but under control once more. He held out a hand and glanced to his left as the officers he'd told to stand down approached.

Dani took Carmen's hand, the strength in her grip saying she didn't care what Mateo saw. They were three steps from the river. The moment they moved, one of the men would shoot. Would they have time?

In the tension of Dani's fingers around hers, Carmen could feel that she was ready. That she would go when the signal was given.

The pistol came around Mateo's body as if in slow motion, and Carmen tapped once, twice, three times on the inside of Dani's wrist, her heart hammering so hard she was sure Mateo could hear it across the clearing.

Their bodies moved in perfect synchronicity, their hands never unclasping as they turned in a whirl of dress and hair and skin reflecting moonlight. The first shot hit where

Carmen had just been standing, but she didn't turn, just planted her feet, watching Dani's bare toes dig into the earth beside her as she followed suit.

"No!" Mateo cried, coming closer, losing precious seconds.

Carmen and Dani locked eyes, and without a word leapt from the bank and into the water.

The current pulled at them, attempting to tear them apart as they approached the falls, but they clung even more tightly, the pounding of the water drowning out Mateo's anger though it couldn't mask the gunshots. Another, then another, then another. The water exploded around them as they were carried toward the center of the river, but there the current turned straight as an arrow and twice as fast.

This time Carmen couldn't hang on.

She lost Dani's hand just as the water bearing them crested the cliff, and for a brief moment all of lower Medio was laid out to her: the forest, the city; she even thought she could see the sea at the horizon line.

If this is my last breath, she thought, spreading her arms out, keeping her eyes open until the last possible second. *So be it.*

At first it was pure free fall, almost joyful, but the dream turned almost instantly dark as Carmen's body picked up speed and her joy turned to terror. Eyes closed, she tried to tuck her arms and legs in to avoid jutting rocks and branches, but it was no use; the inertia was too much. It teased her limbs open like a blooming bud until all she knew was pain.

And then the treetops were rushing up to meet her, and then the ground, and was that little stripe of water all she had to aim for? Was it even worth it to try?

At the moment of impact, Carmen couldn't have said whether it was water or earth that rattled her bones, only that something had. Dani was nowhere to be found, and it felt softer to let the darkness take her.

So she did.

When the fight has tried to bring me to my knees, I will rise.
—La Voz Membership Pledge

⊹⊱✳⊰⊹

FIRST THE LIGHT RETURNED, and with it, pain. Carmen tried to chase the darkness back down its warm tunnel, but it was done with her, spitting her out like a fragment of chicken bone.

Her first thought was that she wished she had died.

Every square inch of her skin felt bruised, with sharp pain gathering like a thousand needles digging into bone at her shoulder and ankle, and a white-hot blaze at her temple that left her dizzy when she tried to sit up.

She collapsed again, face meeting gritty dirt, and discovered her mouth was full of it, crunching between her back teeth and stinging her tongue.

Carmen raised her head and spat once, then again, and the whole world was that patch of dirt and the haze of green beyond it. But it opened up quickly. Too quickly.

Next there was the sound of water nearby, and the humming of morning insects. The sun was coming up, she could tell by the purplish quality of the light as it stained her hand and reflected off the wet pebbles.

It would be day soon, then, but which day?

The memories assaulted her before she could investigate, coming back all at once as she returned to full consciousness, much more abrasive than the dirt or the light. Sota. The gunshot. The hatred in Mateo's eyes. And . . .

"Dani . . . ," Carmen croaked, her throat raw. It was the thought of her that dragged Carmen to her knees, her head pitching and rolling like a ship at sea, her arms shaking and unsteady beneath her. "Dani!"

This time, it was a whisper, raspy, toneless, but something. She would keep working at it.

Trying to get to her knees was harder. The pain at her shoulder reared up like a spooked horse, blotting out everything, nearly taking her under again. But this time she fought the blackness when it came to the edges of her vision. She fought, because she had something to fight for.

Bracing her hands on her knees, gritting her sandy teeth, Carmen pushed herself up to her knees. Her shoulder was dislocated, she was almost sure; it had happened once before when she was training with Alex at eleven. There was only one way to get it back in; until then her arm would be useless.

On your feet, soldier, she told herself in El Buitre's voice, the thought of him soothing, even though she wasn't sure she'd ever see him again. And there was every chance he would kill her if she did. But for now, she would take her comfort where she could.

One bare foot was flat on the ground when her temple throbbed again, sending her spinning and nearly back to the ground. She held on through the pain, waiting for the nausea to pass before placing the other next to it.

Her ankle buckled. *Sprained at best,* she thought clinically as she went sprawling sideways.

Spitting dirt for the second time, she hauled herself up again, scooting on her knees to a fallen tree nearby and using its branches to pull herself to her feet, letting the hurt ankle rest gingerly on the ground.

"Dani!" she called again, and this time there was some volume to it.

But still no answer.

Hobbling, stopping every few feet to drag in a raspy breath or wince or clutch at her shoulder, Carmen surveyed the area. The falls were miles behind her, not even visible through the thick tangle of trees. It was a miracle she had woken up at all.

What are the chances of miracles coming in pairs? she asked herself, shoving away the thought as quick as it landed. Dani hadn't died. Not alone. Not here, of all places. It was a reality Carmen refused to face. Not when Sota . . .

She reeled under the weight of his memory, more painful than any physical injury. She could feel it trying to suck her in, down into a place deeper than the river, a place where no amount of kicking would bring her back to the surface.

Survive, she told herself, locking away his face, his smile, that casual kiss on the forehead their last night together. *Survive, and make it worth it.* Somehow, she stayed on her feet.

As the sun climbed in the sky, Carmen got to know her new body and its limitations. The ankle barely held weight, but a branch—twisted, one-handed, from the fallen tree— served as a walking stick as long as the brush wasn't too thick. Her arm she folded protectively inside her shirt, across her body like an injured baby bird. She would have to put it back in its socket, but that would come later, when she was stronger.

Carmen called Dani's name as often as her voice allowed, watching both sides of the river, feeling the enormity of the forest around her like a sort of reverse suffocation. How could she find her? How could she even know where she'd landed?

Logically, Carmen knew Dani could be at the base of the falls still, her body broken by the rocks. Or she could be twenty miles downstream.

Or she could be . . .

"There," Carmen said aloud, her grating whisper allowing a little wonder into it.

Across the river, the black of her dress barely visible in the dark of the forest, was Dani, sprawled out over the sand as Carmen had been, her face half in the water, but her mouth and nose blessedly free.

"Dani!" Carmen tried to scream, tears welling up in her eyes, but her voice was too ravaged to be heard over the water, and either way Dani did not stir. Carmen tried again and again until her whisper was more worn than before, but her cries had no effect on Dani.

Was she breathing? Carmen wondered, wading closer with her stick, slipping, recoiling already at the depth of the river, the swiftness of the current beneath the deceptively calm surface.

The first step to crossing was obvious, and Carmen knew she had to do it fast, before she lost her nerve or spiraled any further. Heading for the next tree she deemed large enough, Carmen laid her walking stick down and braced the hand of her injured arm gingerly against the trunk.

Her breath came hard and fast, her heart racing as it anticipated the pain to come. *Haven't we been through enough?* her screaming nerve endings seemed to ask. But Carmen remembered the moment Sota had disappeared into the trees, his cry of pain, and she knew she deserved whatever agony she felt now and more.

It was Dani who deserved better.

With that thought in mind, Carmen steeled herself, drawing back—even the river seemed to still as every sensation coiled inside her, bracing for the moment.

She threw her weight into her shoulder and screamed, the pain freeing her voice at last as she collapsed into the tree, clutching at her shoulder, tears running down her face. But she had felt it. The moment of connection amid the agony. The moment she had become whole again.

Slumped at the base of the tree, catching her breath, Carmen flexed her fingers and felt the dull ache of the place the separation had been. Her body was already forgetting the pain, folding it into the rest of her history.

Ripping a piece off the bottom of her already tattered shirt, Carmen bound her ankle as tightly as she could. She winced, but the pain was nothing compared to her shoulder and she made quick work of it, standing gingerly to find her foot could almost take her weight, even without the stick.

Next, she walked up and down the bank, keeping Dani in her sights, looking for the best place to cross without being swept under. There was a thick branch balanced across the river at a narrow point just a few yards down, and Carmen tested it, bouncing it up and down with the flat of her palm until she was . . . mostly satisfied it wouldn't snap under her weight.

She had never considered her ample hips or the curvy rest

of her a detriment, and she had to believe this body she loved wouldn't become one now.

The climb onto the branch was nerve-racking, and Carmen's injured ankle threatened more than once to give out, but she got her balance eventually. She began to shuffle her feet, creeping out into the center of the river and keeping her eyes on where she needed to step next. She avoided the dark, rippling depths, trying not to remember the feeling of drowning in the tunnel, the way the bones had stared.

One step, then another; she wobbled for a moment at the deepest point and feared she'd lose her step, that it would all be for nothing. But Carmen regained her balance and kept on, sweat beading her brow in the early morning heat, her battered body barely obeying her commands but somehow inching her over the river.

When her feet hit solid ground, Carmen collapsed to her knees, trembling, not sure if she was laughing or crying. She wrapped her arms around herself, loving her body even more fiercely than usual for surviving this, too.

The moment she could stand, she stumbled her way to Dani, black threatening the edges of her vision again, the exhaustion of nearly dying and everything that had come after finally taking its toll.

Then she was there, beside her, kneeling down. Dani's skin was so cold as Carmen pulled her out of the water and onto drier ground. And she was crying again—why was she always crying now?—and Dani's lips were blue and her brown skin had gone gray near her eyes and mouth.

"Dani, no, please no, just wake up, just breathe, Dani, please breathe . . ." Carmen barely knew what she was saying, just babbled as the tears fell. She put her shaking hand in front of Dani's parted lips. She felt nothing, and when she searched for a heartbeat she felt nothing again, but she wasn't quite sure where to look, so she felt again, and finally, Dani across her lap, her hands against her chest where her dress had split open, she felt it. The rise and fall of lungs expanding. The soft puff of air against her palm.

Dani was alive. Alive and breathing. Carmen was sobbing now, gathering her close and pressing their cheeks together, not sure if the words she was saying were really words, or if they were some ancient love song being funneled through her as unconsciousness dragged at her heels.

She laid Dani beside her, checking once more for breath, feeling the slowness in her own muscles and her thoughts that meant she wouldn't be conscious for long. Lying beside Dani, Carmen intertwined their fingers and prayed for her. To the gods Dani believed in, the ones Carmen never could. She prayed to the goddess in the water, and the tricksters in the shadows, that they would be safe.

That they could rest before they had to run again. . . .

"Carmen . . . Carmen . . ."

When she heard the faraway voice, Carmen's consciousness

swam for the shore, but it was reluctant to surface when it got there. Content to bathe in the warmth of this blackness for a little longer.

Once again, without her permission, the darkness pulled back, leaving Carmen exposed in the light of evening with a worried face hovering above her own.

"You're okay?" Dani asked, her face badly bruised along one cheekbone, a laceration the length of Carmen's thumb at her hairline. But she was alive.

"Relatively speaking," Carmen said, her voice half-gone but more mellow now.

"Where did you come from?" she asked. "When I dragged myself out of the water I was alone. . . ."

"I found you," Carmen said, sitting up, her head throbbing still, her shoulder aching and her ankle swollen in its wrapping. "I crossed the river and I . . ."

"You *crossed* the river?" Dani asked, her eyes going wide. "On that?"

She pointed to Carmen's ankle, which upon further reflection was even more swollen than she'd realized. It puffed out of the wrap, purple and pale and mottled in places. Carmen reached down to unwrap it, but Dani stilled her hands with her own.

"Let me," she said.

Slowly, carefully, wincing when Carmen winced, Dani removed the section of shirt, and the blood filled Carmen's ankle again, doubling its size in half a minute.

"It might be broken," Dani said, but Carmen shook her head.

"I walked on it," she said, but even she knew it was a feeble argument.

She had been in shock. Numb. Half-crazed with pain and grief. She barely remembered making it here, lying down beside Dani. It was all a haze in her mind.

"Besides," she said. "We have much bigger problems than my ankle right now."

A silence fell between them then, a place for all their unspoken problems to eddy in like the tide returning to its pools. Sota was dead. Shot by Mateo and his men, who were certainly still hunting for Carmen and Dani, if only for the peace of mind that the fall had, in fact, killed them.

That there were no more miracles in store for the former Garcia wives.

Then there were the uncrossable miles between them and the border wall, and the fact that the last time Carmen had seen El Buitre or Alex it had been under threat of treason with bullets hitting the ground at her feet. Would she and Dani even be welcome there if they made it that far?

And then, *then*, there was the dead president of Medio, and all the partygoers who knew Carmen had killed him. Carmen's previous experience as a wanted woman was *nothing* compared to what she had unleashed with that knife, and she knew it.

"One thing at a time," said Dani, ever practical, and Carmen wondered when they'd talk about it. Who she'd pretended to be. Who she was. What it all meant.

"Is that a line from the Primera handbook?" Carmen asked instead, and Dani smiled, just as Carmen had hoped she would.

"I thought the only thing in the Primera handbook was *don't cry.*"

It was ridiculous, the way she remembered that line like it hadn't been said by someone else a hundred lifetimes ago, but now Carmen was the one smiling. Somehow, smiling.

How could she want to kiss this girl, broken and battered and lying half in a creek, with at least half if not the whole country calling for their heads on spikes? And would Dani let her, even if she wanted to?

This beautiful girl, who had never killed. Did Carmen deserve her when she wasn't pretending to be someone more worthy?

"So," she said, clearing her throat, something awkward slithering in around the sound. "One thing at a time, huh?"

Dani smiled again, but this time it looked a little sad. "It's all we can do."

"Can the first thing be learning to fly?"

"The first thing should probably be getting away from the river in case they're still looking for us," Dani said. "And then maybe food? And after that—"

"I thought you said *one* thing at a time," Carmen interrupted, getting to her feet, groping for the walking stick she'd dropped beside her when she passed out.

"Sorry." Dani's cheeks flushed along the tops in a way that was so heartbreakingly familiar Carmen almost forgot where they were. But there was no time for forgetting now.

"Get away from the river, get food," Carmen said. "I think even we can manage that."

The berries and edible leaves Carmen managed to scrounge together didn't do much to satisfy them, but checking something off the list felt good, and after binding her ankle again with a section of Dani's dress, it was time to plan their next move. As peaceful as the clearing they'd found was, they couldn't stay there forever.

Although Carmen had considered it, just for a moment.

"So we just . . . try to find a way to get to the wall, then?" Dani asked, her voice stiff in a way that told Carmen she was nervous.

Unfortunately, she had every right to be.

"There . . . might be a slight problem with that course of action." Carmen wondered how much to tell her, how much to ask. There was so much Dani needed to know before they walked into *that* vulture's nest.

"Why?" Dani asked. "I mean, you killed the president, and rescued me—you'll be a hero, won't you? That has to be better than whatever your assignment was."

Carmen chuckled, a dark edge to the sound. "I wasn't exactly sent here on an assignment," she said, pausing to buy herself some time.

"What does that mean?"

"I sort of . . . left," Carmen said. "Came back on my own."

Dani's pause was so long Carmen had to physically bite her tongue to keep from speaking.

"You came back on your own," she finally echoed.

Carmen shrugged.

"For me?" Dani's voice was small, and the trees around them all seemed to be holding their breath for what came next. Carmen's eyes snapped to Dani's, and in them she found no judgment for what she'd done. Nothing that said she saw Carmen as a ruthless murderer, undeserving of her love.

Carmen had longed for this moment, but as much as she wanted to melt into the question, to answer it decisively, emphatically, something else was taking root. The last time she'd crossed the space between them, the last time she'd let herself feel . . .

Gunshots rang out in her memory. Sota's cries went silent.

Carmen recoiled.

"Things were . . . complicated when I left," she said, grasping for an answer that didn't equate kissing Dani with the death of her closest friend.

Dani's face fell, just slightly.

"Loyalties were called into question. . . ." Carmen knew it sounded feeble, but Dani didn't seem to notice.

"Yours or mine?"

"Both."

"So you came back to clear your name?" Dani asked.

"Prove I wasn't a traitor, so you weren't, either?"

"No," Carmen said, closing her eyes tight against Sota's face, their last night together. "Just . . . people thought that our . . . relationship was getting in the way of my objectivity," she continued, feeling like she was wading into quicksand. "So I had to tell them that it . . . that we . . ."

"You pretended I was just part of the act." Dani's voice was flat.

"I had to." Carmen opened her eyes now, committing to the explanation. It was true, even if it wasn't the thing weighing on her heart.

"So when we get back, *if* they believe somehow that neither of us are traitors to the cause, I'm just the sad girl who actually believed the spy's big act and we, what? Avoid each other? Forever?"

Carmen shrugged, helpless. With Sota's ghost between them, with the scrutiny of the resistance trained on them like a spotlight, what could they do?

Dani looked at the ground, blinking hard, and Carmen thought it should have been easier. Coming back together. But nothing was ever easy.

"I'm sorry," she said, meaning it. Dani only nodded.

As much as home called to her, Carmen had always lived in one world or the other. She'd never considered for a moment what she'd do if she actually survived long enough for them to collide. Now they had, and Sota was dead, and Dani was here, and Carmen didn't know how to mourn him and love her and fight them all at once.

"We're alive," she finally said. "We're together. There are so many impossible miles between us and the resistance, and we don't even know if they'll let us live long enough to explain how we got there, let alone our relationship status. Can we just . . . focus on staying alive for now?"

It was a cop-out, and Dani's face said she knew it, but she sighed, nodding. "Okay."

"Good." Carmen hated the fake decisiveness in her tone, wishing they could sit right here and pull every secret out one by one until there was nothing left between them but light. "We need to find somewhere to lie low, somewhere to heal and plot our next move."

"Anywhere in mind?" Dani asked, a valiant effort at playing along.

Carmen shrugged. "Depends on how lucky you're feeling."

Neither of them said that their luck had probably already been tested enough for one day.

CARMEN'S ANKLE WAS STILL SIGNIFICANTLY swollen, and though she'd never admit it, every step was agony.

Dani was gracious about the slow pace and frequent stops, but between the pain and the awkwardness of their last conversation, the day was spent mostly in silence.

Eventually, they came to a place where they could no longer travel in the jungle. Through the trees, they could see signs of a residential neighborhood. Easy enough to reach from the road, but from the trees it would be a solid twenty minutes on foot—more if Carmen's ankle didn't behave.

At the tree line, they took stock. Dani was still in her

tattered evening gown, walking with a limp from a deep gouge in her hip she had been trying (and failing) to hide from Carmen all day. Her face was bruised and scraped, her short hair sticking up at odd angles, one of her knees mostly skinless from her fall.

Carmen was sure she didn't look much better. Several strips of clothing had been torn off to bind her ankle, leaving her in black pants ripped to the knee and a shirt that hugged her chest but did nothing to cover the majority of her midsection. Even without the haircut she'd given herself with a throwing knife in the safe house, she was in a sorry state.

"We need to try to make ourselves as presentable as possible," she said, her words stiff and formal even though she tried to relax them. Had they really just been kissing like it was the end of the world a day and a half ago? It seemed like a hundred years since then.

"Of course." Dani immediately reached for her hair, her face flushing. It tugged at Carmen's heartstrings, calling up all the conflict that kept her from acting on her feelings.

Sota, she reminded herself, letting the pain seep in for a moment, just as a reminder. *No mistakes.*

When they were finally ready to leave the shadow of the trees, Carmen gave Dani another once-over. Her dress had been torn again, removing the sleeves and most of the skirt so it looked intentionally short instead of ripped to ribbons by a fifty-foot fall and near drowning. Her hair had been smoothed into some semblance of order.

There wasn't much to be done about the bruises and scrapes, though. They would just have to hope no one was looking too closely.

At the end of her examination, Carmen met Dani's eyes by accident, scrutinizing the gash on her forehead, getting drawn in at the last moment. Dani was already looking at her, and she didn't look away.

The moment flared to life in the cold space they'd been carrying between them all day, and for a moment the warmth was enough to keep Carmen there. To make the rest fade into the background. Dani smiled, her slightly crooked front tooth making Carmen's heart ache. It would be so easy, to take that step, but there was the cold weight of her grief again, holding her back.

She almost hoped Dani would ignore it. Forget Carmen's indecision and cross the distance between them.

But she wrenched her eyes away before that hope could show on her face. The last time she'd let herself forget the world, put Dani at the center of it all, Sota had died. This was not the time to forget what she owed him.

"The cause has friends on the middle island," Carmen said, looking at the ground as the moment deflated, turning luke-warm again. "But they can't exactly advertise it. There's a code. Purple flowers to the right of the door means a safe place, red to the left means a healer."

"We need both," Dani said quietly, and Carmen couldn't argue.

They limped through the streets, glancing without staring at doorways, hoping they wouldn't meet anyone before they found friends.

"I'm surprised Alex wasn't with you," Dani said when they'd been walking in silence for a while. "Seemed like you guys were pretty close."

Carmen couldn't help it; she laughed. A sad chuckle that turned quickly into a wince of pain. "We were, until I fled the compound on a motorcycle while she shot at me for betraying La Voz."

"She *shot* at you?" Dani asked. "Wow, and I thought she hated *me*."

"Don't worry," Carmen said grimly. "She does."

"Great," Dani mumbled, and with that they took their first steps into civilization.

The sun was setting, which was probably the best time to be attempting this, Carmen reasoned. The dead of night would be too suspicious, and in the middle of the day their injuries would be too visible. This was their best shot.

Even so, if she was being honest with herself, it wasn't a great one.

In this neighborhood, the roads were dirt, the walls patched over with plaster, the windows dingy and small. They'd have better luck here than any of the affluent neighborhoods close to the capital, and Carmen found herself almost thankful to the river for taking them so far.

But after an hour of walking, darkness was settling, and

they'd seen nothing friendly at all. Fatigue was settling in Carmen's creases, sore muscles tightening as her thoughts took a dark turn.

What if we have no friends here? Would her ankle make it to the next town?

Would that gash on Dani's head?

"There," Dani said, pointing past Carmen, the bruises livid on her arm.

Carmen looked, heart in her throat, hardly daring to hope.

But for the first time all night, Carmen felt her shoulders relax. Red to the left, purple to the right. Friends and healers both.

Carmen's legs were weak from relief and pain. She was more aware than ever of their shredded clothing and hard-won bruises, but she held her head high as they approached the front door of the house, knocking three times in quick succession, then once, then twice again after a short pause. The signal.

"Be on your guard," Carmen muttered to Dani. "With how I left things . . . I can't guarantee even friends will be happy to see us right now."

The seconds passed like hours, and Carmen swayed on the spot as a wave of dizziness overtook her. When had she last slept? In the safe house before the party?

It felt like a lifetime. The last time she'd woken up in a bed, Sota had been alive to do the waking. She swallowed the grief that blocked her throat, threatened to take over and force her to her knees.

Keep going, she told herself. *He would want you to keep going.*

The door swam in front of her, but when it opened her relief kept her upright. They were so close now, so close to safety and rest . . .

"Are there others?" The woman was slight but muscular, her hair dark with streaks of gray in the fringe. Her eyes were bright and sharp as she took in the sight of the two of them, and Carmen was immediately comforted by her competence.

"There's no one else."

To her credit, the woman didn't hesitate, just opened the door and ushered them in.

The house was homey inside, with a crimson wall in the front room and a marigold one in the tiny kitchen. Fresh flowers on every surface. Woven tapestries and paintings on the walls. It was cozy. Loved. Maybe it was the sleeplessness, or the girl beside her and all the impossible things between them, but Carmen felt almost sentimental about it. It was so different from Mateo's massive, cold palace. So different from the tents and slapped-together barracks of her childhood.

Carmen had never lived in a place like this. A real home.

"Stay here," said the woman, a little terse. "Your timing could be better. Lu is *not* going to be happy." This last bit she muttered under her breath as she disappeared into the back of the house.

"You were right," Dani said, her eyes wide. "She didn't seem too happy to see us."

"No one is very happy to see us right now."

The conversation from the other room began, and grew steadily in volume. Carmen looked down, bringing her fingertips to her temples, trying to keep the guilt at bay for one more hour. One more minute. Just until they were officially invited to stay. Just until they were allowed to exhale.

There was pleading, and shouting. Carmen and Dani stood still and silent on weary, aching bones. It seemed like hours passed. But finally, the voices grew softer, and a lamp went on in the window of a back bedroom, and footsteps could be heard in the hall.

Carmen expected to come face-to-face with the woman's more conservative husband, but it was another woman leading the way down the hallway. They wore matching embroidered nightdresses that looked handmade. They stood too close to be sisters.

"Marisol," said the dark-haired woman, gesturing beside her to the other, her gunmetal-gray hair cropped close to her head. "This is Lu. She's the healer. Please, make yourselves at home."

"I want you to know you have two days," Lu said, her face stony. "Preferably less. We're loyal, but we know exactly who you are. We won't let everything we've built here be destroyed by whoever's looking for you. We didn't sign up for that."

Carmen bit back the reply that sprang to her lips. The one that said this was exactly what they had signed up for. That this was what El Buitre's protection bought them. She had always operated in the world as a La Voz agent, with the full might of its leader's power behind her.

Without that, she would have to tread more carefully.

"I understand," Carmen said. "And I'm sorry for imposing on you. If we had anywhere else to—"

"Save it," Lu said. "The only reason this door is open is because of Mari. But it closes the morning after next, whether you walk out or I throw you out."

"You won't have to do that," Carmen said. "We'll be gone the moment it's safe."

Beside her, Dani nodded, and when Lu walked back inside without another word, they followed. By the time they reached the living room, the bedroom door had already slammed behind her.

"I'm sorry," Carmen said to Marisol. "We wish we didn't have to impose, but . . ."

"Sit, queridas," said the older woman, kindness in her voice. "You must be exhausted." The kindness didn't eclipse the keen intelligence in her eyes. "Being dead is hard work."

"So you really *do* know who we are," Carmen said, but she sat. There was no point in being stubborn now; her legs wouldn't last much longer whether she liked it or not. If Mari and Lu weren't really their friends, they were helpless here.

"Everyone on this island knows who you are. But almost everyone thinks you're dead." Coming out from the kitchen, Mari set a glass of water with mint and a bowl of black beans in front of each of them. "Eat. It's not much, but it will help."

"Thank you," Carmen said. "Truly. I didn't know how many friends we still had on this part of the island, and we wouldn't have made it another hour out there."

"We've been friends of the cause a long time," she said, sitting down opposite Carmen as Dani settled in beside her. She slid a plate of warm tortillas toward them, the smell of them making Carmen weak.

She ate too quickly, forgetting manners in the face of her hunger. The warmth of the food and the comfort of their home acted on her immediately, her eyelids growing heavy before her dish was empty. She fought the exhaustion. She couldn't afford to sleep.

Across the table, Mari was looking at them like she expected answers.

"Again, we're so sorry," Carmen began. "And thank you."

"It's my job to help," she said, her tone light, not accusatory. "I'm loyal, even if I can't run missions and travel to new headquarters every few months."

"Yeah, well, if you know who I am, you know La Voz isn't overly thrilled with me right now," Carmen said. "Have they been in contact?"

"A message went around when you first left the compound. A description. A mandate for your safe return."

Safe *return*, Carmen thought. That was something.

"Anything else?"

"Nothing. But I've heard stories about you, mijita," she said. "You're a daughter to them. Whatever you did, I think it can be undone."

Maybe it was the meal, or the relief of taking the weight off her ankle for the first time in hours, or just the fact that she'd have a safe, indoor place to sleep tonight, but Carmen teared up at the words. She could feel Dani's eyes still on her, watching the salt spill up and over, its own kind of curse.

"Do you really think they'll forgive me?" she asked when she was sure her voice wouldn't break. "If I go home?"

Mari considered for a moment before meeting Carmen's eyes. "Is it true what they're saying out there? Did you really kill El Presidente?"

Carmen couldn't help but go back when she asked. To the glade. To the anger that had boiled over in her when he'd called Dani a whore. To the feeling that the man in front of her was responsible for absolutely everything she hated in the world. Everything she'd fought against her whole life.

After a moment, Carmen looked at Mari and nodded. Just once.

It felt like poisoning him all over again.

Mari whistled, a long, low sound. "Well then, my guess is that it will depend on how they feel about whoever is going to replace him."

It was an incredibly incisive observation, and one Carmen hadn't considered. There was so much at play, so many individual threads that could snap and unravel it all. The thought was overwhelming.

"What are you doing on the outskirts, Mari?" Carmen asked, taking her empty bowl to the sink, grateful for the grounded feeling the meal had given her. "Why not come to the hideout, take assignments? Why not fight?"

Mari smiled, and Dani sat up a little straighter next to Carmen, listening. "I would," she said. "It was my dream for a long, long time."

"But?" Carmen asked, just as the back bedroom's door opened.

"But I have different dreams now," she said simply.

Lu still wasn't smiling, but she wasn't scowling anymore, either. When she put her hand on Mari's shoulder, something relaxed in the other woman. She looked freer. Lighter. The sight of it made Carmen's chest ache.

"Everything is set up in the back," Lu said. "I'd like to take a look at your injuries before you get some rest, if you don't mind." Her tone was a little stiff, but not unfriendly, and for the second time that night Carmen wanted to cry.

"Thank you," she said.

Lu's wordless nod was all she would get in return, but it was more than enough.

Carmen's ankle was a bad sprain, but nothing was broken. Miraculously, she hadn't done more damage to her shoulder when she slammed it back into its joint, and Lu said it would heal nicely, her face hiding some grudging admiration when Carmen told the story.

The laceration on Dani's hip was deep, though, the muscle visible when Lu peeled away her dress. Carmen felt herself recoil inwardly, but she forced her face to remain passive, her body still. She deserved to see what her recklessness had cost them.

But Lu's hands were deft, and her supply cabinet was well stocked. Soon they were both on the road to healing.

"I'm not sure how *either* of you survived that fall, let alone both of you," she said. "But I'd stay away from cliffs for a long while, because it won't happen twice."

"Thank you," Carmen said again, looking Lu in the eye.

This time, she didn't turn away before nodding. It was something.

Carmen wondered, as she watched her move through the room, if Mari had ever regretted her decision to choose love over her rebellion. She could see it in Lu's face: patching up rebels wasn't what she had planned for her life, and domestic life clearly wasn't what Mari had planned for hers. But they had found a way to compromise, hadn't they?

It was strange, the way love changed your course, Carmen thought. But was it for better or worse? She didn't know. She didn't know if she would ever know.

"You two can stay in here," Lu said as the last of the bloody bandages went in the trash. "I . . . hope you'll make yourselves at home."

Carmen looked around at the small room, clearly made for a single guest, or two who didn't mind limbs overlapping as they slept.

"Oh," Carmen said, at the same time as Dani said, "Uh . . ."

"We just . . . ," they said together, looking at each other, flushing, and then going silent.

Lu laughed silently, shaking her head. "I'm gonna leave you to work out . . . whatever that was on your own." She headed for the door, turning at the last second. "But if you want some unsolicited advice? You"—she pointed at Carmen—"just alienated yourself from your entire organization and went to the last place in the world you should have to do a lot of things you shouldn't do. And from what I gathered based on a lot of things I didn't want to be overhearing . . . it was because of her." She pointed at Dani, whose flush deepened.

Carmen looked at the ground, unsure what to say.

"There's more to life than this," Lu said. "More than jumping when they say jump and coming home cut to ribbons. And it looks like you two have a shot at finding it if you'd just get your priorities in order."

She was gone before there was time to respond, leaving Carmen and Dani alone in a room with a single, narrow bed and a whole lot of things unsaid.

"Well," Dani said. "That was . . . interesting."

Interesting was an understatement. It was the polar opposite of everything Carmen had ever been told in her life. But she didn't know how to explain that to Dani. She didn't know how to explain anything.

"Are you tired?" Carmen asked.

"Not really," Dani said. "But I guess we should sleep anyway."

Small as the bed was, it was the largest thing in the room. It kept drawing Carmen's gaze. How ridiculous that on a silent night, surrounded by the most dangerous soldiers in Medio, collapsing into Dani's arms had felt as easy as breathing. But tonight, safe for the moment, no disaster bearing down, it had never felt more impossible.

"It's so quiet," she said.

"Yeah, I guess it doesn't feel quite right without fire and chaos and the threat of arrest or death hanging over us, does it?"

"It's still there . . . ," Carmen said, regretting it immediately. "A little farther away, though."

Talking helped ease the tension in the room, and Carmen slid into bed first, not wanting to risk being rude by taking the couch. They had barely gotten Mari and Lu on their side in the first place.

And also, if she was being honest with herself, despite all the confusion still swirling through her, Carmen didn't want to be alone tonight.

Sota's death had circled her like a bird of prey since the moment the shot had rung out, waiting for a quiet moment to nestle in her hair. She grasped for anything else. Her uncertainty about going home, even the fear that despite Mari's best guess, she would be killed the moment she did. The president's death. Mateo's fury. Her desperation to get home and warn them of what was coming.

None of it worked tonight. It all seemed too far away, and Sota's death was so close. It was in every shadow. In the muggy air. It was in every breath she took, and they came less and less easily until she was curled in on herself, gasping for the next, the weight too heavy to bear.

"Carmen?" Dani's awkwardness had vanished by the time she reached the bedside. "Are you okay?"

She could barely breathe, let alone speak, but she tried anyway: "It's my fault," she said again and again. "He's gone, and it's all my fault."

By the third repetition, Dani seemed to have finally understood what was crushing Carmen's chest.

"Carmen, I'm so sorry." She was trying to be strong, but Carmen could hear it in her voice, the fraying at the edges of her composure, the devastation beneath. She had loved him, too.

Maybe that was why Carmen didn't stop her as she eased in beside her, sliding close, fitting her body around Carmen's until there were no empty spaces between them. Carmen could feel the unbearable heat in every place they touched, and she hated herself for wanting it, for wanting more. . . .

In their grief, in the darkness, they held each other like the world was ending, and maybe it was. Carmen knew she shouldn't let herself turn, shouldn't let herself act on the electricity now replacing the blood in her veins.

It was wrong to seek distraction in the place that had killed him, and she knew it, but Dani's breathing came harsher the longer they were pressed together, stirring at the shorn hair on the back of her neck, and Carmen's pulse pounded so hard she knew Dani could feel it against her skin.

Her breath hitched in her throat. Dani pressed closer, and Carmen couldn't help it; she reached up to intertwine their fingers, both their hearts hammering frantically, audibly in the tiny space.

"Carmen . . . ," Dani whispered, like it had been torn out of her, and Carmen gripped her hand tighter. "Please . . ."

The word was a spark to kindling. A match to gasoline. Carmen turned in Dani's arms before she gave herself permission. Then their noses were brushing each other's, and Dani's hands rose up to bury themselves in Carmen's hair, and there was no pain in the world, no grief, no sadness, there was only the charged space between their lips, and every day Carmen had wanted this stretching out behind them.

"Dani," Carmen said, her own whisper harsh against Dani's teeth. "I . . ."

But Dani's eyes were wide open, reflecting the moonlight outside the window, and the question in them was one Carmen had never wanted to say no to.

And so the space shrank in on itself, and Sota's ghost kept his distance. For the first time since the roadside, Carmen let herself remember who this girl was. What she felt for her. What she always had.

Their lips met like a lightning strike, thunder reverberating through their bodies as they pressed frantically into each other, hands tugging at clothing and hair, mouths open in agony and relief as the friction built to a fever pitch between them.

Carmen felt them on the edge of a precipice there, knowing that they'd have to push forward to whatever was next or tear themselves apart trying to stop it. They inched closer with every whispered sigh, every pillow-muffled gasp. . . .

A sharp rap on the door doused the flame in an instant, and they sprang apart, the cool air a reminder to all the places there had just been such heat.

"Towels outside the door!" Mari said cheerfully, and then her footsteps took her away from the door.

But there was space between them now. Everything heavy and impossible had crowded back in. Sota's loss was thick in the room, made worse for Carmen by the fact that she'd tried to find solace in the very place that had caused it.

"I'm . . ."

"It's . . ."

They stopped, words overlapping, bodies still stiff and separate in the tiny bed.

"Good night, Dani," Carmen said quietly.

"Good night."

But neither of them slept for a long time.

18

*Though the road to victory may be littered with loss, I will sol-
dier on in service of my cause and my family.*

—*La Voz Membership Pledge*

⊬⊱✳⊰⊬

IN THE MORNING, CARMEN WOKE up alone.

The sun streamed through the window, and for a moment
she just remembered. Dani's mouth on hers, frantic and
everywhere. The places they could have gone if they hadn't
been interrupted.

But her grief was hot on the heels of her memories, telling her she was unworthy and cruel, that seeking comfort in
Dani's arms when their weakness had killed Sota made her
a monster.

"Good, you're awake," Lu said, leaning in the doorway,

oblivious to Carmen's tangled thoughts. "You'd better come into the kitchen."

Carmen made her way into the small, light-filled living room, gathering herself and preparing to see Dani after last night. Despite her inner turmoil, she was struck again by the beauty of the home Mari and Lu had made here, the love built on the things they'd sacrificed for each other.

She couldn't help it; she pictured herself and Dani in a place like this, hair a little grayer, wrinkles at the corners of their eyes from smiling. A garden out back with tomatoes and a few chickens. Clothes on the line. Dani balancing the books for their little market stall while Carmen folded blue linen napkins at the worn kitchen table that had seen a thousand meals and fights and kisses. A table that had seen a lifetime.

"Well, well, well," came a smug voice from the kitchen, and Carmen's blood ran cold, the warm nostalgic feeling of the memory evaporating faster than it had come.

Not him, she thought. *Not now.*

But she'd been right about them being out of miracles. Because in the kitchen doorway, his hand clamped too tightly on Dani's upper arm, was Ari Vasquez.

Carmen gaped as it all slammed into her with full force. Everything he'd done. The marketplace fire, Jasmín's mission, Ari's face, cold and unfeeling as he advocated for the murder of the girl he now had at his mercy. "What are you doing here?" she finally managed.

"Cleaning up a mess," he said, tightening his grip on

Dani's arm until she winced. "Say goodbye to your new friends, Cuervita."

"I won't go until you promise you won't hurt us," she said. "We have information. We need to see El Buitre immediately."

"You left this organization," Ari said. "You disobeyed direct orders, stole La Voz property, and abandoned the cause. You're hardly in a position to make demands."

"Ari, you have to listen to me," Carmen said, hating the way she had to plead. She had never expected to have to make her case to him like this, alone, without El Buitre or Alex or their history on her side.

She took a deep breath, trying not to see the way Dani was going pale in his grip, the fear around the edges of her eyes. If she looked too closely, she would kill him, and that would only make things worse.

"There's no time for any of this," she said through gritted teeth. "You can hate me, or call me a traitor, whatever you want. But Mateo is coming for La Voz with the full strength of his army. We were there when he revealed the plan. We're out of time. You have to—"

"The only thing I have to do," he said, cutting her off, his voice icy, "is follow the orders given to me by the leader of La Voz. Orders which are now above your security clearance as my prisoner."

"You don't understand," Carmen said, one more last-ditch effort to make him see. "Mateo will assume we've told you everything. He's too paranoid to believe we're dead. He's coming, now, he already killed Sota—"

"And whose fault is that?" Ari interrupted, his eyes deadly.

The grief was back, choking Carmen, whispering that he was right, that she deserved whatever she got. . . .

"Get your things," Ari said when she didn't respond, shoving Dani toward her. "Be outside in three minutes. I'll know if you try to run."

There was nothing to do but obey.

Dani tried to catch Carmen's eye, but she couldn't look back. What did she have to offer her besides more uncertainty? She obviously couldn't save her, any more than she'd been able to save Sota.

With grim determination, Carmen took the salves and borrowed clothes Mari and Lu had given them. He would kill them, or he would take them home. As long as La Voz found out what Mateo was planning, she would take whatever punishment El Buitre had decided to mete out.

Her only regret was that no one else knew of her suspicions about Ari. The botched missions. The strange hold he had over El Buitre. With Sota dead, Carmen was the last one who could have discovered what he was up to.

She hoped Alex would see, eventually. That he would show them who he really was.

Whoever he was.

The mystery of his motivation still tugged at Carmen's subconscious, even now. Even when she was probably marching toward her death. If he was planning to do any-thing but kill them, after all, would El Buitre really have sent Ari?

At least if she died, she could do so with the satisfaction that Mateo hadn't been the one to pull the trigger.

"Ready?" asked Mari, tapping on the door, rousing Carmen from her thoughts. "He doesn't seem like a patient man."

Carmen was holding a single bandage. She wasn't sure how long she'd been staring at the wall. "Thank you," she said, shaking her head, shouldering the small backpack Mari had given her and adjusting the straps.

Mari smiled at Carmen, but it didn't reach her eyes. "It will be alright," she said. "Get home. Tell your story. They'll listen. They love you."

Carmen shook her head. It was a nice sentiment, but the fact that El Buitre loved her would make her crimes all the worse in his eyes. He had trusted her. If he believed she had betrayed him . . .

And that was if they even made it home.

"Thank you," Carmen said again, not wanting to burden Mari with her dark thoughts. If she was never going to see this kind, spirited woman again, she wanted to leave her with something gracious. "Thank you for everything. I'm so sorry for what we asked of you."

"Shh," Mari said, hugging her in a way that made tears spring to Carmen's eyes even through the numbness that had stolen in like fog. "You're brave, and beautiful, and loved, mijita. Don't let anyone take that from you. Especially not some rat-faced boy."

Carmen sniffed into Mari's hair, her throat blocked with emotion. Carmen had been raised by a grizzled resistance leader. She barely remembered her own mother, and La Voz had been rather low on female role models. She didn't know how to be nurtured like this. She had only been trained and molded.

When they pulled apart, Carmen had composed herself, but she knew her eyes were still shining.

Dani was waiting in the living room, and Carmen's chest tightened again. She wanted to tell her to run. To go back and forget she'd ever met Carmen or heard the name La Voz. She was willing to pay the price for what she'd done, but if she had doomed Dani by trying to save her, she would never forgive herself.

"Time's up," came a voice from outside the front door. "Let's go."

"Be safe," Mari said, and then the door was open, the illusion of safety gone as Ari leered into the house. Outside, the sun had just reached the treetops. It was a beautiful day.

Ari gestured in front of him, lifting his shirt just enough to show the shiny pistol tucked into his waistband. "Don't try anything," he said in a low, dangerous voice. "I have the authority to do what's necessary if you run."

But Carmen had never felt less like running.

Shoulder to shoulder with Dani, all of last night's ghosts

252

still hovering between them while Ari stalked behind like a feral dog, Carmen walked out of the city toward home. Or death. Whichever came first.

When they reached a clearing a few miles out of town, Carmen's ankle was screaming. The sun was already high in the sky. The road widened at the end of the lane, dead-ending at a massive tree.

No, Carmen corrected herself as they moved closer. It was two trees that had twisted around each other as they grew. They were massive, haunting and beautiful. Were they holding each other up or stunting each other's growth? Carmen wondered, but if they had an answer, the trees weren't giving it up.

"Stand there," Ari barked, the first time he'd spoken since they'd set out, gesturing toward the trees' massive combined trunk.

Carmen obeyed. What else was there to do? He had a gun, and her only hope was getting home. She would do what it took to stay alive until a better opportunity presented itself.

With the nylon rope in his backpack, Ari tied Dani to the tree first before moving on to Carmen. He was rough with her, the rope chafing at her wrists, her shoulder screaming where she'd jammed it back into the socket.

"I'd say stay put, but . . . ," Ari said when he was done, his smirk infuriating.

Carmen's hands strained at their bonds without her permission. "Where are you going? What is this?" But Ari didn't answer, just disappeared into the trees, leaving the two of them alone in silence.

After what had happened between them last night, he couldn't have devised a better method of torture if he'd wanted to.

Carmen growled in frustration, the knots too tight to shift her arm, her shoulder getting no relief from the awkward position he'd tied her in.

Where had Ari gone? Was he going to leave them here to starve, tied to a tree? Was that El Buitre's punishment for what they'd done? Or was he off digging graves somewhere? She kept these thoughts to herself.

But time passed so slowly, until even the silence between them grew thorns.

"Was it real?" Dani asked abruptly, just as it became unbearable.

"Was what real?" Carmen replied carefully, the cold fingers of her grief wrapping slowly around her accelerating heart. The memory of last night buzzed in her veins now that they were alone, and Carmen hated herself for feeling it. For feeling anything other than her guilt.

"You and me," Dani said, and Carmen surfaced at last. "Then, now, the beginning, the middle, the end? Was any of it real? You said you lied to them about us, but . . . were you lying to me? I just want to know."

Carmen stopped, her eyes widening, feeling a different weight now. The weight of Lu's words the night before, of the weathered table in her mind's eye, of the expectation that she would somehow effortlessly find a place for this in the midst of everything else.

But there was nothing effortless about it.

"It was real," she said. There was no reason not to be honest now. Not when they might not survive the next hour. "It was complicated, and I should have shut it down instead of acting on it. But it was real."

"Do you regret it now?"

Carmen sat with the question for a long time. So much of what they had been, what they still were, was tangled up with her failure at the Garcias'. With Ari's incompetence. With Sota . . .

"I don't know," she said finally, and she should have explained the rest, told Dani about her guilt and her inner conflict. About the way the threads were snagged and tangled together into a mess she couldn't possibly decipher.

About how she felt the closeness of Dani even now. Even in captivity. Even when death could be right around the trunk of this tree.

But she didn't.

"I'm not stupid," Dani said when Carmen didn't elaborate. "I know we might die. I know what it all looks like. I guess I just wanted to know who I'm really walking into it with."

Carmen shook her head, surprised when her hair brushed the tops of her shoulders. "And what about you, Dani?" she asked, suddenly frustrated by how one-sided this conversation had become. "What would have happened if I didn't show up in the capital this week? Were you ever gonna meet with Sota? Or were you just gonna slide back into your cushy life and watch Mateo mow us all down like weeds?"

"How dare you," Dani said, her eyes narrowing. "How dare you reduce my role in this fight to our relationship. Not everything is about *you*, Carmen. I know that has to come as a shock."

It had been Carmen's argument, too, when she'd gone toe to toe with Alex and El Buitre. That Dani's loyalty wasn't tied to their relationship.

But look where that got you, said a snide voice in her head.

"Oh! Right, not everything is about me. So, tell me then, why didn't you show up where you were supposed to? Why were you standing up there smiling and nodding like a puppet while he doomed us all?"

"The same reason you did it for weeks!" Dani said, raising her normally calm voice, turning her head. "Because those were my orders, Carmen, so can you blame me for wanting to know if I was one of yours before I *die* for you."

"You think you're the only one who's sacrificed something here?" Carmen asked. "The only one who's risked something?" She craned her neck, trying to see Dani's face, to do more than feel the warmth of her just out of reach.

She was unreachable.

Typical, Carmen thought as pain shot through her shoulder.

"Let me tell you why I came back to the capital," Carmen

said, all the things she'd been holding back since the moment she took off in a shower of Alex's bullets finally bubbling to the surface. "Let me tell you why I walked out on the man who raised me and my best friend in the world. Lied to the boy who was like my brother in the last hours of his life. Let me tell you why I risked my future, and my cause, and everything that matters to me in this world."

"Tell me," Dani said, her voice low and sharp edged.

"Because I was weak," she said. "Because I let you matter more. Because I didn't confront what was happening and I let myself believe I could care about you, and *want* you, and stay the same soldier with the same motives. But I couldn't. After you, I couldn't."

"And you hate yourself for it," Dani said, like she was discovering something dangerous and glinting at the bottom of a cave.

Carmen didn't answer.

"And you hate me for it."

Did she? Carmen wondered. But she didn't get the chance to answer, herself or Dani. The sound of a rumbling engine interrupted them, tires crunching leaves and fallen branches before a squeaking brake was set.

"Miss me?" came a voice from just out of Carmen's sight line.

Ari had returned.

┽⥽✳⥾┾

THE SOUND OF A TARP being retracted had Carmen's stomach twisting, her hands trembling.

Her imagination (made more overactive by the pressing darkness) pictured Ari dumping their lifeless bodies into the bed of a truck just big enough for the two of them.

If this is the end, it's the end, she told herself, trying to make her peace with it. In her darkest moments at Mari and Lu's, she had felt she deserved it for losing Sota. For all the harm she had done.

But the fierce, stubborn version of her that had made it through the tunnel of bones was back now, clinging to every spark of life, telling her to run, to fight, to survive no matter the consequences. To save La Voz from Mateo, from Ari, like Sota had wanted.

Carmen felt Dani struggling at her bindings behind her and felt a surge of pride. Even if everything else was unclear, they had the most important thing in common.

Ari appeared in front of them then, his face giving away nothing but how pleased he was with himself. It was a look Carmen knew couldn't spell anything good for them.

He untied Carmen first, the metal of the gun still visible at his hip. For a moment, the blood rushing painfully to her one free hand, she thought she could reach it. End this at last.

But what good would it do? Carmen had tried to murder her way out of this situation already, and all it had done was get Sota killed. Ari smirked, like he knew.

"Don't even think about it."

"If you knew what I was thinking right now you'd be half-way home to your mami."

Ari twisted her arm unnecessarily before letting her go, and Carmen saw stars as her wounded shoulder wrenched in its socket.

"Don't forget who has the power here." His voice was more dangerous than smug now. "You're alive because I'm allowing it. See that you don't forget your manners."

Carmen bit her tongue until it bled, watching as Ari jerked Dani's ropes off and shoved her toward Carmen. Only then, when the other girl was safe, did she look around.

The truck was parked just behind where she'd been tied, a massive thing with a cargo hold and two doors in the back standing open to the afternoon sunlight.

"Get in."

"If you're going to kill us, you have to tell them about Mateo." Carmen knew he probably wouldn't listen, but she needed to try anyway. "Ari, he'll kill every one of them if you don't. Please. Not for me; do it for La Voz."

Ari drew the gun and pointed it square at Carmen's forehead. "Get in."

Trying to hide the way her knees had gone weak at the sight of the weapon, Carmen led the way around the back of the truck, pausing just before the double doors.

Was he going to shoot them? she wondered. Making them climb inside first was a smart move if he was. Less awkward moving corpses that way. . . .

Carmen watched herself climb in as if from a distance, wondering if the stress had caused her to snap, feeling the absurd urge to laugh bubbling up inside her. She squashed it before it could take hold. She had a feeling if she started, she'd never stop.

Inside, though she could barely make them out, were water barrels, the kind that the government sent too few of to the outer island villages in an attempt to make it seem like they were making a difference. Carmen remembered setting them out at night once they were empty, hoping in vain to catch the rain that never fell.

"Water barrels?" Dani asked in a panic-hoarse voice as Ari tested the padlock on the door.

"Either to smuggle us over the border or to hide our bodies after he kills us," Carmen answered, deadpan.

Ari was back in the doorway before Dani had time to answer. He closed them in without a word, plunging them into darkness in the windowless space, the engine roaring to life beneath their feet.

Fortunately, Carmen thought, he hadn't shot them yet.

Unfortunately, there was little space that wasn't occupied by cargo, and she and Dani ended up sitting side by side in it, consciously not touching, the echoes of their argument springing up in the closeness even though neither of them said a word.

There were other echoes in the space as well. Carmen tried to ignore them, but her heartbeat wasn't taking her cues.

The truck rolled on for what felt like hours, never stopping. Sometimes it would jerk to a stop or take a corner too sharp and Dani would fall into her shoulder, or Carmen's knees would collide with Dani's ribs. They straightened themselves up as best they could and acted like it hadn't happened.

Carmen was preoccupied by the knowledge that any minute could be their last, that if they died, the knowledge of Mateo's plans might die with them. She saw her vision from the benefit again and again in the darkness—the compound burning. Her family, gone.

The truck lurched again, then braked suddenly. Dani

fell into, then somewhat sheepishly removed herself from, Carmen's lap. The electricity was back, muddling Carmen's thoughts and priorities. The same feelings that had sent her grasping at hair and hems last night flaring back to life between them here.

"Sorry," Dani breathed, her mouth too close to Carmen's.

Carmen turned her head away, as if it was enough.

As if anything would ever be enough.

After a while, when the road had been straight for long enough to risk it, Carmen slept, wedging herself in against the water jug beside her in the hopes that she would avoid unintentional contact with Dani. But of course, when she woke to the sound of the double doors opening at last, they were curled around each other in the narrow space like feral kittens looking for warmth.

They sat up at the sound, Carmen disentangling herself quickly enough that Ari didn't catch a glimpse of them intertwined.

Dani scoffed. "Like it matters *now*," she muttered under her breath.

"Where are we?" Carmen asked the moment his silhouette was visible. It was evening, early by the look of the light. She couldn't see where they had stopped.

Ari didn't answer, but the smugness was gone from his face. Something heavier had settled there, something more tense. That's when Carmen smelled it. The salt in the air.

They weren't going to some random hole in the ground

to be killed and left to rot, after all.

They were going home.

"Get in," he said, gesturing to the barrels.

This time, Carmen didn't hesitate to comply. Her heart was singing in relief. No matter what they decided at the table, she would get a chance to tell them everything about Mateo's plans. Their one chance to prepare themselves wouldn't die on a nameless dirt road with two girls no one would remember.

But trapped in water barrels, separated, Dani and Carmen had no chance to plan their strategy, what they would say if they were allowed a trial. Carmen would just have to hope they could work together in the moment.

That they could survive one more time.

Beside her, Dani took the top off the nearest barrel. It was full of water.

"Aren't there empty ones?" Carmen asked, but Ari's contemptuous look was answer enough.

It was humid in the back of the truck, and the water wasn't cold, but it was still unpleasant enough fully dressed. Dani climbed in without fanfare, and Carmen, of course, took it as a challenge, forcing her complaints down, sinking in until only her face was above the water.

Once they were still, Ari fitted the tops back on, and the darkness was absolute.

They bumped along the road to the border wall, and for the first time since they'd left the clearing, Carmen stopped thinking of her life like it was made up of minutes. She started to wonder what was going to happen when they reached headquarters. When they were finally forced to reckon with the choices they'd made. The disaster they'd set in motion.

Maybe there would be time to get Alex alone. To tell her about Ari, if the worst was going to happen. La Voz had been a man passing down a mask for hundreds of years. It wasn't about the individual, it was about the collective. The cause.

All Carmen needed was enough time to warn them; then she would accept her fate.

They rolled to a stop a moment later, the water sloshing around Carmen until it splashed her face and plugged her ears.

Ari got out, speaking rapidly to a man Carmen assumed was a checkpoint agent. It was early evening, which was a strategic time to cross, she had to hand it to him. It was a busy time. With a line of trucks building up behind you, angry drivers honking and revving their engines, people got sloppy.

Carmen had never known it to be difficult, crossing in this direction, but of course the pressure would be on now. If they believed Dani and Carmen were alive after the president's death, they would expect them to flee to the safety of the outer island as soon as possible.

Safety, thought Carmen wryly, remembering Ari's gun pointed at her head. *Right*.

The back doors opened a few minutes later, and the sounds

of two heavy pairs of boots clanged on the metal floor.

"What's in here?"

"Agua, señor." Ari sounded every inch the harassed delivery driver, tired after a long day's work, ready to get his shipment delivered and make it home for supper.

Much as she hated him, Carmen would have to hope he'd learned *something* useful during his time as a La Voz operative. Otherwise, they were all dead, and Mateo's plans with them.

One set of boots came closer.

"You know we're on the lookout for two murderers, right?"

"Those girls?" Ari asked. "I thought they were dead. Jumped off a cliff, I heard."

"Until their bodies wash up, we're not assuming anything."

Beside Carmen, there was the sound of a lid being removed and replaced. Her heart was pounding so hard she was surprised it wasn't making ripples in the water around her.

"Listen, look in every barrel if you want. Dump them out for all I care. Every one of those savages dies of thirst, it'll be a better world if you ask me. I get my pay either way, amigo."

There was the sound of a pipe being lit, the creaking of the truck door as Ari leaned against it. The other set of footsteps walked away from Carmen. More lids being removed and replaced. There were easily a hundred barrels in the truck. Would he really search them all?

Carmen moved silently down in the water, making sure only her face and one ear were out. If she had to, she would submerge herself entirely and hope the reflection on the water's surface and the dark sides of the metal barrel hid her, praying that Dani would stay hidden, too.

If the officer found one of them, he'd turn every barrel in this truck upside down until he found the other. They survived together or not at all.

As she waited, Carmen thought of the twisted tree again.

After a long moment of lids opening at random and closing again, of holding her breath every time the officer's boots came near, Carmen heard a beautiful sound. The next barrel he approached, the officer kicked it instead, hearing the water sloshing inside and moving on.

He was getting tired of their game, and if Carmen guessed correctly, that line of delivery trucks was starting to build up behind them.

The man kicked the barrel next to her, and then his boots finally stopped in front of Carmen. He kicked once, twice, and Carmen felt the water around her splash against the side.

"Alright, get on with it," he said after a long, breathless moment, and Carmen's body went weak with relief. They had done it. They had fooled him.

The next stop was home.

No matter where my missions take me, I will always return home to La Voz.

—*La Voz Membership Pledge*

THE COMPOUND WASN'T THERE, and then, just as surely, it was.

They left the truck in the vehicle outbuilding to continue on foot, and Carmen watched Dani's face as the structures revealed themselves like magic. Made of the tree trunks themselves and canvas the same color as the rocky ground, spaced out enough to appear random at first.

Suddenly, there was the blacksmith's tent, and an area where sand-covered hammocks hung open to the sea air. There was the med tent, and the mess, and the armory, and in the distance, the training ring.

The deeper they traveled, the more populated the make-shift paths became, but the silence continued to fall in their wake, and soon Carmen's nostalgia turned somber. No one spoke to them and, chin high, she refused to see if they met her eyes.

When she'd ridden up to this camp with Alex on a dirt bike, she had been a hero returning from a dangerous mission. Now, with a suspected traitor and her rumored ex-lover at her side, escorted at gunpoint by the smug boy who'd taken her place at the table, Carmen felt like an outsider.

The knot of kids from the doorway of her tent that last morning were the first to follow, but they weren't the last. More and more joined the procession, their curiosity getting the better of them, until they'd amassed a modest crowd.

Carmen didn't need Ari steering her to know where they were headed, and they reached the center of camp in no time at all, the meeting tent closed, silhouettes visible inside.

There weren't many. They didn't want this trial to be public, and with her strategist's mind, Carmen understood why. Division in the ranks was bad for morale, and defecting for love was a story people might get behind. El Buitre—under Ari's influence—didn't want anyone feeling sorry for Dani and Carmen.

Not before he knew what he was going to do with them.

Ari put his gun away before opening the meeting tent doors, gesturing Carmen and Dani through ahead of him. The conversation inside died down immediately, the occasional hissing whisper the only sound as they crossed the tent.

At the opposite end from El Buitre's chair, two seats stood empty and waiting.

Chairs for the accused.

Along the sides of the table sat a few people Carmen recognized. The woman from the field whose dirt bike she'd probably stolen. A man with kind eyes and a bushy beard who wouldn't meet her gaze.

Alex, who looked down at her hands, a disgusted sneer on her lips as Carmen and Dani took their seats.

Seeing her cut through Carmen like nothing else had. They had been Sota's sisters. Daughters of La Voz. Besides childhood squabbles over who had drawn first blood or who took the kitchen shift when they both got punished for something, they had never been divided.

"Alex," said Ari, nodding respectfully in her direction.

Alex nodded back, but Carmen's worries were momentarily eclipsed by the look on her face. It was an expression Carmen would have known anywhere. One that said Alex didn't like Ari any more than she liked Carmen right now.

She filed the information away for later use. An enemy of her enemy was . . . well, useful to know about, anyway.

"Mi gente," El Buitre said when everyone was seated. "Welcome. Thank you all for being here." His voice was sad, grave, like he was giving a eulogy instead of sitting in judgment.

It wasn't an encouraging sign.

Carmen tried to meet his eye, but he wouldn't look at her. He was performing now, and it told Carmen he had already made up his mind. Her heart sank.

"You all know what's at stake here," he said as Ari leered down the table at Dani and Carmen. "Two of our operatives, one known to us for years, and one a new recruit, are accused of betraying our organization for their own gain. Putting personal loyalty above the cause."

"These are trying times for our rebellion," Ari cut in, and El Buitre, incredibly, yielded the floor rather than chastising him for interrupting.

Carmen had never seen anything like it. Even a second in command didn't dare interrupt the Vulture when he was speaking. And yet Ari went on uncontested, nothing of the cruel, smug bully he'd been during their journey in his voice.

"Loyalty is the one thing we have that they don't. Single-minded devotion to our cause and our goals. When one member of this organization weakens those bonds, we are all more vulnerable."

Around the table, heads nodded; assent was murmured.

"Daniela Garcia, after a personal altercation with her lover, took the trust this table placed in her and disappeared, aiding our enemies, refusing to check in with vital information even when repeatedly prompted."

Eyes swiveled in Dani's direction. Carmen didn't dare look, but she felt her shoulders stiffen. Her chin jutted forward.

"Carmen Santos set this betrayal in motion, began an

inappropriate relationship with an asset and, when it became clear her bad judgment had cost us, stole La Voz property and fled this compound against direct orders to the contrary, interfering with a mission years in the making, haphazardly committing a high-profile murder at a society benefit, and getting one of our key operatives killed in the field in the process. All because she didn't know how to keep her *feelings* separate from her mission."

Carmen had listened with growing horror up to this point, almost amazed at Ari's ability to twist their circumstances until they sounded positively criminal. But with this last line, he gave her a gift. A spark of her old energy.

"May I speak?" she asked El Buitre directly, showing him the respect Ari's interruption had been lacking.

The effect was immediately visible.

"Jefe, I hardly think—" Ari began, but El Buitre held out a silencing hand, looking like a leader for the first time since they'd entered the tent.

"In this organization, we don't hand out judgments without allowing for explanation."

Ari still looked mutinous.

"Take your seat," El Buitre said, his voice ringing out, and Ari did. "Cuerva, you've heard the charges against you," he said. "What do you have to say in your defense?"

Shakily, with the full knowledge of what was at stake, Carmen got to her feet. "First, I have to commend Ari for his ironclad grasp on the chronology of events," she said. "But

I'm afraid his assumptions about our decisions have missed the mark."

Everyone in the tent was fixated on Carmen now, save Alex, who was determinedly looking down.

"I apologize for the way I left," Carmen said, spreading her hands open, hoping to convey innocence and remorse. "I'll admit I felt lost in the new direction La Voz had taken." She took a deep breath. "I love this cause, this rebellion, with all my heart, but the innocent lives lost at the marketplace weighed on me. The careless way we sent Jasmín Flores to gather information, nearly sacrificing her life . . ."

She was focusing on decisions Ari had made, taking her cues from Alex's expression, gambling everything on the fact that he wasn't as beloved as he seemed to believe.

And it was working. Alex's eyes flicked up to Carmen's face momentarily. Around her, the hard faces of the members she didn't know looked interested rather than condemning.

"With those . . . forgive me, uncharacteristic decisions fresh in my mind," Carmen continued, "I saw this table's unwillingness to fight for the protection of one of our operatives as a troubling trend toward forgetting what this resistance was built on." She looked around the table. "Family. Love. The belief in a world that sees people as human, and not as pawns in some larger scheme. Using people that way is what I've been taught to fight *against* my whole life."

Carmen locked eyes with El Buitre here, and he didn't look away.

"I'm not saying I've ever been perfect," she said. "But I'm not a traitor. I went to the capital to prove that by doing what we've always done. Protecting the people who are loyal to us, fighting against those who seek to oppress us. And that's what I . . ." She gestured at Dani. "What *both* of us, have done."

"How?" Ari asked, getting back to his feet, spit flying from his mouth. "By murdering the president without anyone's approval? By getting Sota killed?"

"By rescuing a loyal asset in grave danger, and gathering intel that will save this compound and every one of our lives."

Ari was speechless. El Buitre's eyes locked on Carmen's. "What do you mean?"

Feeling secure in the knowledge that she had their attention, Carmen gestured to Dani. They needed to hear this from her, to know her, if they were ever going to forgive her.

"May I?" Dani asked El Buitre, and he gestured her to her feet.

Ari was beside himself. Carmen fought the urge to smirk in his direction. The battle wasn't nearly over.

"I've been Mateo's closest confidant since Carmen's extraction," Dani said, effortlessly assuming the affect required to address the table, her Primera skills on full display. "He was emotional after the betrayal, unstable; I saw the chance to grow closer to him and took it."

"A likely story," Ari sneered, but El Buitre raised his hand again to silence him, and everyone else at the table was still looking at Dani.

The tide is turning, Carmen thought.

"Unfortunately he rarely slept; he was suspicious of everyone who entered or left the house. He moved us to a secure location in his paranoia; it was guarded day and night at every entrance. He never let me out of his sight because he feared the rebels were going to kill us next."

"And he didn't suspect your involvement with La Voz?"

"His father did," Dani admitted, "but Mateo was adamant about trusting me. I believe he was too fragile mentally to admit he could have been wrong twice. If I'd stayed much longer, I believe Señor Garcia would eventually have changed Mateo's mind. Carmen arrived just in time."

El Buitre nodded thoughtfully. Ari fumed. Alex was looking in their direction now, the scowl gone from her face.

"And what did you learn during your time in confinement with him?"

"The details of the announcement he made at the benefit two days ago," Dani said. "His plan to eradicate La Voz."

Fists clenched around the table, shoulders stiffened. The woman with the dirt bike gasped softly.

"They can't," Ari said. "There are laws that . . ."

"The mother of the future president of Medio was murdered by a rebel living in their midst less than a mile from her home," Dani said coolly. "Laws can change."

Ari fell silent.

"The broad strokes he discussed at the benefit are only the

beginning," Dani said. "They approved emergency amendments that allow more invasive interrogation techniques, searches and identification checks without cause or suspicion. They're marshaling an elite military force trained to cross the wall and make directly for this hideout with all the resources of the capital behind them."

"To search for it," Carmen corrected her. "To search for our headquarters. You said *make for* like he knows where we are, but no one knows . . ." She trailed off at the look on Dani's face.

"I've seen his maps," Dani said gently. "He knows."

"The exact location?"

Dani's silence was answer enough.

"Well, isn't it obvious?" Ari said, cutting through the sound of hearts sinking into stomachs around the table. "They told him! They've been spying on us all along!"

"A predictable theory," said El Buitre, his voice almost cold. "But we all know neither Carmen nor Dani was in possession of our location at that time."

Ari didn't have an answer for that, and Carmen felt a rush of vindication.

Dani cleared her throat.

"There's more. In the morning, Mateo will be named acting president of Medio. They planned to force the current president out for his ineffectiveness to contain the rebel threat even before his death."

Carmen glanced at Dani in shock. This was news even to her.

"Now the process will only be faster. The military force was close to being assembled even before the events of the benefit. Mateo's swearing-in will be tomorrow evening; they've been planning it for a week. After that, it's only a matter of how fast he and his forces can reach us."

Carmen was delirious, they all were. They had days, if that. And someone inside this compound had leaked their location to Mateo. No one was safe.

But who? Who would sell out La Voz? Carmen had been so busy proving she wasn't a traitor, she hadn't stopped to wonder if there were real traitors in their midst.

"I've seen schematics of weapons in development," Dani was saying. "Plans for outer-island bases and strategies for dealing with terrain. I was unable to smuggle hard copies out of the house, but I memorized enough to be useful. To prepare for what's coming. . . ."

She left the rest wisely unsaid. That if they killed her today for treason she hadn't committed, her information would die with her.

"Señor Garcia's suspicions had begun to take their toll on Mateo," Dani reiterated as the silence stretched out. "I was already beginning to fear what would happen in my confinement if he turned on me. If I hadn't been extracted when I was, I would have been tortured, interrogated, and most likely killed. Carmen saved my life."

Carmen didn't know if it was true. They'd had so little hope, no chance to discuss what would happen if they lived. But there was no denying it had been effective in this room.

"Carmen *killed* Medio's president!" Ari said. "Recklessly, and with no authorization! She put all of you in danger!"

El Buitre got to his feet. "If Daniela's information can be verified, the president was already on his way out. And there's hardly a greater danger than the one the Garcia boy's new initiative had already placed us in."

"Sota died," Ari said, grasping at straws. "Because of her terrible decision-making."

"Sota was a member of La Voz," came a voice, heavy with grief.

Alex, Carmen thought, her eyes filling with tears.

"He knew the risks. And if he died to get us this information, to protect us from the threat, he did it with pride. Just as any one of us would."

Tears ran down Carmen's face. Alex still wouldn't look at her, but there was no doubt her contribution had been the turning point they needed.

"We were prepared for increased border presence after the death of the Garcia Segunda," El Buitre said. "We've trained for that as best we can. But a strike of this magnitude would have leveled us, without advance notice."

Carmen held her breath. Beside her, Dani leaned ever so slightly forward, awaiting the decision of the table. Carmen wanted to take her hand more than she'd ever wanted to do anything. She balled up her fists to stop the impulse.

"Our Cuerva made a reckless choice, leaving the compound, disobeying orders. But I believe her motives were pure, and there is no doubt Daniela's information will be vital in the war to come."

Carmen's heart, so heavy when she entered this tent, dared to lighten, just a little.

"With this new information in mind, I propose we focus our efforts on unity. On survival. And forgo punishment at this time."

Could this really be happening? Carmen wondered. Had they really done it?

"But hear me now," he said, looking at Carmen alone. "Any more transgressions of this magnitude, any more transgressions *at all*, and you will receive no mercy from this table. Do I make myself perfectly clear?"

"Yes," Carmen said, and Dani nodded beside her.

"Well then. All those in favor?"

"Sí," came Alex's voice, first of the bunch.

"Sí," El Buitre echoed.

The woman with the dirt bike gave her *sí* next, and the bearded man after her, until Ari was the only one left.

"Jefe, if we could just speak in private," he said, an edge to his voice.

"You're a voting member of this table, Ari," El Buitre said, irritation in his own. "Feel free to vote."

He only needed a simple majority, Carmen knew. Ari's

vote hadn't mattered since the woman across from him had cast hers. But everyone watched him anyway.

"Fine," he said at last, and stormed out of the tent.

Carmen wanted to jump up and down, to embrace El Buitre and Dani and even the bearded man whose name she didn't know. But Alex was passing them without pausing on her way out of the tent, the pain of losing Sota etched in every line of her face, and Carmen knew celebration was the last thing on anyone's mind.

The Vulture approached them as the rest filed out, his face neutral. He clapped Carmen on the shoulder before extending his hand to Dani.

"It's nice to see you face-to-face," he said. "Little bird."

Dani smiled, taking his hand. "I'm grateful to you for my life that day," she said. "And today."

"Let's not make a habit of meeting like this," he said, before releasing her and facing them both.

"If what you say is true, we can only guarantee two days until the capital's forces arrive."

Dani nodded, and Carmen felt dread settle around her like a shawl. With the resources they had, a year wouldn't have been enough time to prepare.

"I'll need you working with our blacksmith on weapons and armor that can combat what the Garcia boy's forces will bring; do you remember enough?"

"I do," Dani said, and Carmen saw the determination in her eyes, the fierceness she'd always loved. Dani had never backed down from a fight. Not even in school.

"We're outnumbered," El Buitre said. "They'll be expecting an easy fight."

"We won't give it to them," Carmen said, and El Buitre embraced her, pulling away with a tear streaking down his face.

Carmen was taken aback. She'd never seen him cry.

"I may be an old man," he said, his voice gruff. "But I have some fight left in me, too. Get cleaned up, fed, and into uniform. Let's see what this ragtag bunch can do, hmm?"

"Jefe," Carmen said. "How do we find out who leaked our location? Someone should be punished for this, someone . . ."

"We have to live, before we can punish anyone," he said.

He was gone before they could answer, leaving Dani and Carmen alone once again. Only this time, they were free.

—⟩✳⟨—

CARMEN TURNED TO DANI, the relief of being alive adding to the cacophony of other emotions between them.

The electricity, the guilt, the fear, it was all still there, but when Dani met her eyes, it was clear which one was pulling ahead.

"You were brilliant," Dani said.

"Me?" Carmen asked, her jaw dropping. "Mateo's becoming president and you had schematics committed to memory? Why didn't you tell me?"

"To be honest," Dani said, her eyes distant for a moment, "I never thought we'd make it far enough for any of it to matter."

"But in the truck?"

"I thought it would be better if you looked surprised," Dani said, her face inscrutable. "Like I'd saved my intel for the leadership, instead of letting them think I was telling you everything during pillow talk or something."

Carmen couldn't help it, she blushed at the phrase, the memory of their night at Mari and Lu's springing up unbidden and swelling between them.

"It was the right call," she said instead of kissing her, almost forgetting why she shouldn't.

"Thank you."

An awkward pause unspooled between them.

"Everything you said up there," Dani said after a moment. "About the cause being a family, protecting its people . . . That's why I joined. It's what Sota always believed."

"He was my best friend," Carmen said. "My brother. We grew up together. Family was what we always wanted."

Dani turned to look at Carmen, her eyes liquid, that familiar brown disarming. "I didn't know . . . ," she said. "There's so much I don't know."

"I'll tell you," Carmen said, without thinking about what it meant. "I want you to know me, Dani, I want . . ."

But what she wanted would have to wait, because the tent doors flew open at just that moment.

"There you are," Jasmín said, sauntering forward. "They said you didn't die, so I had to see for myself."

Carmen's first reaction was shock, followed quickly by

relief. Jasmín was alive, and awake. Her hand was on her hip and one eyebrow was raised and she was still her mischievous, beautiful self.

Carmen's second thought was that she was looking at the only two girls she had ever had real feelings for, together, right in front of her, and that she'd like nothing better than to sink into the ground she'd just been so grateful to be standing on top of.

"You know, sneaking out while I was unconscious wasn't very nice," Jasmín said. "But I guess it's not the first time, right?" A smile played around her plum-stained lips.

Where did she get lip stain *out here?* Carmen wondered. "Sorry," she said, heat rising in her cheeks. "Duty called."

"That's not exactly what I heard," Jasmín said, eyeing Dani speculatively. "In fact, I heard something like the opposite of that."

"Semantics," Carmen mumbled, plotting her escape until Dani cleared her throat. "Sorry, right, uh, you guys obviously know each other. . . ."

Jasmín turned her wicked smirk on Dani. "Right, yeah, the former roommate who got me arrested and almost killed."

"I didn't . . . ," Dani sputtered. "I mean it wasn't . . ." She fell into a rare undignified silence, and Jasmín watched her with that one arched brow, refusing to let her off the hook for a minute or more while Carmen pretended to find the toes of her borrowed shoes fascinating.

At long last, Jasmín burst out laughing, throwing an arm

over Dani's shoulder while the other girl stood stiff as a post, enduring it, her eyes now locked on Carmen's in a way that said she might not escape death today after all.

"Primera, chill!" Jasmín said, pulling Dani forward through the tent flap, where a crowd had gathered. "I was only teasing. Come on, everyone's outside."

Carmen had wanted a few more minutes alone with Dani, to continue where they'd left off, to figure out what they were doing now that the stress of potential execution had been momentarily lifted. But Dani followed Jasmín out into the dusk without looking back, and all Carmen could do was join them.

The story of what had happened in the tent, of what Dani and Carmen had told them, was spreading, and Carmen could sense the purpose in all their movements. This was a compound preparing for war.

"I need to find the blacksmith," Dani said when Carmen had caught up to her. Jasmín disappeared into the crowd with a wink that said they had more to discuss.

"You need to eat, and get your wounds looked at," Carmen said. "At the very least." She wanted to suggest sleep, too, but with two days until Mateo-watch began she knew the likelihood of that was slim.

"I need to be useful," Dani said, but the tension beneath her words said she was doing more than that. She was creating distance between them because of Jasmín. Because of everything about Carmen she didn't know.

It's for the best, Carmen told herself as Dani disappeared into the crowd, toward the sound of the hammer ringing out on metal. But she didn't really believe it.

Carmen drifted, knowing she should bathe, change, eat, even sleep, but too restless to settle. Around her, the compound readied itself. Alex had been running daily drills in the ring since before Carmen left, getting ready for increased military presence after Mama Garcia's death. With the help of Dani's troop strategies, they could train harder, more efficiently, getting ready for whatever Mateo had to throw at them.

The blacksmith would be repairing weapons and armor, reinforcing what they had to stand up to the new task force and their vastly superior weapons. Dani was probably already there, relaying the designs she'd seen, contributing in a meaningful way.

Carmen, on the other hand, was at loose ends. She'd been a spy her entire career with La Voz, more at home in enemy territory than with her own people. But what use did they have for a spy when they knew war was coming?

El Buitre had said the identity of the leak wasn't important—at least not more important than the immediate threat facing them—and he was probably right. But what if Carmen could find it? Prevent more information from changing hands before they fought?

The only question was, how? She barely knew the names of the people at headquarters anymore. She didn't know their faces, their histories. And there was no one to ask.

All around, as the details of the coming fight were passed by word of mouth, as people found ways to be useful, Carmen sensed the energy rising. Snippets of conversation, eager looks on young, untested faces—they told her people were excited for this fight. That they were ready.

They're fools, Carmen thought. She had meant what she said to El Buitre in the tent; she didn't intend to make things easy on Mateo and his men. But there was a reason La Voz had never fought Medio's military in the open field. Never fought them head-on at all.

Near the kitchen tent, the folks who couldn't fight laid out tarps and blankets, getting ready to gather supplies, food, first aid, what little water they could muster. They needed to have resources available in case the fight dragged on, places for their people to be doctored, to eat and drink and rest.

Carmen thought she'd join them for now, put her Segunda training to good use, when she saw him. Ari. On the other side of the massive cook-fire being stoked in the compound's biggest clearing. He looked like he was waiting for someone, but his gaze darted back and forth in a way that raised Carmen's hackles.

Ari had made it his business to know everything about the goings-on in this compound. Even if she despised him, he was still her best chance of finding out who had leaked the intel.

And if he had just found out about the leak himself, he'd

be headed to deal with it, wouldn't he? It was what Carmen would have done.

She waved hello to the señoras who recognized her, thanking them for their efforts, passing through like she'd always intended to make her way to the fire. By the time she reached it, Ari was walking away, glancing over his shoulder, but not soon enough to see Carmen as she eased into the evening shadows to follow him.

Carmen's heart raced as she tailed him, sticking to the trees, reveling in the thrill of doing something she was good at when she'd felt nothing but useless for days.

Ari clearly didn't want to be seen, wherever he was going, and as she slid in and out of the shadows, Carmen theorized endlessly about where they were headed. Was he going to confront the person he believed responsible for the leak? Going to meet a contact who could help him find out?

When the sounds of camp life had faded away behind them, though, Carmen wondered how far he would go. What if he knew she was behind him? What if he was just leading her somewhere remote to do what El Buitre hadn't done in the meeting today?

Using her nature against her? Baiting her into a spy maneuver? It was another thing Carmen would have done.

She was about to talk herself out of it, go back, find another way to investigate the leak, but that's when he finally stopped. It was a dense part of the grove, obscured by ghost trees. Carmen got as close as she could, then lowered to the ground, listening intently as two voices began to speak.

"Took you long enough," said the first, a female voice Carmen recognized immediately. But what was Ari doing meeting Jasmín in the middle of nowhere?

"I was looking for the old man, to ask him what the salt he was thinking," he said, his frustration evident even from a distance. "But he disappeared. No one's seen him since the meeting."

"What now, then?" Jasmín asked, her voice sharper than usual, less flirtatious. "You can't exactly confront him with this in front of everyone."

"I'm not an idiot," he snapped. "Here."

Carmen peered around the tree an inch at a time, barely catching Ari's movement as he handed something off to Jasmín.

"Make sure it gets where it needs to go, and fast. Everything changed when those brats walked free."

Jasmín didn't answer, and for too long no one said a word. When Carmen looked again, she understood why. Against the trunk of a ghost tree, the darkness settling around them, Ari had Jasmín locked in an embrace more intense than any of the ones Carmen had shared with her.

Mind reeling with all she had just learned, and all she hadn't, Carmen retreated into the trees and made as quickly as she could for camp.

Ari? Jasmín? El Buitre himself? Carmen had wanted to

find the leak, but of her three main suspects, two of them were the last people she'd ever have imagined capable of treason like this.

Don't react emotionally, she told her Segunda self, who was ready to confront them all in turn, emotions high, make a scene in front of everyone. But she didn't have enough information. Not yet.

Luckily for La Voz, getting it was what she did best.

Back at camp, Carmen tried to blend in, taking a cup of fermented pineapple juice when it was offered to her, thankful for the cover of darkness for hiding her flushed face, her preoccupation.

Someone had betrayed La Voz. And based on what she'd just overheard, it was one of three people. Jasmín was the least likely, practically speaking. She'd only been awake for a couple of days, and before that she hadn't had the compound location, either. El Buitre . . . Carmen shuddered at the thought. He was the lifeblood of the resistance; he had dedicated his life to the cause. How could he possibly be working against it? Against all of them?

Then there was Ari. Carmen had thought of him as an overzealous brownnoser, after the top job, willing to do what it took to get there. But what if there was something more sinister beneath his pandering, his manipulation?

"You okay?" The voice took her out of her thoughts just before the spiral turned dark.

Dani approached from behind her, a cup in her own hand, her face open and curious, no longer suspicious.

"I'm tired," Carmen said, embarrassed when her voice broke. Had it really only been one day since she woke up at Mari and Lu's?

"Me, too."

Dani's shoulder touched hers, and for a moment, in the darkness, they just leaned against each other, drawing comfort and support from the closeness, their problems seeming a little farther away when they faced them side by side.

╍┼⟩*⟨┼╍

CARMEN WOKE BEFORE THE SUN, feeling peaceful and rested for the first time since she could remember. Feeling ready for what came next.

She had a plan.

Before the camp woke up around her, she dug into the little basket on the table of her tent, untouched since before she went to the capital. The charred remains of her silk Segunda's dress were there, nestled beneath her bandages, right where she left them.

She didn't need the talisman now, the reminder. Not when the flesh-and-blood girl was sleeping just three tents away.

In the quiet of the early morning, Carmen walked to the cliffs overlooking the sea, letting the crash of the waves calm her, bring her back to herself. First, she would reckon with the past, then she would say goodbye to her brother. Then she would get the information she needed to save her family.

Remembering Dani's eyes in the firelight last night, her lips in the narrow bed at Mari and Lu's, Carmen held the charred, braided silk in her fingertips for a moment before letting it drift away on the breeze.

Whatever they were going to be to each other, they would have to base it on the present, not the past. On who they were, not who they had pretended to be.

Walking back through the compound, Carmen saw it with new eyes. When you were raised inside something, its rules were a given. But Carmen had been outside. She had seen the god of bones. She had lost her brother. She had witnessed a declaration of war.

There were so many things that had once mattered to her that didn't anymore.

So many things she had underestimated that now seemed more important than ever.

She loved this place, loved the people in it, loved the cause they had all pledged to fight. It was as simple as that. She would do whatever it took to make sure La Voz survived.

The compound was silent. A calm before a storm. Carmen made her way toward the center of camp, toward the kitchen fire where last night the señoras had built a tribute to the fox-faced boy they'd called son. Called brother.

The altar was arranged at the base of a massive silver ghost trunk. Flowers didn't grow out here, but someone had made twenty or so out of orange paper and laid them around bowls of water and wine, plates of food.

Carmen approached with a knot in her throat, feeling Sota in the air, in the flowers, in the tree itself. They had built this to say goodbye, and for a moment the guilt fell away, leaving nothing but her grief.

She stayed off to the side, allowing the other mourners a respectful distance, but she was too consumed with the beautiful display to look at their faces, so when Ari spoke, it caught her by surprise. She'd thought she'd have to find him when the time came, but here he was.

"You shouldn't be here," he said, his voice carrying in a way that felt intentional.

"What does it matter to you?" Carmen asked, keeping her tone light, aware of all the eyes on them.

"I mean it," Ari said. "He's dead, and it's your fault. Do you think any of us want to see your face while we mourn him?"

Muttering started as the small crowd created distance between themselves and the brewing altercation. Carmen sized Ari up, wondering what his motive was. To discredit her in front of everyone? To keep her from reclaiming his seat?

"I made a call, Ari," Carmen said, her voice low and even, but loud enough for everyone to hear. "Because I was there, not you. We had an objective, and an opportunity arose, and

I took it. You don't have to like it, but Sota trusted me, and he was willing to give his life for this organization. Just like any of the rest of us would."

"*You* made the wrong call," Ari said, stepping closer, his eyes positively murderous.

He was a good actor, Carmen thought clinically. His face looked every inch the grief-stricken boy, mourning a friend. Only Sota had never been Ari's friend, and using him this way made the anger she'd tried to keep at bay surge toward the surface.

"Although I suppose we can hardly blame you, right?" Ari asked, raising his voice further as more people came to investigate the source of the commotion. "The pampered princess, sitting in your big fancy school being fanned by servants who eat better than we do. Married to the richest papi's boy in the country. Becoming weak and *indulgent.*" He spat this last word, and unfortunately for them both, Dani chose this moment to approach.

"What's going on?" she asked, and Ari turned to the crowd now, their attention on him and him alone.

"Just discussing how your *girlfriend* made a shortsighted, showboating decision based more in personal glory than the good of the people," Ari said, too close to Dani for Carmen's comfort before he turned abruptly to face Carmen, their noses just inches apart. "What the hell do *you* know about the people anymore?"

The crowd was deadly quiet.

"I know better than to get them killed on sloppy missions," Carmen said through clenched teeth, refusing to back away. "I know better than to use our people as pawns and undermine our cause for my own gain."

"No, you just leave against orders to save your traitorous girlfriend, and then wipe out years of planning with one completely ill-planned assassination," he said.

"You were at the table during my trial," Carmen said. "You heard the answers to all of this. Just because things didn't go your way doesn't mean I belong here any less than you."

But Ari, whether he knew he was outmatched or for some reason of his own, decided to pivot. He drew two knives from the belt at his waist, and for one wild moment Carmen thought he meant to stab her right here. El Buitre's judgment be damned.

Instead, he slammed one of them, hilt first, into Carmen's chest. The other he raised, backing away.

"If you really belong here, prove it."

So this was the goal, Carmen thought, strangely detached. She couldn't turn down the challenge, not in front of all these witnesses, not without giving credence to everything Ari had just said about her forgetting where she came from.

If he couldn't get her killed or excommunicated, he would turn the people against her. Mitigate her influence on El Buitre, which seemed to be eclipsing his own.

"Or don't you remember how to fight to first blood?" he asked.

Dani was watching, her eyes wide as she stood at the front of the crowd. The Carmen she knew wouldn't fight. She would find some clever way to get out of it. Some Segunda's way. But the people here wouldn't respect a Segunda any more than a traitor.

And Ari's eyes said he knew it.

Carmen lunged before she could talk herself out of it.

Ari was caught off guard, but he couldn't complain. Anything went in a fight like this. He reacted quickly, jumping backward to dodge the blow, and the crowd moved out of the way, forming a loose circle around the two of them.

If this had been the practice ring, Carmen would have pressed her advantage, attacking again while Ari was on his heels. But she waited too long, congratulating herself for making the first move, and Ari was too ruthless not to make her pay.

He exploded with a series of slashes, his arm a blur. Carmen stumbled backward to avoid the onslaught, barely getting her feet under her again. To go down this early would have been an embarrassment, not to mention it would likely have ended the fight, but somehow, miraculously, the island's salt-ravaged soil held on to Carmen's heels.

She felt Dani's eyes on her. She didn't dare look at her expression.

Back, to the side, back, to the other side, Carmen dodged strikes without getting in a single one of her own, doing nothing but treading water until at last, Ari overreached. Carmen stepped forward, going for the skin of his extended arm, but by the time she reached it, the arm was gone, already drawing back for another offensive.

They danced, settling into a rhythm, and Carmen relished the sweat beading up along her hairline, at the back of her neck. The battles she fought in the capital were much different ones, battles of outward charm and quiet scheming. There was something honest about sweat and dirt and blood, even if the problems that hung between them were much more complicated.

In a flash, just when she was getting comfortable with the back-and-forth, Ari spun behind her, one arm like a steel bar around her chest, blade pressing into Carmen's collarbone.

Right before it broke skin, Carmen ducked out of his grasp, falling to her knees and spinning out of reach.

When she got back to her feet, Ari was already there, and the look in his eyes said this would be finished in the next stroke. His knife was driving, a flashy thing that was more for the benefit of the crowd than the desire to win.

That's when Carmen knew she had him. And the irony tasted so sweet.

The strike was so subtle no one noticed until Ari hissed, pulling back. Carmen had nicked the wrist of the hand making the showy strike. A nonlethal blow, but first blood. A win.

Very few people realized what had happened until Ari held his arm aloft—only for the barest second to fulfill the rules of good sportsmanship. The stripe of vivid red dripped down his wrist like a ribbon.

A few people clapped, but even the ones who didn't looked grudgingly impressed. Carmen didn't care what they thought. She went straight for Dani, finding her face in the crowd, her stricken expression sinking in Carmen's stomach like a stone.

"Fine. Pay your respects," he said, seething, his showy plan thwarted. His eyes looked a little crazed. Like something had snapped in him, losing to her two days in a row. "But don't expect us to stand here and watch you make a mockery of his memory."

The real mockery was that he'd pretended to care about Sota's memory at all, and Carmen's goodbye, here, at this beautiful altar, was tainted by it.

Just one more thing he'd answer for before they were done.

"Hey," she said to Dani when he had stormed off in a huff. "Sorry you had to see that."

Dani's eyes were still wide. "It was . . . impressive?"

Carmen was out of breath; fighting was twice as difficult when she had to favor her bad ankle with every step. She didn't know what to say. "I didn't want to fight him," she said. "I didn't have a choice."

"Of course," Dani said. But she didn't look at Carmen. Not really. "I need to get back to the blacksmith. See you . . . later."

She disappeared before they could discuss it, before any resolution could be found. Carmen kicked the base of a tree, hard, feeling like she'd lost somehow even though she'd won.

There was a restlessness building in her again. Something that said she couldn't sit around and do nothing. That she had to be useful. Mateo could be here as soon as tomorrow, and the camp was busy preparing for the threat, but Carmen was the only one who knew about Ari's secret meeting the night before. The mysterious object he'd given Jasmín.

Sore, wounded, exhausted, it didn't matter. It was time to carry out her plan.

"Hey, stranger," she said when she reached Jasmín's tent. The other girl was just waking, her hair a tangle atop her head, too sleepy and seductive for her own good.

"Good morning, gorgeous," she purred.

The tone was lost on Carmen. All she could see was the girl she'd once had feelings for with her arms around that snake.

"Figured we hadn't gotten much of a chance to catch up," Carmen said, easing into the room, trying to hide the way she cast around for a hiding place. Somewhere to keep a palm-sized object before you used it to betray your cause.

"I was going to find you anyway," Jasmín said, sitting up, all business. "I need to tell you something before you hear it from someone else."

Had she underestimated Jasmín? Carmen wondered. Come here to catch her in a lie only to get the truth instead?

"It's Ari," Jasmín said. "He and I. We're . . . you know." She waggled her eyebrows in a way that would have made

Carmen laugh, if things weren't so dire.

She groaned aloud, playing along. "From me to that guy?" Carmen asked. "I'm insulted."

"Don't be jealous," she teased, crossing the room to thwack her on the shoulder. "He's very misunderstood."

"He didn't seem misunderstood when he challenged me to first blood at Sota's memorial altar this morning," Carmen said, keeping her tone mild. *Or last night, when you were meeting him in secret. . . .*

"Oh, sun and skies," Jasmín said, the upper-class curse still her default. Today, it put Carmen on edge. "He's so fussy about you. I never should have told him about us."

"He knows about *us*?" Carmen asked, losing track of her mission for the moment.

"Of course; you think I wasn't going to brag?" Her smirk was criminal.

"It doesn't matter. He's a snake, Jasmín. You need to be careful."

"Ari's not a snake," Jasmín said, draping herself in a dressing gown. She seemed more thoughtful than defensive. "He's . . . passionate."

Carmen rolled her eyes.

Jasmín laughed. "No, I mean it. He believes in this cause, but he's tired of the bureaucracy dragging it down. He wants to cut through the traditions and the rules and really take the fight to the bad guys, you know?"

Carmen gritted her teeth, thinking of the demonstration,

all the lives that had been lost. Thinking of the marketplace fire that had almost ruined everything. This was what he had been after? Chaos? Breaking with tradition?

How did that explain the secret meeting, and El Buitre's involvement, and whatever he'd given Jasmín to pass along?

"There are reasons why we've done things the way we have," she said, trying not to be defensive right away. "But I'd be lying if I said a more radical approach didn't seem attractive sometimes."

"See?" Jasmín said. "You two aren't so different, really."

"What's his angle, then?" Carmen asked. "Besides trying to get me killed." Maybe she could play the ex card to get information. Maybe she wouldn't have to resort to distrusting Jasmín. Maybe there was a simple explanation for all of this.

"Ick, so boring!" Jasmín said. "What do I know? He wants to kill all the bad guys, just like all of you. He just doesn't want to stand on all these codes and social niceties while we do it."

It was a dodge, and not even a good one. Nothing that could possibly explain what Carmen had seen last night. The dressing gown hit the floor, another distraction, and Jasmín wiggled back into her blacks.

"Anyway, you didn't come over here to talk about Ari," Jasmín purred. "It's nothing serious anyway. It's not easy like it was with us."

Carmen let go of the interrogation tactics and embodied

the Segunda, eyeing the pocket of Jasmín's blacks, knowing closeness was the answer if talking wouldn't work.

"There wasn't really an us," she said gently, letting her eyes linger a beat too long.

"I know," Jasmín said. "But I wanted there to be."

So many lies, Carmen thought. It was almost sad.

"I knew better, though," Jasmín said with a self-deprecating chuckle. "There was no room in there for anything but the precious cause."

"And Ari is different?" Carmen asked, taking a step closer.

Jasmín smiled, almost sad. "No," she said. "Ari is exactly the same."

She sat on the bed. Carmen sat beside her. Close enough to touch.

Closeness is a weapon, her maestras had always said. But what if you were both armed?

"When I left school to start my married life, I cried every night," Jasmín said after a few long moments. "I missed you. But I'd try to picture you missing me and I couldn't. Not even my imagination was that good."

"I'm sorry," Carmen said, easing closer. "I didn't know you felt that way. Maybe if I had . . ."

"It wouldn't have made a difference," Jasmín said. "Why do you think I never took my shot?"

"So why tell me now?" Carmen asked, not faking her curiosity. "What changed?"

"You did," Jasmín said simply, spreading her hands in

302

her lap. "I heard about what happened. You stormed out of a meeting, defied El Buitre. Alex *shot* at you. You put Dani before all of this."

"Yeah, and it nearly got us both killed," Carmen said. "Maybe I had it right before."

But Jasmín was already shaking her head. "You think it makes you weak, to love her, but it doesn't. Even I can see how much stronger you are."

Was she lying now? Carmen wondered. Was all this a means to some terrible end of Ari's? And did it make it any less true if it was?

"I just thought you deserved to know," Jasmín said, kneeling down beside her. "That you aren't weak. That you deserve happiness just as much as anyone else. Maybe even more."

"But what if I can't have both?" Carmen asked, thinking of Mari, who had traded it all in for love.

"You're Carmen Santos," Jasmín said, getting to her feet. "Of course you can."

Carmen stood, seeing her moment, extending her hand for Jasmín's, pulling her to her feet.

"You were wrong about one thing," she said, bringing her closer. "I did miss you."

Jasmín's arms went up around her neck, Carmen's around her hips. They stayed like that for a long time, bodies pressing close, Carmen's heartbeat reacting to the memories without her permission.

The other girl's hands were in her hair before she knew it,

and Carmen tightened her grip, hands drifting closer to the pockets at the front of her jumpsuit.

"We shouldn't . . . ," Jasmín said, her voice teasing beneath the words.

"We're not," Carmen said, pressing herself closer.

Hands wandered, lips drifted to necks. Jasmín's hands grew bolder, and Carmen didn't wonder whether it was wrong. When they pulled apart, she didn't have to fake her sigh of regret.

"You'll always be my first," she said, leaning in, kissing Jasmín on the cheek as she smiled ruefully. "I hope he's a worthy follow-up."

"He's not even in the same arena," Jasmín replied with a smirk. "Now get out of here before I get us both in trouble."

Carmen didn't need to be asked twice. She walked out without a backward glance. But the moment she reached her tent, she pulled the folded letter out of her own pocket and smiled.

23

When it comes time to make difficult choices for my cause, I will act without hesitation.

—*La Voz Membership Pledge*

†≻✳≺†

ARI'S LETTER, OF COURSE, was written in code, and there was only one person Carmen knew who could decipher it.

The only trouble was, Carmen hadn't talked to Alex since her return.

Alex had spoken up in her defense at the trial, which Carmen took as a good sign, but still she was far from certain of her reception when she arrived at the training ring just after the mess tent emptied from breakfast.

"You here to practice?" Alex asked tersely. "Because I don't have time to chat."

"I'm not here to talk," Carmen said. "I need a code breaker."

Alex tried her best not to look interested, but Carmen knew her too well not to recognize the set of her lips, the slight rise of her eyebrow.

"I'll be here for another hour."

"Fine, meet me in my tent."

She didn't say no.

Carmen paced in her quarters for every minute of the hour, but when the tent flap opened exactly at the end of it, she knew she had Alex's full attention.

"What is it?" she asked, but her fidgeting gave her away. She was eager.

Carmen hid her smile. "Here," she said, handing over the sheet with its symbols and strange letters.

"You didn't answer my question."

"Do you want to know?" Carmen asked.

"Salt, you never change, do you? Who'd you steal this from?"

Alex's eyes were already flying over the page, and Carmen knew she was searching for patterns and meaning in the nonsense. Alex had been creating the Vulture's codes since she was ten—but the furrow in her brow said this one was unfamiliar.

Carmen waited, remembering a million lazy days like this, Sota creating codes for her to crack, Alex racing through them effortlessly, frustrating him.

He'd gotten better, with time, she thought sadly.

Half an hour passed, then another. The thrill wore off as Carmen waited, the tent heating up around them as the morning aged. Alex muttered under her breath, holding all the symbols in her head as always.

"Aha!" she said when Carmen was sure she couldn't take another moment.

"What?" Carmen asked. "Did you get it?"

"Shh," Alex replied, eyes unfocusing again as she counted in her head. "Almost."

It was obvious when she had it, Carmen thought. The thrill of victory that quickly made its way to confusion, and then something adjacent to anger.

"Why the hell would you give me this?" she asked. "Where did you get it?"

"What does it say?" Carmen asked, watching her brandish the page like a venomous snake.

"It *says*," Alex replied, her eyes flashing, "that La Voz has advance warning about what's coming. And it's addressed to Mateo Garcia. And it's *from* your little girlfriend, who just walked free from La Voz justice on my recommendation."

Dani, Carmen thought. There was no way she could be the traitor. And this letter had come from Ari, not her. Carmen's mind raced, putting together the implications of what Alex had just said with what she'd seen the night before.

Alex was already halfway to the door, scowling.

"Wait," Carmen said. "Just . . ."

Alex whirled on her. "Just what? Just wait for you to weasel your way out of punishment again? I can't *believe* I stood up for you, for that little . . ."

"Dani has never seen this letter," Carmen said, before Alex could gather more steam.

"Oh, that's what you're going with, huh? Do I look stupid to you?"

"Alex, I stole this letter from Jasmín. I watched Ari give it to her last night after the trial. I followed him into the grove. If it says it's from Dani, Ari is trying to frame her."

From the doorway, Alex let the tent flap fall shut. "*Mateo,*" she read aloud. "*Arrived. Rebels informed of military intervention as you ordered. Black Guard strike must happen as quickly as possible for any hope of success. They're preparing now. We're free of suspicion and will be in contact when I can. Yours, Daniela.*"

Carmen took the letter, incredulous, like the symbols would suddenly make sense once she read them.

"So he frames her," Alex said, sitting heavily on Carmen's cot. "And you by extension. He really doesn't like to lose, does he?"

"You believe me?" Carmen asked.

"Please, you think I can't tell when you're lying by now?"

Carmen allowed herself a small smile, but it faded quickly. "The question is, is he framing us because he wants to get even for losing at the table? Or to cover up for whoever's really leaking information?"

"Depends where the letter was supposed to go. Was he really going to send it to Mateo? Or was he going to present it to El Buitre as proof of her treachery?"

Carmen thought hard, but Alex was quicker.

"You said he gave this to Jasmín to deliver, right? If she's working with him, she's the first place we go. But if he's really trying to frame a member for his own personal gain, that's reason enough to call for a trial."

"And that's if he's *just* trying to frame her," Carmen said darkly. "That could be just the beginning."

"Let's not get ahead of ourselves," Alex said. "We need more information before we can make any more accusations."

"We?" Carmen asked, hardly daring to hope.

"You think I'm gonna let you be the one to catch this son of the salt? If he's going down, I want to be there, too."

"Fair enough," Carmen said. "But there's a stop we have to make first."

Dani wasn't thrilled about being ominously removed from the blacksmith's tent in the middle of an armor test, but when she saw the look on Carmen's face—not to mention Alex beside her—she came without argument.

She walked beside them, tall and slim in her La Voz issued blacks, hair curling into her eyes on one side. Dani looked at home in this place, in this uniform, and despite the seriousness of everything unfolding, Carmen couldn't help but be proud.

No one said a word until the sounds of camp had faded away behind them.

"This is good enough." Alex came to a halt and turned to face them with the letter still clutched in her hand.

"What's going on?" Dani asked; the only sign of her anxiety was in the stiff set of her shoulders.

Suddenly, with her standing there brave and ready, Carmen found she couldn't begin. How could she tell this girl who had given up so much that she was a pawn in some scheme of Ari's? That even after everything they'd been through, she wasn't safe.

That Carmen might never be able to keep her safe.

"Whatever it is, just tell me," Dani said. "I can handle it."

But it was Alex who spoke. "We found this letter, addressed to Mateo Garcia. It says it's from you."

To her credit, Dani didn't say a word. Her face remained impassive, waiting.

"We know it isn't," Carmen jumped in, ignoring a withering look from Alex. "I stole it off Jasmín this morning."

"Jasmín's trying to frame me?" Dani asked, swift and sharp. She looked at Carmen, who felt her face flush.

"We don't know what her involvement is. The letter was given to her by Ari. I saw them together last night."

"So *Ari* is trying to frame me, and he's using Jasmín to do it?" Dani said, almost to herself. "But why?" And then: "Who else has seen this?"

"No one," Alex said.

"And they won't," Carmen promised her. "We know you had nothing to do with this."

Dani looked at Carmen, then Alex. "What does the letter say, exactly?"

Alex read aloud, and Carmen watched Dani, who kept her gaze on the ground until the end.

When she was finished, Dani was quiet for a long time. "Unfortunately," she said, "we have bigger problems than just me being framed." She took a deep breath. "It isn't me, but whoever wrote this letter *is* in communication with Mateo. Framing me was secondary to getting him this information."

Even though she'd had the same fear herself, having it confirmed was another story. Carmen's heart sank.

"How do you know that?" Alex asked, instantly suspicious.

"The Black Guard," Dani said. "It's his private name for the new military force, the one he used to talk about in secret before he'd gotten it approved. No one knew it but him and his father—he never even said it when he knew I was in earshot."

Silence settled over the three of them, heavy and thick. Carmen had distrusted Ari since the moment she met him, believed he was self-righteous and incompetent and out for himself above the cause.

But she had never expected him to be a traitor.

"The fire," she said almost to herself. "Jasmín . . ." Her eyes found Alex's. "What if all his botched missions were an attempt to destabilize us . . . to give Mateo an easier path to destroying La Voz?"

"It's an incredibly serious accusation," Alex said. "And one we can't make lightly. Especially with everything that's barreling toward us right now. We'll be weaker squabbling among ourselves than we will united against a common enemy."

"We'll be *weaker* if one of our members is working *with* our enemies," Carmen said, temper flaring.

"I'm sorry, but I just don't see any reason why a high-ranking La Voz operative would take a risk like this," Alex said. "What possible benefit would there be to betraying us that would be worth the cost?"

"You don't know what Mateo could have offered him," Carmen said, remembering the power, the money, the luxury and security of their life in the complex. "The resources he has, the access, it could have been anything."

"Now you're just speculating," Alex said, dismissive. "We need *information* if we're going to go to El Buitre with this. I'm not willing to take a stranger's word as reason enough to cut my entire organization in half."

"Believe me or don't," Dani said, her voice flat, her slender shoulders relaxed. "But there's no way he could have known that term otherwise. Either he's working with Mateo or he knows who is."

All around them, the camp was alive with the sounds of the resistance preparing for war. Trying to build armor to stop bullets, and weapons that would give them an advantage with their inferior numbers and subpar equipment.

Was it all for nothing? Had Ari doomed them before it even started?

And if he had, what had Mateo offered him to make him do it?

"We need to go to El Buitre," Carmen said. "Tell him what we know. Tell him . . ."

"We don't *know* anything!" Alex said, finally losing her temper. "We're not going to him with unfounded suspicions like a couple of children."

"So what, then?" Carmen asked, stepping toward Alex, fed up with her cautiousness, her inability to do what needed to be done. "What's your opinion here? Besides just that everything we've come up with is wrong?"

Alex took a deep breath, her exhale slightly shaky. "We talk to Jasmín," she said decisively. "And then if—*if*—there's a reason to, we talk to Jefe. But not unless we all agree. Deal?"

Carmen didn't like it, but she stuck out her hand to shake anyway, squeezing Alex's a little harder than absolutely necessary in the process, trying not to wince when she squeezed back.

"You're both very tough," Dani said, tossing her short hair out of her eyes. "Now can we go? Mateo's swearing-in ceremony is tonight. If we have to confront your precious Jasmín, we better do it fast."

When they found Jasmín in her tent, she was frantic, turning chairs over, digging through blankets and clothes, a stricken expression on her face.

"Looking for this?"

"I . . . what? I just lost an earring . . . ," Jasmín said, but it was a feeble lie and even she knew it. Her face was pale, her eyes too wide.

"Don't play dumb," Carmen said. "It's beneath you. Whatever you did, it can be undone; just tell us what you know."

From wide-eyed and fearful, Jasmín's expression had gone sly. It was a dangerous look, and Carmen knew it.

"So *that's* what your little visit this morning was about," she said, sauntering forward hips first. "It was a rookie move, falling for it. But can you blame me? I mean . . ." She looked Carmen up and down once, slowly.

"Don't try to change the subject," Dani said coldly. "Why are you and Ari trying to frame me?"

Jasmín rolled her eyes. "You think I know what that letter said? Doing a favor for your lover isn't a crime."

"You expect me to believe you'd do a *favor* for someone if there was nothing in it for you?" Dani asked, her businesslike expression fast becoming a scowl. "I lived with you for years. I know you better than that."

"Mateo is coming," Carmen said, stepping forward, pleading with her eyes. "We know what this letter says. Jasmín, if you know something and you don't tell us, you're responsible for what happens."

She turned to leave, calling Jasmín's bluff, pleased when Dani and Alex took her lead.

"It's not a crime to want better for La Voz, okay?" she called after them, but her voice was shaking. "He told me what it's like, moving from hovel to hovel, always a blink away from being wiped out. Doing dangerous things for dangerous people with no hope that you'll ever be any closer to changing anything."

Everything inside Carmen had gone deadly still; time itself seemed to have slowed down.

"What did you do?" she asked softly. Was this what Mateo had promised Ari? Security for La Voz? Resources? A better life? And how had he been stupid enough to fall for it?

"He was doing what none of you could," Jasmín said, her voice pleading. "La Voz is dying, Carmen, everyone can see it. They're circling us like hyenas, and someone had to *do* something! Make the hard choice so the resistance could survive!"

"Is that what he told you?" Alex asked, derision in every word. "That he was *helping* La Voz by betraying us to our worst enemy? What exactly do you think he's saving besides his own skin?"

From fearful, Jasmín's expression shifted to confused. "Worst enemy? What are you talking about?"

"I'm talking about this letter!" Alex took it from Carmen and shook it in Jasmín's face. "The one that tells Mateo Garcia everything he needs to know to wipe out our entire organization."

"Mateo . . . ? No." Jasmín's face fell. "Not Mateo. The letter was for friends of Ari's in the capital!" Her voice pleaded with them to believe her, to understand. "Sympathizers with resources he said could establish us . . . help us . . ."

"You poor, naive idiot," Alex said. "He betrayed all of us, and he used you to do it."

"There were never any sympathizer friends," Dani said as gently as she could. "This letter is addressed to Mateo from me. He's been passing information to Mateo. He wanted to send this last piece and get me killed for treason all in one fell swoop."

Jasmín's face was frozen in horror. Seconds ticked past like hours, and all the while the threat from the capital was moving closer.

Carmen waited for her to plead her case, to say she hadn't known what she was doing. She waited for her to shirk responsibility and fall on their mercy.

When Jasmín looked at her, however, it was with resignation in her expression.

"I failed you," she said, more serious than Carmen had ever seen her. "It doesn't matter what my intentions were; I betrayed this organization. I'll accept my punishment, whatever it is, but know I'm sorry. I never meant to do anything but help. I should have known he was—" She shook her head, a rueful smile on her face. "I'll accept my punishment," she repeated, and then she was silent.

Carmen looked at Alex, grateful for the wordless communication they'd perfected as little more than children. When they were on the same page, Alex turned to Jasmín.

"I want to confront him, take him to El Buitre to confess his crimes. We have less than a day now before the true threat is upon us. It will move much faster with your help."

"I'll do whatever you ask. Anything to make up for what I've done."

"Good," said Alex. "We can discuss your transgressions once we've stopped him. Any objections?"

Carmen wondered if Dani would speak up, take this opportunity to rid herself of her former roommate, Carmen's former lover. She felt a rush of pride when Dani shook her head, and then shame for believing she'd do anything else.

"Ari's checking in with scouts," Jasmín said. "He won't be back until tonight."

Carmen nodded, anticipation coiling like a snake in her belly. "We'll be ready for him."

I will draw strength from my comrades-in-arms, and allow them to draw strength from me.

—*La Voz Membership Pledge*

⊹⊱✳⊰⊹

THEY PARTED WAYS TO PREPARE for the night. Alex insisted on staying with Jasmín in case she decided to run, but Carmen wasn't worried. In that tent, in the face of all that had happened, they were unified.

The only question was how Ari would react when they confronted him. Would he confess? Or would they have to drag him to El Buitre to get the truth? But then Carmen remembered how the Vulture had stood up for Ari at the meeting table, the access he'd been allowed to have . . .

Dani eased into the tent as Carmen paced, wrestling with her thoughts.

"Can I help?" she asked, leaving space between them. Too much. Not enough.

"Just wondering who I can trust anymore," she confessed. "How deep this thing goes. And, you know, if any of this matters when we might all die tomorrow."

"When has the threat of death ever stopped you?" Dani asked, half smiling.

"Not nearly as often as it should have," she replied, thinking of Sota.

It was his ghost, again, that stopped her when Dani moved close.

"I can't," she said.

"Now?" Dani asked. "Or ever?"

"I don't know." It was as honest as she knew how to be.

"You came back for me," Dani said, stepping back, widening the space between them. "You disobeyed orders. You risked everything."

"Yeah, and look how it all turned out," Carmen said, feeling her frustration, her disappointment breaking through. "You lied, I lied, we did dangerous, stupid, destructive things from the moment we met until the moment we got someone killed. We have to stop the bleeding sometime, Dani."

"You don't mean that," Dani said, her eyes wide. The shape of her mouth would have broken Carmen's heart if there was anything left to break. "That can't be how you saw it."

"It's not about how I see it," Carmen said, shaking her head, hating the words but needing them out like a poison.

"It's about reality. When we get close to each other, bad things happen. People *die*." Without warning, her voice broke on the last syllable, the heat of her frustration cooling into steam, billowing around her until she didn't know which way was up.

Dani must have heard it, seen the crack in her armor, because she closed the space between them in an instant.

"People die anyway," she said. "All the time. Carmen, I lo—"

"Don't!" Carmen said, suddenly dry-throated and afraid. "Don't say it."

"Why not?" Dani asked, her eyes blazing. "Even if you regret it all, even if you think we're some toxic thing that has to be tamed before we bring down the whole world, shouldn't I be allowed to say it if I feel it?"

"Do you honestly think it *matters*?" Carmen asked. "Because it doesn't. It doesn't matter how you feel, or how I do. It's about so much more than just that."

"Like what?" Dani asked, her own fire rising up to meet Carmen's, dancing in her eyes and in the heat that was growing between them.

Carmen, unwilling to back down, exploded instead. "Like the fact that I don't trust you! And you can't trust me!" she said too loudly, but Dani, ever the Primera, did not react. "Because I don't know if you would have come back without a gun to your head! Because I don't know how to fit you into my life here without turning into someone I don't recognize!

Because there's a war starting and Ari betrayed us and Mateo is on the way and here I am, fighting with you over our feelings because we make reckless, bad decisions when we put each other first!" She took a deep, shaky breath.

"You know what this sounds like?" Dani asked, looking up into Carmen's eyes. "It sounds like you being scared, Carmen, and let me tell you something: we're all scared. You're not special because you're some tortured renegade facing down a war. Wondering if you can trust someone? Wondering what you mean to them and how to fit them into your life? That's called being a human! It's called falling in love!"

The tent was silent, but Carmen swore she could hear a faint ringing in it, like the air after a thunderclap, before the next lightning strike.

There it was, sitting between them—an undetonated explosive. The thing Carmen had wanted so much to prevent her from saying. The thing that made this even harder to walk away from.

This was the thing that made people like Mari turn their backs on the fight in their bones, made people like Lu patch up bullet wounds with steady hands and scowling lips. Carmen could feel it teasing at stone walls inside her, the ones she'd been so sure would hold.

She wasn't ready. She didn't know if she'd ever be ready.

Carmen opened her mouth to end the silence, to end it all, but Dani wasn't finished.

"So let me say it as clearly as I know how," Dani said, slowly, precisely. "One last time. Whether it changes anything or not."

Carmen let her silence be permission. She waited. She couldn't not know.

"When you told me who you were, when you left me on that road alone, I was crushed. I was lost. I didn't know what or who to believe, or what I was supposed to do next." She took a deep, shaky breath. "Even through all that," she said, "I never wavered in my commitment." Her words were steel striking flint, lighting something steady and long-burning in her voice. "Because my desire to be part of this world, to fight for what I believe in, never had anything to do with you. So, you can leave me again, and you can lie to me a thousand more times, or you can go out there and get yourself killed and I'll mourn, Carmen, but I'll still be here. Because it's where I belong. Because it's where I choose to be. Because I believe."

Carmen believed her. In this moment, Dani was resistance personified. Her chest rose and fell in an intoxicating rhythm, her face flushed with passion and the glow of late afternoon outside the tent walls. Her eyes were dark and her hair was everywhere and her lips were slightly parted and Carmen believed her.

She felt stronger because of who Dani was. More committed. Ready to risk it all. Not for the girl in front of her, not to the exclusion of the people she wanted to stand up for, but for both. To make a world where they didn't have to be afraid to love.

Carmen stepped closer. And she wondered how something that felt like this could possibly be wrong. And she wondered, for the first time, with a tiny sprout of her just breaking through the stone, if love could be part of rebellion, too.

Out of the corner of her eye, crawling across the inside of the open tent flap, a tiny, fuzzy caterpillar inched along in search of something green. Carmen could barely believe her eyes. It was a sign. The caterpillars were paler out here, sun-bleached and wiry. Survivors.

This wasn't the same caterpillar Carmen had rescued from a bossy bird in the bushes of the Garcia estate, of course, but it was almost possible to believe it was. That Hermanito had traveled all this way to give her a sign.

"I'm afraid, too," Dani said, quieter now, unaware of the metaphor unfolding in Carmen's memory, the words coming in a rush. "I'm afraid that you're two people, and I only knew the one that doesn't really exist. I'm afraid I'll never matter to you as much as you matter to me. I'm afraid of Jasmín, and everything that happened between you guys. Everything you know that I don't. Everything you've done that I . . . haven't." She looked into Carmen's eyes like she was using all the courage she had left. "I'm afraid we won't know what to do with each other when we're not surrounded by people who want to kill us."

Carmen chuckled at this, a low, rough sound that betrayed the effort behind it. "I'm not sure you have to worry about that one. We never seem to be short on enemies."

323

Dani smiled, then stepped a little closer.

Carmen didn't back away.

"I'm afraid of how much I want this," Dani breathed into the space between them.

"I'm afraid of that, too," Carmen said, and she meant it.

Everything inside her was reaching forward, straining, swelling and beating and ready, and she could feel it in Dani, too, rising off her like heat from a sunbaked stone.

But the iron-hard bar of guilt still held one last piece of her back.

"I'm afraid," Carmen said, her voice low, her face already crossing the space a slow centimeter at a time. "That if I come any closer I'll forget what's at stake. I'll make mistakes. I'll let bad things happen because you're the sun to me, and you make me forget there's anything waiting in the darkness. . . ."

"I won't let you forget," Dani said. "We'll fight what's in the dark together. If we have to put each other last sometimes, we'll understand. But we'll do it together. We'll do it with our eyes open."

There was nothing left to say, no more space to close. The fear was still there, lurking, and Ari would be back in a matter of hours, and Mateo was coming. Coming to kill them all.

But even through all of that, the sun was shining.

Dani's lips brushed Carmen's and the light faded outside as afternoon made way for evening. It didn't matter. They were the brightest thing in the sky.

They kissed until they were too aware of the vast expanse

beyond, until Carmen was sure she'd combust if they didn't find out what was waiting there. But the clock was ticking too loudly in their ears.

"It's time, isn't it?" Dani asked in a husky voice, their hearts still hammering against their ribs. Carmen wanted to scream no, but instead she nodded.

"I don't know what's going to happen," she said, because it was true.

"I'll be here, whatever it is."

And even on the edge of a precipice, even as everything Carmen knew unraveled, it was enough.

I will defer to the Vulture in times of uncertainty; his authority will be my law.

—*La Voz Membership Pledge*

✛❧❋❧✛

THEY MET IN THE CENTER of camp, where the road opened up, heading out of the compound and beyond.

Though Alex stood distrustfully close to Jasmín, Carmen could feel it in the air between them as they fell in step. Tonight, they were four strong. Each with an axe to grind. A cross to bear. Each with their demons and their dreams and their fierce, stubborn desire to live through this.

But they didn't make it far.

"Cuervita," came a voice from behind her. "Alex. Can I have a word?"

Carmen turned first, aware of Dani on one side, Alex on the other. Drawing strength from them. She hadn't expected to have to face him so soon. What would she say?

El Buitre stood before them, shoulders slumped, the authority she was so used to seeing in his demeanor almost gone. His face was splotchy and red, his hair tangled, his hands inexplicably filthy.

"What's wrong, Jefe?" Alex asked, concern in her tone. "Is it Mateo? Have the soldiers come early?"

"No, no, it's not that," El Buitre said. "It's something else. Something . . ." He took a deep breath, letting it out in a frustrated huff. "It's something I should have done a long time ago."

The hairs on Carmen's arms stood up. What was happening? What did this mean?

"Should we go inside?" Alex prompted when he didn't speak again. "To your quarters?"

"No," El Buitre said, seeming to steel himself. "Best to do it here. Now." He met each of their eyes in turn. "My girls. You were as close as daughters. You've made me so proud. But I have failed you."

"What do you mean?" Carmen asked, stepping closer instinctively. "What is this?"

"You were right to think there was a leak in our ranks," he said, aging another decade with every word. "And it's all my fault."

Carmen felt as if she'd been tossed into cold water. The shock left her breathless. "You?" she asked, her voice barely audible. "You're the leak?"

"I might as well be," El Buitre said. "When the boy came to me, I knew there was something off. In my younger days I would have trusted my instincts, done my due diligence. I never would have let it get to this point."

It was a mark of the respect and love they had for him that they didn't interrupt, that they listened as their sadness enveloped them like a fog.

"When things started going wrong, I ignored it; I didn't want to face what I'd allowed to happen, so I spent more time away, let things progress without my influence. I wasn't a leader; I was a coward."

Carmen's mind was racing. Was this how the marketplace fire had happened? Jasmín's botched mission? Carmen's own extraction-gone-wrong?

"When he finally revealed the level of his treachery," El Buitre continued, "it was too late to stop him. I should have dealt with it then. I should have stayed true to the title and the mask. But I was afraid to confess how spineless I'd been, to reveal that I'd failed La Voz. So I helped him. I betrayed you all to avoid facing justice for what I'd allowed to happen. I turned the other way. I actively assisted with missions in opposition to La Voz's goals."

Carmen felt like her limbs were made of stone. This couldn't be true. It couldn't. Not El Buitre. Not the man who had raised her. Who had rescued her. Who had taught her everything she knew about resisting.

"Who?" Alex asked, though of course, they already knew.

But when the answer came, it wasn't from El Buitre.

"Who do you think?" Ari's voice was cold, amused, unrepentant. He approached with two massive men flanking him. Two men wearing La Voz blacks who wouldn't look El Buitre in the eye.

From stone, Carmen turned to kindling, anger blazing against the night. "You," she growled, ready to lunge, but Ari pulled a pistol from his belt and pointed it straight at her.

"Call off your bitch," he said lazily to El Buitre, whose expression gave away nothing.

Dani stepped forward, right into the crosshairs, fury in every line of her body.

"If you want her, you'll have to go through all of us."

"It's not her I want," Ari said, still smirking. "She's not the one who broke our agreement."

"It was time, Ari," El Buitre said, his voice ancient and exhausted and weak. "To tell the truth. To end this."

"End it?" he asked, laughing quietly. "Old man, it hasn't even begun."

Carmen didn't have time to react. None of them did. All they could do was watch as Ari turned the gun from Dani to El Buitre. As he fired without hesitation. As the bullet ripped through their leader's chest, sending him to the ground, blood splattering and pooling and absolutely everywhere.

"No," Carmen whispered. "No!" She lunged at Ari, but she had forgotten the men in black. One of them had her arms pinned behind her back before she could scratch a newly bare nail across Ari's unblemished skin.

Carmen struggled against the man, but he was easily twice her size. It was futile.

"Let her go." It was Jasmín, stepping up at last, her eyes on Ari's face, unapologetic.

"Don't think I'm finished with you, you dumb whore," Ari said. "I gave you one job."

"About that job," Jasmín said, undaunted. "The one where I help you gain assistance from your 'sympathizer friends' in the capital to overthrow the Vulture? Would have been nice of you to mention the details."

"Like I could trust you with them," he sneered. "Or with anything."

"Why did you do it?" Alex asked, stepping up beside Jasmín, her hands at her sides in a nonthreatening gesture. "Why betray us when we took you in? When we offered you a family?"

"*Family?*" Ari asked, his cold exterior slipping for just a moment, showing the anger beneath. The desperation.

Alex's eyes flicked to Carmen for the briefest moment, then back to Ari.

"You think this is a family?" he asked. "We didn't choose to be here; we were cursed into being here. I didn't ask to be born in a dirt-floored shack, to starve for half my life, to watch my friends and family drop like flies around me until I finally stumbled into some crackpot's vigilante den."

Carmen's heart twisted in her chest. She could still see El Buitre's body, limbs spread unnaturally, his eyes still open. She choked back a sob as Ari continued, the words pouring out of him like he couldn't stop them.

"I'm here for the same reason as anyone. To find a way to survive. But huddling together in this hovel waiting for them to pick us off? Waiting for the water to dry up or the food to run out? That's not surviving. That's just waiting to die."

He was wrong, Carmen thought, about what La Voz was. But then, he had never truly belonged. And in that moment, not knowing if she would live or die, the only parent she could remember dead on the ground in front of her, Carmen was grateful. At least she had known she was loved. At least she had fought for the right things.

"So you destroyed it?" Alex asked, stepping closer to him so slowly she didn't even seem to be moving. "Just because you didn't belong?"

"You think I cared about destroying your dirty rebels club?" Ari scoffed, but there was still too much emotion in his expression. "I cared about getting out! Making a life for myself that didn't involve eating barely enough gruel or planning battles we could never win. Why shouldn't I want a house with walls? Running water? Why shouldn't I wake up every day without the fear that it's my last one?"

As he spoke, the words like toxins leaving his body,

Carmen saw Alex's strategy at last. She held Ari's eyes while Jasmín and Dani edged around behind, shadows, barely noticeable in the torchlight. El Buitre's body was at Alex's feet. She didn't dare move, but Ari's eyes flickered between Alex and their leader's lifeless form, distracted.

Carmen, moving as little as possible, dug her heels into the grit, leaving her arms in her captor's hold deceptively limp.

"So I took what Mateo Garcia offered," Ari said, not noticing the shifting bodies around him. "The safety. The security. The chance at a real life, and not just some dangerous sham we cover up with the idea of family."

"Now."

Alex's voice was the gunshot at the start of a race. Carmen used the element of surprise to twist her body in the large man's grip, catching him off balance. He was on the ground with her bootheel in his chest before he knew what hit him.

Dani had edged her way behind the second bodyguard, sweeping his legs out from under him, holding his arms behind his back with a triumphant smile that made Carmen's desire to kiss her even harder to ignore than usual.

But it was Jasmín who took Ari, her blade to his throat, her slender fingers resting on his shoulders. "What were you saying?" she asked sweetly.

"Either of you move a muscle, we open his throat. And you'll be next," Alex said to the guards on the ground. Neither of them dared disobey.

The grove was darkening around them, the ghost trees standing out white against the dusk. It was a fitting place, Carmen thought, to expose the last of La Voz's secrets. To leave them standing bare, ready to rebuild.

"Ari Vasquez," Alex said, kneeling beside El Buitre's body, taking the gun from his belt. "You're charged with betraying the cause you claimed to champion. With manipulating Jasmín and trying to frame Dani."

Ari, in Jasmín's hold, was laughing. "Charged by who?" he asked.

"By me." Alex straightened up, the gun in one hand. With the other, she slid on the Vulture's mask. It fit perfectly. Chills chased each other up and down Carmen's arms.

For the first time, there was real fear on Ari's face. "You know fighting them this way will never work!" he said. "You're doomed! All of you! He'll be here with the whole army by tomorrow!"

"So we're doomed," Alex said quietly. "To go out doing what we vowed to do. And to take as many of those bastards out with us as we can along the way."

Carmen could sense it now as she straightened her shoulders, leveled the gun. Something was settling. Something that had been a long time coming.

"Do you recognize my authority to sentence this traitor?" Alex asked, her face somber, her eyes glittering within the Vulture's mask.

"You've always been my leader," Carmen said, a smile on

her face as she raised her palm. "It's my honor to serve you."

Jasmín raised her palm as well. "You showed me mercy," she said. "I won't let you down."

Dani was next. "We didn't have the easiest start," she said, smiling at the memory. "But I'm proud to be part of your resistance."

"Thank you," Alex said, emotion saturating her voice. "Thank you all."

"You can't be serious!" Ari said, his voice two octaves higher in his panic. "That's not how this works! You can't just—!"

"For your crimes against your comrades in arms," Alex said, speaking over him, her voice deeper and more authoritative than Carmen had ever heard it. "For your disregard of the principles and tenets of this organization . . ."

Jasmín stepped away, leaving Ari exposed to El Buitre's gun, and the girl in the mask wielding it. Ari didn't dare move.

"I sentence you to die. All those in favor?"

The trees in the grove seemed to stretch higher, the air crackling with intention.

"Sí," said Carmen, loud and clear. Dani's voice followed, then Jasmín's, but the loudest vote of all was Alex's. The gunshot rang out in the clearing, waking the camp, and for the second time that night there was one less beating heart in the grove.

⊦⊱✳⊰⊦

Night had fallen in earnest. They were gathered in El Buitre's quarters. "Are you ready?" Alex asked Carmen, clapping her shoulder as they prepared to address the remaining members of La Voz at the practice ring.

Carmen hesitated. There was so much swirling between them, inside her. She needed weeks to process everything that had happened today, with Dani, with La Voz. El Buitre was dead. Ari was dead. Instead, they had almost no time left, even to live or die.

"What is it?" Alex asked as Dani and Jasmín peered around the tent's walls to make sure everyone was accounted for.

"I'm not ready to die, too," Carmen said, looking her square in the face.

"So let's not."

When she walked out into the darkness, Carmen followed. They all did.

Alex stepped up to stand before the assembled crowd, El Buitre's gun hanging ostentatiously from her hip. Carmen was on her right, with Dani on her other side. Jasmín took position at her left, her hand resting on the hilt of her knife.

If Carmen had expected confusion, questions, demands to know where El Buitre had gone, she was surprised by the reality. But of course, it made perfect sense.

While El Buitre spent the year hiding from his demons, not to mention committing secret betrayals to cover them up, Alex had been here. Teaching children to hold their swords. Talking with the older women over the washing. Playing cards with the men in the cantina at night.

They would mourn their leader, when the battle was over. They would find a way to honor what he had done without forgiving the ways he had failed them. But there was no time for that tonight.

For now, the assembled comrades weren't looking to Alex with confusion. They looked to her with respect, and as the sun lit the severe angles of her face, Carmen understood why. She had already been their leader in all but title. They accepted her. They trusted her.

And it was a good thing—because they were going to need every one of them to survive what was coming.

"You are all here," she began, her voice quiet but carrying in the early morning hush. "Because you have chosen to give your lives to this cause."

There were murmurs of assent, but no one interrupted. Carmen could see on the faces around her that the shift had been noticed, even if no one was quite sure of the details.

"We have seen more than once this year what that truly means," she continued, bowing her head for the briefest of moments. "We have lost brothers, sisters. But we have also gained them." Here she nodded at Dani and Jasmín. "And though battles have been lost, the war is only beginning."

She stepped forward, drawing her sword but letting it hang loose at her side. An invitation, not a threat. Around them, steel left sheaths in unison, the sound sharp and bright as the first rays of the sun.

"The tide is turning," Alex said. "And this night has brought us news of a betrayal that could have crippled us. But from where I'm standing, you all look stronger than ever."

Hissing and murmurs caught like a grass fire, spreading throughout the ranks until Alex lifted the hand not holding her sword to regain their attention.

"They're expecting an easy win," she said, her tone inviting them to disagree. "Barefoot campesinos with pointy sticks who don't know the butt from the business end of a rifle. They're expecting us to be caught unaware. To lie down and be crushed."

They hung on her every word, their eyes tracking her as she paced back and forth before them like the wolf she had taken for her symbol at twelve years old.

"Do La Voz soldiers *lie down*?" Her words rang out across the field.

"No!"

There wasn't a single person who held back their answer. The sound of them all shouting together gave Carmen chills. Beside her, she felt Dani shift infinitesimally closer, not daring to do more with hundreds of eyes trained on them, but clearly wanting to let Carmen know she was there.

"Are we willing to lay down our lives?"

"Yes!"

"Are we *willing to lose this fight*?" She thrust her sword into the air, and hundreds more points rose to mimic it.

The shouted *no* became a chant, repeated, growing louder

until birds took flight from the ghost trees and the space between them sizzled and crackled with revolution.

By the time the moon rose, they were as prepared as they would ever be.

Carmen, Dani, Jasmín, and Alex huddled around a table in the cantina, which was full to bursting with exhilarated rebels ready to draw blood.

Alex had told them to get some sleep, but in a half-hearted way that acknowledged the impossibility of it. In El Buitre's quarters, over an hours-long strategy session, they had decided the highest probability was of a night attack. Mateo still wasn't aware he'd lost the element of surprise, so he would hope to get as many unprepared rebels out of the way as he could before engaging with them in unfamiliar territory.

If he expected them to be unaware, he had another thing coming.

On a stump against the tent wall, Carmen sat thigh to thigh with Dani, their hands intertwined between them, as close as they could be while trying to keep their heads clear.

Not that that was really working.

The plan had been set, the lookouts were in position, and there were scouts heading up the road to the wall. There was nothing left for them to do but wait. For the horn that meant the army was coming. For the fight to begin.

Outside the cantina, the air seemed electric. Whether it

was distraction she sought, or an end to the feeling that this might be her last night with Dani, Carmen felt the charge at the end of each of her nerves, in the skin of their hands pressed palm to palm, in their bare knees touching just enough to be distracting.

"I'm going to check the perimeter," Alex said abruptly, getting to her feet.

Carmen knew there were plenty of guards patrolling the perimeter already—she had sent them there herself. But if Alex needed to be alone, she wouldn't question it.

"We'll be waiting for word," Jasmín said. "We'll come for you if there's any news."

It was kind of her to play along. But when Alex was gone, and it was just the three of them there, Carmen felt the electricity ramp up another notch. And when she glanced sideways, seeing the spots of color high on Dani's cheeks, she knew she wasn't alone in it.

Earlier they had cracked open a door, and between them the light was still pouring in it, beckoning them both.

Really? Carmen asked the voice demanding she get Dani alone. *Now?*

"Well!" said Jasmín, slapping her hands on her knees. "As much fun as it is to third wheel with your ex and the girl she looks like she wants to trade saliva with, I'm gonna take a walk!"

For a split second, Carmen wondered if Jasmín was hurt, but when she looked up at her, she was smirking as ever.

"Be safe, kids," she said, shaking her head as she wandered off toward a card game.

Dani's blush had spread like wildfire. She looked like she was ready to sink into the ground, or at the very least run for the cliffs.

"Sorry about her," Carmen said, the awkwardness palpable between them, though the electricity was still there, too. How could one girl be so all-consuming? Carmen wondered. Especially just hours before a fight for their lives?

"Oh, it's fine," Dani said, her voice high and a little unnatural. She seemed to know it, too, because she cleared her throat. "I remember how she can be."

The energy between them was almost too much, and Carmen could tell Dani was nervous. The memory of earlier in the tent still sizzled between them, even in these dire circumstances. How had she gone her whole life without kissing this girl?

"So, I got you something," Dani said, stopping in a grove a little ways beyond the cantina.

"When?" Carmen asked, amused.

"Shh, it's a present, don't question it." She pressed her finger to Carmen's lips as she held her hands up in surrender.

From the pouch at her waist, Dani drew a piece of rolled leather.

"I'm not amazing with the smithing stuff yet, but I designed these and the blacksmith's daughter did the crafting. . . ." She was almost shy when she handed it over, and

Carmen unrolled it, curiosity unfurling along with it.

Inside, secured by tiny leather bands, were the lightest, sharpest, most beautifully crafted throwing knives she'd ever seen.

"I know it was hard for me to accept at first," she said haltingly, like she'd practiced it. "This version of you. All the things I didn't know. But I want you to know I see who you are, and I see your world, and I want to be part of it."

Tears pricked the backs of Carmen's eyes. "Dani . . . I . . ." She trailed off, emotion closing her throat for a moment.

"So," Dani said, filling the silence. "Dipping the knife tips in poison is risky, but these have glass bubbles at the tips that will shatter on impact and deliver the dose. There's three different kinds."

She pointed at the first group, Carmen grateful for the chance to get her voice under control.

"These will kill on contact," Dani was explaining now, her voice rambling, color splotches in her cheeks. "Like the one you used on the president. We used all the stores they had left, which wasn't much. So these"—she gestured to the middle row—"are the sleeping draft. Unconsciousness for a few hours depending on how much gets in the bloodstream. Not ideal, but better than nothing." She glanced at Carmen, who smiled. "Oh, and these last ones cause hallucinations, madness, eventually death. So that's basically the gist."

Carmen rolled the leather back up carefully, making sure to leave the precious poison bubbles intact. Once, she'd taken the knives from the safe-house weapon stash because they were the only thing left: ineffectual, but better than nothing.

These knives made her feel lethal, like her biggest mistake had somehow become part of her legend. Honing it until she was as much a blade as the things in her hands. And Dani had designed them, seen who she was and refined it into who she had always wanted to be.

"They're perfect," she said, her voice husky. "I don't know what to say."

"So don't say anything," Dani said, and pulled Carmen's lips to hers.

How many times had they kissed like this? Carmen wondered as Dani's breath hitched against her lips and she pressed in closer. Like it might be the last thing they ever did?

The scene from after the meeting, after their fight, loomed in Carmen's memory. The things they'd done. The things they hadn't. The feeling of *almost* that had been alive between them ever since, whether they'd acknowledged it or not.

She tried to stay in the moment, to let lips and bodies finding more places to press against each other and wandering hands on bare skin to be enough. But whether it was the prospect of impending doom, or the new trust that had blossomed between them, or something else entirely, Carmen found herself hungry for more.

It was Dani who pulled away first, but not far, just to look into Carmen's eyes, and the feeling of wanting wasn't just sparks; it was an inferno.

"Carmen . . . ," she said, her voice ragged at the edges.

"I'm here," Carmen said, even though she wasn't sure it made sense.

"I want . . . to . . . I mean, can we . . . ?"

"Stop?" Carmen asked, everything in her rebelling against the word. "We can, I'm sorry; was it too much?"

"I kind of meant . . . ," Dani said breathily. "Like . . . the opposite of stop."

"Oh," Carmen said, a blank buzzing taking the place of her rebellion. "Oh!"

Dani giggled, her hand pressed to her mouth in a gesture that was becoming all too familiar. It tugged at Carmen's heart, the familiarity, the way they were just building a whisper of a thing and someone was already threatening to tear it down.

"Unless . . . I mean, if you don't want to . . ."

"No!" Carmen said. "I mean, yes, of course I want to. I just . . ." She ran her hands through her hair, laughing a little at herself. She had gone to five years of school, the express purpose of which was to make this moment smooth and effortless. She had lived these moments. But none of them had ever been like this.

"You just . . . ?" Dani prompted, an almost teasing tone to her voice.

Carmen dropped her hair and took Dani's hands again, gathering them to her chest. "I just want to make sure this isn't because you think we might die tonight," she said, blunt, honest, the opposite of everything she'd been trained to be. "Too much of this has already felt like an ending. I want beginnings. . . ." She squeezed Dani's hands, her answering smile sending that fizzing feeling through her veins again.

"What about middles?" Dani asked. "I think middles are underrated."

"Definitely middles," Carmen said, her lips drifting closer to Dani's. "Lots of middles."

They were kissing again then, lips slipping and sliding, something building beneath them and traveling through them until Carmen was sure they were glowing against the twilit sky.

When Dani pulled back this time, Carmen wanted nothing more than to put her right back where she'd been. But when she saw the look on Dani's face she forced her pulse to calm, her cheeks to cool.

"It's not because I think we might die," Dani said. "It's because I love you. I think I have for a long time. But now it's more than just love. It's scars. It's history. It's trust. I trust you, Carmen Santos. And I want this . . . you. I want all of you."

"You have me," Carmen said, meaning it, no part of her pulling away.

When Dani's lips met hers, it was a question, the final question, and she was ready to answer it. Once she had, there were heartbeats and lips that wouldn't pull away, there were stubborn buttons and swallowed laughter and fumbling.

There were sighs and splayed fingers, as the familiar gave way to the new, and the night, maybe the whole world, held its breath. All the scars, and all the questions, and all the history since that first moment, culminating in the one thing they had never been allowed.

The one thing they had never allowed themselves.

As they moved, the breathlessness and the laughter gave way, uncovering something timeless beneath it. Something reverent. Carmen had been here before, but this was different.

This was magnetic and imperfect and went by a million different names. This was the earth moving up to meet them and the sea crashing in and the stars and the moon and everything powerful Carmen had ever let herself feel.

This was poles shifting.

This was wars being fought and won and lost and won again.

This was something she had never thought she could feel.

As the waves crashed up against them again and again, taking everything out on their tide, Carmen felt she was being left somehow cleaner than she had been found. Purer. How could something that was said to be so wrong do all of that? How could something the *gods* supposedly denied feel like a baptism? How could it feel like faith?

Afterward, Carmen lay on her back, not minding the grass that poked between the patchwork blanket they'd made of their clothes, Dani's cheek against her slowing heartbeat.

She reached up to brush her hair from her face and got

Dani's instead, and they laughed, the first sound that hadn't been torn from them since the moment the final *yes* had been said. The laughter built a cocoon around them, something light and bright and ephemeral. Something Carmen knew couldn't last the night. But they had this moment, and Carmen vowed to remember it for the rest of her life. No matter how long (or short) it might be.

26

When the fight finds me, I will meet it with everything I am.

—*La Voz Membership Pledge*

✦✦✦

THEY WERE DRESSING WHEN THE horn sounded, and Carmen found she wasn't afraid. Dani's eyes mirrored her feelings, anchoring her in this place, where she was ready to fight for them. For the right to a million more nights like this one.

"I love you, too," Carmen said, kissing her once on the mouth. It wasn't an ending kiss, or a beginning, but Carmen was starting to think Dani had been right: middles were underrated. "Sorry I forgot to say it earlier." She grinned, and Dani grinned back.

"You were a little distracted."

"I love you," she said again.

"I love you. And if we live through this . . ."

"When," Carmen corrected her, strapping her new knife belt to her waist.

"When we live through this," Dani agreed, "I want to do that again."

"And again and again and again," Carmen said. One more kiss and they were on the move, covering ground quickly though their hands stayed clasped between them. They would be separated soon enough; there was no need to rush it.

Alex was in front of the cantina, her face hard lines and angles. In the distance, there was a rumbling sound. Had it come from the road? Carmen wondered, but there was no time to find out.

"Good," Alex said. "You're here. Remember what we talked about. Mateo's motivations are emotional, which means you two will be his main targets. Stick together. Make him look for you. Vargas, do your best fighting wise; I know you haven't had much time to train. Santos?"

"I am chaos personified," Carmen said, patting her poisoned knives with her free hand, feeling almost eager for the fight.

When they were all assembled, Alex hopped nimbly onto a large wooden crate and drew her weapon. In the flickering torchlight, hundreds of blades left their sheaths in answer.

In the hand that wasn't holding her sword, Alex held the vulture mask. The mask worn by every leader of the resistance for hundreds of years.

In front of them all, with time running out and Mateo's

forces on their way, she dropped it at her feet and stepped on it.

The cracking sound traveled.

Around them, everyone wearing a mask removed it. The air filled with cracking sounds as faces tilted up toward the moonlight. It was waxing, and even though the light would make them easier to spot, Carmen found she was glad for its company.

The crowd watched Alex's every expression as she looked out at them, and Carmen saw something in their eyes that made her believe. In this. In tonight. In all of them.

In the cause she had almost lost trying to come home.

"This is our home. This is our family. They might have guns and armor and numbers, they might have money, but we have heart. We have faith."

Carmen started it. The low, humming sound they'd used to close the protest in the government marketplace. It felt like a lifetime ago, but it had always stuck with her.

First, the low tone was only in her throat, but then she heard Dani's voice join hers. Jasmín, stepping up at Alex's left, added hers as well. Soon the vibration was coming from within and without, the sound swelling with all its disparate parts to form something powerful. Something earthshaking.

"They expect level ground!" Alex shouted over the noise. "A well-lit game board where both sides are lined up to face each other. But we will give them darkness! We will give them fear! We will be everywhere and nowhere. We will be *devastating.*"

349

The wave of sound was cresting, growing frenzied, stomping feet and the hilts and handles of weapons hitting the ground in rhythm.

"And then!" Alex cried. "When we have shown no mercy! When we have made them pay! When we have *won!*" She held out her hands then, and a blanket of silence fell over the crowd.

"We will be free."

The horn blew again, two blasts, and Carmen squeezed Dani's hand once more before dropping it.

"Torches out," Alex said. "We are shadow. We are smoke. We are the ghosts and demons that haunt their nightmares. We are La Voz!"

"We are La Voz!" came the answering cry, and in the faces turned toward them there was no fear, there was only faith. That was what a good leader did, Carmen thought, her own heart on fire as the lights around them went dark one by one, the moon growing brighter in the absence.

Dani's hand found Carmen's, intertwining their fingers as a rumbling began in the distance. *Engines*, Carmen thought. *They're coming by the truckful.* She reached her own hand up to touch Dani's cheek as well, and for a moment it all melted away. The war, the speech, the night, even the moon.

"Be safe," Dani said. "If we get separated . . ."

"There isn't a god or a person living who could keep me from coming back to you," Carmen said.

"I'd like to see them try."

The last torch extinguished as their lips met, plunging the compound into darkness. In the distance, the rumbling grew louder.

Their fingers stayed tangled until the final moment, when the ground forces moved forward and it was time to take to the trees.

When they had ascended, Carmen surveyed the aerial territory. Dani would be her eyes, and with her knives, Carmen could stay out of the fray and cause chaos from a distance. It would keep them both out of Mateo's sights, and allow Carmen to keep an eye on the bigger picture.

Though the trunks of the ghost trees were bare until at least twenty feet up, the branches that spread in their canopies were sturdy, forming a web across the compound that would allow Carmen to move like a venomous spider, biting at will.

The rest of the force was split into zones of the compound, sticking to the shadows, watching for the moonlight's glint off a rifle barrel or a well-polished helmet. Waiting for their moment to strike.

But the strike didn't come all at once. From her perch in a ghost tree in the center of the compound, Carmen watched the dark shapes of soldiers advancing down the road. Groups of two and three, on their guard after El Buitre hadn't arrived to guide them in. They found a desolate compound, bodies missing from their beds, fires cold and torches extinguished.

"Cowards," one of them hissed, approaching the base of Carmen's tree. "They ran."

He straightened up, and Carmen took aim, her first of thirty poisoned knives hitting him directly in the neck. Dani tensed beside her, a silent, beautiful shadow against the dark.

It was a superficial wound, and he slapped at it like a bug, but the knife's glass bubble must have shattered just as designed, because he slumped into a heap on the ground only a second later.

The three men around him stepped closer, missing the glint of the blade where it lay in the dirt, one of them slapping his face, then checking for a pulse. Before they could discover the source of his sudden death, three rebels had slid out from the shadows, slitting their throats where they stood.

A small, hopeful sunrise was taking place in Carmen's chest. She didn't know how many there would be, but was it possible their plan would continue to work so flawlessly?

Her optimism was cut short by the first scream. It pierced the night, and as it died out, Carmen realized she couldn't tell whose side had taken the hit. Peoples' lives ended the same way regardless of their loyalties.

From quiet footsteps and hidden blades, the night turned deadly, black-clad soldiers tearing apart everything they found, dislodging the rebels from their hiding places. Carmen loosed three more knives into the closest knot of combat, choosing the sleeping poison in case one went wide, trusting her comrades on the ground to take care of the unconscious men.

Dani whispered in Carmen's ear when a target was outside

her sight line; they traveled back-to-back through the trees for the most part, seeing everything, deadly and devastating together in a way neither could have been alone.

Mateo's soldiers dropped as Carmen's aim held true, but with only the moonlight to illuminate the scene below, it was hard to tell where to strike.

Restless, Carmen slid from branch to branch, Dani at her back. She searched for a better vantage point, itching to drop to the ground and start tearing into flesh. But Alex's orders had been ironclad. She was to stay above, no matter what happened. To find Mateo and hope she could knock him out before the fight claimed too many rebel lives.

Plus, she could never take Dani, untrained and untested, into the battle. She had to protect her now. Make her part of the way she resisted.

But the first time she saw one of their own fall, Carmen almost forgot her obligation to Alex, her desire to protect the girl she loved. It was a man, but his face wasn't visible. Had it been someone she'd sparred with in the ring? Someone from the mess? Someone's husband? Brother? Son?

Dani squeezed her side sympathetically, unobtrusively. Lending her support in the way she could, bringing Carmen back to herself. She choked on a sob before ruthlessly hurling a knife from behind the trunk of a massive ghost tree. It hit the killer square in the forehead, so hard it stuck from his skull at an angle. But this one hadn't been sleeping poison, or the instant-kill formula she was saving for key moments.

This one was the madness potion, and Carmen pressed against the trunk, out of sight, Dani at her side as she watched the man's shoulders go slack, his face contorting in pain and confusion.

In a moment, he was roaring, his rifle in his hands, spraying bullets in every direction. The rebels knew the look of a man possessed by the poison, and they dropped to the ground immediately, but full of a false sense of camaraderie this man no longer knew, Mateo's soldiers stayed on their feet.

Four of them fell, then five, as the pain and rage gripped him, wringing out his heart until at last, he fell beside them.

Carmen moved on before his body hit the ground, firing into groups, keeping an eye on her knives. There were twelve remaining—less than half of what she'd started with—but the battle seemed to have barely begun. And from her bird's-eye view, Carmen had to admit: it wasn't going their way.

The lack of light and the familiarity with the terrain gave them an advantage, to be sure, but it was nothing compared to the sheer military might of Mateo's force. There were so many of them, cocooned in gear that was proving troublesome for the battered weapons that were the best the resistance had to offer.

And they were learning the terrain, Carmen thought desperately, loosing two more knives when she found groups where things were going especially badly. Aiming carefully where Dani's whispers guided her blades.

No one had spotted them yet, which should have made

Carmen glad—it had been the plan, after all. But instead it made her feel guilty, removed from the action while blood was being spilled and the intimacy of the dance between life and death was palpable below her.

The instinct almost took over. The same one that had let go of the first knife, taken the president's life and set all this in motion. But Carmen had learned. She had a purpose here, an order borne of reason, based on her skills and the faith her commanding officer had in them.

It was time to stop reacting out of fear, wasting ammunition and precious time trying to control outcomes that weren't for her to decide.

It was time to do what only she could do.

"I have to find him," she said to Dani, not bothering to keep her voice low in the noise of the pandemonium below her.

Carmen cast off her shoes, Dani following suit, allowing the bare soles of their feet to grip the petrified bark of the ghost trees. Carmen closed her eyes for a brief moment, saying a prayer to the spirits of these long-dead guardians to hold her high as she crossed them.

From there, she flew.

It had been El Buitre who saw her as the Cuerva, the girl from the legends, but even though he was gone, she still felt the rustle of black wings. She was ruthless. A survivor. A scavenger. And she was done hiding from the only man who'd ever managed to own her.

Below her, the battle had only grown deadlier. She saw

three more fall and told herself she had to keep moving. That her mission was the only reason she couldn't look down and identify them.

Against her palm rested one of her final nine blades. Its glass bubble held the sleeping draft, though Carmen would have relished the chance to kill Mateo on sight. Alex wanted him alive, for now, and more than that: when Carmen showed Mateo exactly what kind of enemy he'd made, she wanted to do it on the ground. At his level. Face-to-face.

But she would have to find him first, and the urgency thrumming alongside her pulse said she'd have to do it faster than this. Everywhere she looked, there were more bodies. More La Voz members. More soldiers. More family. And from the looks of it, they weren't taking enough soldiers with them to do more than break even.

Hopelessness choked her, panic pulling at her like the dark ocean's undertow. Breaking even wasn't enough. It was only a matter of time before their superior equipment and training turned the tide.

Would this be it? she wondered, stopping short, trying to force back the feeling that she couldn't breathe. Was this how La Voz ended? Ari's betrayal and a swarm of men in black? Was it the salt curse, after all? The one Carmen had never believed in?

"You can do this," Dani said, her whisper hot against Carmen's neck. "They need you."

Off in the distance, a now-familiar rumbling sounded.

More trucks? Carmen wondered. Reinforcements would spell the end of this new resistance just hours after Alex broke the mask. Their hard-won stalemate would be over.

But Carmen had come back to herself. She squeezed Dani's fingers, hard, then she straightened herself up, checking her knives, counting them once more.

Nine.

To take out Mateo, she only needed one. And if she was going to die tonight—if she was going to lose everything she'd ever fought for or believed in, everyone she'd ever loved—she was damn sure not going down without a fight.

So eight. Eight knives. Eight chances to affect the outcome of this fight. Eight lives like cupped water in the palms of her hands.

One knife went into the back of a soldier's neck as he towered over a woman with a slight build. He slumped sideways, and she scampered off into the grove before Carmen could see her face.

Seven.

The next went into a bare shoulder, Dani catching sight of a group and turning Carmen with a featherlight touch. The madness poison spread quickly, taking out a group of conferring officers before they could wrestle him to the ground.

Six.

A pair of eyes darting up to the web of branches, widening as they caught sight of her, lungs inflating to scream. They deflated before a sound could be made, sleeping draft rolling their eyes back into their head.

Five.

A man with Mateo's cruel smirk, but none of his self-preservation, bent over a woman, tearing at the front of her shirt. This one, they saw together. The instant-kill poison extinguished the light in his eyes before their fury could run its course. The woman righted herself instantly, plunging her dagger into the man's chest just to make sure, glancing up at Carmen and Dani and holding up a palm before diving back into the fray.

Four.

An exposed left thigh above torn uniform pants.

Three.

A slice across a sweat-slicked cheek.

Two.

An eye.

With one knife in each palm, Carmen knew it was now or never. Madness or sleep. There was no killing potion left.

And then three things happened in quick succession:

First, across the wide-open space where Sota's memorial altar had been built, Carmen spotted Mateo, locked in combat with someone who was holding their own.

Next, the rumbling sounded again, building to an elemental boom, shaking the branch beneath her feet.

And last, for the first time in living memory, rain began to fall onto the thirsty outer-island soil.

There is nothing I won't do for my La Voz comrades, or to our enemies.

—*La Voz Membership Pledge*

⊦⟫✳⟪⊦

THE TREE BRANCH BENEATH HER feet became slick as the first drops hit it. Carmen turned her face up to the sky for a moment in wonder, feeling them on her skin.

But only for a moment.

Her eyes darted back to where Mateo had finally appeared, her entire body tense as a bowstring. She only had one objective now: get to him before he could hurt anyone else she loved. End this, once and for all.

Carmen's bare feet had no trouble with the branches, even as the rain continued to fall on their smoothly petrified surfaces. Trusting Dani to keep pace, she made her way across them like a wraith, like death herself, hair hanging loose around her face, a knife in each hand.

Sleep or madness. Sleep or madness.

Lightning struck from the direction of the mess tent, illuminating the grove in its violet-white glare for the briefest moment, the resulting crack of thunder threatening to throw Carmen from her perch.

The rain increased in intensity until it was a downpour. Carmen's hair grew heavy against the back of her neck, but the feeling was refreshing, heartening. Another lightning strike, and then another, and she held on for a moment, keeping Mateo in her sights, knowing that to fall into the fray before she reached him would be a disaster.

"Carmen," Dani whispered, her eyes wide, disbelieving. "Look."

And as they hovered above the action, steeling themselves, vengeful spirits of the grove choosing their moment to strike, Carmen saw the tide of the battle turn. The inner-island soldiers had weathered a storm like this a week; the rain was no more than an annoyance to them. But to outer-islanders who had lived a lifetime and more of drought, it was nothing more than a miracle. An act of god, when they'd too long believed all their gods had abandoned them.

Everywhere Carmen looked, her people were fighting back with a ferocity she couldn't have imagined, like the rain was feeding them as it swelled the thirsty ground beneath their feet, washing years of dust from the branches of the grove and leaving a moonlit shine on everything around them.

The scales, balanced dead center so far, were beginning to tip.

She saw three of Mateo's soldiers fall, then four, five, each at the hand of a rebel who sprinted joyfully back into the fray in search of another. If La Voz had been waiting for a sign, they had seen it at last.

Steady on her feet, Carmen knew it was time. She would not slip tonight.

At the edge of the clearing, there were no more branches to follow, and it was time to return to the ground, to fight alongside the family she'd chosen. She turned, hands full of blades, and pressed her lips fiercely to Dani's in a clashing, promising kind of kiss.

"Stay here," she said, and then she was gone.

There was no fear as she descended, landing on the balls of her feet, soundless. The ground was damp beneath them, the soil dark as the night sky as it drank in this offering.

This miracle.

Another fork of lightning split the sky, illuminating the massive waves rearing up beyond the cliffs. Around her, miraculously, there was whooping, triumphant, primal screaming that spoke to something deep in Carmen's soul.

Irreverent as she'd always been, even Carmen couldn't keep herself from remembering the story of the brothers. The Salt God's final message to the island that had given his brother everything and sent him into exile.

Maybe it was only a coincidence, but there was a feeling of curses breaking tonight. Of things long taken for granted being held up in a new light.

Mateo's back was to her as he fought someone lithe and slim in the center of the clearing. She couldn't see his face, but she knew the shape of him in the dark by now. It looked like the past. Like something she was ready to bury for good.

Whoever was fighting him now wasn't giving any ground, Carmen thought, a surge of fierce pride jolting her as she caught a glimpse of Jasmín's face. The three of them were alone in the clearing, Mateo without his men as they all struggled to make sense of the surge in energy the downpour had given the rebels.

They never had understood lack, or desperation, and they were paying for it now.

Jasmín saw Carmen first, over Mateo's shoulder, and her eyes widened. The strategic part of her hoped he wouldn't notice, but blood was roaring in her ears, remembering every snide comment, every unwelcome look or gesture, every time he'd casually treated her like he owned her, and she'd been in too deep to fight back.

Turn around, said the pounding of her pulse. *Turn around and face me.*

But he didn't turn. Because ahead of them, dropping from the trees, ignoring Carmen's attempt at an order, was Dani.

She should have known. If it had been Carmen, there was no way she could have stayed put. It had been coming for a long time, the storm finally drawing them all together for this last reckoning.

The sight of Dani acted on Mateo like the rain had on the rebels. Where Jasmín had taken the advantage, Carmen saw rage increase his stature. Anonymity forgotten, Carmen took off at a sprint, just in time to see him hit Jasmín across the face with the butt of his gun—which had clearly run out of bullets—and leave her sprawled in the mud.

He advanced toward Dani then, dropping the rifle on the ground, the rain darkening his hair and clothes.

She didn't draw a weapon, but his hand was on his knife already.

The reassuring rise and fall of Jasmín's chest was enough. Carmen crossed the remaining yards between herself and Mateo before he could draw, every moment, every insult, every degrading memory inside her coiled to spring.

Her poisoned knife was in her palm, and though Dani's eyes had flicked to her once, that Primera's stillness kept the secret of her location from Mateo. If she could just get to him before he turned, she could have him on the ground before he did any more damage.

Carmen was only a few feet away when she was thrown from her feet, the clearing illuminating in a blinding flash as lightning struck one of the grove's trees. The world was too bright, then too dark; her head was spinning, ears ringing, drowning out every thought but one:

Where were her knives?

She clawed her way along the grass, the world coming back in bits and pieces. A pale trunk, the rain on her face, the sizzling sound of flames being doused. There was the ground, and the sky, and here she was between them. But her hands were empty, and before she could look for the glint of moonlight on her blade, there was an arm like an iron bar around her middle, hauling her up.

"Well," Mateo said, shoving Carmen toward Dani the moment she was on her feet. "What a nice surprise. A family reunion." His voice was calm, but a muscle twitched in his jaw, and his eyes were molten.

"You're losing," Carmen said, reaching for Dani's hand, squeezing it once to reassure her she was there. That they would get out of this. That she had meant it when she promised he would never hurt them again.

"You're an amateur," Mateo said dismissively. "And if you think I'm going to let you bait me into a long conversation while you plan your escape, you're even more out of your element than I thought." He walked toward them, the mania in his eyes terrifying, but then Carmen saw it, just behind his boot: a glint of silver in the grass.

Her knife.

Carmen shrugged, shifting toward him just a little. "Worked last time, didn't it?"

"Yes, well, some of us learn from our mistakes. Although I can't say the same for your . . . organization."

The rain had let up after the lightning strike, though the

dark clouds still swirled over the ocean to the south.

The eye of the storm, Carmen thought. In more ways than one.

"So what's the plan?" Dani asked. "Exterminate us all and—"

But Mateo was as good as his word. He lunged for her before she had even finished the sentence. Carmen threw herself in front of Dani on instinct, weaponless, knowing that the better choice would have been to go for the knife and hope for the best.

She caught both his forearms, pushing them up against the full force of him, her arms trembling as he bore inexorably down on her, the blade of his short sword pressing closer and closer as her arms threatened to give out.

Only when Dani had gotten clear of him did she let her arms go limp, the sudden lack of pressure throwing him off balance, sending him pitching forward. Carmen rolled out of the way, searching frantically for Dani, who she found just straightening up behind Mateo, Carmen's knife in her hand.

As if in slow motion, Carmen saw Dani come to her decision, the weight of it settling on her face as she pulled her arm back. Carmen's stomach dropped, and faster than she thought possible she was on her feet, sprinting toward Dani, shouting *no* as Mateo got his bearings and charged toward her, too.

There had been two knives in Carmen's hands when the lightning threw her. One was the sleeping draft that would make it possible to get Mateo to Alex, to move the plan they'd spent hours in El Buitre's quarters perfecting forward.

The other was dosed with madness poison. A venom that would make him lose his mind slowly, flooding his brain with adrenaline until he eventually succumbed to the overdose and died.

And she didn't know which was which.

As counterintuitive as it was, in this moment, Carmen only knew one thing: she had to stop Dani from hurting Mateo at all costs.

But as she drew closer to Dani, Carmen realized it was too late. The knife was leaving her fingertips, Mateo directly in its path. He didn't know the knife was poisoned. That all it had to do was break his skin and one tiny glass bubble. He wouldn't even bother to get out of the way.

Changing course, she did the only thing she could. She put herself in the path of the knife. Better her life than the future of Alex's resistance. Of *their* resistance.

In that endless moment, Carmen tried to memorize everything. The raindrops in Dani's curls. The way the stormy air felt against her bare skin. The life she'd just learned to love.

She prayed it wouldn't end tonight.

She said goodbye anyway.

When she stretched out her hands, she felt the blade bury itself in the flesh of her palm, heard the tiny shattering that meant the poison had been released, and then the guttural scream from Dani as she realized what Carmen had done.

Please, let me sleep, she thought, but in seconds it was the reverse that was true. Her heart sped up, pounding painfully at her rib cage, her breath coming in sharp pants that seemed to scald her throat. She tried to find Dani, hoping her face would keep her grounded, remind her what was real, but as she turned the ground became snakes beneath her hands and she screamed, scrambling away, only to find more behind her and at every turn.

She had no weapons, only her hands, and she swung them at glittering, red-eyed heads with forked tongues until she could feel the skin of them scraping, bleeding.

A terrible red sun was rising in front of her, a white and staring eye at its center, boring into her soul, seeing everything unworthy she had ever thought, every black mark, every death she'd caused, every hurt. It whispered to her in a serpent's hiss that it would be over soon, she would die. But dying would bring her little comfort.

Her throat was raw from screaming but she could not stop. There were hands reaching for her, green and rotting, too many of them, she swung her fists wildly, falling to the ground, kicking at them, biting when they came too close.

The first face that leaned over hers had eyes like that terrible sun. It whispered to her, its hands with their too many fingers trailing down her body, leaving black slime behind. Had she stopped moving? Stopped screaming? Things were getting lost in the whiteness of those eyes, but when Carmen looked down at her own hands there were black feathers sprouting from them.

Carmen stared at them in wonder, glossy black, glinting in the moonlight.

This isn't real, she thought as they took flight, leaving her unarmed and afraid.

But in the air, the crows danced, wheeling around each other, screeching. The sound burned in her chest like a brand; it chased away the pain, the madness, and as she watched with her mouth open, the sky and the ground filled with creatures, haloed and shining in the rain.

All shapes, all sizes, they came to the crow's call, slithering and galloping and prowling and stalking and flying. *Flying.* Carmen closed her eyes and felt them like points of light as the sun-eyed boy stood, afraid, lashing out with a sword like fire.

This isn't real, she told herself again, but then the crows dove, and chaos broke loose.

The masks had been broken, the men within them freed or destroyed. The island was responding, the primal storm drawing them. The crows drawing them.

The sun-eyed boy screamed, and the crows scratched his face, pecked at his hair, pulling tufts of it away that caught fire as they drifted to the earth.

"Stop!" he screamed, the cries echoing around the grove, again and again.

But they did not stop.

A wolf lunged for his arm, shaking him like a doll. A fox

slinked in, content just to watch, to lap at the blood running like a river.

And just before the boy grew still, a final, dark shape passed over them, the shadow blotting out the horrible pale eyes.

El Buitre, Carmen thought. But not the man. The legend.

The vulture dove, and the other animals scattered. The boy screamed again, higher than before, and at Carmen's feet a bloody eyeball fell.

She reached for it with arms heavy as stone. She couldn't reach it. The screaming would not stop and the pain was back. The terrible whiteness was everywhere. The sun too close, her death looking down at her from the center of it with a yawning mouth.

Another face eclipsed the sun, with twelve eyes at least, black and glittering like a beetle's, long, sharp incisors moving hungrily toward the flesh of her hands. It would eat her fingers first, she thought, her heart pounding so hard she was sure it would explode. Its final rebellion.

Nothing could stop it. There was nothing to do but wait. Frozen. For the end.

When its poison green tongue darted out to touch her skin it burned, and she thought she screamed again, but she couldn't hear the sound. Could anyone? The blinding whiteness was back, taking over everything, terrible and so hot it froze her to the bone, and she wanted to run, she had to, but her limbs were stone.

As the cold crept into her veins, calcifying them, her flesh turning pale as the trees of the ghost grove, she saw the monster's tongue turn red.

It's drinking my blood, she thought, and it spat a river of black at her feet, only to begin again.

When the fight has bested me, I will lean on my comrades for strength.

—*La Voz Membership Pledge*

✦❯✳❮✦

THE WHITENESS FADED IN and out.

The beetle-eyed creature came and went as the smell of burning and blood filled her nose and throat. Her stomach filled with wriggling poison eels, and she retched and retched but the creature would not let her go.

For a long time, there was nothing but screaming. Clashing. Scuffling, her body being battered like it was in a strong undertow.

Carmen tried to remember the creatures, the island that had brought them just in time, the way she'd felt when the crows took flight from her hands. The eye. That horrible eye.

But it was gone now. It was all gone.

The whiteness came back, cold and vicious and full of pain, only to recede before it could take her with it. Carmen squeezed her eyes shut against the visions and prayed for sleep. For death. For anything to stop this.

A minute passed, or an hour, or a year, she couldn't know. But once when she opened her eyes the creature was staring at her through two instead of twelve.

Next, her heart slowed.

Next, her hands were back.

When the whiteness receded, she kept her eyes open.

Everything hurt. The awareness of her eyelids against her eyes was like glass grinding. Every one of her bones was raw and sharp-edged against her insides.

Had it been a dream? Was she dying?

Was she already dead?

Something leaned over her and she flinched, expecting the demon-eyed man, the twelve beetle-black eyes, but neither of them came.

Is she awake?

And then: *If she dies I will kill you myself. I don't care how useful you are.*

And then: a scream of pain, not hers, lower.

"I'm in here . . ." Her voice grated on her throat, and she was aware of the rain still falling on her face. She was rewarded by the dark shape returning, the voice.

"Santos!"

And then: "Carmen!"

Her heart lurched at this second voice, things settling back into place. Dani. This was Dani's voice. She was alright. They were alright.

"Dani?"

A sound, somewhere between a laugh and a sob, and one dark shape replaced another, only this time she could see features. Eyes, a nose, hair plastered to a forehead by rain. And hands were squeezing her hands, and she was struggling to sit upright even though everything screamed.

"Mateo," Carmen said as Dani helped her sit up. "Where's Mateo?"

"He's here," Alex said, stepping into view, pushing him along with the butt of a rifle Carmen had never seen her carry before. A glossy one, black. Certainly nothing they'd ever had in the La Voz arsenal. She took it as a good sign. "Don't worry," Alex reassured her, "you were only out a few minutes."

Mateo's face was no longer his face. Scratches marred one side of it, so many you could barely see the skin. His hair had been pulled from the roots in patches, leaving bald, mottled scalp beneath.

But worst of all was the yawning, bloody socket where once there'd been a dark, clever eye. This was no longer the cruel boy who had haunted them all.

He looked like he'd been ravaged by beasts.

Or punished by gods.

"Witch," he said, pointing at her, his remaining eye too wide in its socket. "Get her away from me. She's a witch!"

The clearing spun. She dropped her head into her hands. Her memories were already leaking away, like water through the rocks as the tide went out. The line between what was real and what she'd experienced as the madness poison coursed through her was blurring. She couldn't bring herself to ask what had happened.

Maybe she never would.

"Tell us what the deal was," Alex said, in a tone that said she'd asked before. "Before I take your other eye."

"He said this would be easy!" Mateo shrieked, his eye still on Carmen, watching her like she'd attack him again. "That we wouldn't lose anyone! He said it would be . . ." Mateo trailed off, gritting his teeth against another scream.

"The end of La Voz," Alex said, and Carmen could hear the grief in her voice.

Carmen thought of the vulture's shadow, the eyeball at her feet.

Mateo fell to his knees, dizzy, and Carmen could see the blood. There was so much blood.

The demon with the terrible empty eyes.

Her hands, turning to crows.

The wolf and the fox and the vulture . . .

But did that mean . . . ?

"How did I survive?" Carmen asked, not sure she wanted to know.

"I sucked the poison out of the wound," Dani said, her voice shaking.

The beetle-eyed creature. Carmen shuddered.

"It was all my fault, Carmen, I'm so—"

"Shh," Carmen said, doing her best to smile. "You saved me."

Mateo groaned behind them, breaking the moment, bringing reality back.

"Put something over his eye," Alex said, and Dani got up, the stiffness in her spine making it clear how little she wanted to approach him.

"Don't worry." Alex had noticed it, too. "It's only temporary. By the time I'm done he'll be dead, or wishing he was."

"I'm not a coward," he snarled, but his voice was weak. He had marched in here like a boy with toy soldiers, victory already assured. He hadn't been afraid because the only danger had ever been to his reputation. But now?

Carmen could see it. He was wavering. His convictions flagging in the face of real sacrifice. He had been the golden boy. Beautiful, rich, victorious before he ever lifted a finger to fight.

He was none of those things now.

He was right where Alex had wanted him all along.

In minutes, he was upright and tied to a stump. Carmen got to her feet, swaying, but she didn't fall. It was a small victory.

The sun was beginning to filter through the grove as they

faced him, shoulder to shoulder, Alex out front, and Dani and Carmen on her right. The open space where a sergeant at arms should be was glaring, and Carmen felt a swooping in her stomach until:

"You weren't really about to start this party without me, were you?"

Jasmín limped badly, but she crossed the clearing under her own steam, taking her place and a grateful nod from Alex before turning to face Mateo.

"I've been looking forward to this for a long time," she said, and her voice, though ragged with pain, was menacing enough.

They stared him down. This pathetic boy who had lost much more than an eye today. Who had made a deal with a puffed-up pretender and walked into a fight to the death instead.

We did that, Carmen thought, her chest on fire with pride, and she thought for a moment she caught the smirk of a ghostly fox in the predawn light through the grove.

Had he been here? Truly?

"What's the status?" Alex asked Jasmín, loud enough for Mateo to hear.

"The soldiers are all dead or captured," she said, her voice strong and clear now, fierce with pride of her own. "We sustained significant losses but retained enough to secure the perimeter. Guards and scouts are on their way to the road now, the med tent is fully staffed, and injuries are being looked after."

Alex nodded. "You hear that, boy?" she asked. "Your men are all gone. There's nowhere to run now. No grand victory to take home like a dog with a bone. What do you have to say? For yourself. For your men."

Mateo, weak as he was, only spat blood at her feet.

Jasmín stepped forward and backhanded him across the good side of his face. The next time he spat, Carmen thought there were fragments of his teeth in it.

At least, she could hope.

"You have a choice here," Alex said, stepping closer to him, speaking as if nothing had happened between her first question and now. "You're standing at the edge of a precipice. There's history to be made. You lead the nation of Medio, through whatever divine blunder, and Medio needs healing."

"Don't patronize me," he snapped, pale and disheveled, bleeding but not broken. "Flattery will never win me to your cause. This pathetic dust heap deserves to crumble into the sea, and I for one—"

For the second time, Jasmín slapped him.

"Easy," Alex said when she took her place again. "We need him conscious at least." She paused, an ominous thing. "For now, anyway."

Somehow, despite it all, Carmen felt the urge to laugh. She leaned on Dani instead, her legs growing weak in the aftermath of the poison. But she would meet this moment on her feet.

"You misunderstand me," Alex said now, her voice like ice splintering. "Flattery was never on my agenda. You are a worm, and you deserve a worm's death, crushed between the jaws of something feral." She paused again to let that sink in, sending Carmen's memories spinning again. "But you have access, and access is what we need. So, I offer you an alternative to your death, which, should you refuse this generous offer, will begin soon and last a long, painful time. Is that clear?"

His silence was all the assent she needed.

"Good," she said, and the first rays of morning sun broke through the clouds above, causing the rain-drenched clearing to sparkle in a way that felt like hope. "Now, as I said, you're the leader of a broken nation, Mateo Garcia. And as long as it remains broken it will never prosper. My offer is this: take me and a few of my people with you to the capital. Propose a new policy that will allow us space to voice our concerns, and work with us to integrate this island once and for all. Be remembered as a leader who lifted a god's curse. A hero."

Carmen felt Dani's fingers tighten around hers as they held one breath between them.

"Or die," Alex said bluntly. "A little boy who went off to fight his father's war and came home in a box thanks to a few barefoot girls with sticks and stones."

The rays of sun continued to spread. The sea sparkled

over the cliff's edge. The smell of rain was everywhere, and it smelled new, and it smelled like life. Carmen let out her breath. She had been to the edge of reason, the edge of death, to pay for this moment and every one after.

She already knew what his answer would be.

Jasmín favored her right hip, and Dani's face and arms were scratched and purpling with bruises. Sota was gone, and many more names were only waiting to be uttered in the soft, reverent tones of loss.

But they had won the day, against insurmountable odds. Taken a stalemate, and with the help of a miracle storm, turned it to victory because they believed.

With this victory, they had won the right to fight for more of them.

And maybe to do it differently this time.

And beyond all that, Carmen thought, maybe they had lifted a curse tonight.

"They'll never agree to this," Mateo said at last, his voice weak from pain and blood loss and bitter disappointment. "They'll laugh me out of the capital for suggesting it even *with* both my eyes."

Alex stepped even closer, their faces just inches apart. "You're their leader," she told him, with all the authority of someone who had earned the title. "You don't ask them. You tell them. You *show* them."

Mateo's gaze darted toward the ground, his sneer half-hearted at best as Alex's words sank in.

"You *lead* them," she said finally, and then she stepped back.

There would be no more discussion, her posture said, and Carmen's near-buckling knees were glad of it. He would agree, or he would die and they would find another way. But they would find a way, the divine whisper off the sea told her as much.

The beating of her heart told her.

The fingers intertwined with hers told her.

"I'm not making any promises," he snapped at last. "And you better not make me look like a fool."

"Trust me, you don't need any help in that department," Jasmín said, irreverent as ever.

Alex laughed, just once, a short, sharp bark of a thing. Then she turned to Jasmín. "Take him to my tent. Keep him tied up and under guard."

Jasmín lifted a palm and pressed it to Alex's before turning to Mateo with a terrifying joy in her eyes.

"Get to the med tent and get yourselves patched up," Alex said to Dani and Carmen, pressing palms with each of them before turning back to Carmen and embracing her like a sister. "We have plans to make."

And so they did.

No matter the stakes, I will lead my cause to victory, one step at a time.

—*La Voz Membership Pledge*

⊢✦✳✦⊣

IN THE LIGHT OF THE next day, they assessed the aftermath of the battle and the storm, taking stock, looking ahead to what was next. They had lost nearly half of their fighting force, but those who could not fight had remained safe in the beachside cave.

Ari was laid to rest in a patch of earth near the cliffs. Carmen had protested, but relented when Alex pointed out he had been wraithlike enough in life. They didn't want him haunting them because he hadn't been buried properly.

For El Buitre, they had a quiet memorial, nothing showy, nothing befitting a leader of the cause. But enough for the people who had loved him to mourn.

Carmen kept the story of the final fight to herself, the memory of the legends come to life, but she thought about it all the same. About what they had wrought by taking La Voz back from the pretenders. About what would come next.

Mateo, in restraints in the med tent while his injuries were tended to, spoke to no one, but it was whispered that he'd broken every reflective surface within reach the moment they'd untied him for an examination.

After they were gone, he'd submitted to his bonds again. The goal had never been escape.

Carmen hoped he was broken. That he wondered, on those long nights of captivity, who he was. That he ached with the feeling of not knowing. He deserved it all, and worse, and sometimes Carmen genuinely wished he hadn't survived.

That they hadn't needed him to.

But not every story had a neat, just ending, she supposed. The world as it was didn't lend itself to them. Her life had been proof of that.

The aftermath of the poison still lingered, making her limbs tire easily and causing strange things to unfurl in the shadows at the corners of her vision. She sought comfort in Dani's arms, her heartbeat slowing, her tight-lipped panic turning soft between them.

Alex sent out missives on the first day to every friend and family member of La Voz, inviting them to be part of the rebuilding process, emphasizing the differences in policy this resistance would be implementing. There was no black-mail, no threatening, only a renewal of friendship, and an invitation.

Carmen waited especially eagerly for an answer from Mari and Lu, who had given her so much hope. For her and Dani.

For love, wherever and however it took root.

They would wait a week for arrivals, but the grove was already being dismantled, piece by storm-tossed piece. Despite the changes that had occurred in leadership, La Voz was a nomadic organization, and it was far past time to be moving on. To put this grove and all its ghosts in the past—the ones they'd found here, and the ones they would leave.

The kitchen outdid themselves as they used up anything that would not travel, and for days a perpetual feast of simple but hearty food was spread across the tables. People gathered, ate, drank. They laughed and threw dice. Sometimes they cried. But they were together.

Too soon, the fifth day dawned, a low cloud cover promising more rain this afternoon. Carmen rose from another night in Dani's arms to bid her best friend, her sister, goodbye.

The truck that had brought Mateo and his murderous soldiers in looked out of place in the grove, among the rag-tag bunch that remained after the battle. But children raced around the massive tires, clambering up onto the step outside the driver's door only to be chased down again.

By the time Dani and Carmen arrived in the clearing, Mateo was already secured in the passenger seat, restrained by the chains he hadn't rattled once since he had accepted Alex's terms.

Still, Carmen had warned her, you couldn't be too careful with a rabid dog.

"You clean up nice," she told Alex as she approached, dressed in neat blacks with silver buttons, her normally flyaway hair slicked back.

Carmen tried to keep the emotion out of her voice, but it was no use. The tears welled up the moment their eyes met, and Carmen did not brush them away. Gone were the days she had spent believing her passions made her weak. Life had shown her the error of those ways.

"Don't do that," Alex said, but her long-suffering look bloomed into a nostalgic smile, and Carmen stepped forward, hugging her fiercely.

"Are you absolutely sure about this?" she asked for the hundredth time. "I know he's docile with most of his pretty face missing, but trusting him seems like a stretch."

"Trust isn't on the table," Alex said, patting the shining pistol on her hip. "But if *you* could handle the snake pit, I figure *I* can probably do it blindfolded." She considered Carmen. "And left-handed."

Carmen rolled her eyes, thwacking Alex's shoulder with the back of her hand, and for a moment they were two gap-toothed preteens again, racing each other along the ocean cliffs, Sota lagging just behind, the sun setting as the dinner bell rang.

"Besides, if he doesn't stick to his word, I'll just use him as a bartering chip. I hear his mother's fond of him."

"That's an understatement," Dani said, her voice darkly amused.

"In any case, I don't think this one is going to let anything bad happen to me," Alex said as Jasmín sauntered up, two ostentatious curved swords hanging from her belt.

"Jasmín Flores, take-no-prisoners bodyguard, reporting for duty. Won't my parents be proud."

"Remind me again why you're going, too?" Carmen said, her lower lip jutting out into a pout.

"Please, like she could manage without me," she said, rolling her eyes as Alex smiled. "And it'll be a lot more fun than sitting around here watching you two gaze longingly at each other all day."

Carmen swatted at Jasmín, but when Dani's warm hand found hers, she allowed herself to be pulled back, Dani's chin resting on her shoulder, cheeks already heating up at the closeness.

Maybe Jasmín had a point. There were more battles to be fought, wounds to heal, shadows of enemies everywhere they turned, but when had that ever stopped them before?

Three lanky guards, young but capable, escorted the officers they'd taken prisoner into the truck. There were fewer than twenty. The rest would be buried at the edge of the grove before La Voz found a new home.

"You take care of her," Alex said to Dani, and she nodded,

the gravity in the gesture making her look older than her seventeen years.

But weren't they all? Carmen wondered, her hands still holding Dani's where they met at her belly. Hadn't they seen and done enough to prove they were ready? That they didn't need the greed of a single leader, a single man, to tell them what they were capable of?

Looking around at Alex and Jasmín, Dani, even herself, Carmen could feel it in her bones. The real revolution was here. In the place where girlhood met womanhood. In the bonds of a sisterhood that would never be torn apart.

If they couldn't trust anything else, with that as their foundation, whatever followed would be good. It would be worthy of what it had cost.

"Time to go," Alex said then, her guards waiting patiently behind her, Jasmín practically bouncing on the balls of her feet in her eagerness.

Carmen held out her arms, feeling the familiar imprint of her once more as they hugged goodbye. "Be good," she said, and Jasmín rewarded her with a wicked smirk.

"You of all people should know that's not in the stars," she said, winking as she turned to Dani, whose own embrace was noticeably tepid after that last remark.

That left Carmen and Alex, one more time, and though they'd embraced before, Carmen lifted both palms, as she'd once done to the man who'd raised them. He was gone, while

386

they were here, ready to fight whatever came. Ready to live on their own terms.

Alex pressed her own palms into them, respect and love blazing in her eyes. *"We* are the revolution," she said. "You are the revolution. It all starts here."

"I won't let you down," Carmen said, her words heavy, her throat tight around them.

"Hadn't even considered it."

Be safe, she wanted to say, thinking of the capital, the government complex, the million ways to get lost. To get hurt. "Be great," she said instead, and was it her imagination, or did Alex wipe at her eyes before swinging herself into the truck?

The horn blared—Jasmín's doing—and the children screeched and giggled as the engine roared to life, their mothers frantically gathering them as Carmen stood with Dani, ready for anything.

They watched until the truck was gone, until even the dust cloud had disappeared, and for a moment after, Carmen felt the weight of everything to come. Of the precious thing she had been left.

But Dani's hand was sliding into her back pocket then, pressing them together, and Carmen drew a weapon and shouted at everyone in earshot to meet in the practice ring in ten minutes.

Dani tugged on Carmen's back pocket until she spun

around to face her, giggling, breathless, their noses just an inch apart.

"Are you ready?" Dani asked, her lips just barely brushing Carmen's, and Carmen didn't know what she was asking exactly, because the whole world was spooling out in front of them like glittering threads just waiting to be gathered and spun.

She crushed their lips together, unable to hold back for one more minute. "Yes," she said when they pulled apart, knowing it was true, whatever she was agreeing to. "Yes, yes, yes."

Acknowledgments

✦✧✶✧✦

When I first came up with the idea for the world of Medio, I couldn't have possibly imagined the places this story would take me, or the places I would take its poor characters. So, to be sitting here, finally finished with the story of Dani and Carmen, feels surreal in the most bittersweet way.

First, I have to thank from the bottom of my heart every single reader who has picked up this story. Who has lost or found something in its pages. Who has reached out with a kind word or a story of their own, who has stood in line or taken a photo or listened during a panel or asked a question. This series would be nothing without you.

I couldn't have survived this series without my agent, Jim McCarthy, who fields my middle-of-the-night celebrations and panic. Who translates the world for me and me for the world. Who believes. Always. Even when he's the only one.

Then there's the amazing team at Katherine Tegen books, who has carried this story through to the bitter end. There are horror stories about second books for a reason, and Claudia Gabel and Stephanie Guerdan have showed tremendous patience with me and these thorny characters while we navigated the twists and turns. Thank you both for believing in this book, for creating time out of thin air, and for your hard work in making this story shine.

To my three comadres in arms, Lily Anderson, Nina Moreno, and Michelle Ruíz Keil. I pinch myself on the daily because you all decided to keep me around. Thank you for being my smile through the tears, my eyes in the dark, my safe place to come home to. That, and all the chisme, por supuesto.

My family has been a constant source of inspiration and motivation to me since my first scribbled sentences, and of course I have to thank them for sticking by me through yet another round of all-night edits, thousands of unreturned texts, and calls from random airports when I forget about time changes. I love you all so much.

Alex, my love, you're always sure, and it makes me so much braver. Thank you for reminding me to stand tall, and for being there when I stumble. Everything about this life is more beautiful because you're walking beside me.

And to my little A, who named all her imaginary friends Carmen for half a year. Every word I write is for you. Everything I do is for you. Te quiero para siempre, and even after that.